D0032018

AMULET BOOKS
NEW YORK

A NOVEL BY
A. G. HOWARD

SPLIN

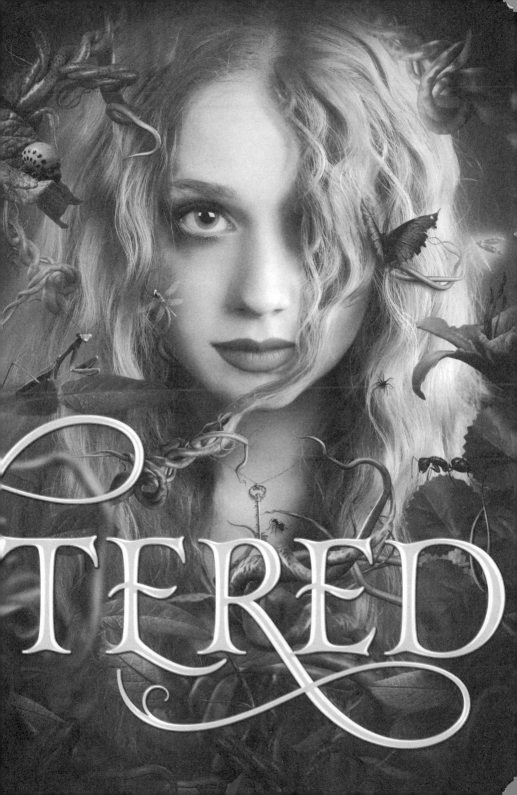

The Library of Congress has catalogued the hardcover edition of this book as follows:

Howard, A. G. (Anita G.)
Splintered / by A. G. Howard.
p. cm.
Summary: A descendant of the inspiration for Alice's Adventures in Wonderland, sixteen-year-old Alyssa Gardner fears she is mentally ill like her mother until she finds that Wonderland is real and, if she passes a series of tests to fix Alice's mistakes, she may save her family from their curse.
ISBN 978-1-4197-0428-4 (hardback)
[1. Supernatural—Fiction. 2. Characters in literature—Fiction. 3. Blessing and cursing—Fiction. 4. Mental illness—Fiction. 5. Mothers and Daughters—Fiction. 6. Hargreaves, Alice Pleasance Liddell, 1852–1934—Fiction.] I. Title.
PZ7.H83222Spl 2013
[Fic]—dc23
2012011538

ISBN for this edition: 978-1-4197-0970-8

Text copyright © 2013 Anita Howard
Title page illustration copyright © 2013 Nathália Suellen
Book design by Maria T. Middleton

Printed and bound in U.S.A.
10 9 8 7 6 5 4 3

THE ART OF BOOKS SINCE 1949
115 West 18th Street
New York, NY 10011
www.abramsbooks.com

❈ · I · ❈

*To my husband and real-life hero, Vince, and to my two
wonderful children, Nicole and Ryan. You embraced my dream
as if it were your own and gave me the courage to keep flying
until I grasped that beautiful shooting star.*

❈ · I · ❈

ONE-WAY TICKET TO UNDERLAND

I've been collecting bugs since I was ten; it's the only way I can stop their whispers. Sticking a pin through the gut of an insect shuts it up pretty quick.

Some of my victims line the walls in shadow boxes, while others get sorted into mason jars and placed on a bookshelf for later use. Crickets, beetles, spiders . . . bees and butterflies. I'm not picky. Once they get chatty, they're fair game.

They're easy enough to capture. All you need is a sealed plastic bucket filled with Kitty Litter and a few banana peels sprinkled in. Drill a hole in the lid, slide in a PVC pipe, and you have a bug snare.

The fruit peels attract them, the lid traps them, and the ammonia from the litter smothers and preserves them.

The bugs don't die in vain. I use them in my art, arranging their corpses into outlines and shapes. Dried flowers, leaves, and glass pieces add color and texture to the patterns formed on plaster backgrounds. These are my masterpieces . . . my morbid mosaics.

School let out at noon today for the upperclassmen. I've been passing the last hour working on my newest project. A jar of spiders sits among the art tools cluttering my desk.

The sweet scent of goldenrod breezes through my bedroom window. There's a field of herbs next door to my duplex, attracting a genus of crab spider that changes color—like eight-legged chameleons—in order to move undetected among the yellow or white blooms.

Twisting off the jar's lid, I dip out thirty-five of the small white arachnids with long tweezers, careful not to squish their abdomens or break their legs. With tiny straight pins, I secure them onto a black-tinted plaster background already covered with beetles selected for their iridescent night-sky sheen. What I'm envisioning isn't a typical spatter of stars; it's a constellation that coils like feathery bolts of lightning. I have hundreds of warped scenes like this filling my head and no idea where they came from. My mosaics are the only way to get them out.

Leaning back in my chair, I study the piece. Once the plaster dries, the insects will be permanently in place, so if any adjustments need to be made, it has to be done quickly.

Glancing at the digital clock beside my bed, I tap my bottom lip. I have less than two hours before I have to meet Dad at the asylum. It's been a Friday tradition ever since kindergarten, to get chocolate-cheesecake ice cream at the Scoopin' Stop and take it to share with Alison.

Brain freeze and a frozen heart are not my idea of fun, but Dad insists it's therapy for all of us. Maybe he thinks by seeing my mom, by sitting where I might one day live, I'll somehow beat the odds.

Too bad he's wrong.

At least one good thing has come out of my inherited insanity. Without the delusions, I might never have found my artistic medium.

❈ · 1 · ❈

My obsession with bugs started on a Friday in fifth grade. It had been a rough one. Taelor Tremont told everyone that I was related to Alice Liddell, the girl who inspired Lewis Carroll's novel *Alice's Adventures in Wonderland.*

Since Alice was, in fact, my great-great-great-grandmother, my classmates teased me during recess about dormice and tea parties. I thought things couldn't get much worse until I felt something on my jeans and realized, mortified, that I got my period for the first time and was totally unprepared. On the verge of tears, I lifted a sweater from the lost-and-found pile just inside the main entrance and wrapped it around my waist for the short walk to the office. I kept my head down, unable to meet anyone's gaze.

I pretended to be sick and called my dad to pick me up. While I waited for him in the nurse's office, I imagined a heated argument between the vase of flowers on her desk and the bumblebee buzzing around them. It was one powerful delusion, because I really *heard* it, as sure as I could hear the passing of students from one class to the next on the other side of the closed door.

Alison had warned me of the day I would "become a woman."

Of the voices that would follow. I'd just assumed it was her mental instability making her say that . . .

The whispers were impossible to ignore, just like the sobs building in my throat. I did the only thing I could: I denied what was happening inside me. Rolling a poster of the four basic food groups into a cylinder, I tapped the bee hard enough to stun it. Then I whisked the flowers out of the water and pressed them between the pages of a spiral notebook, to silence their chattering petals.

When we got home, poor, oblivious Dad offered to make some chicken soup. I shrugged him off and went to my room.

"Do you think you'll feel well enough to visit Mom later tonight?" he asked from the hallway, always reluctant to upset Alison's delicate sense of routine.

I shut my door without answering. My hands shook and my blood felt jittery in my veins. There had to be an explanation for what had happened in the nurse's office. I was stressed about the Wonderland jokes, and when my hormones kicked in, I'd had a panic attack. Yeah. That made sense.

But I knew deep down I was lying to myself, and the last place I wanted to visit was an asylum. A few minutes later, I went back to the living room.

Dad sat in his favorite recliner—a worn-out corduroy lump covered with daisy appliqués. In one of her "spells," Alison had sewn the cloth flowers all over it. Now he would never part with the chair.

"You feeling better, Butterfly?" he asked, looking up from his fishing magazine.

Musty dampness blasted into my face from the air conditioner as I leaned against the closest wood-paneled wall. Our two-bedroom duplex had never offered much in the way of privacy, and on that day it felt smaller than ever before. The waves of his dark hair moved in the rattling gusts.

I shuffled my feet. This was the part of being an only child I hated—having no one but Dad to confide in. "I need some more stuff. They only gave us one sample."

His eyes were blank, like those of a deer staring down traffic during morning rush hour.

"The special talk they give at school," I said, my stomach in knots. "The one where boys aren't invited?" I flashed the purple pamphlet they'd handed out to all the girls in third grade. It was creased because I'd shoved it and the sample sanitary pad into a drawer beneath my socks.

After an uncomfortable pause, Dad's face flushed red. "Oh. So that's why . . ." He suddenly became preoccupied with a colorful array of saltwater lures. He was embarrassed or worried or both, because there wasn't any salt water within a five-hundred-mile radius of Pleasance, Texas.

"You know what this means, right?" I pressed. "Alison is going to give me the puberty speech again."

The blush spread from his face to his ears. He flipped a couple of pages, staring blankly at the pictures. "Well, who better to tell you about the birds and the bees than your mom. Right?"

An unspoken answer echoed inside my head: *Who better but the bees themselves?*

I cleared my throat. "Not that speech, Dad. The nutso one. The 'It can't be stopped. You can't escape the voices any more than I could. Great-great-gran never should've gone down the rabbit hole' speech."

It didn't matter that Alison might be right about the voices after all. I wasn't ready to admit that to Dad or myself.

He sat rigid, as if the air conditioner had iced his spine.

I studied the crisscross scars on my palms. He and I both knew it was less what Alison was going to say than what she might do. If she had another meltdown, they'd slap her into the straitjacket.

I learned early on why it's spelled *strait*. That particular spelling means *tight*. Tight enough that blood pools in the elbows and the hands become numb. Tight enough that there's no escape, no matter how loud the patient screams. Tight enough that it suffocates the hearts of the wearer's loved ones.

My eyes felt swollen, like they might burst another leak. "Look, Dad, I've already had a really sucky day. Can we please just not go tonight? Just this once?"

Dad sighed. "I'll call Soul's Asylum and let them know we'll visit Mom tomorrow instead. But you'll need to tell her eventually. It's important to her, you know? To stay involved in your life."

I nodded. I might have to tell her about becoming a woman, but I didn't have to tell her about becoming *her*.

Hooking a finger in the fuchsia scarf tied around my jean shorts, I glanced at my feet. Shiny pink toenails reflected the afternoon light where it streamed from the window. Pink had always been Alison's favorite color. That's why I wore it.

"Dad," I mumbled loud enough for him to hear. "What if Alison's right? I've noticed some things today. Things that just aren't . . . normal. *I'm* not normal."

"Normal." His lips turned up in an Elvis curl. He once told me his smirk won Alison over. I think it was his gentleness and sense of humor, because those two things kept me from crying every night after she was first committed.

Rolling his magazine, he shoved it into the recliner between the seat cushion and the arm. He stood, his six-foot-one height towering over me as he tapped the dimple in my chin—the one part that matched him instead of Alison. "Now, you listen, Alyssa Victoria Gardner. *Normal* is subjective. Don't ever let anyone tell you you're not normal. Because you are to me. And my opinion is all that matters. Got it?"

"Got it," I whispered.

"Good." He squeezed my shoulder, his fingers warm and strong. Too bad the twitch in his left eyelid gave him away. He was worried, and he didn't even know the half of it.

I tossed and turned in bed that night. Once I finally fell asleep, I had the Alice nightmare for the first time, and it's haunted my dreams ever since.

In it, I stumble across a chessboard in Wonderland, tripping over jagged squares of black and white. Only I'm not me. I'm Alice in a blue dress and lacy pinafore, trying to escape the ticktock of the White Rabbit's pocket watch. He looks like he's been skinned alive—nothing but bones and bunny ears.

The Queen of Hearts has commanded that my head be chopped off and stuck into a jar of formaldehyde. I've stolen the royal sword and am on the run, desperate to find the Caterpillar and the Cheshire Cat. They're the only allies I have left.

Ducking into a forest, I slice the sword at vines hanging in my path. A thicket of thorns sprouts from the ground. They snag my apron and gouge my skin like angry talons. Dandelion trees tower in every direction. I'm the size of a cricket, along with everyone else.

Must've been something we ate . . .

Close behind, the White Rabbit's pocket watch ticks louder, audible even over the marching steps of a thousand playing-card soldiers. Choking on a cloud of dust, I plunge into the Caterpillar's lair, where mushrooms loom with caps the size of truck tires. It's a dead end.

One look at the tallest mushroom and my heart caves. The place where the Caterpillar once sat to offer advice and friendship is a mass of thick white web. Something moves in the center, a face pressed against the filmy case, shifting just enough that I can make out the shape of the features yet see no clear details. I inch closer, desperate to identify who or what is inside . . . but the Cheshire Cat's mouth floats by, screaming that he's lost his body, and distracts me.

The card army appears. Within an instant, I am surrounded. I toss out the sword blindly, but the Queen of Hearts steps forward and snatches it in midair. Falling to my knees at the army's feet, I plead for my life.

It's pointless. Cards don't have ears. And I no longer have a head.

❈·1·❈

After covering my starry spider mosaic with a protective cloth while the plaster dries, I grab a quick lunch of nachos and drive over to Pleasance's underground skate park to kill time before meeting Dad at the asylum.

I've always felt at home here, in the shadows. The park is located in an old, abandoned salt dome, a huge underground cave with a ceiling reaching as high as forty-eight feet in places. Prior to the conversion, the dome had been used for storing bulk goods for a military base.

The new owners took out the traditional lighting and, with some fluorescent paint and the addition of black lights, morphed it into every teen's fantasy—a dark and atmospheric ultraviolet playground complete with a skateboard park, glow-in-the-dark miniature golf, an arcade, and a café.

With its citrusy neon paint job, the giant cement bowl for skateboarders stands out like a green beacon. All skaters must sign a release form and put orange fluorescent grip tape on the decks of their boards to avoid collisions in the dark. From a distance, we look like we're riding fireflies across the northern lights, sweeping in and out of one another's glowing jet streams.

I started boarding when I was fourteen. I needed a sport I could do while wearing my iPod and earbuds to muffle the whispers of stray bugs and flowers. For the most part, I've learned to ignore my delusions. The things I hear are usually nonsensical and random, and blend together in crackles and hums like radio static. Most of the time I can convince myself it's nothing more than white noise.

Yet there are moments when a bug or flower says something louder than the others—something timely, personal, or relevant—and throws me off my game. So when I'm sleeping or involved in anything that requires intense concentration, my iPod is crucial.

At the skate park, everything from eighties music to alternative rock blasts from speakers and blocks out any possible distractions. I don't even have to wear my earbuds. The only drawback is that Taelor Tremont's family owns the place.

She called before the grand opening two years ago. "Thought you would be interested in what we're naming the center," she said, voice dripping with sarcasm.

"Yeah, why's that?" I attempted civility because her dad, Mr.

Tremont, had contracted my dad's sporting goods store to be the sole supplier for the megacenter. It's a good thing, too, considering we had been on the verge of bankruptcy because of Alison's medical bills. Also, as an added bonus, I got a free lifetime membership.

"Well . . ." Taelor snickered softly. I heard her friends laughing in the background. I must've been on speakerphone. "Dad wants to call it Wonderland." Giggles bubbled through the line. "I thought you'd love it, knowing how proud you are of your great-great-great-grand-rabbit."

The jibe hurt more than it should have. I must've been quiet for too long, because Taelor's giggles faded.

"Actually"—she half coughed the word—"I'm thinking that's way overused. Underland's better. You know, since it's underground. How's that sound, Alyssa?"

I recall that rare glimpse of regret from Taelor today as I carve the middle of the skateboard bowl beneath the bright neon UNDERLAND sign hanging from the ceiling. It's nice to be reminded that she has a human side. A rock song pipes through the speakers. As I come down the lower half of the skating bowl, dark silhouettes swoop around me against the neon backdrop.

Balancing my back foot on the tail of the board, I prepare to pull up on the nose with my front. An attempt at an ollie a few weeks ago won me a bruised tailbone. I now have a deathly fear of the move, but something inside me won't let me give up.

I have to keep trying or I'll never get enough air to learn any real tricks, but my determination goes much deeper. It's visceral—a flutter that jumbles my thoughts and nerves until I'm convinced I'm not scared. Sometimes I think I'm not alone in my own head, that there's a part of someone lingering there, someone who chides me to push myself beyond my limits.

Embracing the adrenaline surge, I launch. Curious how much air I'm clearing, I snap my eyes open. I'm midjump, cement coming up fast beneath me. My spine prickles. I lose my nerve and my front foot slips, sending me down to the ground with a loud *oomph*.

My left leg and arm make first contact. Pain jolts through every bone. The impact knocks the breath from my lungs and I skid to a stop in the basin. My board rolls after me like a faithful pet, stopping to nudge my ribs.

Gasping for air, I flip onto my back. Every nerve in my knee and ankle blazes. My pad's strap ripped loose, leaving a tear in the black leggings I wear beneath my purple bike shorts. Against the neon green surface slanting beside me, I see a dark smear. Blood . . .

I draw my split knee up, inhaling a sharp breath. Within seconds of my crash landing, three employees blow whistles and Rollerblade through the lines of slowing skaters. They wear mining caps, with a light affixed to the front, but they're more like lifeguards—stationed for easy access and certified in the fundamentals of first aid.

They form a visible barrier with their bright crossing-guard vests to deter other boarders from tripping over us while they bandage me up and clean my blood from the cement with disinfectant.

A fourth employee rolls up in a manager's vest. Of all people, it has to be Jebediah Holt.

"I should've bailed," I mumble grudgingly.

"Are you kidding? Nobody could've seen that slam coming in time." His deep voice soothes as he kneels beside me. "And glad to see you're speaking to me again." He wears cargo shorts and a dark tee beneath his vest. The black lights glide over his skin, highlighting his toned arms with bluish flashes.

I tug at the helmet's straps beneath my chin. His miner beam is singling me out like a spotlight. "Help me take this off?" I ask.

Jeb bends closer to hear me over the wailing vocals overhead. His cologne—a mix of chocolate and lavender—blends with his sweat into a scent as familiar and appealing as cotton candy to a kid at the fair.

His fingers curve under my chin and he snaps the buckle free. As he helps me push the helmet off, his thumb grazes my earlobe, making it tingle. The glare of his lamp blinds me. I can only make out the dark stubble on his jaw, those straight white teeth (with the exception of the left incisor that slants slightly across his front tooth), and the small iron spike centered beneath his lower lip.

Taelor raked him up and down about his piercing, but he refuses to get rid of it, which makes me like it all the more. She's only been his girlfriend for a couple of months. She has no claim over what he does.

Jeb's callused palm cups my elbow. "Can you stand?"

"Of course I can," I snap, not intentionally harsh, just not the biggest fan of being on display. The minute I put weight on my leg, a jab shoots through my ankle and doubles me over. An employee supports me from behind while Jeb sits down to strip off his blades and socks. Before I know what he's doing, he lifts me and carries me out of the bowl.

"Jeb, I want to walk." I wrap my arms around his neck to stay balanced. I can feel the smirks of the other skaters as we pass even if I can't see them in the dark. They'll never let me forget being carried away like a diva.

Jeb cradles me tighter, which makes it hard not to notice how close we are: my hands locked around his neck, his chest rubbing against my ribs . . . those biceps pressed to my shoulder blade and knee.

I give up fighting as he steps off the cement onto the wood-planked floor.

At first I think we're headed to the café, but we pass the arcade and swing a right toward the entrance ramp, following the arc of light laid out by his helmet. Jeb's hip shoves the gym-style doors. I blink, trying to adjust to the brightness outside. Warm gusts of wind slap hair around my face.

He perches me gently on the sunbaked cement, then drops beside me and takes off his helmet, shaking out his hair. He hasn't cut it in a few weeks, and it's long enough to graze his shoulders. Thick bangs dip low—a black curtain touching his nose. He loosens the red and navy bandana from around his thigh and wraps it over his head, securing it in a knot at his nape to push back the strands from his face.

Those dark green eyes study the bandage where blood drips from my knee. "I told you to replace your gear. Your strap's been unraveling for weeks."

Here we go. He's already in surrogate-big-brother mode, even though he's only two and a half years older and one grade ahead of me. "Been talking to my dad again, have you?"

A strained expression crosses his face as he starts messing with his knee pads. I follow his lead and take my remaining one off.

"Actually," I say, mentally berating myself for not having the sense to fall back into my silent-treatment bubble, "I should be grateful you and Dad allow me to come here at all. Seeing as it's so dark, and all sorts of scary, bad things could happen to my helpless little self."

A muscle in Jeb's jaw twitches, a sure sign I've struck a nerve. "This has nothing to do with your dad. Other than the fact that he owns a sporting goods store, which means you have no excuse for not maintaining your gear. Boarding can be dangerous."

"Yeah. Just like London is dangerous, right?" I glare across the gleaming cars in the parking lot, smoothing the wrinkles from my red T-shirt's design: a bleeding heart wrapped in barbed wire. Might as well be an X-ray of my chest.

"Great." He tosses his knee pads aside. "So, you're not over it."

"What's to get over? Instead of standing up for me, you took his side. Now I can't go until I graduate. Why should that bother me?" I pluck at my fingerless gloves to suppress the acid bite of anger burning on my tongue.

"At least by staying home, you *will* graduate." Jeb moves to his elbow pads and rips off the Velcro, punctuating his point.

"I would've graduated there, too."

He huffs.

We shouldn't be discussing this. The disappointment is too fresh. I was so psyched about the study-abroad program that allowed seniors to finish out their final year of high school in London while getting college credits from one of the best art universities there. The very university Jeb's going to.

Since he's already received his scholarship and plans to move to London later this summer, Dad asked him to dinner a couple of weeks ago to talk about the program. I thought it was a great idea, that with Jeb in my corner I was as good as on a plane. And then, together, they decided it wasn't the right time for me to go. *They* decided.

Dad worries because Alison has an aversion to England—too much Liddell family history. He thinks my going would cause a relapse. She's already being prodded with more needles than most junkies on the street.

At least his reasons made sense. I still haven't figured out why Jeb vetoed the idea. But what does it matter at this point? The sign-up deadline was last Friday, so there's no changing things now.

"Traitor," I mumble.

He dips his head down, forcing me to look at him. "I'm trying to be your friend. You're not ready to move so far from your dad . . . you'll have no one to look out for you."

"You'll be there."

"But I can't be with you every second. My schedule's going to be insane."

"I don't need someone with me every second. I'm not a kid."

"Never said you were a kid. But you don't always make the best decisions. Case in point." He pinches my shin, popping the torn knit leggings with a snap.

A jolt of excitement runs through my leg. I frown, convincing myself I'm just ticklish. "So, I'm not allowed to make a few mistakes?"

"Not mistakes that can hurt you."

I shake my head. "Like being stuck here doesn't hurt. At a school I can't stand, with classmates whose idea of fun is making cracks about the white rabbit tail I'm hiding. Thanks for that, Jeb."

He sighs and sits up. "Right. Everything is my fault. I guess your eating cement in there was my fault, too."

The strain behind his voice tugs at my heart. "Well, the slam was *kind* of your fault." My voice softens, a conscious effort to ease the tension between us. "I would've already aced an ollie if you were still teaching the skateboard class."

Jeb's lips twitch. "So, the new teacher, Hitch . . . he's not doin' it for ya?"

I punch him, releasing some pent-up frustration. "No, he's not *doing* it for me."

Jeb fakes a wince. "He'd sure like to. But I told him I'd kick his—"

"As if you have a say." Hitch is nineteen and the go-to king for fake IDs and recreational drugs. He's a prison sentence waiting to happen. I know better than to get tangled up with him, but that's my call.

Jeb shoots me a look. I sense a talk coming on about the evils of dating players.

I flick a grasshopper off my leg with a blue fingernail, refusing to let its whispers make the moment any more awkward than it is.

Mercifully, the double doors swing open from behind. Jeb scoots away to let a couple of girls through. A cloud of powdery perfume wafts over us as they pass and wave at Jeb. He nods back. We watch them get into a car and peel out of the parking lot.

"Hey," Jeb says. "It's Friday. Aren't you supposed to visit your mom?"

I jump on the subject change. "Meeting Dad there. And then I promised Jen I'd take the last two hours of her shift." After looking at my torn clothes, I glance into the sky—the same striking blue as Alison's eyes. "I hope I have time to drop home and change before work."

Jeb stands. "Let me clock out," he says. "I'll get your board and backpack and drive you to Soul's."

That's the last thing I need.

Neither Jeb nor his sister, Jenara, have ever met Alison; they've only seen pictures of her. They don't even know the truth about my scars or why I wear the gloves. My friends all think I was in a car accident with my mom as a kid and that the windshield messed up my hands and injured her brain. Dad doesn't like the lie, but the reality is so bizarre, he lets me embellish.

"What about your bike?" I'm grasping at straws, considering Jeb's souped-up vintage Honda CT70 isn't anywhere on the lot.

"They predicted rain, so Jen dropped me off," he answers. "Your dad can take you to work later, and I'll drive your car home. It's not like it's out of my way."

Jeb's family shares the other side of our duplex. Dad and I went over to introduce ourselves one summer morning after they first moved in. Jeb, Jenara, and I became tight before sixth grade started the next fall—tight enough that on the first day of school, Jeb beat up a guy in the breezeway for calling me the Mad Hatter's love slave.

Jeb slides on some shades and repositions the bandana's knot at the back of his head. Sunlight hits the shiny, round scars peppered along his forearms.

I turn to the cars in the lot. Gizmo—my 1975 Gremlin, named after a character in the eighties movie Dad took Alison to on their first date—is only a couple of yards away. There's a chance Alison will be waiting in the lounge with Dad. If I can't count on Jeb to back me up about London, I can't trust him to meet the biggest nut who's fallen from my family tree.

"Uh-uh," Jeb says. "I see that look. No way you can drive a standard with a sprained ankle." He holds out a palm. "Fork 'em over."

With a roll of my eyes, I drop my keys into his hand.

He pushes his shades to the bandana at his hairline. "Wait here and I'll walk you."

A burst of air-conditioning hits my face as the door to the complex slams shut behind him. There's a tickle on my leg. This time, I don't swish the grasshopper away, and I hear its whisper loud and clear: *"Doomed."*

"Yeah," I whisper back, stroking its veined wings and surrendering to my delusions. "It's all over once Jeb meets Alison."

BARBED WIRE
& BLACK WINGS

Soul's Asylum is a twenty-five-minute drive outside the city limits.

Afternoon sun beats down, glaring off the car's hood. Once you get past the buildings, strip malls, and houses, there's not much landscaping in Pleasance. Just flat, dry plains with sparse growths of shrubbery and spindly trees.

Each time Jeb starts to talk, I mumble a monosyllabic response, then crank up the volume on the newly installed CD player.

Finally, a song comes on—an acoustic, moody number I've heard Jeb listen to when he paints—and he drives in silent contemplation. The baggie of ice he brought for my swollen ankle has melted, and I move my foot to let it roll off.

I fight drowsiness, knowing what waits on the other side of sleep. I don't need to revisit my Alice nightmare in midafternoon.

As a teenager, Alison's mom, Alicia, painted the Wonderland characters on every wall of her home, insisting that they were real and talked to her in dreams. Years later, Alicia took a flying leap out of her second-story hospital room window to test her "wings," just a few hours after giving birth to my mom. She landed in a rosebush and broke her neck.

Some say she committed suicide—postpartum depression and grief over losing her husband months earlier in a factory accident. Others say she should've been locked away long before she had a child.

After her mom's death, Alison was left to be raised by a long line of foster parents. Dad thinks the instability contributed to her illness. I know it's something more, something hereditary, because of my recurrent nightmare and the bugs and plants. And then there's the presence I feel inside. The one that vibrates and shadows me when I'm scared or hesitant, prodding me to push my limits.

I've researched schizophrenia. They say one of the symptoms is hearing voices, not a winglike thumping in the skull. Then again, if I were to count the whispers of flowers and bugs, I hear plenty of voices. By any of those measurements, I'm sick.

My throat swells on a lump and I swallow it down.

The CD changes songs, and I concentrate on the melody, trying to forget everything else. Dust slaps against the car as Jeb shifts gears. I glance sideways at his profile. There's Italian somewhere in his bloodline, and he has a really great complexion—olive-toned and clear, soft to the touch.

He tilts his head my way. I turn to the rearview mirror and watch the car freshener swing. Today's the first day I've had it hanging in place.

On eBay, there's a store that sells customized fresheners for ten bucks apiece. Just e-mail a photo, and they print it onto a scented card, then snail-mail the finished product to you. A couple of weeks ago, I used some birthday money and bought two of them, one for me and one for Dad—which he has yet to hang in his truck. He has it tucked in his wallet; I wonder if it will always stay hidden in there, too painful for him to see every day.

"It turned out good," Jeb says, referring to the air freshener.

"Yeah," I mumble. "It's Alison's shot, so it was bound to."

Jeb nods, his unspoken understanding more comforting than other people's well-intentioned words.

I stare at the photo. It's an image of a huge black-winged moth from one of Alison's old albums. The shot is amazing, the way the wings are splayed on a flower between a slant of sun and shade, teetering between two worlds. Alison used to capture things most people wouldn't notice—moments in time when opposites collide, then merge seamlessly together. Makes me wonder how successful she might've been if she hadn't lost her mind.

I tap the air freshener, following its sway.

The bug has always seemed familiar—eerily fascinating yet at the same time calming.

It occurs to me I don't know its history—what species it is, where it lives. If I found out, I would know where Alison might've been when she shot the picture and could feel closer to her somehow, but I can't ask. She's sensitive about her albums.

I reach behind the bucket seat, dig my iPhone out of my backpack, and open a search for *glowing moth*.

After twenty-some pages of tattoos, logos, Lunesta ads, and costume designs, a moth sketch catches my eye. Not a perfect match to Alison's, but the body's a bright blue and the wings shimmer black, so it's close enough.

Clicking on the image turns the screen blank. I'm about to restart the browser when a strobe of bright red stops me. The screen throbs as if I'm looking at a heartbeat. The air seems to pulse around me in synchrony.

A Web page flickers to life. White font and colorful graphics stand out vividly against the black background. The first thing that hits me is the title: *Netherlings—denizens of the nether-realm.*

Next follows a definition: *A dark and twisted race of supernatural beings indigenous to an ancient world hidden deep within the heart of the earth. Most use their magic for mischief and revenge, though a rare few have a penchant for kindness and courage.*

I scroll past images every bit as violent and beautiful as Jeb's paintings: luminous, rainbow-skinned creatures with bulbous eyes and sparkly, silken wings who carry knives and swords; hideous, naked hobgoblins in chains who crawl on all fours and have corkscrew tails and cloven feet like pigs; silvery pixielike beings trapped in cages and crying oily black tears.

According to the text, in their truest forms, netherlings can look like almost anything—they can be as small as a rosebud or larger than a man. Some can even emulate mortals, taking on the likeness of existing humans to deceive the people around them.

An uneasy knot forms in my chest at the next line of text: *While wreaking havoc in the mortal world, netherlings stay connected to their kind by using plants and insects as conduits to the nether-realm.*

My breath catches. The words dance around me, a dizzying rise and fall of broken logic. If this were true and not just some Web weirdo's fantasy, it would mean Alison and I share the traits of some creepy, mystical creatures. But that's not even possible.

The car bounces over a bump and I drop the cell. When I pick it up, I've lost the website and any signal. "Crap!"

"Nope. Pothole." Downshifting gears, Jeb sidles a lazy gaze my way—Mr. Cool behind those shades.

I glare at him. "You should probably keep your eyes on the road in case there's any more, genius."

He shifts back from third to fourth gear, grinning. "Fierce game of solitaire?"

"Bug research. Make a right here." I drop the phone into my backpack. I'm so uptight about going to Soul's, I probably read the words wrong. Even though I'm almost convinced of that, the kink in my stomach won't loosen.

Jeb turns onto a long, winding road. We pass a faded sign: SOUL'S ASYLUM: OFFERING PEACE AND REST TO THE WEARY MIND SINCE 1942.

Peace. Yeah, right. More like drug-induced catatonia.

I roll down the window and let in a warm breeze. Gizmo idles while we wait for the automatic wrought-iron gates to respond.

Flipping open the glove compartment, I dig out a small cosmetics bag along with the hair extensions that Jenara helped me make out of shimmery blue yarn. They're strung together and clip in for a dreadlocks effect.

We cruise toward the four-story brick building in the distance; it stands out bloodred against the clear sky. It could've been a gingerbread mansion, but the white shingles on the gabled roof look more like jagged teeth than icing.

Jeb finds a parking space next to my dad's Ford pickup and cuts the engine. The motor grinds to a stop.

"Has the car been making that sound long?" He tosses his shades onto the dash and concentrates on the panel behind the steering wheel, checking out dials and numbers.

I lift my braid over my shoulder, sliding the elastic band from the end. "About a week." Hair hangs across my chest in platinum waves just like Alison's. Per Dad's request, I don't dye it or cut it because it reminds him of hers. So I've had to find other creative ways of ramping up my style.

I bend at the waist until my hair flows like a stream over my knees. Once the dreadlocks feel secure, I flip my head upright and catch Jeb watching me.

He jerks his gaze back to the dashboard. "If you hadn't been ignoring my calls, I could've already taken a look at your engine. You shouldn't drive this until it's fixed."

"Gizmo's fine. Just a little hoarse. Maybe he needs to gargle some salt water."

"This isn't a joke. What are you going to do if you get stalled out in the middle of nowhere?"

I twirl a strand of hair around my finger. "Hmm. Show some cleavage to a passing trucker?"

Jeb's jaw clenches. "That's not funny."

I giggle. "Oh, come on. I'm kidding. All it would really take is a little leg."

His lips curve slightly, but the smile is gone in a blink. "This from the girl who's never even had a first kiss."

He's always teased that I'm a mix between skate glam and American sweetheart. Looks like I've just been downgraded to prude.

I groan. It won't do any good to deny it. "Fine. I would call someone on my cell and wait safely in my car with all the doors locked and Mace in hand until help arrived. There, do I win a cookie?"

He thumps a finger against the dash. "I'll come over to look at it later. You can hang with me in the garage. Just like we used to."

I pull some eye shadow out of the cosmetics bag. "I'd like that."

His smile makes a full appearance—dimples and all—a glimpse of the old, playful, teasing Jeb. My pulse quickens at the sight of it.

"Great," he says. "How about tonight?"

I huff. "Right. Taelor would have a litter of kittens if you left prom early to tinker with my car."

He drops his forehead to the steering wheel. "Ugh. I forgot about the dance. I still have to pick up my tux." He glances at the clock on my dash. "Jen said some guy asked you but you didn't want to go. Why not?"

I shrug. "I have this character flaw? Called dignity?"

He snorts and picks up a bottle of raspberry-flavored water wedged between the emergency brake and console and drinks what's left.

I open my compact and apply a smear of kohl eye shadow atop what's already there, and then elongate the outside corner like a cat's eye. Once I finish both eyes with a sweep along the bottom lashes, my ice-blue irises stand out against the black like a fluorescent shirt beneath the UV lights at Underland.

Jeb leans back in his seat. "Well done. You've managed to destroy any resemblance to your mom."

I freeze. "I'm not trying—"

"C'mon, Al. It's me." He stretches out a hand to bat the air freshener. The moth spins, reminding me of the website. The pinch in my sternum tightens.

I drop my eye shadow into the bag and fish out some silver gloss to spread over my lips, then stuff the bag back into the glove compartment.

Jeb's hand rests next to my elbow on the console, his warmth seeping over to me. "You're scared if you look like her, you'll be like her. And end up here, too."

I'm speechless. He's always been able to read me. But this . . . it's like he's crawled inside my head.

God forbid.

My throat dries, and I stare at the empty water bottle between us.

"It's not easy to live in someone's shadow." His face darkens.

He would know. He's got the scars to prove it, deeper than the cigarette burns on his torso and arms. I still remember after they first moved in: the blood-chilling screams next door at two in the morning as he tried to protect his sister and mom from his drunken dad. The best thing that ever happened to Jeb's family was when Mr. Holt wrapped his truck around a tree one night three years ago. His blood alcohol level was at 0.3.

Thankfully, Jeb never touches the stuff. His dark moods don't mix well with alcohol. He found that out a few years back, after nearly killing some guy in a fight. The court sent Jeb to a youth detention center for a year, which is why he graduated at age nineteen. He lost twelve months of his life but gained a future, because at the center a psychologist helped him rein in his bitterness through his art and taught him that having structure and balance was the best way to contain his rage.

"Just remember," he says, weaving our fingers together. "With you, it's not hereditary. Your mom had an accident."

Our palms touch with only my knit gloves between us, and I press my forearm to his to align the ridges of his scars against my skin.

You're wrong, I want to say. *I'm exactly like you.* But I can't. The fact is, alcoholics have programs, steps to take so they can fit into society and function. Crazies like Alison—all they have are padded cells and blunted utensils. That's their normal.

Our normal.

Looking down, I notice blood has seeped and dried on the bandage at my knee. I run a hand over it, worried about Alison. She flips out at the sight of blood.

"Here." Without my even saying a word, Jeb works the bandana off his head. Leaning over, he ties the cloth around my knee to hide the soiled bandage. When he's done, instead of moving back to his side of the car, he props an elbow on the console and runs a finger along one of the blue falls in my hair. Either it's vibes from our unresolved issues or from our intimate conversation, but his expression is serious.

"Those dreadlocks are wicked tight." His voice is low and velvety, filling my stomach with knots. "You know, you really should go to prom. Show up just like this and knock everyone on their asses. I guarantee you'll still have your dignity."

He studies my face with an expression I've only seen when he paints. Intense. Absorbed. As if he's considering the painting from every angle. *Me* from every angle.

He's so close, I smell the raspberry on his hot breath. His gaze shifts to the dimple in my chin and my cheeks flame.

In the back of my head, that shadowy sensation rouses, not so much a voice as a presence, like a shudder of wings scrambling my insides . . . urging me to touch the labret beneath his lower lip. Instinctively, I reach out. He doesn't even flinch as I trace the silvery spike.

The metal is warm, and his stubble tickles my fingertip on either side. Hit full-on by the intimacy of my action, I start to draw back.

He grabs my hand and holds my finger against his lips. His eyes darken, thick lashes narrowing. "Al," he whispers.

"Butterfly!" Dad's shout carries through the open window. I jump, and Jeb boomerangs to his side of the car. Dad saunters down the immaculate lawn toward Gizmo, wearing khaki pants and a royal blue polo embroidered with TOM'S SPORTING GOODS in silver thread.

I soothe my racing pulse with a few deep breaths.

Dad bends over to look through my window. "Hello, Jebediah."

Jeb clears his throat. "Hey there, Mr. Gardner."

"Hmm. Maybe you should finally start calling me Thomas." Dad grins, arm propped on the window's edge. "After all, you graduated last night."

Jeb smirks, proud and boyish. He gets that way around my dad. Mr. Holt used to tell him he'd never amount to anything, pressuring him to drop out and work at the garage full-time, but my dad always encouraged Jeb to stay in school. If I wasn't still ticked over how they'd teamed up against me about London, I might actually enjoy their moment of bonding.

"So my girl lassoed you into being her chauffeur?" Dad asks, shooting me a teasing glance.

"Yep. She even sprained an ankle to get her way," Jeb ribs back.

How can his voice sound so steady, while I feel like a hurricane has been set loose in my chest? Isn't he even a little rattled by what happened between us two seconds ago?

He reaches into the backseat and tugs on the handles of the wooden crutches he borrowed from Underland's medical supply room.

"What did you do?" Dad opens my car door, worry apparent on his face.

I swing out my legs slowly, gritting my teeth against the throb as blood rushes to my ankle. "The usual. Skateboarding is trial and error, you know?" I glance at Jeb as he comes around to the passenger side, mentally forbidding him to tell Dad about the worn-out knee pad.

Jeb gives his head a shake, and for a second, I think he's going to turn on me again. Instead, our eyes lock and my insides tangle. What made me touch him like that earlier? Things are weird enough between us as is.

Dad helps me stand and crouches to look at my ankle. "Interesting. Your mom was convinced something happened. She said you'd hurt yourself." He stands, an inch shorter than Jeb. "I suppose she just assumes the worst any time you're late. You should've called." He cups my elbow while I position the crutches under my arms.

"Sorry."

"It's okay. Let's get you inside before she does something—" Dad stops himself in answer to my pleading gaze. "Uh, before our ice cream melts to cheesecake soup."

We start toward the sidewalk lined with peonies. Bugs dance atop the flowers and white noise grows around me, making me wish I had my earbuds and iPod.

Dad throws a glance over his shoulder when we're halfway to the door. "Could you park the car in the garage, in case it rains?"

"Sure thing," Jeb's voice answers back. "Hey, skater girl . . ."

I pause behind Dad and pivot on my good foot, fingers tight around the cushioned crutch grips as I study Jeb's expression in the distance. He looks as confused as I feel.

"When do you work tomorrow?" he asks.

I stand there like a brainless mannequin. "Um . . . Jen and I are on the noon shift."

"Okay. Get a ride with her. I'll come by then to look at Gizmo's engine."

My heart sinks. So much for hanging out like old times. Looks like he's going to avoid *me* now. "Right. Sure." I bite back my disappointment and turn to hobble with Dad up the path.

He catches my eye. "Everything all right between you two? I can't remember a time you didn't tinker in the garage together."

I shrug as he opens the glass door. "Maybe we're growing apart." It hurts to say it, more than I'll ever admit out loud.

"He's always been a good friend," Dad says. "You should work it out."

"A friend doesn't try to run your life. That's what dads are for." Raising my eyebrows to make my point, I limp into the air-conditioned building. He steps in behind me, silent.

I shiver. The hallways here unsettle me with their long, empty stretches and yellow blinking lights. White tiles magnify the sounds, and nurses in peppermint-striped scrubs blur in my peripheral vision. The uniforms make them look more like candy stripers than certified health-care professionals.

Counting the barbs painted on my T-shirt, I wait for Dad to talk to the nurse behind the main desk. A fly lands on my arm and I swat at it. It swoops around my head with a loud buzz that almost sounds like "*He's here,*" before darting down the corridor.

Dad pauses beside me as I stare after the fly. "You sure you're all right?"

I nod, shaking off the delusion. "Just don't know what to expect today." It's only a half lie. Alison gets too distracted around plants and insects to go outside very often, but she's been begging for fresh air, and Dad talked her doctor into trying. Who knows what might come of it?

"Yeah. I'm hoping this doesn't unbalance her too much . . ." His voice trails off, and his shoulders slouch, as if all the sadness of the last eleven years weighs on them. "I wish you could remember her the way she was before." He places a hand on my nape as we head toward the courtyard. "She was so levelheaded. So together. *So much like you.*" He whispers that last part, maybe in hopes I won't hear.

But I do, and the barbed wire tightens once more, until my heart is strangled and broken.

THE SPIDER & THE FLY

Other than Alison, her nurse, and a couple of groundskeepers, the courtyard is deserted. Alison sits at one of the black cast-iron bistro tables on a cement patio that's been stamped to look like cobblestone. Even the decor has to be chosen carefully in a place like this. There's no glass anywhere, only a reflective silver gazing globe secured tightly to its pedestal base.

Since some patients are known to pick up chairs or tables and throw them, the legs of the furniture are bolted into the cement. A black and red polka-dotted parasol sprouts up from the center of the table like a giant mushroom and shades half of Alison's face. Silver teacups and saucers glisten in the sunlight. Three settings: one for me, one for Dad, and one for her.

We brought the tea service from home years ago when she first checked in. It's an indulgence the asylum caters to in order to keep her alive. Alison won't eat anything—be it Salisbury steak or fruit cobbler—unless it's in a teacup.

Our pint of chocolate-cheesecake ice cream waits on a place mat, ready to be scooped out. Condensation rolls down the cardboard packaging.

Alison's platinum braid swings over her chair's back, almost touching the ground. She has her bangs tucked beneath a black headband. Wearing a blue gown with a long bib apron to keep her clothes clean, she looks more like Alice at the Mad Hatter's tea party than most of the illustrations I've seen.

It's enough to make me physically sick.

At first I think she's talking to the nurse until the woman stands to greet us, smoothing out her peppermint scrubs. Alison doesn't notice, too intent on the metal vase of carnations in front of her.

My nausea escalates when I hear the carnations talking over the drone of white noise in the background. They're saying how painful it is to be snipped at the stems, complaining about the quality of the water they're swimming in, asking to be put back into the ground so they can die in peace.

That's what I hear, anyway. I have to wonder what Alison thinks they're saying in her own warped mind. The doctor can't get details, and I've never brought it up because it would mean admitting I inherited her sickness.

Dad waits for the nurse, but his gaze, heavy with longing and disappointment, stays locked on Alison.

A slight pressure on my right arm shifts my attention to the unnaturally tan face of Nurse Mary Jenkins. The scent radiating off her is a mix of burned toast and talcum powder. Her brown hair is pulled up in a bun, and a white, high-voltage smile nearly singes my vision.

"Howdy-hi," she sings. As usual, she's over-the-top bubbly—like Mary Poppins. She studies my crutches. "Yikes! Did you hurt yourself, honey drop?"

No. I've sprouted wooden appendages. "Skateboard," I answer, determined to be on my best behavior for Dad's sake, in spite of how the yammering flowers on the table have gotten under my skin.

"Still skateboarding? Such an interesting hobby." Her pitying stare implies *"for a girl"* better than words ever could. She studies my blue dreadlocks and thick eye makeup with a grim expression on her face. "You need to keep in mind that a calamity like this can upset your mother."

I'm not sure if she's talking about my injuries or my fashion sense.

The nurse looks over her shoulder at Alison, who's still whispering to the flowers, oblivious to us. "She's already a little high-strung today. I should give her something." Nurse Poppin' Stuff starts to pull a syringe from the arsenal in her pocket. One of the many things I despise about her: She seems to enjoy giving her patients shots.

Over the years, the doctors have discovered that sedatives work best to control Alison's outbursts. But they turn her into a drooling zombie, unaware of anything around her. I'd rather see her alert and conversing with a roach than like that.

I scowl at my dad, but he doesn't even notice because he's so busy frowning himself.

"No," he says, and the deep, disciplinarian edge to his voice makes the nurse's penciled-in eyebrows snap up. "I'll send Alyssa for you if things get difficult. And we've got the gardeners over there for manpower if we need it." He gestures to the two hulking men in the distance who are pruning some branches from a bush. They could be twins with their huge mustaches and walrus-shaped bodies stuffed in brown coveralls.

"All rightio. I'll be at the front desk when you need me." With another glaringly fake smile, she bounces into the building, leaving the three of us in solitude. Or the eight of us, if you count the carnations. At least they've finally stopped talking.

The minute Dad's shadow glides across the vase, Alison looks up. One glance at my crutches, and she launches from her seat, rattling the tea set. "He was right!"

"Who was right, hon?" Dad asks, smoothing back the loose hairs framing her temples. Even after all the years of disappointment, he still can't resist touching her.

"The grasshopper . . ." Alison's blue eyes glitter with a mix of anxiety and excitement as she points to a thick web in the parasol's ribs. A silver-dollar-size garden spider scuttles across it, securing a white cocoon against the gusting wind—dinner, no doubt. "Before the spider wrapped him up, the grasshopper shouted something." Alison's hands clench together in front of her waist. "The grasshopper said you'd been hurt, Allie. He saw you outside the skating place."

I stare at the mummified lump in the spider's web. There was that insect that kept climbing my leg at Underland. What, did it hitch a ride on the car?

My stomach turns over. No way. No possible way it's the same bug. Alison must've overheard me and Dad talking to the nurse about my fall. Sometimes I think she pretends to be oblivious because it's easier than facing what's happened to her, or what she's done to our family.

She grips her hands so hard, the knuckles bulge white. Ever since the day she hurt me, she avoids any physical contact between us. She thinks I'll break. That's one of the reasons I wear gloves, so she won't see the scars and be reminded.

Dad pries her hands apart and laces his fingers through hers. Alison's attention settles on him, and the chaotic intensity melts away.

"Hi, Tommy-toes," she says, her voice soft and steady.

"Hi, Ali-bear."

"You brought ice cream. Is this a date?"

"Yeah." He kisses her knuckles, flashing his best Elvis smirk. "And Alyssa's here to help us celebrate."

"Perfect." She smiles back, her eyes dancing. No wonder Dad's helplessly in love with her. She's pretty enough to be a fairy.

Dad helps her back to her chair. He lays a cloth napkin in her lap, then slops some drippy ice cream into a teacup. Placing the cup on a saucer, he eases it in front of her along with a plastic spoon.

"*Il tuo gelato, signora bella,*" he says.

"*Grazie* meatball!" she blurts, in a rare moment of levity.

Dad laughs and she giggles, a tinkling sound that makes me

think of the silver chimes we have over our back door at home. For the first time in a while, she *feels* like home. I start to think this is going to be one of our good visits. With everything going on in my life lately, it would sure be nice to have a moment of stability.

I sit, and Dad takes my crutches, laying them on the ground, then helps me prop my ankle on an empty chair between Alison and me. He pats my shoulder and takes a seat on the opposite side.

For several minutes, we laugh and sip sticky cheesecake soup from our teacups. We talk about normal things: the end of the school year, tonight's prom, last night's graduation, and Tom's Sporting Goods. It's like I'm in a regular family.

Then Dad ruins it. He takes out his wallet to show Alison snapshots of my mosaics that won ribbons at the county fair. The three photos are stuck in the plastic sleeves along with an assortment of credit cards and receipts.

First is *Murderess Moonlight*, all in blues: blue butterflies, blue flowers, and bits of blue glass. Then *Autumn's Last Breath*—a whirlwind of fall colors made up of brown moths and orange, yellow, and red flower petals. *Winter's Heartbeat*, my pride, is a chaotic tangle of baby's breath and silvery glass beads arranged in the image of a tree. Dried winterberries dot the end of each branch, as if the tree is bleeding. Jet-black crickets form the backdrop. As morbid as it sounds, the mixing of bizarre and natural somehow creates beauty.

Alison wriggles in her chair as if disturbed. "What about her music? Is she still practicing her cello?"

Dad squints my way. Alison's had very little to do with my education. But one thing she's always insisted on is my participation in orchestra, maybe because she used to play the cello herself. I dropped out this year when I only had time for one elective. We haven't mentioned it because it seems so important to her that I continue.

"We can talk about that later," Dad says, squeezing her hand. "I wanted you to see her eye for detail. Just like you with your photographs."

"Photographs tell a story," Alison mutters. "But people forget to read between the lines." Breaking her hand out of Dad's, she becomes deathly quiet.

Eyes filled with sadness, Dad's about to close the wallet when Alison spots the air freshener with the moth's picture . . . the one he hasn't yet hung in his truck.

With trembling hands, she grabs it. "Why are you carrying this with you?"

"Mom . . ." My tongue strains with the effort to form the word, unnatural and stiff, like trying to twist a cherry's stem into a knot. "I had it made for him. It's a way to keep a part of you with us."

Jaw clenched, she turns to Dad. "I told you to keep that album hidden. Didn't I? She was never supposed to see this. It's only a matter of time now . . ."

It's only a matter of time till what? I end up here where she is? Does she think the photographs made her crazy?

Frowning, she tosses the air freshener across the table. Her tongue clucks a steady rhythm. The sound snaps inside me, as if someone is plucking my intestines with a guitar pick. Her most violent outbursts always start with the tongue cluck.

Dad stiffens his fingers around the air freshener, wary.

A fly alights on my neck, tickling me. When I swat it away, it lands beside Alison's fingers. It rubs its tiny legs together. *"He's here. He's here."*

Its whispers rise above the wind and the rest of the white noise, above Alison's clucking tongue and Dad's cautious breaths.

Alison leans toward the bug. "No, he can't be here."

"Who can't be here, Ali-bear?" Dad asks.

I stare, wondering if it's possible. Do crazy people share delusions? Because that's the only explanation for Alison and me hearing the exact same thing.

Unless the fly really did talk.

"He rides the wind," it whispers once more, then flits off into the courtyard.

Alison locks me in her frantic gaze.

I tense, stunned.

"Hon, what's wrong?" Dad stands next to her now, his hand on her shoulder.

"What does that mean, 'He rides the wind'? Who?" I ask Alison, no longer caring about giving my secret away to her.

She glares at me, intense and silent.

Dad watches both of us, looking paler by the second.

"Dad?" I lean across my propped up leg and tug at my sock. "Could you get some ice for my foot? It's throbbing."

He scowls. "Can't it wait a second, Alyssa?"

"Please. It hurts."

"Yes, she's hurt." Alison reaches over and touches my ankle. The gesture is shocking—so normal and nurturing, it chills my blood and bones. Alison is touching me, *for the first time in eleven years.*

The monumental event rattles Dad so much, he leaves without another word. I can tell by the twitch in his left eyelid that he'll be bringing Poppin' Fresh back with him.

Alison and I don't have long.

The minute he vanishes through the door, I jerk my leg off the chair, wincing against a jolt of pain in my ankle. "The fly. We both heard the same thing, right?"

Alison's cheeks pale. "How long have you heard the voices?"

"What difference does it make?"

"All the difference. I could've told you things . . . things to keep you from making the wrong choice."

"Tell me now."

She shakes her head.

Maybe she's not convinced I hear the same voices she does. "The carnations. We should honor their last request." I pick up a plastic spoon and, carnations in hand, hop on one crutch to the edge of the cement courtyard where the landscaping begins. The earth smells damp and fresh. The sprinklers have been on recently. Alison follows close behind.

I don't see the walrus gardeners anymore. In the distance, the shed door is open. The men must be inside. Good. There's no one to interrupt us.

Alison takes the flowers and spoon and drops to her knees. She uses the spoon to burrow into the soft earth. When the plastic snaps, she digs with her fingers until there's a shallow grave.

She lays the blossoms within and rakes dirt back over the top. The expression on her face is like a sky filled with churning clouds, undecided whether to storm or dissipate.

My legs waver. For so many years, the women in our family have been pegged as crazy, but we're not. We can hear things other people can't. That's the only way we could both hear the fly and carnations say the same thing. The trick is not to talk back to the insects and flowers in front of normal people, because then we *appear* crazy.

We're not crazy. I should be relieved.

But something else is going on, something unbelievable.

If the voices are real, it still makes no sense that Alison insists on dressing like Alice. Why she clucks her tongue. Why she rages for no reason. Those things make her look crazier than anything else. There are so many questions I want to ask. I shove them aside, because one other question is most binding of all.

"Why our family?" I ask. "Why does this keep happening to us?"

Alison's face sours. "It's a curse."

A curse? Is it possible? I think of the strange website I found when I searched for the moth. Are we cursed with mystical powers like those netherling things I read about? Is that why my grandmother Alicia attempted flight—she tried to test the theory?

"All right," I say, making an effort to believe the impossible. Who am I to argue? I've been chatting it up with dandelions and doodlebugs for the past six years. Real magic must be better than being schizophrenic. "If it's a curse, there's a way to break it."

"Yes." Alison's answer is a croak of misery.

The wind picks up, and her braid slaps around her like a whip.

"What is it, then?" I ask. "Why haven't we already done it?"

Alison's eyes glaze over. She's withdrawn somewhere inside herself—a place she hides when she's scared.

"Alison!" I bend over to grip her shoulders.

She refocuses. "Because we'd have to go down the rabbit hole."

I don't even ask if the rabbit hole is real. "Then I'll find it. Maybe someone in your family can help?"

It's a stretch. None of the British Liddells even know about us.

One of Alice's sons had a secret affair with some woman before he went off to World War I and died on the battlefield. The woman ended up pregnant and came to America to raise their love child. The boy grew up and had a daughter, my grandma, Alicia. We haven't been in touch with any of them . . . ever.

"No." Alison's voice pinches. "Keep them out of this, Allie. They don't know any more than we do, or we wouldn't still be in this mess."

The determination behind her expression shuts down any questions her cryptic statement might raise. "Fine. We know the rabbit hole is in England, right? Is there a map? Some kind of written directions? Where do I look?"

"You don't."

I jump as she pulls down my sock to expose the birthmark above my swollen left ankle. She has an identical one on her inner wrist. The mark is like a maze made of sharply angled lines that you might see in a puzzle book.

"There's so much more to the story than anyone knows," she says. "The treasures will show you."

"Treasures?"

She presses her birthmark to mine, and a warm sensation rushes between the points of contact. "Read between the lines," she whispers. The same thing she said earlier about the photographs. "You can't lose your head, Allie. Promise you'll let this go."

My eyes burn. "But I want you home . . ."

She jerks back from my ankle. "No! I didn't do all of this for nothing—" Her voice cracks, and she looks so tiny and frail at my feet.

I ache to ask what she means, but even more, I just want to hug her. I lower myself to my knees, ignoring the wound behind Jeb's bandana as I lean in. It's heaven, feeling her arms around me. Smelling her shampoo as I bury my nose at her temple.

It doesn't last. She stiffens and pushes me away. A familiar jab of rejection scrapes through my chest. Then I remember: Dad and the nurse will be back at any second.

"The moth," I say. "It plays a part in this, right? I found a website. The picture of the black and blue moth led me to it."

Overhead, clouds dim the sunlight to a grayish haze, and Alison's skin reflects the change. Terror sharpens her gaze. "You've done it now." She lifts trembling hands. "Now that you've gone looking for him, he won't be breaking his word. Not technically. You're fair game."

I lace my fingers through hers, trying to ground her. "You're freaking me out. Who are you talking about?"

"He'll come for you. He'll step through your dreams. Or the looking glass . . . stay away from the glass, Allie! Do you understand?"

"Mirrors?" I ask, incredulous. "You want me to stay away from mirrors?"

She scrambles to her feet, and I struggle to balance on my crutch. "Broken glass severs more than skin. It will sever your identity."

As if on cue, Jeb's bandana slips from my knee, revealing the bloody bandage. A tiny yelp leaps from her mouth. There's no tongue cluck to warn me before she lunges. My back slams against the ground. The air is pushed from my lungs and pain bursts between my shoulder blades.

Alison straddles me, peeling off my gloves as tears stream down her cheeks. "He made me hurt you!" She sobs. "I won't let it happen again!"

I've heard her say those words before, and in an instant, I'm back in that place and time. A five-year-old child—innocent, oblivious—watching as a spring storm gathered outside the screen door. The scent of rain and wet dirt rolled over me, making my mouth water. Right against my nose, a moth landed on the screen, the size of a crow with a luminous body and wings like black satin. I squealed and it took flight, hovering, teasing me, asking me to play.

Lightning flashed, a flood of light. Mommy always told me it wasn't safe to go outside when it's storming . . . but the moth fluttered, beautiful, taunting, promising it would be all right. I piled up some books to reach the lock on the latch and tumbled outside to dance with the bug in the flower beds, mud squishing between my toes. Mommy's scream made me look up. She sprinted toward us with a set of pruning shears.

"*Off with your head!*" she yelled, and snipped every flower where the moth perched, cutting the petals from their stems.

I followed, hypnotized by her energy as rain pelted us and lightning torched the sky. I thought she was dancing and flung my arms in the air behind her. Then I tripped over my feet. White petals were bleeding on the ground. Daddy came running out of the house. I told him we needed Band-Aids for the daffodils. He gasped at the sight of me. I was too young to understand that flowers don't bleed.

Somehow I'd gotten into the line of fire, and the pruning shears sliced my skin—from my palms to my wrists. The doctor said I didn't feel the pain because of shock. That was the last time Alison lived at home, and the last time I called her Mommy.

A clap of thunder snatches me back to the present. My heart hammers against my sternum. I'd forgotten about the moth. That bug was my secret pet as a child and the catalyst for my scars. No wonder its photograph seemed familiar to me. No wonder it made Alison so crazy to see it again.

She wails, holding my bare palms up to the dim light. "I'm so, so sorry! He used me, and I failed you. You're meant for so much more than this. We all are."

She rolls off me and digs up the carnations. Dirt crumbles from the stems as she stands. "He can't have her! You tell him that . . ." Alison squeezes the petals into a clump between her fists, as if trying to strangle them. Then she tosses the tattered blossoms aside and stumbles over to the gazing globe, trying to shove it off its base. When it won't budge, she pounds the ball with her fists.

I grab her elbows, worried she'll hurt herself. "Please stop," I plead.

"Do you hear me?" she shouts at the silver globe, jerking out of my hold. "You can't have her!" Something moves in the reflection, a blur of a shadow. But on second glance, it's only Alison's image staring back, yelling so hard the veins in her neck bulge.

What happens next is like a dream. The clouds swirl overhead. Rain starts pounding down. I watch through the downpour as—in slow motion—the wind whips her braid around her neck.

A hacking cough shakes her throat and she doubles over, fingers clenched around the braid to loosen it.

"Alison!" I leap toward her. It barely registers that my ankle no longer hurts.

Alison falls to the muddying earth, gasping for breath. The rain falls harder, as if someone's pelting pebbles at us. Her dirt-caked fingernails gouge at the platinum cord strangling her. In her desperation, she rips some skin from her neck. Blood rises along the welts. Her eyeballs bulge, snapping from side to side as she struggles to inhale. Her house shoes slap against the muddy ground.

"Alyssssss," she hisses, unable to talk.

I'm crying so hard, I can't see my fingers as I wrestle against the braid. Lightning strikes in the distance . . . once . . . twice . . . then the plaited cords tighten around my fingers and tangle me up, a pressure so intense, I fear my knuckles will snap. My fingers pop into place against my will and squeeze her neck.

Something is trying to make me kill my mom!

Nausea, hot and vicious, rips through my stomach.

"No . . ." The more I struggle to free both of us, the more deeply interlocked we become. My yarn dreadlocks cling to my neck like a wet mop. Rain and tears bleed into my eye shadow, and black droplets smudge Alison's dirty apron. "Let go!" I shout at her hair.

"Stop . . . Allie . . ." Her plea is hollow and hissing, like air escaping a tire.

The braid squeezes my fingers again.

"I'm sorry," I whisper, sobbing. "I'm not trying to hurt you . . ."

Thunder rolls through my bones, the taunting laugh of some dark demon. No matter how hard I pull, the strands embed me deeper and tighten around her neck. Her hands go limp. She turns blue, eyes lolling up until the irises disappear.

"Somebody *help!*" The scream strains my lungs.

The gardeners come running. Two sets of meaty hands curl around me from behind, and just like that, the braid releases.

Alison sucks in a deep, raspy breath, filling her lungs and coughing. I go limp as one of the gardeners holds me up.

Nurse Jenkins hovers into view, syringe in hand. Dad's right behind and I slump into his arms.

"I d-d-didn't," I stutter. "I wouldn't, not ever . . ."

"I know." Dad hugs me. "You were trying to keep her from hurting herself." His embrace makes my sopping clothes stick to my skin.

"But it wasn't Alison," I murmur.

"Of course not," Dad whispers against my head. "It wasn't her. Your mom hasn't been herself for years."

I suppress the urge to throw up. He doesn't get it. She wasn't trying to strangle herself; the wind controlled her braid. But what sane person would ever believe that?

Just before Alison's eyes flutter closed, she mumbles something with a drunken stammer: "The daisies . . . are hiding treasure. Buried treasure."

Then she's oblivious—a drooling zombie.

And I'm left alone to face the storm.

BUTTERFLY THREADS

It takes so long to get Alison settled at the asylum, Dad has to drive me straight to work. We pull up to the curb at the only vintage clothing shop in Pleasance. It's nestled in a popular strip mall along the commerce side of downtown, a bistro on one side of the shop, a jewelry store on the other. Tom's Sporting Goods is across the way.

"Remember. I'll be at work. Just one quick call, and I'll take you home." Dad's frown forms wrinkles at the edges of his mouth.

I'm numb, still wondering if I imagined it all. I stare past the pink brick storefront and black wrought-iron fence. My gaze focuses and unfocuses on the curvy black letters over the door: *BUTTERFLY THREADS*.

I hold the moth air freshener at my nose. The scent reminds me of spring, outdoor hikes, and happy families. But winter is all I feel inside, and my family is more screwed up than we've ever been. I want to tell Dad that Alison's delusions are real, but without proof, he'll just think my sanity is splintering, too.

"You don't have to do this," he says, taking my other hand. Even through my gloves his touch feels like ice.

"It's only two hours," I answer, hoarse from all my screaming in the courtyard. "Jen can't get anyone to cover her shift on short notice, and Persephone's out of town."

Friday is our boss Persephone's scavenger day, when she commutes to nearby towns to haunt estate and garage sales in search of merchandise. Contrary to what Dad thinks, I'm not being a martyr. From three o'clock to five is the dead zone at work; hardly any customers show up until after rush hour. I plan to use that time to search the store computer for the moth website.

"I should go." I squeeze Dad's hand.

He nods.

I open his glove box to put the air freshener inside, and an avalanche of papers hits my feet. A pamphlet on top catches my eye. The background is peaceful pink with a generic white font printed across the front: *ECT—Why Electroconvulsive Therapy Is Right for You or Your Loved One.*

I pick it up. "What is this?"

Dad bends across the seat to put away the other papers. "We'll talk about it later."

"Dad, please."

He stiffens and glances out his window. "They had to give her another dose of sedatives while you were in the lounge."

The words punch me. I was too chicken to follow when they wheeled Alison to the padded cell. I cowered on a couch in the lounge, pulling out my ruined dreadlocks like a robot while I watched some stupid reality show on TV.

Reality . . . I don't even know what that is anymore.

"Did you hear me, Allie? Two doses in less than an hour. All these years, they've been drugging her into oblivion." He squeezes the steering wheel. "Yet she's getting worse. She was screaming about rabbit holes and moths . . . and people losing their heads. The drugs aren't working. So the doctors have offered this option."

My tongue absorbs my saliva like a sponge.

"If you'll look at the first paragraph"—he points at some numbers on the pamphlet—"the practice has been making a comeback since—"

"They used eels, you know," I interrupt a little too loudly. "In the old days. Wrapped them around the patient's head. An electric turban."

The words are senseless—mirroring how I feel inside. All I can think of are my pets at home. I learned early on that I couldn't have the traditional cat or dog. It's not that animals talk to me; only insects and plants are on my frequency. But every time Jenara's tabby caught a roach and gnawed it to death, I got nauseated listening to the bug's screams. So I settled for eels. They're elegant and mystical and use a shock organ to stun their prey. It's a quiet and dignified death, similar to the bugs dying by asphyxiation in my traps. Still, I won't touch their water without a pair of rubber gloves. I can't imagine what they could do to someone's brain.

"Allie, this isn't the same as what they did seventy years ago. It's done with electrodes while the patient is anesthetized. Muscle relaxants keep them oblivious to any pain."

"Brain damage is still a side effect."

"No." He reads the upside-down text aloud. "Almost all ECT patients will experience confusion, inability to concentrate, and short-term memory loss, but the benefits outweigh the temporary discomforts." He meets my gaze, his left eye twitching. "Short-term memory loss is a *discomfort*. Not brain damage."

"It's a *form* of brain damage." I haven't been the daughter of a mental patient for the past eleven years and not picked up on the definitions and levels of psychological anomalies.

"Well, maybe that would be a blessing, considering your mom's most recent memories consist of nothing but the asylum and an endless procession of drugs and psych evaluations." The deep lines around his mouth look like they might crack all the way through to his skull. What I wouldn't give to see his Elvis smirk right about now.

My throat constricts. "Who are you to decide this for her?"

His lips tighten to that stern expression reserved for when I've overstepped my boundaries. "I'm a man who loves his wife and daughter. A man who's tired down to his bones." The mix of defensiveness and resignation in his brown eyes makes me want to curl up and cry. "She tried to kill herself right in front of you. Even if it is a physical impossibility for her to choke herself, it doesn't matter. The meds aren't working. We have to take the next step."

"And if this doesn't work . . . what then? A lobotomy with a can opener?" I throw the pamphlet across the seat. It hits his thigh.

"Allie!" His voice sharpens.

I see right through him. He's desperate to get Alison back, but not for me. All these years he's been pining for her, the woman he used to take to drive-in movies . . . who waded with him through puddles in the gutters after it rained . . . who drank lemonade on the porch swing and shared dreams for a happy future.

If he does this, she may never be that woman again.

I shove open the door and drop down onto the sidewalk. Even though the late-afternoon sun has found its way through the clouds, a chill coats my entire body.

"At least let me get your crutches for you." Dad starts to dig them out from behind the passenger seat.

"I don't need them anymore."

"But Jeb said you sprained—"

"News flash, Dad . . . Jeb's not always right." I tug at the bandana covering my bandage. My ankle hasn't hurt since Alison pressed her birthmark to mine. In fact, my scraped knee seems better, too. Chalk it up to more unexplained weirdness. I don't have time to wonder about it. I've got bigger issues.

Dad glances off into the distance, his jaw tight. "Butterfly . . ."

"Don't call me that," I snap.

His face falls as two chatty shoppers walk by. The last thing I want to do is hurt him; he's stayed by Alison's side for years, not to mention raised me all alone.

"I'm sorry." I lean in to see him better. "Let's just do more research, okay?"

He sighs. "I signed the papers before we left."

My mask of understanding slips, anger seeping out the edges. "Why would you do that?"

"The doctor offered this as an option months ago. I've been looking into it for a while. At first, I couldn't bring myself to even entertain the idea. But now . . . they're starting Monday. You can go with me to visit her afterward."

An uncomfortable heat glides up my neck. The humidity from the storm and the white noise of surrounding bugs only make it worse.

"Please try to understand," Dad says, "how much I need her home again."

"I need her, too."

"Then won't you do whatever it takes to make that happen?"

Inside me, the flapping shadow comes to life again. It dares me to say exactly what I'm thinking. "Yeah. I'd even dive down a rabbit hole." I slam the door.

Dad taps the horn, no doubt wanting an explanation for my remark. I rush into the shop without looking back.

The automatic doorbell chirps and a gust jingles the crystal teardrop chandelier centered in the ceiling. I stand there, dazed, while the air-conditioning ices my damp clothes. The rich coconut scent of the candles in the candelabras along the walls eases the crimp in my stomach.

"Is that you, Al?" Jenara's muffled voice carries through the storeroom's open door.

I clear my throat and grip the air freshener. In my rush to escape, I forgot to leave it in the truck. "Uh-huh."

"Did you see my prom dress? It's on the new-merchandise rack."

I lift the only hanger on the rack. The clear plastic cover crinkles. Jen bought two dresses at Butterfly Threads months ago. She sliced and diced them to create a fitted lime halter bodice that flares into a mini zebra print/pink netting combo. Hand-sewn iridescent sequins catch the light as I hang it back on the rod.

"Nice," I say. It's actually amazing, and under normal circumstances, I'd be a lot more enthusiastic over one of her fashion creations. But I can't find the strength today.

I toss the moth air freshener under the checkout counter next to Jenara's makeup bag. It lands on top of Persephone's mythology tomes.

A sense of someone watching slides through my bones and I look over my shoulder at the poster on the wall. It's from a movie called *The Crow*. Persephone's in love with the hero: black leather, white face, black eye makeup, and a perpetual brooding scowl. There was some mystery surrounding the actor. He died on set while filming.

I've always been drawn to the poster. Even on a flat piece of paper, the guy has the most soulful eyes—eyes that seem to know me, just like I know them. Although I've never seen the movie, he's familiar, to the point that I can smell the leather swaddling his body . . . feel the slickness against my cheek.

"He's here . . ." I jump as the words rush my ears—the same ones the fly said earlier. Only it's not a whisper this time, not the white noise I'm used to. It's a guy's deep cockney accent.

Mirrors line the side walls of the store, and a blur of movement races across them. When I look closer, the reflections show nothing but my own image.

"He rides the wind." The voice hums through my blood. A gust of cold air comes out of nowhere and snuffs out the candles, leaving only the afternoon light and the chandelier overhead.

I scramble backward until I hit the counter. The poster's bottomless eyes follow my every move, as if he's the one talking to my mind and turning the wind. Icy tingles run through my spine.

"Al!" Jen's shout breaks the spell. "Can you help me carry some stuff? We need to put up the Dark Angel display before I leave."

I force myself to break the poster's hypnotic gaze and head for the storeroom. The air conditioner clicks off. The gust must have come from the vents.

I laugh nervously. I'm tired, hungry, and in shock. My delusions are real and my family's cursed. That's all. It should be easy to accept, right?

Wrong.

My soggy Skechers squish with each step along the black-and-white checked tiles. Jenara meets me in the doorway, arms stacked so high with clothes and props, she can't see over them.

"So, my dress is *nice?*" Her question drifts from behind the stack. "Way to pull out all the stops for your BFF's ego."

"It's awesome. Bret will love it." Still feeling the poster's eyes, I balance on tiptoe and take the blue wig and miniature fog machine from the top of her armful.

"As if it matters," she says from behind the swaying stack. "Did I tell you Jeb threatened to turn Bret into a smashed pumpkin if I don't get home by midnight? Taking a sweet fairy tale like 'Cinderella' and twisting it into a death threat. That's seriously warped."

"Yeah, he's been on a real role lately."

Everything starts to slide from her tower. I grab several props from the top of the pile, revealing her face.

Her heavily lined green eyes bulge when she sees me. "Ohmyholyshiz. You look like you duked it out with a Sasquatch. Did you and Jeb settle things in a mud pit?"

"Ha." Leading the way to the display window, I drop my stuff in the window next to Window Waif, Persephone's mannequin.

Jenara sets some sooty feathered wings atop the props pile. They sparkle with black sequins.

"Seriously, what happened? I thought you were going to visit your mom. Hey." Jen touches my arm. "Did something go wrong?"

Several tendrils of dark pink hair have fallen from her upswept do. The strands coil like pink flames over her black tube dress, bringing back what they did to Alison's hair at the asylum.

"She lost it," I blurt. "Attacked me."

All other details clog my throat: how they shaved her hair so she wouldn't try to choke herself again—though now I suspect it was preparation for her shock treatments. How they kept wiping slobber from the sides of her mouth and put her into adult diapers, because when you're heavily sedated, you don't have control of your faculties. And, worst of all, how they took her to the padded cell in a wheelchair, hunched and strapped in a straitjacket like a withered old woman. That's why I couldn't follow and say good-bye. I'd already seen enough.

"Oh, Al." Jen's voice is low and soft. She pulls me in for a hug. The citrusy, bubblegum scent of her shampoo comforts me. "I'll do my own makeup and stuff here. Go home."

"I can't." I tug her closer. "I don't want to be around things that remind me of her. Not yet."

"But you shouldn't be alone."

The doorbell chirps and three ladies wander inside. Jen and I step back.

"I won't be alone," I answer. "Not during business hours."

Jen tilts her head, sizing me up. "Look, I can stay for another half hour. Go get yourself together. I'll take care of the customers."

"You sure?"

She flicks a tangle of my hair. "Sure and absolute. Can't leave you in charge of the place looking like a circus clown reject. What if a hot guy comes in?"

I attempt a smile.

"Take my makeup bag," she says. "I have some more hair extensions you can use."

I pick through my layaway stuff in the storeroom, grabbing a pair of platform boots along with the clothes, then duck into the tiny bathroom. The vent above the sink blows frosted air over my skin. A fluorescent glow from the tiny light fixture distorts my reflection. I brush out my tangles and clip on Jenara's purple dreadlocks.

Most of my makeup has been cried and rained off, leaving smudge tracks on my face. Now all I see is Alison. But if I look deeper, it's me wearing a straitjacket and an eel turban, grimacing like the Cheshire Cat as I sip pot roast from a teacup.

How long do I have before the curse kicks in for real?

I lean against the sink, untie Jeb's bandana, and breathe him in. Before this afternoon, all I wanted was to go to London to hang with him and earn college credits. Amazing, the difference a few hours can make.

If I don't find a way to England to look for the rabbit hole, Alison's brain gets fried and I end up where she is in a few years. There's no way I can get enough money for airfare before Monday. Not to mention a passport.

Gritting my teeth, I peel away my torn leggings and bandage. The split in my knee is almost healed, and there's not even a scab. I'm too exhausted and frazzled to guess why. I turn on the cold water and scrub at the physical reminders of what happened, drying my skin and underclothes with the hand dryer.

Once I line my eyes with strokes of dark green and wriggle into some purple, green, and red plaid tights, I top it off with a miniskirt over fluffy red petticoats. A green cap-sleeve tee layered under a red bustier—along with a pair of purple fingerless gloves—and I'm ready to face the customers.

I cast a final glance at the mirror. Something moves behind my image, shimmery and black like the feathered wings in the prop pile. Alison's warped warning skitters through me. *"He'll come for you. He'll step through your dreams. Or the looking glass . . . stay away from the glass."* Yelping, I whip around.

Nothing's there but my shadow. The room seems to shrink, small and off balance, as if I'm stuck inside a box tumbling down a hill. My stomach bounces.

I burst into the dimly lit storeroom and almost trip over the laces of my shin-high boots in a panicked race to get back to Jen.

She rushes to meet me. "Jeez." She leads me to the bar stool behind the checkout counter. "You look like your head's going to pop. Have you had anything to eat?"

"Ice cream soup," I mumble, relieved the customers already left and didn't see my entrance. I'm shaking all over.

Jen feels my forehead. "You don't feel warm. Maybe your blood sugar's screwy. I'm getting you something from the bistro."

"Don't leave." I grab her arm.

"Why not? I'll be right back."

Realizing how crazy I sound, I change tactics. "The window display. We have to . . ." The explanation stalls on my tongue as I notice she's already finished it. "Oh."

"Yeah, oh." Jen eases my fingers off her sleeve. "I relit the candles, too. Why'd you blow them out? You need all the relaxing vibes you can get. I'm going to bring you a croissant and a drink—something decaffeinated. Never seen you this wired." She's across the room before I can respond.

The door swings shut behind her, leaving me alone with her window display. A blue wig and a clingy black angel costume hug Window Waif's form. The giant wings are strapped into place around the mannequin's shoulders with a matching leather harness. Black sequins glitter on the feathers, and smoke pours out of the miniature fog machine, snaking around the macabre scene.

Somehow, those wings and the smoke belong together.

I think of my moth friend. Why was Alison chasing it with the shears? Just because it lured me outside in a storm? It had to be something deeper, some kind of ongoing animosity, but I can't quite grasp it.

Reluctantly, I turn to face the poster. His dark eyes look straight at me, piercing. "You know, don't you?" I whisper. "You have the answers."

Silence . . .

I snort—a hollow, lonely sound. I'm officially losing it. Whispering bugs and flowers are bad enough. Expecting a poster to answer? That makes me asylum-worthy.

Trembling, I move to the computer on the other side of the register and find the site from earlier. I scroll past everything I've already seen, trying to find a connection to Alison's ravings.

There's another group of pictures: a white rabbit, bony enough to be a skeleton; flowers sporting arms, legs, and mouths dripping with blood; a walrus with something protruding from his lower half like tree roots. It's the Wonderland crew after a heavy dose of radiation poisoning. It's also a connection: In some way, the moth and these nether-realm beings are tied to the Lewis Carroll tale. No wonder Grandma Alicia kept painting the story's characters on her walls.

Ever since Alice, my family has been nuts. Could be she really did go down a rabbit hole and came back to tell the tale, but she was never the same after the experience. I mean, who would be?

The hairs on my body lift as if a current runs through me.

After the last of the graphics, there's an antique ivy and floral border on either side of the black background, and a poem centered in a white fancy font.

'Twas brillig, and the slithy toves
Did gyre and gimble in the wabe;
All mimsy were the borogoves,
And the mome raths outgrabe.

I've seen the riddle in the original book. Notepad in hand, I scribble *Wonderland* at the top and copy the poem, word for word.

I open a new search window to look for interpretations. One site has four different possible meanings. What if they're all wrong? I skim over two until the third one catches my eye.

There are illustrations alongside the words—creatures with long curlicue noses digging holes beneath sundials. A sense of knowing overtakes me, and I close my eyes. Children play on the screen of my eyelids. A winged boy and a blond girl dive into a hole beneath a statue of a child that balances a sundial on his head.

I don't know where the images came from. I must've seen them in a movie—but I can't remember which one. They seem so real— and so familiar.

I jot down the definitions from that interpretation of the poem.

According to whoever wrote it, *brillig* is four o'clock in the afternoon; a *tove* is a mythical creature—a mix between a badger and a lizard with a corkscrew nose. They're known for making their nests beneath sundials. *Gyre* and *gimble* are verbs meaning to dig into the earth like a giant screw, turning out soil until a deep tunnel is formed. In the context of the poem, the hole is being dug in a distinctive location, considering a *wabe* is the grass plot under a sundial.

The other words aren't defined, but it's a start.

According to the poem and the images in my mind, it seems that the rabbit hole could be under that little-boy sundial statue.

Now I just have to find it.

I hop back to the netherlings site and scroll down to see if there are any details I missed. At the bottom is a huge chunk of black space all the way to the end. No more text, no more pictures, even though there's plenty of room for them. Could be the Webmaster meant to save the space for later.

I'm about to exit the site and do a search on sundials in England in hopes to find a city and address, when movement in the dark background catches my attention. It's like watching a cricket swim through ink. But instead of a cricket, a simulated black moth flutters across the screen, just like the one from my past.

I'm starting to think the moth is tied to everything: the little boy and girl I saw by the sundial, my family's very real curse. If only I could remember more about the insect. But my memories are blotted and misty, like looking down through clouds from dizzying heights.

The animation catches my attention again. It starts at the top of the empty space. When it gets a quarter of the way down, glowing blue text appears beneath the drag of the moth's wings.

Find the treasure.

I read and reread until my eyes burn, shocked by the similarity to what Alison said. *"The daisies are hiding treasure. Buried treasure."*

Dad plowed the flower garden after she was first committed years ago—destroyed it. There was nothing buried there. So what could she mean?

Another line of text appears onscreen. *If you wish to save your mother, use the key.*

I shove back from the computer, heart pounding and palms sweating in my gloves. I didn't imagine it. The words are staring back at me, blinking.

How is someone talking to me?

How would they know about Alison, and how did they find me?

I look around the empty store.

I should tell someone. Dad's out of the question; he'd sign me up for shock treatments, for sure. Jenara will think it's just one of my tormentors from school playing a sick joke.

But Jeb. Despite the weirdness between us, I know he'll always be there for me. I'll show him the website. Just the thought of his reassuring smile—the one that says he gets me in a way no one else does—coaxes me from the brink of terror.

At the sound of the doorbell, I glance up. Taelor's face looks back and I nearly groan aloud. Her chic, shoulder-length hair glimmers gold in the sun. The words *Glitz and Flash and Everything Panache* are written in shimmery letters across the bag she carries.

I turn again to the computer. The screen's gone blank and an error message flashes.

"Hey, Alyssa." Taelor peruses the jewelry rack on her way to the counter. "Any good sales today?" She holds up a skull rhinestone brooch with glittery crossbone dangles. "Preferably something that doesn't smell like a funeral home."

Ignoring her, I search for the URL. The error message returns. I jiggle the mouse. If I can't find the site again, I'll never be able to convince Jeb what I saw was real.

Taelor strolls closer. One of the straps on her designer purse slips off a sun-bronzed shoulder. "Guess it doesn't matter. People like you don't care who's been wearing this stuff or how dead they are."

After pausing to crinkle her nose at a shirt, she plops her shopping bag and purse on the opposite side of the counter, lithe arms propped on the edge. She was once a force on the tennis court, but when her dad never showed up for her tournaments, she gave it up. What a waste.

The extra four inches of my boots set me almost eye level with her. "Don't you have a prom to get ready for?" I ask, hoping she'll leave.

Her gaze gets all round and innocent. "That's why I'm here. I went next door to pick up Jeb's graduation gift. I thought I'd drop it by his place this afternoon so he can wear it tonight."

I don't even ask what she could possibly be getting Jeb from a jewelry store.

"What's this?" She thrusts a hand across the counter and pulls my notes toward her. I try to grab them away, but she's too fast. "Wonderland, huh? So you're doing some research on the family rabbits."

"Good-bye, Taelor." I wrestle my notes back, accidentally knocking her purse to the floor in front of the counter.

She doesn't bother to pick it up. Instead, her expression hardens. "No good-bye yet. First we're going to talk."

That flittering presence in my brain taunts me to fight back. A surge of adrenaline kick-starts my tongue. "Thanks, but I'd rather talk to a dung beetle."

Taelor's eyes widen, as if she's surprised by the insult. I smile. It feels good having the upper hand for once.

She takes a few seconds to work up a comeback. "You talk to beetles, huh? Glad to know you'll have someone to play with once Jeb's gone. And don't be thinking you can pull your wounded-friend crap to keep him from moving to London with me next month."

"With *you*?" My upper hand just got amputated. I feel like I did when I fell skateboarding—like I have a miner's cap spotlight on me.

"He hasn't told you yet?" Taelor's practically beaming. "I shouldn't be surprised. He's always so worried about your fragile state of mind." She leans across the counter so her face is inches from mine. Her expensive perfume stings my nose. "I'm spending senior year at a prep school in London. I've been offered a modeling contract there. My dad's renting Jeb a flat. It's win-win all around. Jeb can make connections for his art through the people I'll meet, and we can hang out at his place on the weekends. Cozy, right?"

My chest constricts.

She eases back. There's panic behind her expression. Why? She's annihilated my one chance to ever have Jeb's friendship to myself again. She's won everything.

"Wow. You really thought you had a chance, huh?" Taelor taunts. "Just because he asked you to pose for a few sketches, that doesn't mean he's hot for you."

My jaw drops. Jeb's never asked me to pose for anything. There were times he had his pencil and sketchbook out while we were together, but I never would've guessed he was drawing me.

"His art is all about death and tragedy, so of course he likes your mortician style. It's not a compliment. Don't delude yourself that it is."

I'm too stunned to respond.

"We both care about him." Her voice softens, and it's apparent that for once she's being sincere. "But do you care enough to let him do what's best for *him*? He has way too much talent to get stuck babysitting you for the rest of his life like your poor dad. Don't you think that would be a colossal tragedy?"

The urge to scratch out her eyes boils in my veins. "At least I have a dad who cares enough to be there." The words shoot out like poison arrows. Her wounded expression makes me regret them instantly.

The doorbell chirps and the scent of espresso wafts in.

"Oh, fark." Jen evil-eyes Taelor as the door slams behind her. "What are you doing here?" She stops next to me, setting down a croissant and a fruit smoothie.

Taelor clears her throat and her mask of nonchalance drops back into place. "Alyssa and I were just discussing London and why she won't be welcome to stay with Jeb and me." She snatches up her shopping bag. "It stinks here in the land of the dead. I'm out."

The minute she's gone, Jenara turns to me. "One of these days, she's going to slip up and show Jeb her ugly side."

I pluck at the edge of my croissant. "She's why he didn't want me to go. He didn't want me getting in the way of . . . them."

Twisting her fishnet tights with a pen, Jen doesn't answer.

"Why didn't you tell me?"

Her eyes fill with regret. "I just found out about her going this morning. And I didn't know how to tell you when you came in. You've got so much crap going on with your mom."

Folding my Wonderland notes, I study the blank computer again.

What does it matter that the website's gone? Jeb doesn't have my back anymore, and we'll never have what we once did.

"Al?"

The sobs I've been smothering since my fight with Dad gather in my chest. They burst like a thousand acidic bubbles, silently eating away at my heart. But I refuse to cry.

"C'mon," Jen nudges. "If anyone can convince him to give her up, it's you. Tell him already. Tell him how you really feel."

I think of Jeb's amazing paintings. Of all the things he can be if given the opportunity. He doesn't need any more emotional baggage to hold him back. And I've got enough to sink an oil tanker. Besides, I can't bear to have him turn me down to my face. He's already chosen Taelor over our friendship.

I tuck my notes into a skirt pocket. "Nothing to tell. I crushed on him when we were in sixth grade, so it doesn't count." She starts to say something, but I shut her down. "And you're not spilling, either. Pinky swears are forever."

A worried wrinkle appears on her forehead as she gathers her prom dress and makeup. "This isn't over."

"It is. Jeb's made his choice."

Shaking her head, she leaves.

The instant the door closes, I turn to *The Crow*. The emo guy stares back, his eyes bleeding black tears as if he knows my pain. I have the strangest longing to be in his arms—wrapped up in leather.

I'm waiting inside the rabbit hole, luv. Find me. His gaze burns the challenge into my soul like a brand.

Startled by our deepening connection, I step back and topple the pen holder with my elbow. A pencil rolls off the counter in front. I walk around to pick it up and am surprised to see Taelor's purse on the floor. She was in such a hurry to leave, she forgot to get it.

I fight the urge to toss her things out into the street. Instead, I lift the purse's straps to store it under the counter until she comes back. One half of the zipper gapes open, revealing a huge wad of cash.

Almost in a daze, I dig out the money, unrolling the lump of twenties and fifties. There's over two-hundred-and-forty dollars. If I added it to my savings at home, I'd have enough for a one-way ticket to England with a little left over for a fake passport and expenses; then all I'd have left to do is find an address for the sundial.

It wouldn't be the first time we owed the Tremonts a debt. In fifth grade, Dad took out a loan from Taelor's father to help pay Alison's medical bills. That was how Taelor learned about my ancestry to Alice Liddell in the first place.

So, in a way, this is justified compensation. Taelor's payment to me for all the years she made my life miserable.

My fingers quiver as I shove her gutted purse into the bottom of the trash can, piling papers on top. I reach under the counter to grab the air freshener and slide it—along with the money—into Persephone's tome on mystical crystals. The book has an elastic band sewn into the binding that holds the pages shut.

I turn to the poster again. The darkness behind the guy's eyes seems to be driving everything I do, and there's nothing to pull me back from the brink this time.

No mother, no father, and definitely no Jeb. Not even his smile could save me now.

TREASURE

Once Dad and I get home, I add the stolen stash to my savings in a small pencil box secured with a rubber band and hide it behind my cheval mirror.

Plugging my phone in to charge, I text Hitch to meet me outside Underland around midnight and tell him why. He's the only one I know who can make a fake passport. I still can't believe I took Taelor's money and hid her purse. But like Dad said, we'll do whatever it takes to get Alison home. Thinking about how lit Jeb would be if he knew I was meeting Hitch in the dark alone makes me all the more determined to follow through.

A low rumble shakes the windows and rain pelts the roof as another storm closes in.

Spreading a palm along my aquarium's cool glass, I search the back and flip on a soft bluish light. Aphrodite and Adonis perform a graceful dance, entwining their long bodies.

On my way to check my bug traps in the garage, I cut through the living room. Dad's there, sitting in his recliner while staring at those giant daisies Alison appliquéd all over the arms and back. He sobs.

I want to hug him and make up for our fight, but when he sees me watching, he claims to have something in his eye and leaves to pick up burgers for supper.

Dust motes drift in the amber glow of the floor lamp beside his recliner. The weird lighting, coupled with the dark paneled walls, gives the living room a strange aura, like an aged sepia photograph.

Photographs. Why did Alison say that about pictures . . . how people forget to read between the lines?

I stand there, a few feet from the recliner, while everything she babbled skates along my mind like pebbles cast into an endless well. One keeps rising back to the top: *"The daisies are hiding treasure. Buried treasure."*

The explanation is staring me in the face. It has been for years. I drop to my knees in front of the recliner, crumpling the layers of netting and lace beneath my miniskirt as I shove my backpack out of the way. Hard to believe it's only been seven or so hours since I was at school. So much has happened, I've lost track of time.

I pluck at one of Alison's cloth daisies where two appliquéd petals curl down from frayed stitches. On a hunch, I slide my index finger between the appliqué and the upholstery to find a hole burrowed deep into the recliner's stuffing.

Holding my breath, I tug at the appliqué until it's hanging by no more than one petal and a few threads. The dime-size hole stares back, too perfectly round to have been accidental. All this time, I thought she'd sewn the patches on to cover threadbare places. All this time, I was wrong.

Digging into the torn upholstery, I pull out stuffing until I hit something tiny, hard, and metallic. I trace the object, following a round shape that stretches to a long, thin leg with grooves and teeth. *A key.* My forefinger drags it to the hole's opening and tugs it out. An attached necklace chain coils on the cushion like a snake.

The challenge from the website comes full circle: *"If you wish to save your mother, use the key."*

Maybe I should be freaked out, but I'm thrilled to finally have tangible proof that Alison is trying to tell me something . . . that her babbles weren't babbles at all. They were coherent clues.

Tapping the cold metal with a fingertip, I imagine what the key might unlock. I've never seen one like it, so intricate, with strips of burnished brass interwoven like ivy. It looks old—antique, even. As tiny as it is, it might open a diary.

I loop the necklace around my neck and tuck it under my shirt. Alison said *daisies,* plural. Could there be other things behind the rest of the appliqués?

Inspired, I disregard the fact that Dad could come back at any minute. I don't even stop to consider the consequences of ripping apart his favorite chair.

He keeps a Swiss Army knife on the side table for opening mail.

I flip the scissor attachment out, then snip all the daisies in half and gouge out the holes beneath. Batting snows around me.

Soon, I'm sitting at the foot of the recliner with a small trove of Wonderland-related objects: an antique hair clip—more like a bobby pin, actually—with a ruby teardrop attached to its bent end; a feather quill; and a Victorian fan made of white lace and matching gloves scented with talcum and black pepper. I suppress a sneeze and push aside two snapshots of my great-great-great-grandmother Alice in favor of the small book I also found.

I stroke the tattered paperback's cover and study the title: *Alice's Adventures in Wonderland.* Across the word *Alice,* Alison's name is scrawled in red marker.

She wanted me to find these "treasures." Something here is supposed to discourage me from going to the rabbit hole. Instead, I'm convinced these things can help fix Alison, help me break the Liddell curse for good.

Tucked within the novel's front cover is a tourism brochure for the Thames sundial trail in London. On it is a statue of a child balancing a sundial on his head. I sit back in disbelief. It's the one I saw earlier in my mind, the one the children were playing beside. Alison must have looked for the rabbit hole when she was younger; she must have traveled to London on her search. Where else could these keepsakes have come from? More important, what made her stop looking?

The statue is dated 1731—long before Alice Liddell's birth—so it would've been in place when my great-great-great-grandmother was little, which means she could've fallen into the hole beneath it.

I now have an address, but according to the brochure, there's no public access to the grounds. Tourists are only allowed to look at the sundial statue from behind iron railings. Even once I get there, I'll need a miracle to sneak in and explore the sundial up close.

I slide the brochure back into place in the book, skimming the story I know so well. It's full of black-and-white sketches. There are a few dog-eared pages and some excerpts underlined: the Walrus and the Carpenter poem, Alice's tears causing a flood, the Mad Hatter's tea party.

Alison's handwriting fills the margins, notes and comments in different colors of ink. I touch them all, saddened we never sat down together—book in hand—so she could explain what everything means.

Most of her additions have blurred, as if the pages got wet. I stop at the illustrations of the Queen and King of Hearts, where she wrote: *Queen and King Red—here's where it started. And here it will end . . .*

Lightning flashes under the drapes.

After the last page of the story, there's an additional twenty or more pages, hand-glued into place. On each, someone scribbled sketches similar to the mutated Wonderland characters on the moth website: the skeletal white rabbit, vicious flowers with bloodied teeth, even a different rendition of Queen Red—a fine-boned beauty with bright red hair, black designs inked around her eyes, and gauzy wings.

The sketches trigger another vision of the children, more powerful than the one I experienced earlier, because my eyes don't even close. My living room fades and I'm in a meadow somewhere, breathing in the scent of spring. Dappled sunlight blinks around me, keeping time with tree branches rocking in the breeze. The landscape is weirdly fluorescent.

The girl—who looks to be five—wears a frilly red pajama top with long, puffy sleeves and matching pants that cover her ankles. She sits on a grassy knoll beside the boy, who can't be more than eight. They both have their backs to me.

Black wings drape behind the boy like a cloak, matching his velvet pants and silky shirt. He tilts sideways, so I catch his profile, but his face stays hidden beneath a curtain of glowing blue hair as he uses a needle to thread dead moths along a string—making the gruesome equivalent of a popcorn garland.

His feet—snug inside black hiking boots—are propped on a set of sketches, the same ones glued inside Alison's *Wonderland* book.

"There." His young, soft voice rustles like feathers on the wind. Without looking up, he points to the picture of Queen Red with his needle. The line of dead moths trails it, flapping with the movement. "Tell me her secrets."

The girl wriggles her bare feet, pink toenails glistening in the soft light. "I'm tired of being in Wonderland," she mumbles in a milky voice of innocence. "I want to go home. I'm sleepy."

"So am I. Perhaps if you didn't fight me in the air during flying lessons," he says, a cockney accent becoming apparent, "we'd both feel the better for it."

"It makes my tummy kick when we get so high." She yawns. "Isn't it bedtime yet? I'm getting cold."

Shaking his head, the boy prods the picture once more. "First, their secrets. Then I'll take you back to your warm bed."

The girl sighs and captures one of his wings, winding herself up in it. Warmth and comfort surge through me, mirroring what she must feel. She burrows into the satiny tunnel, wrapped up in the scent of him—licorice and honey.

"Wake me when it's time to leave," she says, her voice muffled.

Eyes still hidden behind his wild hair, he laughs. His lips are well shaped and dark against his pale skin, his straight teeth shiny and white. "Sneakie-deakie, trixie-luv." He tugs his wing free, leaving her cold and pouting.

He drops to his belly on the ground. His wings spread on either side like puddles of glimmering black oil as he leans over the pile of moth corpses. After stabbing one through the abdomen, he slides it into place behind the others on the string.

The girl watches, fascinated. "I want to stab one."

He lifts a hand and five fingers splay out—white, graceful, and long. "Give me five secrets, and I'll let you string a moth for each one you get right."

Clapping, the girl grabs the Queen Red sketch and lays it in her lap. "She likes ash in her tea, still glowing with embers."

The boy nods. "And why is that?"

Her head tilts as she's thinking. "Um."

I can't explain how, but I know the answer. I bite my tongue, waiting to see if the girl guesses, rooting for her.

Lifting his line of corpses, the boy teases, "Looks like I shall finish this alone."

She hops up, feet stomping the lime green grass. "Oh! The ash is for her mommy. Something about her mommy."

"Not good enough," he says, and stabs another moth onto his needle, the pile beginning to dwindle. He smiles wickedly.

Her frustration is tangible. He chides her like this often. Pushing her until she pushes back; but there's another side to him, one that's encouraging and patient, because I can sense her affection and respect.

He threads another moth, clucking his tongue. "Shame you'll not get to help. I think you're too much of a baby to hold a needle anyways."

She growls. "Am not."

Tired of his arrogance, I shout out the answer. "The hiss of steam when the embers snuff out in the tea! It comforts the queen. Reminds her of her mother's shushes when she would cry as a baby."

Both children snap their heads in my direction, as if they heard me. The girl's face is exposed—a vivid reality. She's *me* . . . a dead ringer for my prekindergarten school picture, missing front tooth and all. But it's his face—the boy's familiar black eyes leaking ink— that lands me back in my living room on my knees, the meadow vanishing from around me.

I'm numb. Is it possible? These aren't memories of some movie I watched; they're memories I *made*. If I had that memory trapped inside me, what else happened to me that I can no longer remember?

Have I actually been to Wonderland, spending time with some netherling creature . . .

I inhale a ragged breath. No. I've never been there.

My finger traces the lines of Queen Red's flaming hair on the sketch. If I've never been there, how did I know about the queen and her mother? How do I know she was lonely as a young princess after her mother died, because the king couldn't bear to spend time with her for her resemblance to his dead wife, and her sadness when her father remarried because he had to, since queens rule Wonderland?

I know these things because *he* taught them to me. The winged boy.

British . . . I'm reminded of the voice I heard in my head at work, along with the poster and the guy's bottomless, bleeding black eyes. His challenge resurfaces in my mind: *"I'm waiting inside the rabbit hole, luv. Find me."*

Luv. That's what the boy called the girl—what the boy called me—in my resurfaced memory. It's the same person . . . or creature . . . but he's older now, like me. I suddenly feel like I've been missing him for years. My emotions scramble in two different directions—a heady mix between terror and yearning—making me dizzy.

The doorbell rings, crashing me back to the present. Dad's garage-door opener has been on the fritz. It has to be him.

I stand. Stuffing covers the floor. Cottony fluff oozes out from the holes in the chair's upholstery. It looks like one of those toys that squeezes Play-Doh through strategically placed orifices.

The doorbell rings again.

I drag stuffing out of my hair. How will I ever explain what I've done to the recliner?

Mind racing, I hide my findings inside my backpack, making a spontaneous decision to take it all to London. Then, considering the violent nether-realm creatures I saw online and the black-eyed, winged boy who is somehow a part of my past, I drop Dad's army knife in, too.

After setting the bag aside, I stumble to the door and unlatch the lock, glancing over my shoulder at the mess.

As I open the door, Jeb steps up onto the porch, shoving his phone into his tux's jacket pocket. I struggle to maintain a calm appearance. "Hey."

"Hey," he says back. Lightning slashes the clouds behind him. The flash casts shadows of his long lashes across his cheeks. A gust of wind carries his cologne to me.

Maybe he's here to apologize. I hope so, because I could use his help right now.

"We need to talk," he says. The sharpness in his voice pulls my defenses up instantly. He towers over me at the threshold. Despite the tuxedo, he's still grunge, all the way from his unshaved chin to the bandana cinched around his left biceps. His ribbed white tank and weathered black combat boots in lieu of a dress shirt and shoes help complete the look. Paris Hilton of Pleasance High is going to have a hissy when she sees his wardrobe enhancements.

"Shouldn't you be on your way to the powder-puff ball?" I ask, cautious, trying to feel him out.

"I'm not driving."

Translation: Taelor's picking him up in the family limo and is running fashionably late.

He grinds a knuckle into the door's scrollwork, his jaw working back and forth. He's ticked about something, all right. What could it be? I'm the one who deserves an apology. A groveling, in fact.

"Can I come in?" Red sparkles under his lip where a brand-new garnet labret catches the light. The mystery of the bag from the jewelry store is officially solved.

"How adorable," I mock. "Taelor gave you lip jewelry . . . and it's sparkly."

He nudges the piercing with his tongue. "She's trying to be diplomatic."

Anger rises in a white-hot surge as I remember London and all the things Taelor said to me. "Of course she is. Because she's eight kinds of wonderful, and that's just her legs."

Jeb furrows his brow. "What's that supposed to mean?"

"Taelor has all the diplomacy of a black widow spider. Garnet's her birthstone. You're wearing her birthday on your lip. Talk about spinning you up in her web."

He looks down at me, frowning. "Cut her a break. She's had a bad enough day. She lost her purse with some money in it." Pausing, he traces a finger along the door's frame. "The last place she remembered having it was at your store. But she figured you would've contacted her if you'd found it. You didn't see it, right?"

I push down the guilt nudging me. "No. And I'm not her royal majesty's purse keeper, FYI."

"Seriously, Al. A little compassion, okay? Didn't you hurt her enough already?"

"I hurt *her*?"

"Rubbing it in her face that her dad doesn't care like yours does. You don't understand what it's like. Your dad. You're so lucky to have that. Neither of us ever did. You know she's sensitive about it. That was cold."

Speaking of cold, my blood turns to ice. I'm dying to tell him what she said to prod me into being so vicious, but I shouldn't have to. There was a time when he trusted me enough to take my side over anyone's without question. Now he's always trying to make Taelor and me play nice. But I'm not the one with the problem . . . other than being a liar and a theif.

Everything presses down on me: the weird discoveries, my busted-up friendship with Jeb, and my damaged family. I feel like I'm smothering. I try to slam the door. Jeb's foot intercepts it. I jerk clear as the hinges swing open.

His palm rests on the knob so I can't try to shut him out again. Rain droplets glisten along his sleek hair, which no doubt took gallons of glaze and hours to perfect. It's the one part of his appearance

Taelor will actually approve of. As for me, I favor the messy look—hair out of sorts, body slicked in sweat with motor oil or watercolors splashed across his olive skin. That's the Jeb I grew up with. The one I could count on. The one I've lost.

I harden my glare and my heart. "If that's why you came by, to bite my head off about hurting your perfect girlfriend, consider it done."

"Oh, no. I'm not even warmed up. Jen texted me. She heard from Hitch. I guess he's not as bad a guy as we thought, because he was wondering what kind of trouble you'd gotten yourself into. Why you need a fake passport tonight."

My throat shrinks. I want to slip beneath the cracks in the linoleum. "I can't do this now," I mutter.

"When else would be a good time? Maybe you can text me when you're on the plane."

I turn around, but he follows me into the entryway. Rounding on him before he can cross into the living room, I fold my arms over my bustier, trying to subdue the urge to punch him. "You can't come in without an invitation."

He leans a shoulder against Alison's framed photo of a wheat field at harvest. "That so?" His boot heel nudges the door behind him, shutting out the storm and the scent of rain. "Last I checked, I wasn't a vampire," he says, his voice low.

My fists clench tighter, and I step backward onto the line of carpet that borders the edge of the living room. "You sure have a lot in common with one."

"Because I suck?"

"More proof. You just read my mind." I ease one hand up to grip the key hidden beneath my T-shirt.

Jeb reaches for my other wrist, wrinkling my fingerless glove as he pulls me back into the entryway with him—close quarters with my fluffed-out miniskirt rustling against his thighs. "If I could read minds, I would know what's going on in your head to even consider traveling to a foreign country alone in the middle of the night without telling anybody."

I try to break free, but he's not having it. "Hitch is a tool. I said I wanted a fake ID, not a passport. He got them confused."

Jeb releases me, but there's still tension between his eyebrows. "What would you need a fake ID for?"

That fluctuation in my head comes alive, lapping at my skull, teasing me to push Jeb's buttons and watch him squirm. "To hit a few bars and pick up guys. Live a little. Get some life experience. You know, so I'll be ready to go to London in time for your royal wedding to Taelor."

The venomous outburst has the desired effect. Jeb's expression changes to something fierce yet fragile, like a mix between hurt feelings and wanting to strangle someone. "What's going on with us?"

I shrug and stare at my boots, pushing down the prodding sensation inside me. Rain patters against the windows, expanding the bubble of silence between us. I turn to escape into the living room, not even caring about the state I left it in.

Jeb's on my heels. It's like I'm the White Rabbit trying to outrun Time. He catches the tail of my petticoats and spins me to face him. His expression stiffens as he sees the recliner over my shoulder.

"What happened to your mom's patches?" He grasps my arms. "Wait . . . did something go wrong at Soul's today?"

I shake free and hold my hands in front of my stomach to ease the rocking sensation. "Alison had a setback. A big one. Jen didn't tell you?"

His study of my face intensifies, taking in every feature. "She was in a hurry. Just got the text about Hitch. Is your mom the reason you're acting out?"

My cheeks flame. *Acting out.* Like I'm a preschooler having a meltdown. If he could see the things going on inside me right now, he might actually have the sense to be scared.

It finally hits me head-on . . . how close to insanity I'm teetering . . . the madness behind the things I'm starting to believe. I shiver.

Jeb opens his arms. "C'mere."

I don't even hesitate. I let myself fall into his sturdy arms, hungry for one taste of the ordinary and sane.

He guides us to the couch without breaking my desperate hug—his arms around my waist, my feet resting on his boots like we're waltzing. I breathe in his chocolate/lavender scent until I'm drowning in it. We plop down together on the cushions. I don't realize I'm crying until I pull back and his ribbed tank sticks to my damp cheek.

"Sorry about your shirt." I try to brush off the makeup smudged on the left side of his tank.

"Easy fix." Jeb buttons his jacket, concealing it.

"So much for dignity," I whisper, scrubbing my face dry.

He plucks at some stray strands of hair glommed on to the wetness on my temples. "You want dignified? Check this." He fishes something from his jacket's inner pocket. "The prom committee voted for a masquerade theme. Tae bought me a mask."

"A masquerade prom? *Real* original." I force the sarcasm, grateful he's avoiding the subject of the recliner and Alison. Whether it's for my comfort or for his, I don't care.

"No laughing." He slips the mask on, a black satin cutout with an elastic band. Miniature peacock feathers fringe the eyeholes and outer edges, making it look as if a butterfly crash-landed on his face. I can't help myself. I snort.

"Hey." Dimples appearing, Jeb gooses me in the ribs.

I catch his finger, smiling. "So . . . you're a drag queen gone rogue, right?"

"Oh, you're going down for that, skater girl." He tickles me until I tumble backward onto the cushions and he half pins me.

"Ouch." I hug my sides where they ache from both crying and laughing.

"Did I hurt you?" He stops, hands on either side of my waist.

"A little," I lie.

His forehead's really close to mine, long black lashes peeking through the mask's eyeholes. His expression is pure remorse. "Where? Your ankle?"

"Everywhere. Laughing pains."

He grins. "Ah. So, are you gonna take it back?"

"Sure. You look more like a feather duster, anyway."

He laughs, then peels off his mask and uses the elastic band like a slingshot to send it soaring across the room. It hits the wall and splats to the floor in a feathery lump.

"Good riddance," we say simultaneously, sharing a smile.

This is what I've been missing. Hanging out with Jeb makes me feel almost normal. Until I remember I'm not.

I scoot over to put some distance between us. "You should go. You don't want Taelor to see you coming out of my side of the duplex."

He lifts my left ankle into his lap. "I want to look at that sprain first."

I'm about to tell him it's better, but his strong, warm palm under the bend of my knee shuts my tongue down. Biting my lower lip, I watch as he unlaces my boot. When he coaxes an index finger beneath my legging's hem and gently traces my birthmark, the gesture is so unexpectedly intimate, a tremor races up my shin.

His eyes lock on mine, and I wonder if he felt it, too. He's looking at me like I'm one of his paintings again.

Thunder shakes the room, breaking our stare.

I cough. "See? All better." Dragging my leg free, I lace up my boot.

"Al." His Adam's apple moves as he swallows. "I want you to put a stop to this Hitch thing. Whatever's going on, it's not worth . . ." He pauses. "Losing an important part of you."

Unbelievable. He thinks I'm such a prude, he won't even say the word. "You mean my *virginity*?"

His neck flashes red. "You deserve better than some one-night thing. You're the kind of girl who should have a commitment from a guy who actually cares. Okay?"

Before I can answer, a fluttering sound distracts me. At first, I think it's in my mind, until I notice some movement over Jeb's shoulder. A flash of lightning blinks beneath the drapes in the window, illuminating the hallway. Then it's unmistakable. Alison's moth—huge, satiny black wings, glowing blue body—hovers there for an instant in front of the hall mirror before flying into my room.

My head spins.

"No," I say. It can't be the same insect from the snapshot . . . the one from my childhood. Moths only live a few days. Never years.

"No what?" Jeb asks, oblivious to the moth, intent only on me. "Are you still going through with it?"

My pulse kicks up so loudly in my ears, it nearly drowns out Taelor's ring tone on Jeb's phone.

"You'd better leave." I push him to standing and herd him toward the door.

"Wait," Jeb says over his shoulder between reluctant footsteps. He turns to face me at the door. "I want to know what you're doing tonight."

I peer through the drizzle at the white limo in his driveway, considering one last time if I should tell him the truth. *I'm going to London to find the rabbit hole. Even though I'm scared gutless of where it might lead, of who's waiting inside for me. Of whatever I'm supposed to do once I'm there. I have to go.*

But Taelor's words from earlier rip the fantasy to shreds: *"Jeb has way too much talent to get stuck babysitting . . ."*

My stomach clenches and I say the hardest thing I've ever said. "You don't have a say in anything I do. You ditched our friendship for Taelor. So stay out of it, Jeb."

He steps backward onto the porch as if in a daze. "Out of what?" The pain in his voice rips me apart. "Stay out of your plan to hook up with some random loser, or stay out of your life?"

The limo honks and its headbeams cut through the wet haze. Before my resolve softens, I whisper, "Both." Then I shut the door, turn, and collapse against it.

My spine digs into the heavy wood. Regret fills my already crowded heart, but I can't let the pain stop me. The second the limo's wheels grind away on the wet asphalt, I snatch my backpack from the living room. I'm ready to go looking for my past.

Once in the hallway, I hesitate, drawn to my mosaics hung on either side of the mirror. Something is wrong with the *Winter's*

Heartbeat piece. The silvery glass beads forming the tree throb with light, and the crickets in the background kick their legs in unison. Their wings rub together, making an eerie chirping sound.

Gasping, I squeeze my eyes closed until the chirps stop; then I look again.

The mosaic is normal—still and inanimate.

I groan and back away. A crackle shatters the silence in my room. I left the door ajar earlier, and soft blue light radiates from within. It has to be the moth's body causing the glow. I ease inside, both relieved and disappointed that it's just the bulb in the eels' aquarium.

Heart pounding, I reach to flick on the main light switch.

Lightning strikes, shutting off the electricity, and everything goes black.

I'm squeezing the doorframe so hard, my fingernails eat into the wood. The sound of flapping wings darts from one side of the pitch-black room to the other. My pulse bashes and hammers. Every instinct tells me to run into the hallway, out the front door, to try to catch Jeb so he can protect me.

But I heard the limo leave. He's already gone.

Something soft swoops by my face. I yelp. Stumbling forward, I skim my palms along the top of my dresser, find my flashlight, and click it on. Yellow light illuminates a painting Jeb once made for me, and jars of bug corpses.

The hairs on my neck stiffen as I move closer to my cheval mirror. The glass is cracked from top to bottom, like a hard-boiled, crystallized egg that's been tapped all over with a spoon, waiting to be peeled.

What was it Alison said about broken glass? That it would sever my identity?

Jagged puzzle pieces make up my shattered reflection: hundreds of miniature plaid leggings peeking out between shin-high boots and red net petticoat at my thighs; thousands of bustiers draped over another thousand T-shirts. Then a hundred of my faces with ice-blue eyes standing out from smears of green liner.

And there, behind my many heads, fluttering black wings and a soft blue glow. I spin around and shine the flashlight, expecting to find the moth behind me.

Nothing.

When I turn back to the mirror, a scream lodges in my throat. A guy's silhouette appears behind me in the reflection. The image is distorted and broken into countless pieces, all except his inky eyes and dark, shapely mouth. Those I see clearly. It's the boy from my memories—all grown up.

Into the Rabbit Hole

"Lovely Alyssa." The guy's lips purr that cockney accent I heard at the store. *"You can cure your family. Use the key to bring your treasures into my world. Fix Alice's mistakes, and break the curse. Don't stop until you find me."*

What does he mean, "Alice's mistakes"? Something she did inside Wonderland caused all this to happen?

The weight of my backpack holds me steady as I stare at him, captivated. I'm afraid to turn around and see if he's behind me, afraid the silhouette and beautiful voice are only figments of a frantic, failing mind.

"Are you real?" I whisper.

"Do I feel real?" he whispers back, his breath hot against the nape of my neck. A set of strong hands wraps around me from behind, causing every nerve to dance inside my body. I twist around. The flashlight's glow sweeps the empty room, yet the pressure of knowing fingers still trails across my abdomen. Stunned with sensation, I let my hand follow his touch, from my navel to the band of my skirt. My knees give out. Somehow, I'm still standing, as if the phantom guy holds me up.

"Remember me, Alyssa." A nose stirs the hair at the back of my head. *"Remember us."* He starts to hum, a haunting melody. No words ride the music, only the familiar notes of a forgotten song.

The instant his humming ends, so does the embrace. I sway to catch my balance. Within the broken reflections, the moth has replaced him again. Somehow, the moth and the guy are tied together.

I should be terrified. I should be committed. But something about the netherling is sensual and exhilarating, more evocative than anything in my world has ever been.

I reach toward one of the moth's reflections, aiming for a crack where it's severed in two. My finger meets the glass, only instead of sharpness, it feels like sculpted metal. Repositioning the flashlight, I realize it's not a crack in the glass at all . . . it's a keyhole, tiny and intricate.

I dig out the key from under my shirt, fingers shaking as I take aim.

"Tut," my dark guide scolds, though I can't see him anywhere. *"I've taught you better. You're forgetting a step."*

He's right. I remember. "Envision where you wish to go," I say, using his words from years before. The key is a wish granter, and will open the mirror to my desires. Letting the backpack fall to the floor, I dig out the sundial brochure and study it. When I look up again, it's the picture from the brochure staring back at me from the cracked reflection. I insert the key into the hole and turn.

The glass becomes liquid and ripples, absorbing my hand. I jerk back, and the key falls against my chest, suspended on its chain. I hold my fingers up. They look the same as always . . . completely unaffected. They're not even wet.

A crackling sound snaps my attention back to the mirror. The splintered glass begins to smooth, forming a watery window instead of a reflection. It's a portal that opens into the garden bright with sunlight and flowers where the statue sundial waits.

"Want it with all your heart." The command swims in my head, so quiet it's an echo from my past. *"Then step inside."*

I have a moment of lucidity. If I'm about to be magically sucked into London, I need a way home. I snag my pencil box of money and drop it into the backpack. I shove the flashlight in, too. Who knows how dark the rabbit hole might be?

I step forward and let both of my hands sink into the liquid glass up to my elbows. On the other side, a cool breeze meets my arms. Someone strokes my skin, from my elbow down to the wrist . . . fingertips so soft and knowing, they light a firestorm inside my veins.

It's a touch I already know, yet so different now. No longer innocent and calming.

When I look into the portal, my gloved hands appear in the landscape beyond, casting shadows on the grass next to the guy's winged silhouette.

Before I can see him clearly, he's gone.

I hesitate and think of Jeb. It's almost as if I hear his voice calling out for me from somewhere far away. I wish he was here, right now, stepping in with me.

But I can't look back. As deranged as it seems, that guy in the mirror is the answer to everything in my past. This is my one chance to find Wonderland, to cleanse the Liddell bloodline of this curse, and to save Alison. If I can do this, I can finally be normal. Maybe normal enough to tell Jeb the way I really feel about things.

Taking a breath, I plunge inside.

※·I·※

I spin in a haze of greens, blues, and whites, my perceptions unraveling like a roll of gauze. A prickly sensation sweeps in—tiny needles weaving me together once more. I fall backward onto the ground and wait with eyes clenched shut, backpack pushing into my spine.

The wooziness passes, and the scent of moist soil and fresh air drifts over me. I blink at a bright sun and blue sky. Weird. If I'm in England, it should still be early morning here . . . way before dawn. Somehow, I arrived at the same time as the picture in the brochure—the time I envisioned. Blades of grass prickle through my gloves as I push my weight onto my palms to sit up. The sundial statue boy waits a few feet away.

Behind me is a fountain, the water flowing along mirrored panels as tall as I am. They must be the other side of the portal I stepped through, because my hair and clothes are damp. A spiked, wrought-iron fence casts shadows across the garden.

I stand, drop my backpack to the ground, and brush speckles of mud from my skirt and tights.

The birds chirping and white noise from the flowers and insects *sound* real. The breeze shaking the leaves overhead *feels* real. The fragrance of white roses from a bush on the other side of the statue *smells* real. All my senses tell me this isn't a delusion.

My imagination couldn't conjure hands like my guide's—or the song he lit in my memory. A song for which the words escape me, but in some way define me. The melody brings back feelings of comfort and security—like an old lullaby.

I concentrate on the white noise. A distinct whisper spins through my ears.

Find the rabbit hole . . .

The breeze coaxes a soft fragrance my way. It's the roses talking.

I drop to my knees and crawl toward the sundial statue, parting the grass as I go. There must be a hole or a metal lid—something that could hide a tunnel.

An ornate rock border and a ground cover of ivy surround the statue's large platform. I start digging through the leaves. White noise erupts as I upset the sacred dwellings of spiders, beetles, and flying insects. Some scatter beneath my fingers; others light into the air. Their whispers cling like static, leading me.

With the touch of a feather, you can enter the nether.

I scramble to my feet, then step into the ivy, giving the statue a push. It doesn't budge.

The time must be right, or you'll be here all night.

Time. I try to recall the "'Twas brillig" poem definitions. Wasn't four o'clock mentioned? According to the sundial's shadow, it's a little past five. Maybe I have to turn back the clock somehow.

I try to force the gnomon shaft to a new position so its shadow will fall on the Roman numeral IV. It doesn't budge, either. Maybe the statue just has to *think* it's four.

I dig through the backpack, dragging out the feather quill I pulled from my dad's recliner. "With the touch of a feather . . ." I center the plume over the dial and move it until it casts a shadow pointing to the IV. Then I tuck the quill into a crevice to hold it in place. The sundial still reads five o'clock, too, but I'm hoping my improvisation is enough to do the trick.

A series of clicks and clatters emerges from inside the statue's base, like latches being opened. Heart racing, I wedge my shoulder against the stone boy's arms. With my heels rooted into the ivy, I use my legs to push and strain against the stone.

Rock grates along metal, and the statue tips over on its base. A *poof* of dust belches, then clears, revealing a hole the size of a well.

I drop to my knees. Inside the backpack, I push things around to find my flashlight. Flipping it on, I search the depths below. No bottom in sight. I can't dive headfirst into some tunnel if I can't see where it ends.

An overwhelming sense of loneliness and panic wraps around me. I'm not a fan of heights—the very reason I haven't mastered an ollie in skateboarding yet. I love the thrill of the ride, but free-falling has never been my idea of fun. I once went rappelling in a canyon with Jeb and Jenara. The climbing up wasn't so bad, but Jeb had to piggyback me the entire way down while I kept my eyes shut.

Again, I find myself wishing he was here.

I sit up. That stirring pressure inside me comes to life . . . it assures me I'm ready for this.

If reality is anything like the Alice book, she doesn't fall so much as *floats* her way down. The physical laws might be different within the hole.

So maybe it's not how far down but how *fast*.

I drop the flashlight in. It bobs down slowly, like a glowing bubble. I almost laugh aloud.

I take a swig of water from one of the bottles at the bottom of the bag. Then I zip it closed and position the pack on my shoulders.

Perched on my hands and knees at the hole's edge, I have a moment of doubt. I weigh a lot more than a piece of plastic and some batteries. Maybe I should push in a few heavy rocks, just to be sure.

"Al!"

The shout from behind makes me scramble. Dirt gives way beneath my hands. Screaming, I clutch at empty air and tumble in.

Inside, the hole widens. More like a feather on a breeze than a skydiver, I float, my position shifting from vertical to horizontal. My stomach quivers, trying to adjust to weightlessness.

Overhead, someone dives in after me.

In seconds, he latches on to my wrist and tugs to align our bodies. It's impossible . . .

"Jeb?"

His arms lock us together, his gaze intent on the slowly passing scenery. "Sweet mother of—"

"Stuff and nonsense," I interrupt with a quote from the original *Wonderland* book. "How are you here?"

"Where *is* here?" he asks, mesmerized by our surroundings.

Open wardrobes filled with clothes, other furniture, stacks of books on floating shelves, pantries, jelly jars, and empty picture frames all cling randomly to the tunnel's sides as if stuck with Velcro. Thick ivy curls around each item and embeds it in the dirt walls, pinning everything in place.

Each time we pass something, Jeb draws me closer, his expression a mix of dread and awe. At one point, I work my arm free and snag a jar wrapped in leaves. I bring it between us and twist off the lid, then stretch out once more to leave the jar upside down, floating alongside us. A dribble of orange marmalade oozes from it and stays suspended as we drift—down, down, down until our feet gently meet the bottom, as if we've been lowered on ropes.

The entrance to the rabbit hole is nothing but a pinhole of sunlight up above. We stand in an empty, windowless room, domed and dimly lit by candles hanging upside down in candelabras. The scent of wax and dust wafts all around us. My legs wobble, as if I've been running laps for a week. We must have fallen at least a half mile. We're still embracing, but neither of us seems to want to let go.

After a few minutes, Jeb eases us an arm's length apart and stares at me—*into* me.

"How?" I whisper, still unable to grasp that he's here.

He pales, shaking his head. "I . . . I slipped on the porch in the rain. That has to be it. Yeah, that's why I'm wet. I'm dreaming this now. But . . ." He presses our foreheads together and I make a mental note of every other place our bodies touch. His hands glide up my rib cage before stopping on either side of my face. "You feel real," he whispers, his hot breath mingling with mine. Every point of contact between us heats to white flame. "And you're so pretty."

Okay, that's proof he's delusional and in shock. First off, he's never said anything like that to me. Second, my makeup has to look like soggy newspapers by now.

The key. It's a wish granter. My dark guide told me to *want with all my heart.* So when I visualized Jeb by my side before stepping in, because I wanted him with me, he came through, too.

I never meant to drag him into this.

Interlocking our fingers, I coax his palms from my face. "Maybe there's some way to send you back." Although I have a bad feeling there's not. Something he said earlier sinks in. "Wait . . . what do you mean, you slipped on the porch? I heard the limo drive away."

"Tae and I had a fight. She left for prom without me. I wanted to check on you one last time—couldn't leave things like they were. You didn't answer the door. It was unlocked, so I . . . that must be when I hit my head."

I grip his shoulders. "You didn't hit your head. We're really here. This is real."

"Uh-uh." He steps back. "That would mean you really jumped into the mirror. I really dived in to catch you. Then I got stuck in a tree and had to climb down to find you. No. Not possible."

"This shouldn't have happened," I mumble, wrestling my guilt. "Wonderland is my nightmare. Not yours."

"Wonderland?" He points to the tunnel overhead. "*That* was the rabbit hole?"

"Yeah. Alison had clues to this place hidden behind the daisies on Dad's chair. That's why I tore it up."

One look at Jeb's face and I know he doesn't buy it.

Taking a deep breath, I slip off the backpack and draw out the brochure and treasures. I consider telling him about the moth and my dark guide, but those details stick inside me, an immovable mass.

"I haven't had a good look at most of the things yet," I add. "But I think they're leading me here. I think—I think the Lewis Carroll book wasn't exactly fiction. It was a real-life account of my great-great-great-grandmother's experiences, with some discrepancies. For one, there was nothing mentioned about a sundial covering the rabbit hole."

We both look at the wink of light overhead.

Jeb rocks back and forth, as if he's seasick. He gets his bearings and levels his gaze at me again. "Did your dad know about this stuff you found?"

"No. If he did, he would've signed Alison up for shock treatments even sooner."

"Shock treatments? I thought she hit her head in a car accident. Got brain-damaged."

"I was covering. There was never an accident. She's been Wonderland-crazy for years. Now I can prove she's not. That it's all real."

Doubt darkens Jeb's face. "We have to get back first. And that's not going to be easy."

He's right. There's no door. It's like we've fallen into a genie bottle and the only way out is to become smoke and drift up.

"We've got to get help." He fishes his cell phone out of his jacket. After punching several buttons, he frowns.

"No service?" I ask.

He drops his phone into my backpack and sifts through the contents, his expression determined. "What else do you have in here?"

A bee swoops around me and I swat it away. It must have come in through the opening overhead. "Bottled water . . . a couple of energy bars. School junk."

I crouch beside him and reach in, making sure he doesn't open the pencil box; then I push aside Alison's *Wonderland* book to grab the white gloves I found in the chair. I take off my fingerless ones and pull the others on in their place. They're a perfect fit. Next, I secure the hairpin just above my left ear. In a vague, misty memory, I used to play dress-up in these items with my netherling companion. Now it's an impulse I can't resist.

Jeb fishes out Dad's Swiss Army knife. Eyebrows raised, he holds it up.

"I borrowed it from a Boy Scout?" I blink.

He slides it into the pocket of his tuxedo pants. "No dice. I pounded my share of the locals in seventh grade and kept tokens from the battles. Boy Scouts don't carry knives this sweet."

My shakiness eases as he flashes a small smile. I'm not sure if he believes any of this or still thinks he's dreaming, but at least he's trying to keep a sense of humor.

He zips the backpack. The slide of the metal teeth echoes in the room. The bee buzzes around my head again. It registers that these are the only two sounds I hear. No white noise. Not a whisper, not a murmur, not a hint of a word.

For the first time in six years, I know silence.

I close my eyes and let it seep into me, soft and numbing.

Silence. Is. Bliss.

Inspired by that thought, I stand up to explore.

"Stay close, skater girl." Jeb retrieves the flashlight, which ended up on the round table in the middle of the room. I shouldn't be thinking it, after bringing him here, but it's amazing how good it feels to hear my nickname.

I stop next to the purple-striped walls, hung with upside-down candelabras. Black-and-white tiles cover the circular floor. A pile of creamy, fragrant wax the size of an anthill rests beneath each dripping candle. How the wicks stay lit is a mystery. Even though the wax melts, the candles don't seem to shrink.

"I don't believe it," Jeb says. He holds up a dark brown bottle with a label tied around its long neck like a price tag. "'Drink me,'" he reads aloud.

"No way." I'm at his side in an instant.

"Shrinks you or something, right?" he asks.

"According to the guidebook. Is there a petit four in that glass box under the table?"

As I stick the bottle into my backpack, he crouches. "Cake on a satin pillow. Looks like raisins on top. They spell the words 'Eat Me.'"

"Yeah. The cake that makes you big again."

He whips the bandana off his tux sleeve and wraps up the box with the small white pastry. "I'm assuming you want it, too, for evidence?"

I nod. But it's not evidence we're gathering. Something tells me I might need to use this stuff later, once I've sent Jeb home and can continue on alone.

Back at the walls, I search for a way out. Red velvet curtains hang in intervals with golden cords of rope draped over knoblike finials. The coverings are long enough to hide a door. I flap open the first one, hoping to find some antique, ornate door that might have a lock to fit the key around my neck. There's nothing but wall behind it. I try another curtain with the same result.

"Check this out." Jeb pulls a sheet off a wooden contraption propped against the opposite wall. Strings, pulleys, and a giant clock's face form the convoluted frame. A sign reads: JABBERLOCKY'S MOUSETRAP. I think back on the Jabberwocky poem associated with

Carroll's books. The misspelling of the word is yet another inconsistency with a story I thought I knew by heart.

Wonderland characters cover the front in vivid shades of paint. A long platform juts out at the bottom, connected to some pulleys.

"It looks like a Rube Goldberg," Jeb says, cocking his head sideways to scope it out.

"A what?"

"Rube Goldberg—the cartoonist and inventor. He drew complex devices that performed simple tasks in convoluted ways. This one is a mousetrap."

I stare at him.

"What?" he asks.

Laughing, I shake my head. "Your geek undies are showing. I thought you outgrew them in seventh grade." He used to be obsessed with constructing things—building mazes and marble ramps with his dad out in their garage. It was the only time I ever saw them get along.

A sad smile flits across his face, and I know he's remembering, too.

"What's that thing on the platform?" I ask to change the subject, kicking myself for bringing it up.

He taps what looks like a chunk of cheese. "A sponge. Wonder if the trap actually works."

"One way to find out." I reach for a lever with the words *Push Me* written in red.

"Wait." Jeb drops the sheet and pulls me away. "Why would a mousetrap be down here? What if it's set up for bigger prey—like intruders?"

The bee returns, buzzing around me again. I swat it away. Lazily, it hovers in midair, then lands on the same lever I was about to try.

With a whirring sound, the machine initiates a chain reaction.

First, the big hand of the clock clicks into place, pointing to the Roman numeral IV. This activates a pulley's wheel that in turn twists a corkscrew through a nest to a drilled hole. The corkscrew's pointed end pushes through and unbalances a seesaw slab on the next level.

Jeb and I back up several steps, hand in hand.

I've seen this process before. I dig in my shirt pocket and pull out the Wonderland notes from that website, looking over the "'Twas brillig" definitions again.

Jeb eases behind me to read over my shoulder. "Where did you find those?"

"Shh . . ." It's all there: the four o'clock, the nest, the corkscrew. After emitting a piercing whistle, the machine launches the yellowish orange sponge into the air. It flies to the other side of the room.

I chase it, skidding to a stop as it drops to the floor next to one of the curtains I looked behind earlier.

"Pick it up." That British voice fills my mind, a reminder of the reason I've come. Not to gather proof of Wonderland but to cure my family's curse. I have to find the guy from my memories. He'll tell me how to fix my great-great-great-grandmother's mistakes. I pick up the sponge and tuck it into my skirt pocket.

The whirring starts again. Over where Jeb stands, the pulleys and wheels reverse to their original position. As if connected to the machine by invisible strings, the curtain next to me lifts, revealing a trap door that wasn't there two minutes ago.

"Open it."

As if I'm a puppet controlled by my netherling guide, I reach for the door.

"Al, don't!" Jeb shouts.

I slide it open before he can get to me.

A long, dark corridor juts off from the room. I duck my head in. There's enough light coming from behind me to see that the tunnel gets gradually smaller. A flash of movement in the blackness sends me tumbling backward into Jeb. He slips an arm around my waist and holds me against him as a small rabbit-shaped shadow, standing on two legs, appears in the doorway.

"Late," its tiny voice says.

I clench my teeth against screaming. I can't believe it. The White Rabbit is *real*.

"Late, I say. Lady Alice, too late be you." The rabbit hops into the wavering candlelight. His unbuttoned red tailcoat flaps open, revealing his rib cage.

Jeb curses, and I slap a palm over my mouth.

It's not the White Rabbit or any kind of rabbit at all. It's a tiny, dwarfish creature the size of a bunny. The legs, arms, and body are humanoid but fleshless—a bleached-out skeleton. White gloves cover cadaverous hands; white lace-up boots protect his feet. The exception to the skeletal appearance is his bald head and his face of an old man, covered with flesh as pale as an albino's. His eyes—wide and inquisitive like a doe's—glow pink. Long white antlers sprout from behind each of his small human ears.

It's clear how young Alice might've mistaken him for a rabbit. His horns look like ears when viewed in the shadows.

"White Rabbit?" I venture, feeling Jeb's arm tighten around me as he mumbles in disbelief.

"White, *Rabid*," the pint-size skeleton says. "Liddell, Alice . . . you not be. But her hands you have."

I stare at my gloves. "I'm her great—"

"No one," Jeb interrupts as he steps between me and the creature. He won't let me out from behind him. I sense him going for the knife in his pocket and clutch his arm to stop him. Then I peer around his shoulder.

"Great No One, are you?" the creature asks, tilting his antlers to one side to see me.

"No. That's not my name. Did you say Rabid is yours?"

The creature glances at the table, then back to us again, twisting his gloved hands nervously. "Rabid, I am. My family *White* be." Appearing flustered by our lack of response, he bows at the waist. "Rabid White, of the Red Court be I. And are you?"

I can't find my voice. My memories and the online stories were true. We've stepped into a nether-realm and are face-to-face with a netherling. That strange melody sings inside my heart, the one put there by my forgotten childhood playmate. It's even more powerful than the fluttery sensation I sometimes feel. It tells me to embrace my identity, to be proud of who I am.

Without even thinking, I blurt out, "Alyssa Gardner of the human court, I be."

Jeb hisses and his shoulders tense, but he doesn't lose focus on our guest.

"Ohhhh." The cadaverous creature swoons with an odd clacking sound, like a chime made of bones. His lips twist into a hideous snarl, revealing two long, bucked teeth. "Her gloves those be. A thief are you!"

Jeb snaps out the knife and flicks open the blade in one fluid movement, his other arm holding me behind him.

"Everything you'll ruin." Our guest's pink eyes glow hot red. Saliva foams at his mouth. "Not welcome. So says Queen Grenadine, not welcome you be!" His screech hangs in the air as he hops into the shadowed corridor and vanishes.

"What do you mean, Queen Grenadine?" I shout after Rabid. "Since when is there a new queen? What happened to Red?"

Jeb tucks the knife away and grabs me before I can follow the creature into the hallway. "What was that?" His fingers dig into my shoulders as I strain to break free. "Seriously, what was it, Al? There isn't a rabbit alive that looks like that!"

"Jeb! He's getting away!" I thrash like a wild animal. "I know where he's going . . . it's the door my key was made for. Please!" There is fear in Jeb's eyes, and I wonder why I don't share it. All I know is I've always been different in my world. In a place like this, I'm actually ordinary.

"No." Jeb crosses my arms over my chest, then lifts me against one of the curtains on the wall so my feet dangle, pinning me like a butterfly to a corkboard. "We're not going anywhere. That foaming freak thinks you stole those gloves. And now he knows your name. Very smooth, by the way."

"I didn't say it intentionally," I grind out, boots swinging with my effort to get down.

"What does that mean—*intentionally?*"

The same inner melody that gave me courage to speak earlier warns me not to say anything about the moth, the stranger, or the music.

"From what I know about this place," I offer, "it's a magical realm. And the thing we just saw was a netherling . . . one of the occupants."

"'Magical'?" Jeb stares at me as if my head's on crooked. "I don't remember Lewis Carroll's version saying anything about little walking skeletons."

"Alice must've been too young to understand what she saw. Maybe her mind blocked out the darker details." I glance at my gloved palms, empathizing with the desire to hide from bad memories on a level few people could.

"If you're right," Jeb says, "then our guidebook is screwed." He looks at the pinhole of sunlight overhead. "The entrance is still open." He lowers me to the ground but keeps holding my elbow.

I grip his tuxedo's lapel. "Don't you see? It doesn't matter that Wonderland's different than what Carroll wrote. All these years, Alison's been locked up in a psych ward for nothing. It's *real*. You weren't there today. They treated her like an invalid. If they fry her brain, she might end up incapacitated forever. I won't leave without helping her!"

"We've got stuff to help her now. The cake and the bottle."

"It won't be enough. I have to fix something Alice did. He told me—" I stop myself too late.

"*Who* told you?"

"I . . . I found a website." I clench my jaw. I've already said too much.

"Some perv lured you here via a magical website?" Jeb won't let go of my arm.

"Not exactly."

"We're done." He's not even listening to me now. "I'm getting you somewhere safe." He slides one of the tasseled cords from the curtain behind me, and then drops it to the floor in a golden coil. "First, we get every rope and tie them together to make a lasso. Then we'll use the furniture along the tunnel wall to get back up. It'll be like that time we climbed rocks in the canyon a few summers back."

I don't know what scares me more: the fact that his plan's so good it might work, or that I don't want it to.

My guide's voice returns, stern this time, almost angry. *I tire of these games. Drink from the bottle. One sip. Find me.*

I wrestle Jeb's grip, but he's too strong. He's already drawing down his fourth rope when a gritty, grinding sound reverberates overhead. We both watch as the pinhole fades to blackness—the statue shutting us in.

Mouth agape, Jeb drops both the rope and my arm. I make a break for the corridor, grabbing the backpack and a candle from the wall on my way. I duck into the darkness with Jeb's shouts ricocheting all around me.

After nearly tripping over my boot laces, I use my mouth to hold the candle so I can free one hand. I rummage in the backpack for the brown bottle. The candle's flame casts flickers of yellow along the walls.

Jeb's close behind. I don't want him any deeper into my mess, but the only way I can keep him safe is if he's with me.

I hunch down to keep going as the passage gets smaller. Lifting the chain off my neck, I wrap it on my wrist so the key dangles free at the end. Somehow I know that unless I want it to shrink, too, it can't touch me. Far ahead, where the passage is smallest, the miniature door comes into sight.

With the backpack looped over one shoulder, I pull out the

brown bottle and pop the cork, slopping a dash of liquid into my mouth opposite where I still hold the candle. The bitter flavor burns going down. I recork the bottle and tuck it away into the backpack, dropping it for Jeb.

"Just one drink!" I yell over my shoulder, and leave him the candle.

Muscles jerk—bones click. Every inch of my skin warms and tightens, as if I'm tumbling in a clothes dryer, growing smaller with each step. Nausea turns in my stomach while the corridor seems to grow alongside me.

When I look back, Jeb's on his belly, snaking toward me with one arm outstretched to catch me in his hand. I weave between his fingers, stumble forward, and, struggling with a key now the size of my palm, I unlock the door and dive headfirst into Wonderland.

THE OCEAN OF TEARS

I scramble to my feet, as small as a cricket, just like in my recurring nightmare. Only this time I'm not Alice. And so far, I still have my head.

Climbing onto a mound of dirt, I take a look around. A flower garden towers above, casting enormous shadows. Between openings in the trunklike stems, a beach stretches along an endless ocean. An empty rowboat waits on the shore—gigantic compared to me. Salt and pollen season the air.

"It can't be," Jeb's voice thunders.

I spin on my heel to face him, covering my ears. One huge eye peers out from the rabbit hole's door.

"Drink from the brown bottle," I answer.

"I can't hear you." His mumble shakes the ground under my feet.

I mime drinking something and hold out a forefinger, signaling the number one.

Then he's gone.

I hope he wears the backpack for the transition. Judging from the current size of my clothes, everything touching him will shrink.

In a matter of seconds, Jeb plunges through the opening with the backpack in tow. The door snaps shut behind him, with the key on the other side.

Catching me around the waist, he pulls me against him. "What were you thinking?"

"I'm sorry."

"'Sorry' won't fix this mess. We're the size of bugs and locked out of our only exit."

"Well, you're the one who left the key!"

His face flushes. "What are we supposed to do now?"

"We eat a bite of cake and get big again."

He slaps his brow in feigned shock. "Of course. We're just going to eat a piece of hundred-year-old magical cake."

"You can stay this size if you want to. I'll carry you in my pocket."

Snarling, Jeb slips the backpack from his arms. "Whatever. Let's just do this. We're smaller than the stinking flowers, for crying out—"

"The boy thinks we stink, Ambrosia." A craggy, witchlike voice erupts out of nowhere. Movement sweeps along the garden, as if wind blows the blooms.

Jeb and I edge backward, nearly tripping over the fallen pack.

One of the giant daisies bends low, casting a long blue shadow.

A distorted mouth widens in the flower's yellow center, and rows of eyes blink on every petal. "That he did, Redolence. The nerve," she says. "After all, if anyone stinks, it would be him. We haven't any sweat glands."

Jeb drags me behind him, reversing our direction. "Um, Al? I'm not the only one seeing a talking flower, right?"

I clutch his waist, my heartbeat pounding into his spine. "You get used to it." I try to suppress the panic stabbing me.

"What's that supposed to mean?"

I don't have the chance to answer, because Jeb crashes us into a huge stem.

A nasturtium leans down, snarling. A hundred gray eyes nestle on her bright orange petals. "Watch where you're going, would you?"

Several dandelions bob the fuzz on their heads, scolding. Tiny eyeballs protrude from their tufted seeds like snails' antennae.

I swallow a scream as they all start talking at once:

"How long has it been since we've had such delectable visitors?"

"In our living-backward years or their moving-forward years?"

"Doesn't matter, really. I was more just making a point."

Jeb eases us into a small clearing in the midst of the chattering creatures and turns me to face him. "Did they just call us 'delectable'?"

Behind us, a dandelion sneezes. Her seeds burst from her head in tufts, leaving bald spots. "My eyes! Someone catch my eyes!" She reaches out with her leaves to try to grab them.

Two places down, a geranium bends at midstem and opens a bucket on the ground. The word *Aphids* glitters on the side in red paint. Fishing out a pinkish bug the size of a mouse, the flower pokes the writhing victim into his mouth and chews, drool oozing down the petals that make up his chin. His eyelids close underneath the slobber.

Jeb's expression grows wild. "A flower eating an aphid. The eater becoming the eaten! People sometimes eat flowers, Al. *Delectable . . .*"

That stab of unease becomes a full-blown punch. "We should—"

"Run!" Jeb grabs my hand and jerks me into a sprint toward the rabbit hole's door.

"How do we get in?" My thighs strain with each jarring step.

"We break the friggin' lock."

I almost trip on my boot heels. Jeb is unrelenting, dragging me along. "We don't have to go so fast! They're rooted in the ground!"

"Don't bet on it," he says.

I follow his gaze over my shoulder. It's like a zombie movie—the flowers moan and rip their stems up from the dirt; their mouths stretch wide, pressed open by long, spindly teeth, clear and dripping with slobber like melting icicles. The balding dandelion gets free first and sprouts humanlike arms and legs. She uses her roots for added momentum, as if she's being propelled by snakes. She whips out a strand of ivy and loops it around Jeb's ankle, lassoing him. With one tug, she drops him to the ground.

"Jeb!" I catch his wrists in a tug-of-war against the hissing flower.

"There's no out the way you came in," another flower growls as it squirms from its grave of dirt a few feet away. That's when I realize none of them are flowers, not really. Just like with the dandelion, arms and legs appear as they burst out of the ground.

They're part humanoid, part plant—multi-eyed mutants.

"The rabbit hole only opens into *our* realm. The portals that open out to yours are guarded in the castles far across the ocean, inside the pulsing heart of Wonderland," one flower says while waving an arm.

Vines cling to the greenish flesh along its naked biceps. "Therein is the only escape. Don't you think we would've already left, were there a way out of the hole?"

I picture all the furniture pinned up along the tunnel wall with ivy. So, they'd been trying to *build* a way into our world? I shiver.

Jeb struggles under the vines now roped around his waist. "Al, run," he mumbles.

"Yes, run," the dandelion mutant taunts. She cups my chin with mossy fingertips and tilts her head to see me with her three remaining eyeballs. "Run or be eaten."

A fresh wave of terror trickles through my spine. I shake it off as a flash of knowing comes to me: The netherling boy from my memories once taught me how to defeat this flower.

It's as easy as blowing tufts in the wind.

On impulse, I reach up and pluck off what's left of her seeds, leaving her blind. A white, gooey liquid dribbles down my hands from the exposed eye sockets. She shrieks and droops to the ground, incapacitated.

I'm peripherally aware of Jeb fishing the knife from his pocket beneath the greenery binding him. If I can provide a distraction, maybe he can get us out of this.

I hold up the dandelion seeds. The sticklike eyeballs writhe in my hand, trying to stare at me. I toss them down, stomping them. "Who's next?" I hope to sound tough, but my voice quavers.

The zombie flowers howl and fling their vines around my ankles. Ivy snakes around my legs and torso and up my chest, sealing me within a leafy cocoon so thick only my head and upheld arms are free. Then two strands cinch my wrists together. With a yank, they flip me onto my stomach. I can't budge.

Jeb and the incapacitated dandelion are all but forgotten as the others surround me.

Misshapen hands, green with chlorophyll, skim across me—cold and rough like leaves shaken from trees after a storm. Dizziness clouds my head. The vines are too tight. I can't jerk away. I can't even get enough air to scream.

Hot gusts blow over me. Eyes clenched shut, I sob. Slobber drizzles along my nape from someone's mouth, glomming strands of my hair together.

"Wait!" one of them shouts close enough to my ear that it rings. "She's wearing the gloves!"

Sliding my cheek against the gritty ground, I peer up at hundreds of eyelashes blinking in rapid succession.

"It is true!" a white-rose-headed freak gasps. "Do you have the fan, as well?"

Neck craned, I nod. My left nostril fills with dirt at the effort.

"We should celebrate!" They pass the bucket of aphids around among them.

"Do you think it's her? After all this time?" a flower with pink petals asks, munching on her snack.

"She does look rather like *you know who.*"

"Even more of the devil's seed in this one, to be sure," Pinky adds. "The eyes of a tiger lily she has."

"Just think of it." One of the flowers pops a screeching aphid into its mouth as the bucket passes by. "We'll soon be connected to the heart of Wonderland once more!"

The rose-head leans low, intent on me. "So, are you here to set things right?"

My gaze drifts between their body stems. Jeb has almost sawed his way out of the vines. Just a little longer. Over the fear nested in my chest, I force myself to talk. "Yes. Set things right."

"About time. We can pick up roots, but we can't traipse across the water, even in a boat. We must stay connected to the soil. The path to Wonderland's heart has to be opened to us. For that to happen, Alice's tears must be dried up. That's your job!"

"Hear, hear!" they all say in unison. "Your job to fix her messes."

The rose snaps two thorny fingers to silence the rest of the garden. "You must go across the ocean and onto the island of black sands. Inside the heart of Wonderland, the Wise One waits. He has been here since the beginning. He smokes the pipe of wisdom. He knows what must be done."

"Pipe? You mean the Caterpillar?" I ask.

Wicked laughter erupts among my captors.

"The Caterpillar," Pinky scoffs. "Well, I suppose you could call him that. That's what the other one called him."

"The other one?" I ask.

"*Your* other," the rose says. "The one whose tears formed the ocean that now isolates us from the rest of our kind. High time a descendant came down to mend things."

Before I can respond, an orange monstrosity steps up to speak. Spindly fronds fall from her mouth, where they cling to her drool. Stinging nettles tip her fingernails. "We could ask the octobenus to take her across. We'll use the elfin knight as leverage. His blood alone is worth all the white gold in the Ivory Queen's palace. The octobenus can trade it for a bevy of clams. He'll never go hungry again. He cannot refuse such a bargain."

"This boy is no knight," the rose says. "He came down with her."

Orangey shakes her petals. "He was sent to escort her. He has emerald eyes, and the blood droplet beneath his lip has crystallized to a gem. He's indubitably and undeniably an elfin knight of the White Court."

I try to calm my racing thoughts enough to analyze their conversation. They think Jeb's garnet labret marks him as one of the netherlings. I shoot a gaze toward him to see if he heard, but he's no longer trapped by vines.

"Well, he hasn't the uniform!" Pinky screeches. "Let us see if his ears are pointed."

They turn around. "He's escaped!"

They surge toward the sound of the backpack's zipper, but Jeb already has the cake in hand.

In less than two blinks, he grows high above us. Body coiled and tense, he takes a swipe at the garden with one of his giant boots. The blossoms scream, grouped together in a bouquet of trembling petals.

He's as graceful and majestic as a Greek god, lovely and appalling in his wrath. He lifts me so I hang from his fingers by strands of ivy, strung up in my cocoon like a helpless yo-yo.

Nervous energy courses through my limbs. I have to escape . . . the bindings are too tight . . . I can't expand my lungs.

"Can't breathe!" I struggle, but the effort only swings me faster. My stomach flops like a pendulum. The flower creatures cry out and grapple for me, but Jeb curls his fingers and nestles me within his fist—a snug, tender darkness.

"Shh. I got ya, Al . . ." His whispered breath rushes over me as he opens his palm.

My fear of heights battles a newborn claustrophobia. I roll along his warm flesh until his thumb, careful and tender, stops me. I freeze on my back to let him unwind the strands of ivy. His giant, callused fingers are gentle despite their size.

The minute I'm free, I catch his thumb—almost bigger than me—and nuzzle it. He tastes like grass and icing and all the flavors of Jeb, magnified. My heart hammers against his inner knuckle. "Thank you," I say, knowing he can't hear me.

Carefully, he holds me level to his face. His eyes are the size of teacup saucers, huge and framed with eyelashes like a thicket of moss and shadows. "Hang on," he whispers.

He lifts me to his shoulder. I straddle the backpack's strap. With one hand and both boots tucked under for security, I wave.

Taking my cue, Jeb kicks over the bucket of aphids, freeing them. He roars at our captors and they root themselves back into the ground, re-creating the flower forest that once surrounded us. He walks over them in one step. They're lucky he doesn't crush them.

We arrive at the rowboat and Jeb offers a palm to lower me onto the closest seat. The wood grains look like ripples of sand on a desert, and splinters peak like porcupine quills. I find a smooth spot and wait.

Jeb sets the backpack into the hull of the boat. He digs through it, and his hand reappears with a chunk of cake balanced on his fingertip. To him, it's probably nothing but a crumb. I stand and eat from his finger, closing my eyes as my bones and skin strain and expand like rubber bands. When I look again, I'm perfectly proportioned, sitting on the seat, with Jeb crouched in front of me, watching anxiously.

"You okay?" He rubs his palms along my thighs.

I grip my stomach. "Yuck."

"Yeah. Let's hope we're done playing musical sizes. It's hard on the innards." His jacket is crumpled in the bottom of the boat, and his bare arms sparkle with sweat. He rakes a hand through his hair, leaving it disheveled. "Those gloves saved your life," he says. "What gave you the idea to wear them in the first place?"

I'm unable to put into words the fluttery feeling or the memory of a childhood here, so I try to downplay it. "Lucky guess?"

I can still see the flowers morphing into monsters before our eyes. Like Jeb said, this is not the Wonderland Lewis Carroll created. Yet somehow, my instincts have served us so far. Thanks to my absent netherling guide.

I have to find him. The longer I'm here, the more I feel drawn to him. We'll go to the Caterpillar, like the flowers said. In his wisdom, he can help me find my guide and break the curse.

As if reading my mind, Jeb hops out of the rowboat and shoves the bow toward the expanse of glistening waves. Sand grates along the bottom and he leaps inside once we hit the water. "They said there's a way out across the ocean. Guess that's our only option." Taking the seat opposite mine, he works the paddles, biceps straining.

"Do you really think these are Alice's tears?" I ask. "That I'm supposed to make them go away somehow?"

"I'm the wrong guy to ask. I just saw a skeleton with antlers and a forest of aphid-noshing flower zombies."

I prop my elbows on my knees. "I'm sorry I freaked back there, when I was wrapped in the vines." I finally know what it's like to be Alison, trapped inside a nightmare.

"Are you kidding?" Jeb says. "You threw yourself out as bait so I could escape. I'm not thrilled about your putting yourself in the line of fire, but those were great distraction tactics. Hey." He nudges my boot with his. "Get some rest."

I lean back to relax my aching muscles. The sound of lapping waves lulls my eyes closed. I've rested for less than a second when Jeb whistles.

"Look." He gestures behind me.

Instead of the beach we just left growing smaller in the distance, there's nothing. We're surrounded by water in every direction. While I'm trying to make sense of that, the sun vanishes, as if someone flicked a light switch. I stiffen in my seat, fingers clenched on the boat's edges.

"What just happened?" Jeb asks, his voice strained.

"It's nightfall. There's no twilight here," I answer, as sure as I am that we're going in the right direction to find the winged guy from my past.

Jeb just stares at me and keeps rowing.

Stars twinkle in the purple heavens, reflecting in the dark water that swirls all around us. We swirl, too, the boat turning in slow circles until it's impossible to differentiate between water and sky.

Jeb sets the oars in their grooves. "My rowing's not getting us anywhere. We're going to have to leave it to the currents and hope for the best." Starlight flashes across his labret.

"Could you hand me the backpack?" I have a sudden urge to look at those sketches in the Alice book.

Jeb digs out two energy bars and a bottle of water, then steps over the oars toward me, rocking us gently. "You need to eat." He hands off the backpack and the snack, then sits cross-legged in front of me.

I set the bar aside, open the water, and take a swig. Then I slide the *Wonderland* book from the bag. "They thought you were an elfin knight of the White Court."

Jeb rips open his energy bar. "Yeah, whatever that is."

I flip to the sketches. "Here." The likeness could be Jeb's twin: muscular build, square chin, dark hair, jeweled red dots lining the outer corners of his temples and lips. Eyes as dark velvet green as the underside of leaves. The only difference is the pointed ears.

Jeb studies the picture, chewing.

"They serve the Ivory Queen," I explain, "in her castle of glass. Their blood crystallizes when the air hits it. That's how they mark themselves, by piercing holes in their flesh so their blood can leak out and become jewels. They're trained to be emotionless, to act only on instinct. Having so much self-control makes them fierce protectors, but it also makes for a very lonely queen."

Swallowing, Jeb looks up. "You sound like you're reading from an encyclopedia. How do you know all that?"

I turn the pages until I come to the skeletal rabbit. "The same way I know that Rabid White was tortured by an evil spell that was eating his skin from his bones. But Queen Red rescued him, stopping the bad magic before it could get to his face. He swore to serve her and no other until the day he died. So, why's he serving someone named Grenadine now?"

"Huh?"

I shake my head. "Nothing. Look, you saw me back there. I knew how to stop that dandelion creep. I knew how to walk through a mirror. It's because I've been taught."

Jeb crumples his food wrapper and stuffs it into the backpack, then waits for me to explain.

"I don't know how, but before Alison left for the asylum, I came here. It must've been a lot of times—I'm remembering more and more. I think it was mostly at night. In our world, anyway. While my parents were sleeping."

Jeb doesn't budge, just stares up into the sky.

I slump. "You think I'm crazy, right?"

He huffs. "Have you taken a look around? If you're crazy, I'm riding the banana train right alongside you."

I let out a relieved laugh. "Good point."

"Okay, it's time you were straight with me." He digs out the other recliner treasures and lays everything at my feet. "Start with your mom. Why she was really sent to Soul's." He pauses. "And what it has to do with your scars, since you obviously didn't get them in a car accident."

After another slow drink of water, I tell him my history, from the pruning shears to the bleeding daffodils. But I'm not ready to share details of the moth or my dark guide. Those memories feel private, somehow.

When I get to the part about the talking bugs and plants that Alison and I both hear, his gaze intensifies.

He plays with the laces on my boot. "So, you chose bugs for your art because it was the only way you could—"

"Shut them up? Yeah."

He shakes his head. "And I thought my childhood was warped. No wonder you've been scared of ending up at Soul's, too." He leans back on his elbows. "Now I get it. That battle I always see in your eyes. Light and dark. Like my gothic fairies." He's studying me as if I'm a piece of artwork again.

"So the sketches you made of me . . . they're the basis for your paintings?"

His eyebrows rise.

"All those times I caught you looking at me like I'm a palette of paint."

Thumping his fingers on the boat, he frowns. "Not sure what you're talking about."

"I know about the sketches Taelor found."

Something—either shock or embarrassment—flickers through his eyes.

I clench my fingers. "She's right, huh? The morbid and revolting are such fascinating subjects." It hurts to say it almost as much as it did to hear it.

"Is that what she said?"

I lift a shoulder in silent affirmation.

He sits up again and places a hand on my shin. "Look, she lashes out when she feels threatened. After finding the sketches . . . well, she kind of lost it. I mean, the guy she's been dating has an aesthetic obsession with another girl. You can see her side, can't you?"

"Maybe." I never would've guessed I was anyone's obsession, aesthetic or otherwise. If I inspire his art, then why is Taelor the one he chooses to have in his life? "Jeb . . . why do you put up with her?"

He pauses. "I guess because I'm the only stable thing she has."

"And by fixing her problems, you hope to make up for everything your dad did to Jen and your mom?"

He doesn't answer. That's as good as a yes.

Hatred for his father's weakness and violence flashes through me. "You're not accountable for his mistakes. Only for your own. Like going to London with Taelor."

"That's not a mistake. It's going to help with my career."

I stare at my boots. "Right. Just like my 'mortician sense of style' will help with mine." I attempt a laugh, but even to me it sounds false.

"Hey." The insistence in Jeb's voice makes me look up at him.

"Tae was wrong, you know. About that. Do you think my paintings are ugly or freakish?"

I think of his watercolor paintings: darkly beautiful worlds and gothic fairies weeping black tears over human corpses. His depictions of misery and loss are so poignant and surreal they break the heart.

I twist my gloved hands together. "No. They're beautiful and haunting."

He squeezes my shin. "An artist is only as good as his subject."

For one raw, drawn-out moment, we're silent. Then he lets go of me.

I rub my knees, warming my leggings. "Can I see them someday?"

"The sketches?"

I nod.

"Tell you what. We get out of this in one piece, and I'll give you a private viewing." He holds my gaze for a minute too long, and my blood runs hot. How am I supposed to figure anything out when I can't even read my own body's signals anymore?

"Okay." He looks down at the *Wonderland* book in his lap and slides out the pictures of Alice, moving close. "What's up with these?" Flicking on the flashlight, he points its yellow glow at them, effectively distracting me from my whacked-out emotions.

The pictures are faded and worn, one of a sad and lovely young girl with dirty smudges on her dress and pinafore. The words *Alice, seven years of age and fresh from the rabbit hole* are handwritten on the back. The other picture is of Alice as an eighty-two-year-old woman.

I place them side by side. What was it Alison said? *"Photographs tell a story. But people forget to read between the lines."*

She said the same thing when she traced my birthmark—insisting there was more to the story than people realized.

Peering more closely at the pictures, I search the young Alice's face and body. There's a shadow on her left elbow that seems to match the pigmented maze Alison and I share. I study the same spot on the elderly Alice, but there's no birthmark.

"That's it!" I point to the pictures. "There and there. Alice had a birthmark that matches mine and Alison's when she was a kid, but she lost it as an old woman."

Jeb holds both pictures up to the light. "Could be the photo was retouched."

"Why would anyone do that?"

Jeb reaches for the energy bar on the seat beside me, tears the wrapping, and curls my fingers around it—unspoken insistence that I eat. "Are there any answers in the book?"

Chewing a bite of granola, I flip through page after page. I trace a finger over Alison's blurred notes in the margins while Jeb holds the flashlight. "There might've been, if these were legible." I reach the end, past the sketches and final pages, and am just about to put it away when Jeb tugs it out of my grasp.

"Look here."

If he hadn't pointed it out, I wouldn't have noticed the blank page bent in half and glued to form a pocket against the inside of the back cover. I dig out a folded piece of paper. It's old, yellow, and wrinkled.

The word *Deathspeak* is scribbled across the back, followed by a trail of crooked question marks, then a handwritten definition. *Deathspeak: the language of the dying. One can only speak it to the one who was the cause of one's ill fate. It is the final recompense, to appoint a task that the offender must either carry out or die himself.*

Jeb and I look at each other. I unfold the paper so we can see what's written inside. I know after the first sentence that it's something I wish I'd never laid eyes on. Yet I can't look away . . .

November 14, 1934: On the date of mental evaluation, Alice Liddell Hargreaves is an eighty-two-year-old woman of petite height who was brought in by concerned family members. According to relatives, her mental state began deteriorating months ago, when she awoke one morning with no recognition of her whereabouts and only a vague sense of her identity.

The psychologist conducting the interviews notes that the patient is preoccupied with inner thoughts, often brooding and overwhelmed by the size of the room. She occasionally crouches in a corner or perches on a chair when being interviewed. She is inattentive and vague, and has lively interactions with inanimate objects but detached human exchanges.

Patient is not oriented in physicality or place, with a marked impairment of time, inclined to melancholy dissertations over the loss of the seventy-five years she claims to have been locked in a birdcage in "Wonderland," having been "seduced by a statue boy at the age of seven to dive into a rabbit hole."

The examining psychologist attributes this to a grandiose delusion originating from a childhood given to vivid imaginings that were fed by the Liddell family's close friend Charles Dodgson, a.k.a. Lewis Carroll. Patient has fallen back on these fantasies to account for her selective memory loss.

Inasmuch as the patient exhibits the following symptoms: (1) grandiose delusions and selective amnesia, (2) marked diminished interest or pleasure in social interactions unless socializing with bugs or plants, (3) absence of appetite; prefers only fruit and desserts and refuses to ingest nutrition unless drink is served in a thimble and food on a birdcage tray—she is diagnosed as suffering from Mania and Schizophrenia.

Recommended treatment: electroshock twice daily—natural voltage administered by applying an electric eel to the head. Supplement with psychiatric counsel until all delusional lapses are contained, memory is reinstated, and mood of the patient is elevated.

I shove the report at Jeb.

He watches me. "Are you okay?"

How do I answer that? My great-great-great-grandmother tripped so far into her psychosis that she couldn't remember her past or present. The thimble and birdcage-tray idiosyncrasies are too close to Alison's teacup fetish. The consistency disturbs me.

Could something else be going on . . . not a delusion but a manipulation? Is that why Alison is so into the Alice charade? Whatever it is, it's obvious that she's headed for the same fate as my other ancestors.

"Do you see why I can't let her go through with those treatments?" I point to the paper. "The date of Alice's death. She died just two days after the report. The shock treatments must have killed her!"

I yank my dreadlocks out—ignoring the rip at the roots of my hair—and fling them into the ocean. I'm done fighting my resemblance to Alison. Since we're teammates in this bizarre game, we might as well look the part.

Jeb pulls me off the seat to sit me beside him, but the boat rocks, and I end up falling into his lap. We both freeze. When I start to ease off his legs, he holds me there. My heart hammers; I can't deny how amazing it feels to be so close to him. Ignoring the alarms going off inside me, I give in and press my cheek to the soft knit of his tank, my arms folded between us. He strokes my hair as I snuggle beneath his chin, legs curled in the fetal position.

"I'm scared," I whisper. *For more reasons than I can say.*

"You have every right to be," he answers softly. "But we're going to get back home. We're going to tell your dad everything. With both of our accounts and this lab report, he has to believe."

"No. This only proves that Alice was as crazy as he thinks Alison is. In the end, she didn't even remember getting married and having a family. Even with the living evidence of children and grandchildren around her, she still didn't remember."

Jeb is silent.

"I don't want to end up in a straitjacket," I say, holding back a sob. "With every memory I've made lost . . . or so meaningless it could belong to someone else."

Jeb's arms tense around me. "That's not in your future, Alyssa Victoria Gardner." He's never called me by my full name. He says it like my dad would, loading power into every syllable, which is exactly what I need.

"What, then?" I ask, hungry for any crumb he can spare.

"You're going to be a famous artist." His voice is deep velvet—soothing and sure. "You'll live in one of those artsy, upscale apartments in Paris with your rich husband. Oh, who just happens to be a world-renowned exterminator. How's that for a twist of fate? You won't even have to catch your own bugs anymore. That'll give you more time to spend with your five brilliant kids. And I'll come visit every summer. Show up on the doorstep with a bottle of Texas barbecue sauce and a French baguette. I'll be weird Uncle Jeb."

Uncle Jeb? I like the idea of him always being in my life. But as I stare at his ribbed tank and envision those circular ridges on his chest—a tragic dot-to-dot of each time he accidentally spilled a drink or left a toy out for his dad to trip over—I'm floored by how fast old feelings sweep in. Though fabric hides the scars, I know every one by heart. I've seen them countless times when we've gone swimming together or worked in his garage. I dreamed about them in sixth grade, about how it would feel to trace each one with my fingertip.

Right now, I'm wondering the same thing. How it might feel to heal his wounds with my touch.

"Not an exterminator," I blurt against the pulse pounding in my neck.

"Huh?"

I pause. "I'm going to fall in love with an artist. And we'll have two kids and live in the country. A quiet life, so we can hear our muses and answer when they call."

Tipping up my chin to meet his gaze, he gives me a tender, starlit smile—one that melts my insides. "I like your version better."

His mouth is so close to mine, his breath warm, sugary, and tempting, but thoughts of Taelor and London resurface. I can't let my heart get stolen by a guy who's hot for another girl, or be the kind of person who steals another girl's guy. I've already stolen money from Taelor and I've let this go far enough. I slip off his lap, my net skirts scraping his tuxedo pants.

As if waking from a trance, Jeb sits back on his palms and looks out over the rippling water.

"What do you think will happen tomorrow?" I ask, my voice as shaky as the rest of me.

"Whatever it is, don't jump into things without me. We do everything together. Deal?" He lifts one of my hands, smooths the wrinkles on my glove, and curls my fingers into a fist while waiting for an answer.

"Deal," I say.

"Good." He bumps my fisted knuckles with his. I shiver—both from the chilly breeze and the sweetness of the gesture.

"Here." Jeb picks up his tux jacket and helps me slip my arms inside. Then he puts everything into the pack. "Let's try to get some sleep."

He cradles my back against his chest, and we spoon in the hull of the rocking boat. His nose nestles in my hair. A spiral of white stars coils and uncoils in feathery sparks. It looks like curls of lightning, just like the spider and beetle mosaic I worked on earlier today before I went skating at Underland. Another tremor rolls through me. I remember watching these same constellations with my netherling guide years ago. No wonder it came through in my art.

"I hope that's not a storm coming," Jeb whispers against my nape, arms tensing around me. "This boat won't hold up to thrashing waves."

Tucking my hand absently into my skirt pocket, I prod the sponge my guide wanted me keep.

"It's only a constellation," I answer, and Jeb doesn't question how I know.

Without speaking, we watch the display overhead until it bursts into a thousand glittering colors, like silent fireworks. When it's gone, nothing remains but common white stars.

"Wow," we both say.

After a few quiet minutes, Jeb relaxes, and his breath rasps, slow and even, against the back of my head. Although it's Jeb's body keeping me warm, the last things I envision before falling asleep are inky black eyes and a spread of satiny wings.

OCTOBENUS

The Alice nightmare finds me while I'm sleeping . . .

I'm not alone this time. Jeb carries the stolen sword, and we race down the path toward the Caterpillar's lair. The thorns that once snarled and ripped my pinafore elongate into leafy eels. The serpentine strands wrap around our legs and carry us upside down to the chessboard. Our bodies freeze into game pieces. A hand appears, wearing a black glove, and moves us from square to square. It picks me up to claim checkmate, but Jeb comes alive, slashing at the fingers with the sword to free me. The bloody digits fall one by one and morph into caterpillars. Jeb and I race back to the path. The mushroom waits in the center, cloaked in a web. The caterpillars beat us there. They tunnel into the cocoon, filling it until it writhes—a living, breathing thing. A razor-sharp black blade slices from within the webbed casing. Whatever's inside is coming out.

I awaken, startled, and blink against the sun's brightness. My hands are clenched into fists. What woke me up? I was so close to unveiling the face in the cocoon—the one I've been waiting years to see.

Yawning, I focus on the here and now. Sometime in the night, I must've turned toward Jeb in the rowboat, and he pulled me against himself, tucking me under his chin. All I see now is a close-up of his tank. He's still asleep. His heavy breath rustles my hair, slow and rhythmic. His arms clutch my waist.

Yesterday comes back to me in pieces: the rabbit hole, the mutant flower garden, the ocean of tears.

I snuggle into his neck, fingers curled within the sleeves of the tuxedo jacket, determined not to wake him so I can pretend things are simple and perfect for just a few minutes longer.

The boat rocks and I realize that's what woke me. Not a gentle, riding-on-a-current movement. More a something-heavy-sloughed-over-the-edge-and-is-watching-us movement . . .

I freeze—as rigid as the wood beneath us.

Guttural snuffles fill the air, like those of an asthmatic bulldog. The warmth of sun on my shoulders turns chilly as a shadow falls across us. My heart does a somersault. Before I can belt out a scream, Jeb snaps into action, rolling us toward the bow and jerking us to our feet. He was awake the whole time.

"No way," he says.

I wobble with the boat's motion, holding on to Jeb's waistband with one hand and the seat behind me with the other. I peer around him.

At first glance, our intruder looks like a walrus. He has two giant tusks with images of snakes and angry flames carved along the ivory. But beneath rolls of blubber, his lower half is a tangle of slithering octopus tentacles, covered in suction cups. It's as if someone snapped two different creatures together, creating an octo-walrus. He must weigh over five hundred pounds, and his body occupies most of the boat.

As huge as he is, and with his tentacles hanging half in and out, the boat should be capsized. Jeb and I should've been flung like stones from a slingshot as soon as he slithered aboard. Instead, the hull is level and drifting along the shining water as if the creature weighs no more than we do. Wonder what Isaac Newton would have to say about the jacked-up physical laws here?

Jeb nudges me to sit behind him but keeps standing, every muscle in his body tense and ready to snap. "What are you?"

Our uninvited guest scrapes oozing goop from his eyes with the human fingers on the ends of his flippers. "Fair question, elfin knight. I'm an octobenus. Now, let me guess your next question. What do I want? For that, there's a simple answer. I want to stop the endless suffering in my belly." Whiskers—long and blond against a cinnamon brown hide—droop under his nostril holes. His tentacles slap the ocean, spritzing us with water.

From the chain at his neck, he opens a locket the size of a cigar box and digs something out. He lays a clam in his palm, carefully holding its shell pinched shut. "Good morning, little sea cabbage," he taunts it. "Still worried about your family?"

The clam tries to open its mouth in answer. The octobenus repositions his hold to keep it quiet. "Tell you what. If you can stanch my hunger, I'll set all of them free. Willing to give it a try?"

Although the clam can't open its mouth wide enough to talk, a pinkish, hatchet-shaped muscle slinks out from the crack—like a malformed foot or arm—patting the enormous creature's cheek in a final bid for life.

A whimper bursts from my throat. Jeb reaches behind his back and opens his hand. I lace our fingers together.

In a rush of blubber and slobber, the octobenus forces the shell open, seals his mouth around it, and suctions out the contents with a terrible sucking sound. The clam's excruciating scream echoes in my head, then fades to dreadful silence. I grasp Jeb tighter, trying not to gag.

"Nope. Still hungry. Suppose I'll be eating your children next." Our unwelcome visitor laughs, an ugly, grinding sound, then tosses the empty shell overboard. He swats it with a tentacle so it sinks, and the motion makes the boat rock.

Jeb's fingers cinch around my wrist as he struggles to stay balanced.

"You must be swift with slimy prey like that," the octobenus says. "They're tricksters . . . always trying to capture you in their Deathspeak. Can you imagine, being a slave to a clam's final wish?" He laughs again.

Deathspeak . . . that phrase from the back of Alice's psych evaluation. I peer around Jeb as the walrusy creature wedges a monocle over his watery left eye.

"Now," he says, "if you would be so kind as to step aside, Elf, I might get a better look at your ward."

Jeb's stance tightens. "Not a chance."

The octo-freak drops his monocle. "Those bumbling flowers think that your blood has the power to buy me my fill of bivalves!" His shout rattles over us—through us—carrying the scent of fish and death. "But it's never been an issue of *buying* them. I'm a hunter. I must capture them. It is my nature. Clams are such crafty creatures, always using their little arms to move about and escape under their beds on the ocean floor. If only it weren't so dark down there, and with my eyes gone so bad . . . I'm lucky to capture a half dozen before they all hide." He wipes his mouth with a thick flipper. "But the Wise One owns a magic flute that calls my prey from their hiding places. And now I have a way to barter for it."

"By offering my blood in exchange," Jeb guesses.

This can't be happening. I don't care how many fights he's been in at home. Even with a Swiss Army knife, he doesn't stand a chance against a five-hundred-pound sea monster.

"He's not a jeweled elf!" I shout from behind Jeb. "He's human. Look at his ears."

Jeb squeezes my fingers—a plea to keep quiet.

"Doesn't matter either way. Jewels and riches mean nothing to the Wise One. But you, little cabbage, he's desperate for your help. Oh, yes. He's been waiting years for you to find your way here."

The statement churns in my head. The flowers said the *Wise One* is the Caterpillar. So . . . he's been waiting for me? Maybe the Caterpillar sent the moth and my dark guide to find me and bring me here.

Our captor's tentacles writhe along the boat's edges like giant pythons, and the wood creaks. "With you as hostage, I can barter for the flute. He will lay it at my feet for your safe deliverance."

"You'll have to kill me to get to her," Jeb says.

I jerk on his wrist but he ignores me.

The octobenus kneads his flipper-hands. "Ah, a loyal friend. I had one of those, many years ago. He was an artisan. He carved my tusks and crafted a beautiful trunk to hold my reserve of clams. Then I learned he was pilfering my supply. So one night as he slept, I captured him"—the tentacles curl around the boat in demonstration—"and locked him in the trunk with the empty shells. I cast the lot into the ocean to muffle his screams. His bones are fish bait now."

I bite my lip to keep from screaming.

Our captor laughs. "Dismal, isn't it? You see, if I would be so callous with a friend, what's to stop me from killing you? Nothing gets in the way of my belly's needs." He runs the thin, pointed end of a tentacle down to the tips of his slobbery tusks. "I *will* have the girl!"

He thrashes his tentacles and snags Jeb around the waist.

"No!" My arms dart out to hold him. The tentacles rip him away and lift him into the air.

"There's land . . . to your left!" Jeb shouts as he wrestles with the creature, barely missing the deadly tip of a tusk. The struggle jostles the boat.

Choking on more screams, I hold on to the seat to keep from falling. Jeb's right. There's something on the horizon. It glitters like black sequins. It could be the island the flowers told us about.

"Go!" Jeb yells. "I'll hold him off as long as I can!"

He grabs the chain around the monster's neck. With quick thrusts, he wraps up some tentacles so I can make my escape. One of the tusks slices through the knee of his pants. The sound of tearing fabric reminds me of the clam's horrible death. I can't let that happen to Jeb.

We'll never escape the octobenus in the water. How do we fight back? He has no obvious weakness . . . only a raging appetite.

"Wait!" I drop to my knees in front of him, acting on a sudden idea, hoping it works. "Please, free my friend, and I'll help you willingly."

"Al!" Jeb shouts.

"Give your word, nether-girl," our captor says, his face a blubbery sneer. "You know the rules . . . an oath from our kind cannot be broken, else your power will be lost."

I don't know why he's calling me nether-girl, but I'm willing to use it to my advantage. "I promise to help you."

"Not good enough," he says, winding Jeb's ribs tighter in his tentacles until Jeb groans. "Do it properly. Cover your heart . . . swear on your life-magic. And be very specific."

I hold my gaze on Jeb's bluing lips and slap my shaking palm to my chest. "I swear on my life-magic to help tame your appetite."

With a snarling turn of whiskers, he unwinds his tentacles and releases Jeb so he flops upright into the hull.

I throw my arms around Jeb's slimy clothes. He keeps me balanced in the boat as we stand together. He's coughing so hard, I can hardly hear his voice. "You should've . . . bailed."

"No," I whisper. "We stick together, remember?" Then I turn to our captor. "Mr. Octobenus, I know how to fill your belly. We can give cake to your clams."

Jeb frowns at me, finally catching his breath.

The creature eases back to his seat on a nest of tentacles, panting and snuffling from the exertion of the fight. "Do you mean you're offering me some clam cake?"

"No. The cake is *for* the clams," I answer. "To stretch your supply until we get you the flute. We have just the thing to grow your clams to the size of dinner plates." I turn my face to Jeb and mouth the words *Eater becoming the eaten.*

His face lights with understanding. He drags the backpack toward us. It's incredible how composed he is after almost getting impaled, crushed, and devoured.

The mutant walrus watches, curious.

Jeb opens the bandana to expose the cake with the words *Eat Me* spelled in raisins.

The octobenus whoops. "An amplifying pastry! Wherever did you find such a prize? I've never personally seen one work. They were outlawed after the Alice incident. No matter, no matter . . ." He opens the box on the chain again. The newest clam wrestles against him furiously.

"Give it here," the octobenus says. "If this fails, I gore out your mortal friend's entrails and feed them to the fishes." Drool seeps down his tusks and fills the carved images in slow, glistening slathers.

"Oh, it'll work." Jeb slides the cake across the hull. "I'd stake my life on it."

"You just did." The mutant walrus grunts as he bends to pick it up. Breaking off a crumb, he prepares to slide it into the crack of the clam's shell.

"You'll need to give it more than that," Jeb says, inching us toward the edge of the boat, backpack in hand. "As much as you can stuff into its mouth."

"Yes, yes. Just think of it! Clams as big as dinner plates . . ." Without looking up, he chuckles and breaks off a larger piece. Then, forcing the shell open, he shoves the cake inside and snaps it closed again.

Within seconds, the clam starts to shake along with the boat.

"Now!" Jeb dives overboard with my hand in his. A slap of tentacles grazes my legs, but then the warm water folds over us, and we sink. Jeb dog-paddles in front of me, his hair twirling like sea grass in the blue depths. He tugs on my wrist. I kick upward, my boots and clothes heavy and awkward in the water.

We surface and suck in deep breaths, swimming in place long enough to see what's happening in the boat. The clam stretches from the size of a makeup compact to that of a Dumpster.

In a strangely graceful display of blubber, fins, and tentacles, the octobenus realizes his misstep and tries to slide overboard. Too late. The giant shell opens, and a hatchet-shaped appendage springs out—as big and powerful as an anaconda. The muscle wraps around the octobenus and draws him into its mouth, slurping up tentacles like giant spaghetti noodles before slamming shut.

The boat buckles and cracks. In moments, the clam sinks into the ocean, leaving only foam and floating debris behind. Waves ripple around the wreckage, an eerily serene ending to such a violent scene.

Jeb holds my wrist and the backpack with one hand while using his other arm in a one-sided breast stroke to propel us toward the black beach.

Something pulls me downward.

I pump my legs until my calves cramp, trying to stay afloat. It's no use. I let go of Jeb, afraid to pull him down with me.

Swept underwater, I search for what's anchoring me, terrified a sea creature is to blame, yet there's nothing there. The weight seems to be centered at my waist, but I'm descending too fast to find it. I flail, arms and legs straining against the downward momentum. My lungs shriek for oxygen.

Jeb appears above me. The backpack descends behind him into the dark depths. I snap my legs and hands into action, clawing at the water. Jeb tries to pull me up by gripping under my arms. I jerk away, fighting him. Or maybe I'm fighting myself. Fighting my fear . . .

His expression is resolute as he grabs me. He refuses to give up, and that scares me more than anything. I shake my head.

Save yourself! my eyes tell him, but he's too stubborn to listen.

I want to tell him I'm sorry I dragged him into this. Instead, empty bubbles swirl between us.

A hot and heavy ache pushes at my chest. I bat at the water, trying to break through somehow, to make it disappear. My tears mix with Alice's and every thought blackens at the edges. Jeb's still pulling on me, but it's hopeless—we keep sinking.

As I'm about to surrender to unconsciousness, it dawns on me that the weight is coming from my skirt pocket. Numb, I pull out the sponge I picked up at the bottom of the rabbit hole.

What was once the size of a bite of cheese is now as big as a golf ball and growing. It glides down toward the bottom of the ocean, dragging the water with it, creating a whirlpool.

I'm free.

Holding on to each other, Jeb and I surface long enough to fill our lungs before the suction of the funnel captures us. The sponge is the size of a grapefruit now, and I can see the bottom of the ocean far beneath us.

I scream, clutching Jeb for dear life.

My eyes squeeze shut as we slam into something solid.

"Al," Jeb says, and that's when I notice I can breathe.

I gasp hungrily for air, open my eyes, and blink away the wetness. The ocean is gone. Flattened sea grass and piles of wet sand surround us. Puddles of water glimmer in places, reflecting the sun. In the distance, I spot our backpack. The island's black sands tower like a cliff above us—a climb we can't possibly make.

A few yards away, among the debris, the giant clam sits next to a mossy, decomposing trunk and smacks its bloody lips. I guess the octobenus ended up finding his artisan friend again, after all.

A breeze stirs, scented with fish and salt. I expect the sponge to be the size of a mountain. But there it is, next to my soggy boots, no bigger than a basketball. I pick it up. Hard to fathom that an entire ocean is contained inside.

Jeb helps me stand, and I drop the sponge. It lands with a splat.

Even though I'm weak and battered, a sense of accomplishment rushes through me. "We did it," I mumble, hardly able to grasp the meaning of the words. "We drained the ocean. Just like the flowers wanted us to."

"*You* did it," he answers. He pushes hair from my brow. "And you almost drowned in the process." Before I can respond, his warm, soft mouth touches my forehead, my temple, and then my jaw. Each time, his labret gently grazes my skin. He stalls at my jawline and bends to gather me close for a hug, nose tucked against my neck. "Never scare me like that again."

It doesn't matter that we're wet; heat radiates through our sopping clothes. I weave my gloves through his hair. "You came back for me."

He nuzzles closer in the crook of my jaw, and a powerful wave of emotion pulses through him. "I'll always come back for you, Al."

A tiny knock of caution drums in my chest, reminding me of Taelor, of Jeb's determination to go to London without me to be alone with her. But adrenaline surges even stronger. I touch his ear with my lips, tasting Alice's leftover tears on his skin. "Thank you."

He tightens his arms. His nose roots through the hair at my nape, like he's losing himself in the tangles. Our heartbeats thunder between us. Nervous shivers assault me until my limbs quake.

"Jeb," I whisper. He mutters something indecipherable, and my trembling hands clutch his neck.

A groan escapes his throat. I catch my breath as he clenches my hair in his fingers and draws back, eyes intense. He's about to lean into me when a cacophony of clicks and clatters interrupts.

We turn in circles. Thousands upon thousands of clams tunnel out from the sand. I clutch Jeb's hand, worried they're going to attack us for destroying their home. Instead, high-pitched cheers break loose.

Glancing over Jeb's shoulder, I gape. "Behind you."

Beside the clifflike wall, tons of shells pile one on top of another—tumbling in and out, over and over—to form a living escalator.

"We defeated their enemy," I whisper. "They want to help us."

Jeb doesn't hesitate. He takes my hand and leads me toward the ascending steps, snagging the backpack on the way. Together, we ride toward the sparkling black sands of the island.

Once we reach the top, I wave to the clams as they disappear into their ocean bed far below.

Jeb opens the backpack to check on our things. "Maybe I shouldn't be surprised that nothing's wet in here." He opens the pencil box before I can stop him. His jaw twitches. "What's this?"

"It's my . . . savings." Great. Not only did I throw myself at Taelor's boyfriend, but now I've lied about the money I stole from her.

Jeb looks up from counting it. There's something unreadable behind those thick lashes.

"You look different," he says, stashing the money back in the box and shaking wet droplets from his hair.

"Do I?" I rub the skin around my eyes. Are all my secrets blinking across my face like neon signs? "My makeup must be running all over the place."

"You're sparkly—everywhere."

"Oh. Probably just salt residue." I slip off his tux jacket, wring out the water, and hand it over.

"Huh," he says, still intent on me. "So . . . should we talk about it?" He shoves the jacket into the pack.

"About what?"

"What happened down there, between us."

Heat prickles my cheeks. He regrets it. Or maybe he's afraid I'll tell Taelor. Either way, I end up looking like a jerk. "It was the adrenaline. That's all. We were just happy to be alive. No worries. What happens in Wonderland stays in Wonderland, right?"

He doesn't even crack a smile. Just holds my gaze, then shakes his head. Lips drawn into a tight line, he puts all his attention into zipping up the backpack.

I want to believe he felt what I did . . . these things that I shouldn't be feeling at all. But how can that be true? I'm not the one he's going to be living with in another country.

I try to concentrate on something else, like how the water in my boots squishes between my toes, or how I have gaping rips the size of silver dollars all over my leggings.

"Where to now?" he asks.

It's possible he's talking about more than our physical destination, but I'm too scared to take a chance I'm wrong. Instead, I focus on our whereabouts.

The shore stretches as far as I can see . . . an endless, inky desert of shimmery soot. It's not at all what I expected the heart of Wonderland to look like, if that's what this really is. There's no flora or fauna anywhere except for a lone tree standing taller and wider than a redwood just a few feet ahead of us.

Familiarity lures me closer. Jeweled bark covers the entire tree, from the gnarled trunk to the branches that twist hundreds of feet into the air. It glimmers in the sun like a million white diamonds. At the end of each branch, rubies well up like liquid and dribble to the ground, as if the tree is bleeding jewels, the way elves do when their skin is pierced. With the black sands as a backdrop, the scene reminds me of my cricket mosaic back home—a beauty both mesmerizing and bizarre. I tamp down a surge of panic, remembering how the crickets seemed to be alive and kicking the last time I saw it on my wall.

"Winter's Heartbeat," Jeb says from beside me.

I nod. "You see the resemblance, too?"

His jaw spasms. "You've been here before."

I shake off my unease and step up to the tree, kicking a path through the fallen rubies. A spot at the base of the trunk pulses behind the diamond-bark like a heartbeat. With each thrum, it lights up in red lines the same shape as the birthmark on my ankle. The image sparks a memory of me and the winged boy, fuzzy yet unmistakable.

Jeb moves closer and I turn to hold his shoulder for balance, lifting my left leg to unlace my boot.

"What are you doing?"

"Following instructions," I answer, peeling off the boot and hiking up my leggings to expose my ankle. Jeb grips my elbow as I crouch down, pressing the maze on my ankle against the glowing lines of the tree.

A shock of static electricity leaps from me to the trunk; then a loud cracking breaks the hush. Jeb yanks me back as the trunk splits, the glittering bark rolling open like a scroll to expose a doorway. A soft red glow throbs and beckons from within.

"The pulsing heart of Wonderland," I whisper, shoving my foot into my boot again.

The red light reflects off Jeb's labret. "Okay, I'll buy that you came here as a kid and are having some kind of repressed memory flashes. But how is it you have a mark on your body that unlocks anything in this place?"

I hesitate, then tell him what I read about netherlings talking to bugs, and what I suspect about my family curse: that we share some characteristics with the creatures here, including freaky magical marks on our bodies.

Jeb stares at me, and I wonder how much more of this he can take without going crackers.

"You okay?" I ask, biting my lip.

Swallowing, he slides his fingers through his hair. "It's you I'm worried about. So how do we break this 'curse'?"

My heart bounces when he says "we." He's in this with me to the end. Not just because he's stuck here, but because he's the Jeb I grew up with. *My* Jeb. "I have to find someone inside. The one from my past . . . the one who used to bring me here."

Jeb frowns. "Okay. According to the flowers, this is also where the portals are. Right? The doors that will take us home?"

"Yeah," I answer, half expecting him to try to talk me into waiting outside while he checks things out. Instead, he holds me back only long enough to get out the flashlight, reposition the backpack, and take the lead. We descend a winding stairway through a dark tunnel that seems to spiral down forever.

"Don't look down," Jeb says.

Why do people say that? It only makes it impossible not to. My gaze sinks to the steps thudding beneath our boots. Bones, interlocked and bound with some kind of shimmery gold twine, make up the stairs. Most of the bones are deformed in size and shape. Others look humanoid. I press my palm over my mouth.

"What are they from?" Jeb whispers. "Ancestors? Human captives?"

I scan my foggy memories. "I don't remember ever learning about this . . ."

Jeb picks up his pace. We leap off the last step and duck through a curtain of vines. Instead of finding ourselves deep underground, a vista opens in front of us underneath a dark purple sky. The sun and the moon are twisted into one, the moon a blue tinge next to its brighter brother.

The combined light turns everything an ultraviolet hue. Plants of all kinds—bushes, flowers, trees, and ground cover—are neon beneath the blended rays: pinks, purples, greens, yellows, and oranges.

The paler shades of our clothes glow, too. No wonder I always felt so at home in Underland's activity center. On some subconscious level, it reminded me of this place.

A cool gust, thick with the scent of loam, greenery, and flowers, blows across us. Then I catch wind of something else—a fruity incense drifting our way. I know that smell. "Follow the smoke," I say, abandoning the path.

Jeb takes my hand and helps me over a bed of fluorescent marigolds. I squeeze his fingers in gratitude. My body is starting to feel the effects of our insane water ride. I have bumps and bruises everywhere.

As we lumber ahead, I can't stop thinking of the way he came back for me in the water, the way he wouldn't give up, the way he jumped into the mirror in my bedroom without a thought for his own safety. Maybe we *should* talk about what's going on between us, because something is definitely changing on my end. I run my tongue along the roof of my mouth nervously. I've been holding on to this secret so tightly for so long.

"Listen, Jeb." I gulp twice. "About what happened back there on the ocean floor. I—"

"Later." Glancing behind me, he catches my shoulders. "We have company."

He forces me to duck as a glowing cloud swoops over us, glimmering like fireflies.

"It's her!" a tiny voice squeals over the hum of many wings. "It is!"

A swarm of humanoid creatures the size of grasshoppers and the color of lima beans hovers around us. They're all females, naked with glittery scales that curve around their breasts and torsos in swirling designs. Their pointed ears and flowing hair sparkle, and their eyes are bulbous and metallic like a dragonfly's, as if they're wearing copper sunglasses. Wings flutter next to my cheek, milky white and furred with something resembling dandelion fuzz.

One of them gets close enough to pat Jeb's temple, her palms no bigger than a ladybug's body. "I found him. He's my prize!"

"Mine!" three others screech, tunneling into his hair.

Jeb clenches his hands around the backpack's straps.

"No, sister sprites," one answers with a voice like a chime. She hovers in front of Jeb, as enthralled as the others. "Our master said they shall be in my keep."

The others grumble and pull back.

Suspended in midair, the tiny victor bows while flapping her wings. "I am Gossamer. I shall lead you to the one you seek." Her dragonfly eyes glimmer in my direction and brighten, as if she's angry. "To the one who seeks *you*." My stomach flips at her implication.

Then she turns to Jeb. "Elfin knight, do you wish for pleasure on your quest? I can provide it, if you so desire."

Rubbing his labret with his thumb, Jeb glances at me, adorably bewildered. "Um. No thanks. I'm good."

Giggling, the sprite flutters ahead, joining the others.

We follow our luminous guides into a thick forest, weaving through tall, neon grasses until we reach a clearing of lime green moss, bright yellow lichen, and glowing mushrooms. A circle of trees reaches overhead, branches stretched and twisted together to form a domed roof. Slivers of the purple sky break through, just enough to cast shadows.

Each of the sprites takes her place inside the canopy, dotting the branches like lit candles. Their luminance adds a soft, glowing haze to the surroundings. Gossamer motions for us to follow her to the middle of the clearing, where a giant ultraviolet-striped mushroom awaits, wreathed in a fragrant cloud.

An unmistakable sense of knowing curls through me. I recognize this place from my Alice nightmares. We're in the lair of the Caterpillar—the wisdom keeper of Wonderland.

"She doesn't look like anything special, my lord." Gossamer hovers over the thick smoke that cloaks the mushroom's cap, hiding whatever sits atop. "She's covered in mud and reeks of clams."

"That would be because she just drained the ocean, pet. Had to be a rather laborious feat, don't you think?"

My entire being shakes at the sound of that deep accent. Liquid, masculine, and sensual. It's *him*. My netherling guide. If only I could see past the smoke.

"Her apparel appears to be that of a scullery maid," Gossamer says, shooting me a disapproving glance. "Perhaps you should send her home and wait for another. Someone more acceptable."

"One who's naked shouldn't judge apparel," that familiar voice answers. "You well know that clothes do not the lady make."

Humbled, Gossamer joins the other sprites overhead. At last, the smoke clears, revealing a hookah pipe and the crow-size moth—black wings and luminous blue body—perched atop the mushroom like a butterfly on a petal.

It inhales smoke from the hose and releases plumes into the air. Some are shaped like birds, others like flowers. One of the vaporous designs pulls away to form a woman's head—like the carving in a cameo. As it slowly dissipates, it starts to look like a five-year-old girl. A five-year-old *me* . . .

"So good to see you again, little luv. How I've missed you."

Gasping, I fall to my knees. The Caterpillar and the moth and the winged guy. They are all one and the same. They have been all along . . .

"I've seen that bug," Jeb says. "In your car. On the mirror." He drops the backpack and grips my shoulders, trying to drag me to my feet. My legs won't cooperate.

"Tut-tut. You are never to bow to me, lovely Alyssa." The voice drifts from the moth's proboscis on gray puffs of smoke. His attention shifts to Jeb. "You, on the other hand, will bow to *her*."

Smoke streams toward Jeb and transforms into a net in midair, cloaking him. The weight brings him to his knees. A stick slices his kneecap where the hole gapes in his pants from the octobenus's tusk. Blood drizzles out.

"Aha! He's no elf. He's a mere mortal." The moth flaps his wings as if he's made some great discovery.

"A mortal man!" the sprites screech in voices as dulcet as tinkling bells. They plummet from the trees like radiant snowflakes, swarming around Jeb as he slashes at his smoky restraints. The sprites knock the knife from his hand, then wriggle through the net, covering him like ants on a sugar cube.

I leap up to fend them off. "Get away!"

"Oh, don't stop the fun," the moth croons in my direction. "We won't break your toy soldier."

I grab the knife and try the scissor attachment on the net, but the ropes keep disappearing in my hands. I'm so preoccupied, I almost miss the transformation happening atop the mushroom. The moth laughs, and I look up just in time to see his wings fold over his body. The satiny appendages expand to the size of an angel's wings, then swoop open to reveal the guy from my mirror's broken reflection—the one from my memories—all grown up.

The knife slips from my hand. I'm mentally trapped between the past and present.

He's close to Jeb's height and age. He wears a black leather suit with utilitarian boots and lounges on the mushroom's cap with the hookah's hose perched elegantly between two fingers, ankles crossed.

Weathered pants cover his toned legs. He's lankier than Jeb but in great shape. His jacket, unzipped almost to his abdomen, reveals a smooth chest, milky white like his clean-shaved chin.

The sprites steal our knife and abandon us to rush to their master. They preen his hair and smooth his clothes, cooing and laughing.

No wonder Persephone's movie poster always seemed so familiar. My netherling companion grew up to look just like the hero, except his shoulder-length hair is blue and glowing, and he wears a red satin half mask. Other than that, he's the spitting image: porcelain-pale skin, eyes as black as the makeup lining them, lips full and dark.

With the gray smog swirling around his sooty wings, he also reminds me of Jenara's window display: a dark angel.

Although he's more of a devil.

I know, because my childhood memories return in a crashing wave—slamming me with the name I haven't spoken in eleven years.

MORPHEUS

"Morpheus." I say it more as an accusation than a revelation.

The winged devil flashes his white teeth in a stunning smile that draws me in as it puts me on guard. "Mmm." He moves his hand along the hookah as if it's a violin. "Your voice is a song. Say it again." He takes a drag of smoke from the pipe.

I'm so entranced by seeing him alive and real, I don't even try to resist. "Morpheus."

"Beautiful. Your mum should've known it would take more than a pair of pruning shears to snip me out of your life. Though it appears she managed to cut me from your memories for a bit." He puffs out circles of smoke. "I'm wounded, Alyssa. It shouldn't have taken this long for you to find me." Catching the smoke rings on his finger, he tosses them into the air, where they burst into vaporous stars.

Jeb struggles under the net next to me. "This is the joker you've been looking for? The one from the website?" he asks.

"More than that," I answer, not even sure the words I'm forming are coherent. "We grew up together, somehow. He was the one in my dreams when I was little. That's right, isn't it? You came to me in my dreams . . . brought me here. Told me things."

"*Taught* you things, rather. Oh, but we made time for recreation as well. I shall have to see that we continue that tradition." Morpheus hands off his hookah to some sprites with his pale, elegant fingers. I close my eyes, remembering glimpses of us as children, leaping across rocks as Morpheus took flight and lifted me under my arms— a gentle security. When my eyes open again, I blush, remembering how different his touch felt in my bedroom last night. He stands up on the mushroom, wings draped in a flowing arch behind him as he steeples his hands beneath his chin.

"Hospitality Hat!" he shouts, completely off topic.

Several of his attendants flutter over with a black velvet cowboy hat and place it on his head. He tilts it cockeyed. The velvet is accented with a band of decomposing white moths, making him appear both suave and savage.

"She had no right to interfere." He runs a long forefinger across the hat's brim. Lengthy wisps of blue hair touch his shoulders. "It wasn't her place."

It takes me a minute to realize he's on the subject of Alison again. "You knew her?"

"Yes. Of all the other candidates, of all of your ancestors, her mind was the most receptive to me. We connected when she heard the nether-call at age thirteen. But she turned her back on her responsibility the moment she met *Tommy-toes*." He sneers at my father's nickname. Then he composes himself, smoothing his jacket. "Never mind all that. I see you wore the gloves. Did you bring the fan, as well?"

"Along with everything else she had stashed away."

"And she thought her buried treasures would keep you from coming. Too bad the words in the margins were indecipherable, aye? Perhaps she should've kept her mouth shut and played with her carnations."

Carnations? Indecipherable words? Understanding creeps over me. "It was you. You smeared her notes so I couldn't read them. And at the asylum . . . *you're* the one who almost killed her!"

"I admit to nothing. Other than that she was out of control. She needed to calm down for her own safety."

"Of course she was out of control! You messed with her mind half her life!" I clench my jaw. "It's your fault she's in that place."

Morpheus spreads his satiny wings—a move that blocks the glowing sprites from my view and casts me into shadow. "You have yourself to thank for that. She was handling things fine until you came along. Just ask your father. She never talked back to the bugs and plants before you were born. At least, not in front of anyone."

"No," I whisper.

"Don't listen to him, Al." Jeb tries to comfort me. "Your mom loves you."

Morpheus raises his palms over his head and applauds. "Bravo, Gentleman Knight. Did you all see that?" The sprites join the false praise, bouncing around the mushroom, all except Gossamer, who sits on the hookah, observing in dignified silence.

"True nobility," Morpheus continues, strutting atop the mushroom. "Bound and incapacitated, yet his only thought is for the maiden's tender sensibilities. And I must admit, he's right." The sprites silence their mock accolades, confused. With one flap of his wings, Morpheus glides down and lands gracefully in front of me—looming and beautiful. "Your mum does love you. Very, very much."

My legs quiver, but I lift my gaze to his, disdain burning behind my eyes.

"Stay away from her." Jeb thrusts a fist through the net and grazes our host's leg.

Morpheus sidesteps him. "Ah, ah, ah." He coaxes the smoke to merge so the net disappears, leaving Jeb's wrists, ankles, and neck in manacles attached to the mushroom's base. "If you're to behave like a trained monkey, you shall be treated as one."

"Jerk!" I lunge with an open palm, but Morpheus catches my wrist in midair. The impact rattles my bones and shakes my bruises.

"There's that fire." Morpheus cocks his head, the expression on his face somewhere between amused and impressed. "Nice to see it still burns."

"Hands off, you son of a bug!" Jeb struggles against the smoky cuffs, face turning red as he growls with the effort to get to us.

Chuckling, our captor bends low over me, keeping hold of my wrist. "Oh, I do like him," he murmurs. "Such a wordsmith." He's so close that his smoke-tinged breath seeps inside me—sweet as honey and binding as spider's silk—a comfort from my childhood. "As for you . . . is that any way to treat an old friend? After all we shared? Tsk-tsk."

I'm tempted to lean closer, to seek more of the seductive sensations. But the desire is not mine. He's manipulating me somehow. He has to be.

I thrash against him. His fingernails dig into my glove, making my wrist throb.

Black eyes glitter, frigid and harsh, behind his mask. "Stop fighting and listen. Your mum didn't have to turn her back on me. She didn't have to go to the loon-house to protect you."

"Wait." An alarm goes off inside me. "You're saying she *chose* to go there?"

"All she needed was a few miles of distance between you. She could've arranged a divorce, moved to the other side of town, given your father full custody. But she loved you both too much to hurt you like that. She wanted to be a part of your lives . . . yet still keep you safe. So she sacrificed *her* life. That is the purest of loves."

"You're lying." My accusation comes out on a wisp of air.

"Am I? You're the only one I've ever reached quite so young. You and your mum had a bond, stronger than any I'd ever encountered. I was able to use her dreams as a conduit into yours. When she realized what I was doing, she went mad. But that was only temporary insanity. Let there be no doubt—the Alice costume, the tea party obsession, the tongue clucks, talking aloud to the bugs and flowers—every tic she developed was orchestrated by her, so she would be kept away from you. Out of respect for her sacrifice, I vowed not to approach you myself again."

"You broke your word, then," I whisper.

"No. There was a loophole, you see." The knuckles on his free hand graze my temple. His touch is warm and delicate. "*You* found *me*. Since you were the one to seek me out first, you released me of the bonds of the promise. Clever, clever girl. Now you're here to set things straight, aren't you, little plum? To fix what Alice put wrong. Make Wonderland right again, and you'll break the curse that's on your family name. The talking bugs and flowers . . . the ties to this realm. You will no longer be under their spell. At last, your mum can stop pretending to be a raving lunatic, because I'll have no more need for any of your lineage."

My chest hurts, as if someone used my heart for a punching bag. That's why Alison said those things in the courtyard . . . that if I went through with my plan to find the rabbit hole, she'd have done it all for nothing. She put herself through years of overmedicated humiliation and horror because she hoped to keep me away from here. Then I went and ruined everything by searching Morpheus out.

Which makes what my dad and the doctors are planning even more devastating.

"My fault," I whisper, trying not to cry. "Everything that's happened to her . . . my fault."

"Al, don't let him guilt you!" The rustle of Jeb's clothes as he strains against the cuffs barely registers.

Morpheus tips my chin up. "Yes, bear no guilt. Because you discovered the rabbit hole and were brave enough to leap inside. You're the only one who's ever had such cunning and courage since Alice herself. And you've already managed to dry up the ocean she left behind. You're going to fix everything for your mum. For all of us. You're very special, Alyssa. Very special, indeed." He tugs at my wrist, lifting me to stand on tiptoe until my nose touches the lower lines of his mask. He's so close, I can almost taste his licorice-scented lips.

A loud snap cracks the air, and Morpheus breaks his hold on me.

I rock back on my heels. The sprites screech as Jeb's restraints break free of the mushroom.

Jeb rolls on the ground and whips his legs around. The broken cuffs—still attached to his ankles, neck, and wrists—trail him like a scorpion's coiling tail, and catch Morpheus in the spin, slamming him to the ground. The impact knocks off his hat and evaporates the smoke, leaving both guys wrestling in a tangle of wings and limbs.

Jeb straddles Morpheus and cinches his fingers around his neck. "I told you not to touch her." His deep voice is hoarse yet calm, making the hair on my neck stand on end.

Morpheus makes the mistake of laughing, and Jeb snaps. One hand clutching Morpheus's neck, he punches him, crumpling the red satin mask. Morpheus twists his head to dodge the strike. His wings lie wrinkled and hapless beneath him.

My muscles tense. I'm at war with myself. A part of me wants to defend Morpheus—to plead his case with Jeb; the other part roots for Jeb to beat him to a puddle. I bend over, temples throbbing as I drown in a sea of distorted memories and disjointed emotions. The sprites whimper and swarm in the branches above. They've obviously never seen their master attacked by anyone.

Morpheus thrusts his knees out to knock Jeb off and they spin through the neon grasses, leaving a flattened trail. This time, Morpheus ends up on top. His wings enfold them like a tent. The outline of Jeb's face appears, pressed against the black satiny membrane on the other side. A sucking motion reveals an imprint of his mouth.

He's suffocating.

I burst through my mental haze and launch into Morpheus, toppling him. He rolls on the ground, wrapped within his wings like a pupa.

Dropping to my knees, I lower my face to Jeb's. His breath warms my nose, slow and even, but he won't open his eyes. "Jeb! Wake up, please . . ." I drag his shoulders onto my lap to cradle his head.

Morpheus stands and dusts himself off.

"What did you do?" I scream.

He repositions his crumpled mask, then draws each wing over his shoulders and runs his palms across them, checking for damage. "He's merely unconscious." Putting his hat back on, Morpheus touches the handprints on his neck, eyes darkening. "It was a kindness. I could've killed him." He snarls. "Should've, actually. No doubt I'll rue that decision."

Glancing up at his harem, Morpheus motions the sprites down. "Take the pseudo elf back to the manor. Wake him from his slumber. Make him feel welcome as only you can."

Gossamer is the first to descend from the trees. There seem to be even more sprites now. Following her lead, they drop down in torrents, a glimmering rainfall.

"No!" I throw myself across Jeb. I slash at them with my fists. On Gossamer's command, they collide with my arms and ribs at full speed, stinging like hail. I refuse to move until Morpheus snatches my collar and forces me to my feet.

My writhing in his grasp only makes him more resolute. His arm winds around my waist, as hard and strong as a metal clamp. He holds my back pinned at his side with my feet dangling. Fifty or more sprites raise Jeb up by his clothes. His head lolls, and his shirt and pants pucker beneath their grips, as if he's being hoisted on ropes.

"Jeb!" I shout. Tears blur my vision when he doesn't respond. "Be careful with him."

The tiny females are only able to carry him a few inches off the ground, and the long grasses bend under his weight as he's dragged from the clearing. Some of the remaining sprites tug the backpack behind the procession. When the last stretch of grass pops up in their wake, I shove against Morpheus and break free, though it's only because he lets me.

"If our time together ever meant anything to you, you won't hurt him." Hot tears pour down my cheeks.

Morpheus reaches out to catch a teardrop on his fingertip. He holds it up in the pale glow that radiates from the few remaining sprites above us. A curious frown curves his lips. "You cry for him yet bled for me. One must wonder which is more powerful. More binding. I suppose we shall one day know."

My throat dries. "What are you talking about? *Bled* for you?"

He rubs my tear into his skin as if it were lotion. "All in good time. As to your toy soldier, spare no grief for him. He's getting scads of attention. And once he's oblivious in his ecstasy, he'll forget where he is and who he came with. Though I imagine I'll have to send him to some other part of Wonderland to keep him out of my hair."

Terror grips me. Bad enough those pint-size nymphets are going to seduce Jeb, but if they make him forget who he is, he'll be lost here forever. Jeb's here because of me. He doesn't deserve an ending like this. "Please, just send him back to our world."

Morpheus shrugs. "Not possible. We're having a bit of trouble with transportation here in the nether-realm."

"That can't be true."

He steps closer. "Can't it?"

I take two steps away. "You visited me at home, at work. Watched me. Almost choked Alison with the wind . . ."

He throws his head back and laughs, raising his arms as if he's some grand performer. "Imagine that. Me, controlling the wind and weather. Why, I must be a god."

I glare at him. "I know what I saw."

He straightens his sleeve cuffs. "I used reflections to visit you. The gazing globe at the asylum, store mirrors . . . the mirrors in your home. Through them, I projected an illusion, but I couldn't fully materialize because the portals are obstructed. Your mind was my stage. No one else could see or hear or feel me. Only you. And you did feel me, didn't you, luv?"

Thinking of the way his phantom breath tickled my neck as he hummed—hot and teasing—leaves me rattled to the bone. I lift my chin, a lame attempt to hide his effect on me. "There was magic . . . with my mom's braid. It moved, locked my fingers around her throat. That was you."

He buffs his fingernails on his lapel. "It was magic, I'll admit. Misguided magic. And not mine."

"What does that mean?"

"You're not yet ready for me to answer that."

Tired of his manipulations, I shove him off balance and sprint for the opening in the trees where the sprites disappeared, nearly tripping over my heels in my desperation to find Jeb. There's a harsh flapping overhead; then Morpheus drops into my path. I skid to a stop.

He crouches with wings spread parallel to the ground and stares up at me intently, like a giant bird of prey—dark and dangerous. I'm familiar with this side of him . . . his temperamental black moods. There will be no reasoning with him unless I can get the upper hand.

He stands and catches my shoulders before I can bolt again.

"Enough games," he says. "It's time you fulfill your destiny. I did not spend the first third of your life training you in vain. Alice has left ripples in our world that only you can smooth. I've waited over seventy-five years for this day to come . . . made too many sacrifices to watch it all fall to rot. You fix what she broke, and it will open the way for you to break the curse and get back home. Until then, I make the rules."

Alice has left ripples in our world that only you can smooth. The zombie flowers said something like that, too. That only a descendant of Alice could fix this. And the octobenus insisted that the Wise One—Morpheus—was desperate for my help. *Desperate.*

He's the one who prompted me to keep the sponge, the one who's been teaching me about Wonderland for years. Why? He must have some kind of personal stake in this.

"You need me." I raise my voice, taking a chance on my assumption. "It's not that my ancestors couldn't figure out the way here. They didn't *want* to come. It has to be by choice. You can't force them; otherwise, you would've abducted one and already fixed this mess. I'm the first who's ever been willing to come this far, and I don't have to do anything you ask. So what if I'm stuck here? I've always been an outcast. I've already learned to live with it. Alison . . . she'll survive, like she always has."

Morpheus doesn't have to know the truth: that Alison's quality of life teeters on my success. I'm seeing this bluff through to the end.

"This is your one chance." I rest my hands on my waist. "Screw with me, and you could end up waiting another seventy-five years."

A strange expression drifts over my childhood companion's face. If not for the mask, I might get a better read, but it seems like there might be a glint of pride.

His fingers grow light on my shoulders. "What are your demands?"

"Jeb and I will be reunited, today. You'll call off your sprites and leave his memories intact. He'll be treated as your equal, not your pawn. And I want *clarity* . . . how you can claim to be Alison's friend, if you and I grew up together; how you knew my ancestors if you're my age. And what your stake in this is."

He releases me from his grasp. "That's all you ask?"

Recounting what the octobenus said about vows among the netherlings—a fact verified by the promise Morpheus kept to Alison not to contact me—I add one thing more. "I want your word . . . an oath."

"Well, drat." Sighing, he holds a palm over his chest as if pledging allegiance. "I vow on my life-magic not to send away or harm your precious boyfriend as long as he's loyal to you and your worthy cause. Although I reserve the right to antagonize him at every given opportunity. Oh, and I will happily explain all your questions." He bows then—every bit the gentleman.

Leather suit and crumpled mask, that morbidly sexy hat. He thinks he's a rock star. Maybe he is one in this place. But he's given his word and he has to uphold it, or his wings will shrivel up and he'll lose all his mojo.

Straightening, he takes a full step forward so his boot tips touch mine. "There. Since that unpleasantness is out of the way, shall we proceed? Seeing as we're both grown up now, we have some re-acquainting to do."

I scan the trees. All of the sprites have left. Nerves jump beneath my skin. "Where is everyone?"

"Preparing a celebratory banquet for us at the manor. We have no chaperones. Might as well take advantage."

Panicked, I take a step back, but his wings curl around me and hold me in place, blotting out everything but him. It's like we're sharing a cave.

His skin is almost translucent in the dimmed light. "Time to let me inside, lovely Alyssa."

Before I can respond, he peels off his mask and drops it to the grass underfoot. What I thought was makeup around his eyes are actually permanent markings—like tattoos, but inborn. They're black like overblown eyelashes, with teardrop-shaped sapphires blunting the pointed ends. The effect is beautiful, in a macabre, circus-folk sort of way. I can't resist the urge to reach up and touch the glistening tears. The jewels flash through a spectrum of color until they're no longer blue sapphires but fiery topazes—orange and warm. His lashes close as if in bliss for all of two seconds. Then his inky gaze opens and swallows me whole.

"I am ageless." His voice echoes inside my head, though his lips don't move. *"I can use magic to mimic any age I wish. Using this power affects netherlings mentally, physically, emotionally. We* become *the age in every way. So, in essence, the only childhood I ever had was with you in your dreams. Open your memories, and you will see."*

The song comes to life once more—Morpheus's lullaby.

This time, I don't fight it. I wrap my mind around the fluid notes, letting them permeate my every thought until . . .

Slivers of my past play out like movies across the black screen of his wings. I'm a newborn, lying in my crib. A soft satin blanket swaddles me—red with white-ribbon trim. My window is open, and a summer breeze whispers under eyelet curtains, swaying the mobile over my head. Rocking horses and ballerinas dance above me.

It's the song that woke me. Not the mobile's music but his. The moon shines, and he's there, a moth silhouette hanging on the outside of my screen. His deep voice drifts in, cooing and gentle:

"Little blossom in white and red, resting now your tiny head; grow and thrive, be strong and keen, for you will one day—"

Before I can summon the verse's end, I'm thrust into another memory. This one's hazy, as if I'm looking through smudged glass. I realize it's because I'm dreaming. I'm a toddler, not more than three, walking with a six-year-old Morpheus along a black, shining beach. His small wings curl over us for shade. I hold his hand, awed by the glistening spectacle in front of us: a tree made of jewels. Morpheus crouches to point out the maze on the tree's base, then rolls up his lacy sleeve cuff to reveal a matching mark on his forearm. I turn my ankle, making the connection. He helps me press my birthmark against the trunk. As the doorway opens, he jumps to his feet and dances around. "We have the keys! We have the keys!" his small voice exclaims in childlike glee. I giggle, bouncing along behind him.

Then I'm back in my house two years later. It's Saturday morning, and I'm drawn to the screen door by Morpheus's lullaby—now as familiar as the pink-rose linens upon my daybed. The scent of a spring storm breathes through the mesh. He waits in moth form on the other side. It's our routine: I play with him, my childhood friend, throughout my dreams at night—exploring our enchanted world in the glimpses he gives me—then I see him in intervals throughout the day as the insect. Lightning blinks, and I shiver at the door, fearing the storm. But his teachings are already embedded within my head, coming alive in a fluttery sensation of confidence that pushes me to find a way out. Soon I'm dancing with my moth in our garden. Mommy sees. Rushing outside, she carries long, sharp scissors and snips at flower petals while screaming, *"Off with your head!"* When I realize what she's really after, a strange discomfort stirs inside. I've seen how the petals tatter beneath the blades. I don't want her to ruin my moth's pretty wings. I throw my hands over the scissors to stop her. The moth escapes unscathed. But I'm not so lucky . . .

Coming out of the trance, I drop to the ground and clutch aching palms to my chest. The scars throb as if freshly cut. Morpheus bows over me, smoothing my hair. "I told you that you were special, Alyssa," he murmurs, the weight of his palm strangely comforting on the top of my head. "No one else has ever bled for me. The loyalty of one child for another is immeasurable. You believed in me, shared new experiences with me, grew with me. That has earned you my sincerest devotion."

At last, I understand. The other memory, the one I assumed was real all these years, was tinged by what my dad thought had happened. By what he witnessed when he glanced out from the kitchen window where he was making pancakes. He thought I was dancing behind Alison, when all the while I was trying to protect my friend.

Someone I *thought* was my friend. Does a friend fly away and leave you bleeding and heartbroken?

I'm wrung out. All the revelations jumble in my mind, too much to absorb. The trauma my body's faced over the past several hours takes its toll. My bruises throb, and my limbs feel as heavy as stone.

Still on my knees, I droop against Morpheus's thighs—a solid support. The cool leather of his pants cushions my cheek. I close my eyes. Yes . . . I've been here before, held safely against him.

At first, I think I'm imagining it when he bends over to scoop me into his arms. But when the scent of licorice and warm skin surrounds me, I know it's real.

"You left," I accuse him, fighting to stay awake. "I was hurt . . . and you left me."

"A mistake I vow on my life-magic to never make again." Even though he's cradling me close, his response sounds far away. But distance doesn't matter; he gave his word. I'll be holding him to it.

My eyes squint open to see shadows fold over us. Or is it wings?

For an instant, concern for Jeb resurfaces in my mind; then I drift into a dark and dreamless sleep.

CURIOUSER &
CURIOUSER

I'm warm . . . too warm. A blue haze blinks bright, then fades—like the sun refracting off waves. The flow of water trickles somewhere close, and even closer, there's the rustle of clothes.

"Jeb?"

"Take it slow, luv." Morpheus sits beside me—licorice-scented skin, wild blue hair, tattooed eyes with jewel-tipped points. I remember now. He carried me here from the mushroom lair. I woke up midflight before passing out from my fear of heights, then woke again for an instant as he tucked me in his bed.

The blue haze is actually sheets of falling water, drizzling from the elegant canopy attached to the bedframe. Liquidized curtains.

Morpheus's wings slice through the waterfall, which curls back and leaves him dry. Each time he shifts, the watery curtain moves with him, as if some sort of invisible barrier stands between him and the downpour.

I try to sit up, but the pile of blankets is too heavy. Claustrophobia makes my heart pound.

"Morpheus?" My voice cracks, rough and gritty, as if I've been sucking down dry saltines. It must be from all the tears I swallowed in the ocean.

He lies beside me on the mattress, leaning on his elbow. His fingers weave through the strands of platinum hair splayed out on the pillow around my head. "You were crying in your sleep. Are you in pain?"

I nod, working my hand through the blankets to touch my throat. "Jeb," I murmur.

Morpheus frowns. "Your friend's safe and resting in the guest chambers. Which means you are mine for now." He starts to pull the blankets back.

What felt like bindings a minute ago now feels like armor being peeled off. I'm not sure what I'm wearing underneath the covers, so I clamp the last remaining blanket in place at my collarbone.

Morpheus leans close. His hair brushes my exposed shoulder, tickling and soft. "Shy little blossom," he whispers, his sweet breath cloaking me. "We're simply going to meld your pain away."

Meld... that doesn't sound like something my dad would approve of. Jeb, either, for that matter. I start to push Morpheus back, but the blanket slides down my body in the curl of his pale, elegant fingers. I'm left in a long, strappy nightgown of champagne lace and satin. It covers all the right places, yet I feel exposed. Morpheus had to see me naked to put me into this. I cross my arms over my chest, cheeks hot.

He smiles. "No worries. My pets undressed you. When they took your clothes to be burned."

"Burned? But . . . I don't have anything else—"

"Hush now, and be still."

"You said something about a banquet. There's no way I'm wearing this." I tighten my arms around myself.

He shakes his head, then pushes the hem of my gown until it's just above my ankle, exposing my birthmark. I sit up, about to jerk my leg away, but his deep, dark eyes turn to mine. "Trust me."

The fluttery sensation in my mind prods me to listen. Here in this place, where I no longer have the white noise of voices distracting me, I can hear my thoughts distinctly for the first time in years. I can understand that beating in my mind. The fluttering feeling—that's me. I have another side, beyond good girl and obedient daughter, that's instinctive and wild.

It's that side that chooses to trust him, despite our bizarre past . . . or maybe because of it.

Rolling his shirt's cuff to his elbow, Morpheus exposes that matching birthmark at his inner forearm—the one I remember from my dreams. Intrigued by our likenesses, I grasp his wrist with one hand, tracing the lines with my other. The maze glows beneath my touch. His features shift, and a rumble escapes his throat—something between a purr and a growl. His arm tenses, as if it takes his full concentration not to move while I appease my curiosity.

He's a contradiction: taut magic coiled to strike, gentleness at war with severity, a tongue as sharp as a whip's edge, yet skin so soft he could be swathed in clouds.

Holding his gaze, I remember what *meld* means. I take the lead and press our birthmarks together. Heat sparks the joining like when Alison healed my ankle and knee, though this is a more volatile reaction. Warmth simmers through my entire body, leaving me flushed from head to toe.

Morpheus coaxes me to lie back and draws down the gown's hem before spreading a blanket up to my chin. He places his hat on his head at an angle. His wings sweep high as he stands, and the water curtain lifts in an arch around him.

"Don't budge from that spot until I return with something for your throat." There's a raw edge to his voice that makes my body even warmer.

As he backs up, the water curtain drops, blinding me to my surroundings. The minute I hear the door to the room shut, I scoot out from under the covers, press my spine to the headboard, and curl my knees under my chin, shivering as the cool air hits me.

I close my eyes and think of how it felt—the pulse of his magic against my finger, his flesh against mine. Rubbing my birthmark, I shake off the euphoria.

The more I remember of Morpheus and this place, the more I forget myself . . . or the self I thought I was.

Why didn't Alison tell me? If she'd just been honest, I wouldn't be confused out of my mind while Jeb's locked up in another room.

Guilt stabs my heart. No. She was trying to protect me. She's going to suffer unnecessary shock treatments if I don't break the curse and get back soon.

Instinctively, I reach a hand toward the liquid curtain and will the water to react to me as it did to Morpheus. It lifts back like a living thing and leaves me dry. I grab a blanket, tie it around my shoulders in a makeshift cape, and leap through, landing on a plush rug. An echo of soreness remains in my muscles. Other than that, I'm pain-free.

I turn on my heel. The room's decor feels vaguely familiar—wild and stunning, just like its owner. There are no windows or mirrors. Soft amber light falls from the giant crystal chandelier that takes up most of the domed ceiling. Gold and purple velvet hangings drape the walls, intertwined with strands of ivy, seashells, and peacock feathers.

A set of multitiered crystal shelves occupies the wall to my left. Half of them hold hats of all shapes and sizes embellished with dead moths; the other half holds what first appears to be clear glass dollhouses. Then I realize they're terrariums.

Within the terrariums, moths fly from side to side and perch on leaves and twigs. Thick webs coat the glass panels in places, similar to the webbing in my Alice nightmare. They're cocoons—caterpillars transforming into moths. Listening to the waterfall, I think of how Morpheus's wing cut through the liquid earlier, and compare it to my dream in the rowboat, when a black blade was about to slice through the web.

It wasn't a blade at all.

The door creaks open and I spin around, heart pounding.

Morpheus steps across the threshold and shuts us in. "Up and about, aye? And not a drop of water on you." He carries a tray with a teapot and matching china cups. "Well done."

"You." I point a shaky finger toward the cocoons. "The nightmare I've been having for years. You put it into my mind, didn't you?"

His jaw tightens as he sets the tray on a glass table. "What nightmare would that be? I've not been mentally connected to you since your mother was committed . . . not until yesterday." He pours tea into a cup. Wisps of steam fill the room, carrying notes of honey and citrus.

"I'm Alice," I say, "searching for the Caterpillar. They're going to take my head. He's my only ally." I rub my neck. "Wait, no. There's the Cheshire Cat, too. But neither one can help me. The Cat's lost his body, and the Caterpillar . . ." I look at the glass cases. "It's you, stuck inside the cocoon."

Morpheus fumbles the teapot's lid with a loud clatter. When he turns to me, his eyes are wide. "You remember. After all these years, you retained the details."

"The details about what?" My legs waver, and I clutch the blanket tighter around my neck.

Morpheus motions to the chair beside him. "Sit."

When I don't move, he takes my hand and leads me. He's wearing black gloves now, reminiscent of the ones I dreamed of in the rowboat. I'm about to point that out when he hands me a cup.

"Have some tea, and we'll revisit the story."

Revisit?

While he pours a cup for himself, I sip mine. The hot, sweet liquid soothes my throat. I slide a finger against the table beneath my saucer. The surface is a chessboard, black and silver. A glass sheet covers it to protect from spills and scrapes. Jade chess pieces—pawns, rooks, knights, and more—are arranged in an unusual pattern. Sentences hover over three of the silver squares as if by magic, in tiny glowing script. I lean in to read them, catching the words *ocean* and *palm* before Morpheus sweeps his glove across the glass and smears them.

"What was that?" I ask.

"It's how I keep track of your accomplishments."

"'Accomplishments.' Mind explaining?" I take another sip of tea.

His wings hang wide on either side of his chair as he sits opposite me, placing his hat on the table. "I would prefer to show you."

He retrieves a small brass box from a drawer on his side of the table. Its hinged lid pops open, and Morpheus tilts it. The contents scatter onto the chessboard, a whole other set of tiny game pieces. These are also carved of pale green jade: a caterpillar smoking a hookah, a cat with a bold smile etched into place, a little girl in a dress and pinafore. There are other characters, too, all familiar. Morpheus and I played with them when I visited in my dreams.

I reach for the Alice figurine and hold her up, trailing a finger along the lines of her pinafore. With her marbled, green-tinged exterior, she looks different than in the pictures—more fragile. Precious and rare, like the stone she's carved of.

Morpheus lifts his cup and regards me over the edge while drinking, then sets it on his saucer with a clink. "She always was your favorite."

I'm both flattered and frightened over the expression of adoration that crosses his face. A nostalgic fuzziness swells inside my chest. "You used to tell me a story with these."

"I did indeed. Or, rather, we used to watch it."

"Watch it?"

The jewels under his eyes sparkle, flashing to a calming blue. "How are you feeling, Alyssa?"

Puzzled by the question, I frown. "Fine. Why do you ask—" No sooner do I speak, than the room starts to spin, the chess pieces along with it. My teacup topples, half of its contents spilling upward. I clasp both hands to my throat. "You put something in my drink . . ."

"Simply cleansing the palate of your mind. You must be relaxed and as light as a feather to channel your magic in the beginning stages. Otherwise, it will come in bursts and fits and be unruly, like it was at the asylum." Morpheus's disembodied voice floats around me as the chandelier blinks—dark to light, dark to light.

"Are you saying . . . ?" *No, it's not possible.* "I was in control of that magic?" To think I had anything to do with Alison's near choking makes my insides quake.

"Out of control is more like it," Morpheus scolds. "You were too distraught for it to work properly."

I struggle to find him amid the chaos, needing to see his face so I'll know if he's serious. "But how?"

"The moment your mind accepted the possibility of Wonderland being real, it released the vacuum of doubt that once held you trapped," he says from somewhere above me. "Now, stop thinking like a human. Netherling logic resides in the hazy border between sense and nonsense. Tap into that logic, visualize the chess pieces coming alive; see it, and it will be."

Skeptical, I twirl in a circle of weightlessness alongside everything else: the glass shelves, the hats, the table, and the chessboard. The bed's watery curtain forms a funnel around us, swaying and swirling in an effort not to touch anything. The Alice carving slides from my grip as I try to keep my balance in the swimming room. Halfheartedly, I pretend she can reach for me, take my hand, but she falls out of my sight.

"There once was a child named Alice," Morpheus says with a voice of soothing liquid. I still can't see him. "She was innocence and sweetness, happiness and light. Perhaps her only flaw was that she was very—"

"Curious," I finish for him, and in that instant, the chess pieces grow to human size. I try harder to imagine them alive: visualize blood pumping through their carved bodies like clear mountain streams, envision their lungs expanding and sending oxygen to beating hearts of stone.

I'm concentrating so hard that I'm startled when the caterpillar, his hookah smoking in one hand, snags my wrist. "You look like a girl I once knew. Her name started with an *A*. Perhaps yours does, too?" The greenish smoke stretches into a thick, fragrant sheet around me, matching his jade sheen.

The cat floats up beside us. He holds out the sheet of smoke and, using his claws like scissors, cuts eight vaporous letters to spell the word: *Allegory*. He spreads the letters out like a strand of paper snowflakes. The smile on his green-tinged face widens.

"Ah," the caterpillar says, his tobacco puffs making clouds around us, "she's a figurative figure. She shall play on my side, then, as I'm the academician."

The cat shakes his head, his smile vanishing. They start a tug-of-war, jerking me back and forth. I yelp, my arm sockets stretched to the limit. "Let go!"

"Tut-tut. The only things figurative here are you two idjits." Morpheus breaks their hold on me, then folds one hand around my waist while snatching the caterpillar's hookah with the other. "Now, take your places."

At that, the animated chess pieces descend with the others through the funnel of water. Morpheus floats us up, up, up toward the huge chandelier in the domed ceiling—the one part of the room that's still stable. The lightbulbs are as big as we are, and the dizzying height makes me nauseated. I wrap my arms around his neck and tuck my face against his smooth chest as he settles us on the brass fixture. "This isn't happening," I say. But it is, because I can remember it happening before, years ago.

"Find your courage. Look down. Your show is about to begin."

I shake my head, eyes clamped tightly. "We're too high . . . it makes my stomach kick."

He laughs and inhales a puff off the hookah then blows the smoke over me, saturating me in the comforting scent. "That's how you know you're alive, Alyssa. The kicks."

Before I can respond, a loud rapping makes me brave a peek.

The funnel of water forms a curtain, which parts to reveal a stage. Morpheus's bedroom has transformed. The living chess pieces dominate the scene, their milky-green bodies vivid atop a glossy black and silver chessboard that stretches the length of the floor. Everything is arranged in a large circle that reminds me of a circus's center ring.

The queen's husband, king of the Red Court, lounges upon a velvet throne. Another woman in royal robes stands at his right hand, crimson bows tied on every finger. There are bows on her barefoot toes, too. She keeps shushing the ribbons, as if they won't be quiet. Queen Red stands before them both, locked in chains. The jurors' box, which is actually a cage filled with jagged-toothed tigers and bubble-headed seals, sits on the right. Card guards line the walls.

Seated in the witness chair is little Alice, fussing with the hem of her carved dress.

Rabid White stands behind her, his antlers low and his shoulders slumped, looking drained and miserable. His jacket and boots are the same marbled hue of his shiny, bald scalp. A strange assortment of creatures sits upon wooden bleachers and snacks on peanuts and popcorn. Even the Ivory Queen and her elfin knights are in attendance.

A toad-faced creature stands behind a podium, though he's dressed more like a ringleader than a judge. He bangs a gavel. "The Red Court is now in session!" His plumed wig wriggles. Only when it stands on long stick legs do I realize it's a stork. After preening its jade feathers, it settles into place again, and the judge continues. "Queen Red, because *The Alice* entered our world through the rabbit hole, which is in the Red province, and because you failed to capture her before she unleashed her mortal mischief over all of Wonderland, you have been accused of gross negligence and havoc by association. How do you plead?"

Queen Red's wings droop behind her. She glares at the king and the woman with the bows. "I plead temporary preoccupation brought on by a broken heart. My husband left me for Grenadine . . . I was too distracted by his betrayal to note something so insignificant as a mortal child in our midst."

Murmurs explode from the jurors' box. Grenadine looks remorsefully at the ribbons on her feet. The king shifts atop his velvet cushions.

"You're the one who should be in shackles," Queen Red says to her husband. "Wasn't it enough that before his death, my father favored her over me, an amnesiac little brat not even of his blood? But your betrayal is so much worse. My simpering stepsister can't remember what day it is unless one of her chatty ribbons catches her attention. She certainly can't remember whom she's supposed to love. You're responsible for wooing her and distracting me from my duties."

The judge leans over his podium, hugging it with his webbed

hands. "Perhaps you should be grateful to your royal husband for bargaining with this court to waive the harshest sentence. Should you be guilty found, you will be exiled to the wilds. Preferable to losing your head, I should say."

"And as to *The Alice*?" Queen Red shoots a scathing glance at the witness box. "What of her sentence?"

The judge points his gavel at Alice. "She has chosen to read her written confession in exchange for being sent home with the promise never to return and to forget everything she's seen." He nods at the child, urging her to stand.

I lean forward to get a better view, so invested in the outcome I no longer care how high I am, relying solely on Morpheus's arm around my waist to keep me anchored to the chandelier.

Alice curtsies before taking out a piece of paper from her pinafore's bib. She coughs twice, delicately, then reads aloud: "Perhaps my first mistake was whom I chose to befriend. Or did they choose me? The smiling cat and the smoking caterpillar . . . oh, they hatched such fine schemes!"

I glare over my shoulder at Morpheus, who coughs up his puff of smoke and smirks sheepishly.

Below us, the judge waves his gavel, disturbing the stork upon his head. It makes a clucking sound and snatches the gavel's handle with its beak. "Descriptions of the schemes, if you please!" the judge screeches, wrestling the bird for its prize.

Alice clears her throat and inhales deeply. "We put an untimely stop to a tea party, spilled soup over a duchess so we could make her sneeze and steal her gloves and fan, unleashed an accidental ocean, and helped a hungry artisan trick his walrusy friend out of a bevy of very vocal clams, thank you."

Several bivalve audience members throw their popcorn at the witness and squeak out the word, "Scandalous!"

Alice dodges the rain of kernels by ducking behind her chair. The judge—who's managed to salvage his gavel with the loss of his wig and dignity—waves her to stand up straight. "How did you come to hide at the Ivory Queen's castle?"

"I wasn't hiding, in fact. Chessie Cat and Mr. Caterpillar insisted I visit the Ivory Queen and ask her to send me home, as she is more agreeable than Queen Red." Alice slides a pointed glance in Red's direction.

The shackled queen snarls, and her chains move as if alive, nearly catching Alice's ankle before she scrambles onto her chair.

Hammering his gavel, the judge demands order. "Would Queen Red's royal advisor please step forward and wrangle her chains?"

Rabid White moves up to take the metal links and holds them taut.

"Continue," the judge says.

Kneading her gloved hands, Alice clambers down and recites the rest of her confession from memory. "Ivory seemed pleased to have guests. She was, in fact, very fond of Mr. Caterpillar—who *is* debonair, in his own squirmy way. Just as I was preparing to follow the knights to the highest turret of the castle, where my doorway home awaited, an invitation arrived from Queen Red's court—a croquet match. But it was a trap, so you could imprison me and force my confession for this trial." She curtsies once more. "I'm sincerely sorry for the trouble I've caused. May I please go home now?"

"You will never go home, cancerous little polyp!" Queen Red screams.

I almost don't catch what happens next. Rabid's hands move

faster than a shock of lightning, slipping out a blade that magically slices through Queen Red's metal chains. It happens so quickly, no one else even notices until the queen flaps her wings and grabs Alice by her shoulders, lifting her into the air. The judge's stork snatches the blade from the floor and follows Queen Red as she flies with Alice out the courtroom door, along with everyone else.

The minute they're gone, I strain against Morpheus's hold. "Follow them!" I demand.

"Follow them yourself," he says, and releases me. I scream, somersaulting in midair, my stomach bobbing into my throat. An itch begins behind my shoulder blades, as if something is scratching to get out; then it's gone as soon as it started. Inches away from striking the floor headfirst, I flip around and drop into my chair, teacup in hand. The chess pieces lie scattered on the table's surface, as if the re-enactment never happened.

I know better.

Morpheus sits across from me, spinning Queen Red's chess piece as my stomach sinks back into place.

"How does it end?" I ask.

"Your nightmare knows."

I place the Alice figure upon a black square. "The stork and the queen fought in midair. Alice escaped and came looking for you."

"But I couldn't do a bloody thing for her because I had already begun my metamorphosis. I was locked in that cocoon for seventy-five years."

"So how did Alice win?"

Morpheus rolls the statue of the red queen across the board, knocking over Alice. "She didn't. As you know very well, her lineage was cursed."

"And that's why you brought me here."

He nods once. "To set your family free and reopen the portals back home, you must fix all the messes that caused Queen Red to be exiled and lose her crown: drain the ocean, return the gloves and fan to the duchess, make peace with the clams and the tea party guests. Only you can break Red's magic bonds."

A weighty silence follows, broken only by the sound of the cascading waterfall around the bed. I reach for the caterpillar figurine, but Morpheus's hand catches mine. Warmth seeps through his glove and into my bones.

For an instant, I see him so clearly as the teasing child he was when we spent time together in my dreams. I understood him then, why he collected moth corpses, because their wings represented freedom, something that he'd been without while locked inside his cocoon . . . why he loved flying, especially in storms, because outrunning the lightning gave him a sense of power. Just like he understood my quirks: my fear of heights, my hunger for security. But here, he's tortured, seductive, and unreadable. All grown up with just as much baggage as me.

"That's why you're involved," I mumble, testing a hypothesis. "To appease your guilty conscience for failing Alice."

Hissing, he stands in a rushed flurry of wings and leather. Gusts from the movement flit through my hair. "My guilt for what happened with Alice can never be appeased." He snatches up the Cheshire Cat figurine and paces the rug. Despite his impressive height, he's as graceful as a black swan. "And don't delude yourself. I'm not quite that unselfish."

"I know you too well to think otherwise." I lift an eyebrow, toasting him with my teacup.

He looks at me briefly, almost smiling. "In her fight with the stork, Red managed to get the blade. I might've been unreachable in my cocoon, but Chessie was there. He dived for Alice before Red could behead her. He took the strike that was meant for the child." Morpheus balances the cat figurine on his fingertip, holding it up to the light. "Chessie is of a rare strain—not one part spirit and one part flesh but both at once. He can vanish and reappear in midair and twist himself into any shape. Such a being is nigh impossible to kill. When Red cut him with the vorpal sword—the one blade that can slice through any magic in the nether-realm—it cleaved his magic in twain. Split in two, but still alive."

"So he didn't die?" I set my teacup aside.

"Not exactly. His head rolled toward the bushes where Alice was hiding. He managed to catch the vorpal sword in his mouth and spat it at her feet. Chessie's bottom half was captured by Queen Red, and in one last act of defiance, she fed it to her pet bandersnatch before she was captured and banished from the kingdom."

Morpheus shakes the box that earlier held the chess pieces. Out falls the biggest figurine of all: a grotesque creature with dragon's talons and a spiked tail. Its gaping mouth and jagged teeth send a shudder of terror up my spine. When I was little, I used to hide this one while we animated the other pieces.

Morpheus tosses the cat into the air, then lets it plop soundly on his palm, squeezing his fingers around it. "What did I teach you about the bandersnatch?" he asks, testing me.

"It's bigger than a freight car. It swallows its food whole so the victim decomposes slowly in the dark void of its belly—a death that can take over a century to complete."

That glint of pride shines back at me. "Correct. For Chessie, who cannot die, it's like being exiled on a desert island, without any sun or moon or stars. Or wind or water. Just death, all around you. There, half of him resides to this day, trapped and longing to be reunited with its head once more."

A nudge of sympathy knocks at my heart. "You want me to help free Chessie from the bandersnatch, so he can find his head again."

Morpheus turns on his heel to face me, wings drooping. "All I need is the vorpal sword. Only its blade can cut through the hide of the bandersnatch. Alice hid the sword in the one place she knew it would be safe. Somewhere so ridiculous and mundane, no one would look for it there." His gaze falls on the figurines in front of me, and I pick up a character with an odd, cagelike hat.

"The tea party. The Mad Hatter has it," I guess.

"You've forgotten. That is strictly a Carrollism—the name Lewis used in his tale of fiction. His true name is Herman Hattington. And there's nothing mad about him. He's rather jolly, in fact, *when he's awake.*"

I tap the carving's head, waiting for an explanation.

"Alice left the tea party guests beneath a sleeping spell," Morpheus continues. "Wake them, and they can tell you where the sword is. You've already dried up the ocean and made peace with the clams. I've a guest coming to the banquet tonight who will receive the gloves and fan on the duchess's behalf. After that, making things right for the tea party guests will be the only thing left undone."

Standing the Alice figurine up again, I place the caterpillar next to her, thoughtful.

Morpheus returns to the table and drops the cat into the brass box, then sweeps all the other characters in with him. Standing over me, he holds out his palm. "What say you, Alyssa? Are you willing to help me while you're helping yourself? A favor for your childhood friend?"

Once Jeb and I get home, I can tell Alison that the nightmare is finally over, that we'll never be connected to Wonderland again. Just thinking of her smile sparks an ember in my heart.

Taking a breath, I slide my fingers into Morpheus's and meet his gaze. "I'll do it."

He lifts my hand and presses soft lips to my knuckles. "I always knew you would." Then he smiles, his jewels glistening gold and bright.

Jabberlock

I wait in a cold, mirrored hall with a glass table and chairs for company. Jeb's supposed to meet me here. I'm dying to see him again but at the same time nervous about how he'll react to my decision to help Morpheus without talking things over with him first.

I close my eyes, disoriented by the movement all around me. Mirrors line every inch of the ceiling and walls, even the floors. Shadowy figures glide in the reflections.

In our world, mirrors are made by slapping a coat of silvery aluminum paint onto the back of a glass plane. A person can't see anything but their reflection. Here, I can see shadows inside, like they're sandwiched between the layers. Morpheus told me they're the spirits of moths. It makes me wonder about the bugs I've killed back home.

Apparently, in Wonderland, everyone—or thing—has a soul. The cemetery is a hallowed place revered by all netherlings. No one will set foot inside, other than the keepers of the garden: the Twid Sisters.

At the hands of the twins, the dead are cultivated: sown, watered, and weeded out like a virtual flower garden of ghosts. One sister nurtures the souls—singing to the newcomers and keeping the spiritual flora content. The other sister weeds out withering spirits that have languished and turned bitter or angry—something to do with locking them inside other forms for eternity.

The Twid Sisters aren't getting along with Morpheus right now because he refuses to send his dead moths their way. He'd rather let them fly free somewhere between life and death than tie them down in a prison of dirt. So he hides them inside his mirrors.

Some might call that morbid. I see a degree of tenderness there, in his effort to give them dignity. The same tenderness I've glimpsed in our past, and earlier, when he treated my injuries.

The birthmark on my ankle is universal to the creatures of Wonderland—keys to their world and a way to heal one another—and a part of the Liddell curse. I still don't know why, in her old age, Alice lost the marking. Or why she forgot her time in the real world, swearing she lived in a birdcage here instead of having married and had a family. But at least one thing is clear: I'm a part of this realm until I can shatter the curse to pieces.

Heavy boots echo along the mirrored floor and I glance up.

"Jeb!" I race toward him. The floor is slick, and the boots the sprites gave me have little traction. I slip. Jeb drops the backpack, leaps forward, and catches me.

He drags me up until our foreheads touch and my feet dangle above the ground. It never ceases to amaze me how easily he can lift me, as if I weigh nothing at all.

I stroke his clean-shaved face and garnet labret—breathing him in, assuring myself he's all right.

"Did he touch you? Hurt you?" Jeb whispers in the silence.

"No. He was a gentleman."

Jeb frowns. "You mean a gentle*roach*."

I snort, which melts his severity and makes him smile. He spins me around. "I've missed you," he says.

I tuck my chin against his broad shoulder and hug him tightly. My body's thirsty, drinking up his warmth like a sponge. "Never let me go, okay?" Any other time, that might sound lame. But right now, it's the most genuine request I've ever made.

"Never plan to," he whispers, his mouth close enough that his breath grazes the top of my ear.

When I lean out of the hug, he's watching the moving silhouettes race all around us.

"Gossamer told me about them," he says. "I didn't believe her. The guy's moth-crazy."

I prop my forearms on his shoulders, feet still swinging at his shins. "You should see his room. He has tiny glass houses filled with living ones. He keeps them there until they leave their cocoons. When they're strong enough, he sets them free."

"He had you in his room?" A dark cloud crosses Jeb's face. "Do you swear he didn't try anything?"

"Scout's honor."

He squeezes my waist, tickling me. "Too bad you were never a Scout."

I squirm and smile. "Nothing happened." That's a lie. Morpheus got to me in a big way, showing me a side of myself I can hardly believe exists—one I'm not sure Jeb will be able to accept. But I'm thinking maybe he doesn't have to know about the thrummings in my head or my weird powers. Maybe I can hide my cursed tendencies until we get out of here and I'm cured.

Fingers locked around Jeb's neck, I tug his short ponytail. To help us fit in at the banquet, we're both going in costume. He's supposed to be an elfin knight, so the sprites drew his hair across his ears to cover their rounded tips. I like it this way. His strong jawline and expressive features take center stage.

"Figured they'd put you in a hat," I tease.

"Nah. Those are reserved for worms with wings."

I laugh and nudge his shoulders, unspoken permission to put me down.

He sets me onto the floor. "You look amazing."

"Thanks." I don't tell him my outfit is Morpheus's creation: a peach baby-doll sleeveless tunic with cascades of ruffles that start under my breasts and go all the way to midthigh. Red lace trims the ruffles and complements the red bondage-style belt encrusted with glistening rubies that cinches my waist. Five sturdy silver rings embellish the belt, matching the gray blouse layered under my tunic. The blouse's puffy sleeves cover my arms to my wrists, where fingerless red lace gloves peek out. Gray and peach striped leggings coat my legs like candy canes and disappear into knee-high red velvet boots.

The entire ensemble is a calculated effort to make me look wild and untamed, so the eccentric dinner guests will be more receptive to me. To that end, the sprites wove red berries and flowers into the funky, dreadlock-style braids all over my head, then tucked the hairpin from Alison's recliner treasures just above my left temple. For some reason, Morpheus was adamant that I wear it.

I point to Jeb's elfin knight uniform. "I've seen this before. That cross represents the elite of the jeweled elves." The black pants wrap his legs like a well-worn pair of jeans. There's a silver chain linked in and out of two belt loops, forming the illusion of five separate strands, and a cross made of glistening white diamonds on his left upper leg. I slide my fingers along the jewels. "You're not just a knight . . . you're one of the royal escorts."

Jeb stops my palm at his muscled thigh. His eyes grow intense, the way they did when we embraced on the ocean floor.

I slide my hand free and he clenches his jaw.

Embarrassed, I concentrate on the rest of his uniform. The shirt is long-sleeved, made of something clingy. It's silver with vertical black stripes made of semisheer fabric. I search for his cigarette burns, aching to see them, then notice his spattering of chest hair is gone. "You shaved your chest?"

He looks down at the sheer black stripes. "Actually, there wasn't a mirror in my room. Gossamer did it after my bath, when she shaved my face. She said elves are hairless everywhere but their heads."

Everywhere? I picture him naked—Gossamer touching his abs, among other places. "That sprite saw you in the nude?"

He clears his throat. "More than just her. I think there were about thirty of them climbing on me at one point."

A surge of jealousy scalds me. My fists clench. "Thirty sprites touched your naked body?"

"Chill about the sprites, all right? Flying lima beans aren't my thing. Now, come here. There's something I want to show you."

He turns me to face the mirrored wall and stands behind me, chin resting atop my head as he lifts his hands to either side of my face. "Check out your eyes."

My image stares back, transposed over the moth shadows. I noticed the makeup when I first came into the hall. The sprites did an incredible job making it look real. Black eye shadow dips like curvy tiger-stripes beneath my lower lashes. The lines resemble Morpheus's tattoos, just a more feminized version.

"You've been like this the whole time. I noticed it when we first stepped out of the rabbit hole. I thought your makeup had smeared. But then, after the ocean, you still had it. I didn't make the connection until I saw Morpheus without his mask a few minutes ago." Jeb pauses, looking like he might be sick. His thumbs rub the edges of the black designs. "They don't wipe away. And the glitter all over your skin? That's not salt residue. You're starting to look like my fairy sketches, for real."

Feeling nauseated myself, I twine my tunic's ruffles around a finger. That explains why the octobenus thought I was a netherling. "Why didn't you say something?"

"We were too caught up in all the stuff going on."

I turn from my reflection. "So, the curse is getting worse."

"Worse than you think." Jeb gets behind me and smooths his hands down the back of my shoulders. "There are slits in your costume . . . are wings coming next?"

His callused thumbs stroke the naked skin along my shoulder blades. I can't answer. From what we've seen so far, only some netherlings have wings. The idea of something bursting out from my skin makes me woozy. In fact, thinking about the changes I've already undergone is enough to make me feel like I'm riding some kind of crazy, runaway carousel.

Jeb's harsh scowl stares back at me in the reflection. "Why is it that this curse only affects the women in your family?"

"Alice was a female," I answer, still in a spin over the wings question. "Only a female can undo her messes."

"'Messes,'" Jeb says, his frown intensifying. Gripping my arms gently, he turns me around and stares into my eyes. "When I was with the sprites, Gossamer mentioned what you did to the ocean. She didn't call it fixing a mess. She said it was a *test*. And even weirder? She seems resentful that you accomplished it . . . that you're here at all. Something's not adding up. We're not doing another thing to help bug-juice until he's straight with us."

"He's already told me the truth. He told me the steps I have to take." I tell Jeb what I learned in Morpheus's room, though I'm not brave enough to share details about our "melding" moment or the magical chess piece puppet show.

"So, you're just going to take his word?"

"He has noble motivations. His friend's in trouble."

"Stop humanizing the guy, Al!" Jeb slams a palm against the mirror wall. The moth shadows dart away as if startled. "He's not of our world, okay? And he has this power to get inside your head. I watched you with him in the clearing . . . you can't think straight when he's around."

The accusation revives my anger about London. "So, you're going to play that card? Me not being strong enough to think for myself?"

"This is different. Look what's happening to you!"

"But I can stop it by doing one more thing. That's all."

"Oh, yeah? From where I'm standing, the more you do for him, the more you become like him."

"No. You're wrong." I tug on one of my braids, wishing I could convince myself as easily as I spout the words. Wishing I could deny that the longer I'm here, the more deeply this place is ingrained in my blood, or that Morpheus is the tourniquet, twisted tightly around my veins.

Jeb grinds his teeth so hard, his jaw jerks. "We're not going to argue about this, Al. That's what he wants. I won't let him do it."

"Do *what?*"

He wraps the hair I'm playing with around his wrist and tugs me close, bowing his head so our brows touch. "Come between us."

My entire body goes soft and warm at the gruff possessiveness in his voice, but he doesn't have a right to it. "Did you forget? There's already someone between us. You're moving with her to London."

"I was an idiot. To think for one second that being on the other side of the ocean could give me any control."

A fiery knot tightens in my chest and I take a step back. "'*Control*'? Over what? My life? Reality check, Mr. Oblivious: I'm not your 'kid sister' anymore. I'm done being shelved with all your other responsibilities—somewhere between clipping toenails and changing dirty socks." I shove him aside and start toward the glass chair, determined to wait there for Morpheus.

Without warning, Jeb snags one of the rings in my belt and spins me around. In one smooth motion, he lifts me onto the narrow, crescent-shaped table. My skin trembles beneath his touch as he scoots me all the way against the wall, his hips wedged between my thighs. We're level—face-to-face. The fluttery feeling fills my head—and in the shadow of my darker side, a rush of satisfaction wells up, a perverse thrill that I can stoke his emotions to this gut-deep reaction.

I brace my hands against his shoulders to maintain space between us, but it's only for show. My bluff fades to weak-kneed enthusiasm the instant he snags my wrists and pulls them down, leaning in so our noses almost touch.

"Reality check right back at ya," he says, his breath a hot rush in the chilly room. "I know you're not a kid anymore. You think I'm blind?" His fingers lace through mine, pinning my arms against the cold, smooth mirrors so our heartbeats pound against each other. "You're the one who's oblivious. Because there's nothing brotherly about the way you make me feel."

My brain shuts down. I must've swallowed every moth spirit from here to kingdom come. I can swear they're rippling through my stomach.

Jeb releases my fingers and cups my face in his hands, barely touching me, like I'm breakable. "It's me I'm losing control of. Hundreds of sketches, and I still can't get enough of your face." He traces the dimple in my chin with his thumb. "Your neck." His palm moves along my throat. "Your . . ." Both hands find my waist and drag me off the table so we're standing toe to toe. "I'm not wasting another second drawing you," he whispers against my lips, "when I can touch you instead." He presses his mouth to mine.

A spark, hot and electric, jumps between us. Shock and sensation shimmer through me, aglow with his heat and flavor. Six years of secret desire. Six years of denying that he's the orbit of my world.

To think, he's been running from me, too.

Adrift in disbelief and pleasure, I freeze. My arms hang limp at my sides, fists opening and closing. Jeb's mouth vibrates against mine in a groan. He coaxes my hands around his neck, bending closer.

He tastes amazing—like chocolate and salt. Familiar yet new and exciting. I clutch my fingers around his neck. The feelings I've been suppressing uncoil and thrash inside me like electric eels, shocking me to life. Every sensory receptor hums, hyperaware. I taste him, breathe him, feel him.

Only him.

My lips follow his, pulsing slow and soft and warm. His labret scrapes my chin, a harsh and sexy counterbalance.

His hands guide my jaw, showing me how to tilt my face. He teases my lips open with his. I run my tongue along his teeth, finding that crooked incisor before his tongue catches mine.

Maybe I'm breathing too hard. Maybe I'm slobbering too much. Maybe I'll never measure up to the other girls he's been with. But it doesn't matter, because of all the things I've experienced on this journey—shrinking and growing, flying sprites, living chess pieces—not a one of them is more magical than this moment.

His kisses fade to nuzzles along my face and neck, soft and poignant. "Al," he whispers. "You taste so sweet . . . like honeysuckle."

"Don't," I murmur, in a daze.

He draws back, eyes heavy and dark. "You want me to stop?"

"No." *I've fallen asleep praying for you to look at me like this. To touch me like this.* "Don't break my heart."

Moth shadows glide above him in the mirrored ceiling, distracting me from the fierceness of his frown. "I'd cut mine out first."

I believe he would. Stretching to tiptoe, I clasp his ponytail. This time, I kiss *him*. He responds with a spine-tingling growl, fingers digging into my hips. I skim my gloved palms down to find his chest, seeking the scars. Stopping at the chains on his waist, I grip them until the metal bites into my fingers and back us against the wall. A chill seeps into my shoulder blades from the mirror, but the perfect fit of his body against mine lights my blood with a thousand tiny fires, consuming me.

We're both so into it, neither of us hears the footsteps until a snarl breaks us apart. We turn to find Morpheus standing there with enough rage in his black eyes to send the Devil packing for heaven.

Jeb tugs his fingers from the rings in my belt but keeps a hand at my lower back. I touch my lips; they're throbbing and gluttonous, hungry for more.

"Well, now, isn't this cozy?" Morpheus's voice isn't liquid this time. It grates like rusted nails along my eardrums. He peels off his gloves and slaps them against his palm, wings droopy and trailing the floor like a cape. "Perhaps you might give Alyssa her lipstick back. We haven't time to find more before dinner."

Jeb swipes my gloss from his mouth. I lick my lips, struck by an inexplicable stab of guilt.

Morpheus's lullaby plays softly in my head, melancholy and pinched. The words to the song seem to have been altered to fit his mood:

Little blossom in peach and red,
Trapping boys with your pretty head;
Tease and play, be coy and smart,
For you will one day break his heart.

The lullaby sours to shrieking notes in my ears, making me wince.

Grunting deep in his chest, Morpheus turns to a mirror and brushes his clothes with his gloves. He's wearing a white flouncy shirt under a red brocade jacket that swings at his thighs. It's double-breasted with brassy buttons on both lapels. His pants resemble tights—crushed red velvet. Black lace-up boots stop just at his shins. He could be Romeo straight out of Shakespeare's play if not for the blue hair and wings.

He whips his wingspan to its full magnificence. The jewels at the tips of his eye markings flash with his temper, from red to green. "Don't you know, elfin knight"—he turns back to us—"that it is very untoward for a guard to proposition his innocent charge?"

I frown. What, do I have the word *prude* stamped across my forehead? "You don't know anything about me."

Morpheus twists his mouth into a wry grin. "Perhaps you were simply pretending, then? To blush like an unblemished peach?"

Jeb drags me behind him. "She's not having this discussion with you."

Morpheus huffs. "A little late for chivalry. Had anyone else seen that display, your masquerade as a knight would have ended before it ever began. Did you forget to tell him about a knight's first order, pet? About keeping his hands and emotions in check?" Morpheus's attention falls to his right shoulder. Gossamer peers out from beneath his hair. She and Jeb exchange a glance.

Morpheus's eyes fall back on me, slicing like onyx blades. All I want to do is bask in the memory of my first kiss. Instead, I'm wrestling the notion that I've betrayed some nether-realm guy I haven't seen in years, and for some reason, the thought of hurting him is unbearable.

Jeb's stance stiffens. "Change of plans," he says. "Al's not going to help you play out this little game, whatever it is. You're sending us back. Now."

Morpheus lifts one side of his mouth in a sneer. He addresses Gossamer again while still staring at me. "Seems you were wrong. You told me the mortal wasn't a threat. Perhaps you underestimated the allure of our crafty Alyssa."

Gossamer studies her teensy feet. Her wings flap slowly, like a butterfly's at rest. "I thought he preferred someone—"

"Shush! That's not your secret to tell!" Morpheus shouts. The volume of his voice knocks Gossamer off her perch. She flutters in midair, hands slapped over pointed ears.

Morpheus touches a finger to his mouth. "Read my lips, loose-tongued little spriteling. *Get. The. Bloody. Box.* It's time to show our maiden and her toy soldier what kind of welcome they'll receive, should they turn their backs on their one ally."

Gossamer whisks out of the corridor.

"And bring me my Cajolery Hat!" Morpheus calls after her. His command is still echoing when he spins on his heel to study us. Smug, he coaxes his gloves on. "There's a problem with your request, pseudo elf. I can't simply send you back. And Alyssa knows this."

Jeb casts a glance over his shoulder, eyes wide with questions.

"Oh, dear me." Morpheus slaps a palm to his cheek, as if stunned. "Were you too busy to talk about anything pertinent? Or perhaps our innocent maiden was feeling guilty for the money she 'borrowed' from your other girlfriend's handbag, and you, being the noble knight, decided to comfort her."

Jeb turns to me. "Wait . . . that money in your pencil box. Tae *did* leave her purse at the shop? You stole from her."

Morpheus leans in between us. "Well, how else was our Alyssa to skip off to London to find me?"

Jeb's gaze doesn't budge, heavy with accusation. "I can't believe you lied to my face. You stole money to get a fake passport and planned to go to London all along."

"Two for two," Morpheus taunts, behind me now. "A liar *and* a thief. That pedestal's getting slippery, isn't it, little plum?"

I elbow him hard enough that his wings rustle. "I did what had to be done to help Alison," I grind out to Jeb, disregarding Morpheus's smug smile as he walks by in my periphery. "I only *borrowed* the money. I'm going to pay it back."

Morpheus stops beside Jeb. "She has a point. Motivation always justifies the crime. That's the law of the land here."

"Hear that?" Jeb says, piercing me with the mockery in his voice. "The local cockroach has given you his stamp of approval. And you wonder why I can't trust you to go off on your own."

A tiny fire burns at the base of my throat, an annoying need to justify myself rising like acid. "I had a plan."

"Oh, great plan." Jeb motions to the room around us.

"Like I could have ever seen this coming, Jeb!"

Before Jeb can respond, Morpheus steps between us, gripping us each by the shoulder. "Beg pardon, lovebirds," he intones. "But as much as I'm enjoying this, your quarrel is in danger of upstaging my grand unveiling."

He motions to the door, where Gossamer has returned with twenty other sprites. Five of them carry a red top hat with a wide black band holding a peacock's feather in place. A string of iridescent blue moth corpses drapes the brim like a garland.

The other sprites bring a black bag too heavy to lift, so they drag it across the floor.

"All the guests have arrived, Master," Gossamer says, her tiny voice quavering. She and her companions drop the top hat onto

Morpheus's head while the others leave the bag next to our backpack.

"Introduce the appetizers and have the harp play a tune." Morpheus angles his hat. The dead moths tremble with the adjustment, as if they're struggling to escape. "We'll be there shortly."

Gossamer nods and trails behind the others, glancing over her shoulder once before she flits into the adjoining hall.

Morpheus snatches up the bag. As he strolls toward the glass table, his satiny wings skim my left boot. A vibration hums through my birthmark and up my shin before it stops to settle in my thigh, warm and titillating. Frowning, I slide my leg back and tap my boot to ease the sensation. Jeb watches me with disapproval in his eyes.

Morpheus folds down the bag to expose a tall silver hatbox flocked with white velvet. I've never seen anything like it, even in my dreams. Curiosity lures me to the table.

Morpheus gestures to the chair, playing the role of gentleman host again.

"I'll stand," I murmur. I'd like to blacken his already black eyes for stirring up things between Jeb and me just to get back at us for the kiss. Although I'm strangely intrigued that he cares enough to be jealous in the first place.

Jeb settles behind me and squeezes my shoulders—still my protector, even when he's angry. I lean into his body heat, grateful for it.

Morpheus shoots a disgusted glance at us, then drags the box to the center of the table. It's actually made of pewter. White velvet roses cover the sides, and engravings curl across the top of the hinged lid in some archaic language. The longer I stare at the words, the more legible they become. Is that another manifestaton of the Liddell curse? That this language comes naturally to me?

"Time for introductions," Morpheus says, opening the lid an instant before I make sense of the first sentence.

Dark, oily fluid sloshes inside the box. A sheet of glass over the top holds the liquid inside. Morpheus gives the contents a jiggle and a whitish object bobs toward the surface.

It reminds me of a Magic 8 Ball I once saw at a garage sale. The black plastic ball had a window inset. Blue fluid filled the core, and a white die would drift up to the window, marked with phrases on every side. All you had to do was ask the ball a question, roll it around in your hands, and then turn it over. Your answer would appear in the window on the die . . . everything from *Most Likely* to *Ask Again Later.*

Only this floating object is almost the size of a honeydew melon and oval shaped. Thick whitish strands swirl around it, attached to it. Morpheus gives the box another shake. The orb spins to reveal a face.

It's a head!

Yelping, I battle the bile rising in my throat.

Jeb curses and tries to turn me to him, but I can't look away. The liquid must be some kind of formaldehyde. Why would Morpheus have a pickled head in a pewter hatbox? What kind of psycho is he?

"Wake up, fair one," Morpheus whispers, a strained tenderness to the request. I watch, mortified, as he taps a finger along the glass, tracing the face's closed, crystallized lashes. When the eyes flip open, I almost jump out of my skin.

The thing's alive.

Recognition dawns on me from the chess piece reenactment. It's the Ivory Queen, even more beautiful than her jade counterpart, as delicate and pale as moonlight. Black tattoolike marks line both temples in a network of veins, as if dragonfly wings were pressed onto a stamp pad, then transferred to the skin. Her eyes are so light blue, they're almost colorless; long lashes curl upward on each blink. They're just like her eyebrows, silvery and crystalline as if coated with ice. At the outer corners, two black lines dip down to her cheekbones and end in teardrop shapes; it's like she's weeping ink. Pale pink lips—as curved and lovely as a heart—open to an adoring smile as her gaze falls on Morpheus. She tries to talk.

He leans close, sweeping his gloved palm lovingly across her encased cheek. She tries to talk again but can't be heard through the liquid and glass.

Jeb and I stand there, imprisoned in our own silence.

Morpheus breaks the hush. "This is a jabberlock box. It can hold an entire being within, though only the face appears. You've heard the saying, 'Off with their heads,' from the book you carry?"

I glance at my gloved palms, thinking about my scars. That's not the only place I've heard the words, and Morpheus knows it. Is this what Alison meant, when she said she didn't want me to lose my head?

"Well, this is the origin of that phrase," Morpheus finishes. "Little Alice took it much too literally. It used to be a standard punishment here in Wonderland. Though it's now considered barbaric. It's worse than any prison, for its occupant can be seen but not heard. Their jabbers are locked away."

The box shakes under Morpheus's hands. The queen's features change from adoring to desperate. She thrashes back and forth, and bubbles churn the surface. Her hair swirls like albino sea grass. Morpheus wraps his arms around the box to keep it from bouncing off the table. When her mouth stretches in a muted scream, he slams the lid shut. His complexion pales. He rewraps the box in the bag before I can see the inscription again.

Smoothing his cuffs over his gloves with trembling fingers, he sighs. "I didn't wish to upset her. She's at peace when she's left alone. But if she's not freed soon, all her memories will be lost forever."

"You care about her," I say with an unexpected twang of envy. In my long-lost memories of us as children, it was always just the two of us. We "got" each other on every level. Morpheus made me feel adored, special, important. I never considered him doing the same for someone else as a man. "Morpheus, what is she to you?"

He doesn't answer. Not aloud, anyway. His expression is hazy and troubled, and the jewels around his eyes twinkle from silver to black, like stars peering down on a storm-swept night. Alice's confession from the trial comes back to me: *Ivory was, in fact, very fond of Mr. Caterpillar.* Judging by how Morpheus looked at the queen just now, by how she looked at him, he returned to her castle after his metamorphosis.

I imagine his elegant fingers tracing her skin, his soft lips on hers. That stab of envy evolves to something much uglier—a covetous twist of emotion I can't even put a name to. What's wrong with me? Why should I care about Morpheus's love life, when I've finally kissed Jeb after all these years?

Morpheus's wings flap wide, then close again. The dreamlike fog draping his features is replaced by suppressed rage. "In this realm, the mirrors are gateways. But the hall in which we stand leads only to other parts of Wonderland. The gateways back to your world are inside the White and Red castles, and they are connected to the queens. Ivory's portal is frozen due to her state and will remain so until she's freed by the person who put her into this box. That leaves only the Red castle's portal. I understand you've already met Rabid White."

I gulp and nod.

"So you know how well received you would be in the Red province. Set foot there, and you could end up in a box just like this."

An image of me or Jeb locked in dark liquid flashes into my mind. Jeb must feel my shiver, because his grip on my shoulders tightens. "So who put Ivory in there?" he asks.

Morpheus removes his hat and sets it next to the bag, leaving his hair a mass of glowing blue tangles. "After Queen Red was exiled to the wilds, she was never seen again. Her stepsister, Grenadine, married the king and became Queen—a woman so forgetful, she could never handle wearing the crown. And now her king wants to give her two." Morpheus drags a glittering diamond tiara from the bag. "I've a spy stationed in the Red castle. When the White Court came to me with news of Ivory's fate some weeks ago, I sent word for my contact to steal the jabberlock box. I'm harboring Ivory here, along with her crown, to keep them safe from Grenadine and King Red. If they control both the Red and White portals, good luck ever getting home." He tucks the tiara away again. "All this will be ameliorated once Alyssa finds the vorpal sword. It's the most powerful weapon in Wonderland. I can use it to force them to grant Ivory's freedom. Her portal will be open to you then."

Jeb levels his gaze at Morpheus. "Let me get this straight. You lured us down here with promises to save Al's mother, knowing all along we'd have no way home until we freed your freaking girlfriend."

Morpheus lifts a finger. "Seeing as we're laying out the facts, let's not forget that *you* weren't invited to begin with. If this is too much for your delicate constitution, mortal dreg, you're welcome to stay safely tucked away in my guest room until it all blows over."

"I go where Al goes, dances-with-bugs. And just so you know, if anything happens to her, I'll pin you by your wings to a corkboard and use you for dart practice."

Jeb and Morpheus's standoff is only background noise. I'm here to break the curse for Alison—that's all that matters.

Only, I should never have dragged Jeb into this. If I could just have an instant replay.

Something the flower zombies said nudges my memory. Something about time moving backward in Wonderland. What had they meant by that? It's obviously not a literal truth. Time has been moving forward since Alice's visit, or things wouldn't be in such a state.

A sense of urgency rolls over me. Alison goes for electroshock on Monday. "I need to get to that tea party and wake up the guests."

Jeb looks at me. "And how are you supposed to do that? Give a magical kiss to the half-baked hatmaker?"

Morpheus secures his hat on his head and tilts it. "'Half-baked'? Herman Hattington's skills happen to be exceptional. No one can custom-fit a hat like he can. And as for a kiss waking him? Wrong fairy tale, Prince Charming. Although I assure you"—Morpheus grazes my temple with his thumb—"our little luv is going to bring us all a happily ever after."

Jeb catches Morpheus's wrist in midair. Their gazes meet.

"No touching," Jeb snarls.

Morpheus jerks his hand free. "Our dinner guests know why Alyssa's here. Since they've been missing their excursions to the human realm, they're willing to welcome her in hopes they'll get the white portal back. But should they realize *you* are an outsider who dropped in without an invite, they'll not be so accepting. For your own preservation, you must be convincing as an elfin escort. Elfin knights are even-tempered and dispassionate. Time to pretend you have such virtues."

I sense the tension in the air as Jeb struggles to contain his temper. The two face off, staring each other into the ground.

I shove an arm between them. "Shouldn't we get to the banquet?"

Frowning, Morpheus fishes Alice's white gloves from his lapel. The grass stains and dirt have been washed off. "We'll need the lace fan." He directs the command to Jeb, who pauses as if he might deck him. I tug on his elbow—a muted plea.

Jeb stalks down the corridor to retrieve the backpack.

Morpheus and I study each other in electrified silence. I can't decide what upsets me most: my evolving netherling traits . . . the ticking clock on Alison's treatments . . . the jabberlock box . . . why Morpheus seems to care that I kissed Jeb when he's involved with someone else . . . or, worst of all, why it upsets me to know about his love for Ivory.

The thoughts scatter around me like broken glass when Jeb returns.

Morpheus tucks the fan inside his lapel along with the gloves. "Leave your baggage here. If anything goes awry during dinner, come immediately to this hall. It is isolated . . . nigh impossible to find unless you know the secret entrance. Gossamer will see that you're sent to the tea party should we have any unexpected guests."

"Unexpected guests?" I ask.

"Guests of murderous or malicious intent. You are, after all, a fugitive from the Red Court." Morpheus rubs his hands together as if relishing the thought of trouble. "I'm famished. Let us feast."

T H E F E A S T O F B E A S T S

Black-and-white stripes cover the walls of the windowless dining hall. I can't tell where the walls end and the floor and ceiling begin.

It's almost as disorienting as the moving moth spirits earlier. Even the long dining table and chairs at the far end of the room are painted to match, creating a camouflage effect. The guests look like they're hovering in place on a striped background. I feel lost yet strangely at home, like a flea who has taken up residence on a zebra.

A giant chandelier mounted on the cathedral ceiling illuminates our surroundings with swathes of swinging light. I step across the threshold with Morpheus on my right side, my hand curved atop the back of his. Jeb stays two steps behind on my left. In elfin code, it's unseemly for a knight to have any interaction with his charge, other than to protect her life should the moment arise. We can't touch, we can't exchange glances, we can't even speak to each other, or we'll blow his cover.

"Your attention, please," Morpheus says to the guests. Gossamer peers out from under his hair again, and the self-playing harp falls silent along with the dinner chatter and clatter. "Miss Alyssa of the Other Realm." He turns to me and holds out my arm. "These are the solitary of our kind, born neither of the Red Court nor White. We, the wild and woolly of Wonderland, welcome you to the Feast of Beasts."

My hand tightens on his as the guests gawk at me, food dripping from their snouts.

Gathered around the long table is a mishmash of creatures, some clothed, others naked. Though they vary in size and gender, they're all more bestial than humanoid. One looks like a hedgehog, prickles and all, except she has the face of a sparrow. She must be shy, because she rolls into a ball upon our entrance, then bounces under the table. A pink woman with a neck as long as a flamingo's ducks down and gives the hedgehog a thump with her head, sending the ball out from under the table to the other side of the room.

There are more creatures: some with wings; some that are part-frog/part-plant, with wriggling vines growing out of their skin; others as bald as seals with the bodies of primates and the woolly heads of lambs.

The one thing they all have in common is their interest in me. I'm the focal point of fifty-some sets of eyes.

A few muttered whispers break the hush.

"It's her . . ."

"Spitting image, she is."

"I hear she drained the ocean with a sponge. A *sponge*. Cunning and imaginative, that."

They all know about my relationship to Alice and what I'm here to do. Talk about epic fail potential.

My nerves combine with the stenches of food, animal dander, and musk. Dizziness spins the room. Jeb's behind me. I know he'll catch me if I faint. I also know that if I do, it will ruin everything. I have to stay strong for Alison. So I pull it together and glance from one strange face to the next, curious which creature came to collect the fan and gloves on behalf of the duchess.

Morpheus leads me to the table and slides out a chair at the right-hand side of his seat at the head. There's a huge mallet propped beside the table's leg, and one underneath every chair down our row. He settles me next to a small wiry creature that looks like an albino ferret wearing a black baseball helmet on his head, though his serpentine eyes and forked tongue detract from any cuteness factor.

Jeb takes his place behind me, just out of reach. Morpheus stands at his chair and tips his hat to the guests, black wings arched high. "I apologize for my lateness. But on the bright side, our avenging angel has come at last. So, let the celebration begin!"

After a smattering of applause from our guests, Morpheus hands his hat off to Gossamer and several other sprites. They hang it on the chair's arm as Morpheus sits, folding his wings over the back like a cloak. Gossamer perches on his shoulder and everyone else resituates with a creak of wood and a rustle of fur and fabrics. Chatter resumes, along with smacks, gulps, and slurps.

"Have a taste, luv." Morpheus motions to my plate. Then he

turns to have a hushed conversation with a green piggish beast who sits at his left across the table from me. The pig wears a gray pin-striped suit complete with fur cuffs. His sleeves stretch down, barely covering lobster claws. He smiles, and I cringe at his teeth—black and round like peppercorns.

On my plate, a handful of goldfish flap around the center, gasping.

"Twinkle?" the ferret next to me says in a flute-like voice. He points a clawed finger at the fish.

"Are we supposed to eat these raw?" I ask him. "I've never been a fan of sushi."

"Sue-she?" he asks.

"Never mind." I turn from the goldfish to him, grateful for the distraction. "So, your name is Twinkle?"

He tilts his head, his shiny helmet glinting as he gestures to the fish skeletons on his plate. "Twinkle."

Nauseated, I stare again at my own thrashing dinner.

Their fish eyes sag in their sockets, looking right at me. Pity and revulsion twist in my stomach. I can't even imagine my pet eels out of water and unable to breathe. Do the moths and bugs I use in my mosaics suffer like this when they die? Why have I never cared enough to ask?

"Twinkle," the creature next to me repeats. He lifts a silver spoon almost as big as himself, stands in his chair, and proceeds to thwack several of my fish on their heads, knocking them dead. "Twinkle them, see?" His forked tongue flits past his lips.

"Oh, no! Please . . ." On impulse, I reach for my goblet to pour liquid over the remaining live fish so they can breathe again. The mixture oozes out slowly, coating the fish in a gritty glob that smells of cinnamon and apple juice. Desperate, I dig the smothered fish out of the mess, getting the goop under my fingernails and into the weave of my gloves.

Everyone's looking at me again, but I'm too disgusted to care.

"What *is* this?" I snap at Morpheus.

His eyes gleam. "Do you not put sand in the cider where you're from?" He smirks. I remember seeing that same teasing smile in dreams as a child, how it used to mean we were about to do something daring and fun. But now there's an edge of malice behind it. What could've happened to change him from the playful boy to the troubled man he is today?

"Would you rather try the wine?" he asks.

At the other end of the table, the primate netherlings are capturing the wine bottles, which float in midair, and stuffing bits of wool from their lamblike heads into the bottle necks to weigh them down. They then pass the wine around for toasts.

Crinkling my nose, I refuse the offer.

"Ah, poor, delicate little blossom." Morpheus takes a napkin, gently grasping my left hand. "Let us clean you up, aye?" Gossamer lights on the table next to my right hand and proceeds to help with unnecessary roughness, yanking at my gloves and pinching my knuckles while grimacing at me. In contrast, Morpheus smooths the sandy mixture from my fingertips. Heat flares from the contact.

There's heat behind me, too, from Jeb's gaze. I don't have to see it. I sense it. He warned Morpheus not to touch me during the feast.

"Pity we were so preoccupied in the Hall of Mirrors earlier and missed the appetizer," Morpheus says as he glances at Jeb smugly. "You would've loved the spider soup, being so adept at wounding insects."

I wince.

"Even more a pity"—he leans in and whispers low so only I can hear—"that you would waste your kisses on a man who fantasizes about other girls. Little Gossamer can see inside people's minds as they're sleeping. The beautiful young woman in Jeb's dreams was not you. Interesting, that he chooses now to act on 'hidden' feelings. Down here, away from all the others, when he wants so desperately to talk you out of your quest."

A sharp-edged shadow passes through my chest, slicing like a knife.

"Oh, but of course he's sincere," Morpheus continues to taunt. "It's not as if he's ever kept anything from you. He's always been honest."

Jeb's move to London with Taelor fills my mind, leaving me as sullen as the dark clouds behind our host's eyes.

Watching my reaction, Morpheus smiles. "Yes. A man who never lies will never break your heart." Planting a kiss atop the back of my glove, he tosses down the napkin and releases me.

Gossamer glowers at me before she flits back to his shoulder.

Tears build behind my eyes. I will them not to fall but can't will away the sick ache in my stomach. Morpheus must be right. Jeb's never mentioned having feelings for me in our real lives. He's still with Taelor up there and dreaming of her down here.

Morpheus stands and returns his hat to his head, all business now. "Enough playing with these bland morsels. Waiters, bring out the main course!"

Some movement along the walls provides a momentary distraction from my heartache. It's as if pieces of the plaster are sprouting legs. Only when they peel from their places and slink off to one of the adjoining rooms do I realize they're a band of human-size chameleons with suctioned toes.

When the zebra-striped lizards return, bulbous eyes twisting in every direction, they carry a platter garnished with dried fruit and something that resembles a duck. It's plucked and roasted but still has its head intact. A warm, herbal scent tickles my nose. At least it's cooked.

"May I introduce you all to the main course?" Morpheus spreads out an arm with dramatic flair. "Dinner, meet your worthy adversaries, the hungry guests."

My tongue dries to sandpaper as the bird's eyes pop open, and it hobbles to stand on webbed feet, flesh brown and glistening with glaze and oil. There's a bell hung around its neck, and it jingles as the duck bows to greet everyone.

This cannot be happening.

Every nerve in my body jumps, urging me to turn to Jeb. But I can't.

Morpheus drags the heavy mallet from beside his chair and pounds it on the table like a judge's gavel. "Now that we're all acquainted, let the walloping begin."

Gossamer launches from Morpheus's shoulder and leaves the room with the other sprites as mass confusion erupts. All the guests leap to their feet, mallets in hand, to chase the jingling duck.

He's surprisingly agile and bobs out of the way, maneuvering among serving platters, dishes, and silverware.

"What are you doing?" I ask Morpheus. "I've never seen anything so savage!"

"'Savage'?" The green pig snorts an answer for him. "You act as if we're a bunch of animals." His peppercorn teeth form a sneer.

"Stop thinking with your head, Alyssa." Morpheus leans low across the table, his blue hair swinging forward at his shoulders. "Think with this, instead." He taps a finger above my naval. It's a good thing Jeb can't see from his angle, or he'd break Morpheus's hand off.

"My stomach?" I barely breathe the question.

"Your gut. Instinct. The deepest part of you knows that this"—he motions to the chaos around us—"is how it should be. That same part of you that prompted you to look for me and step through the mirror. The same part that gave you the power to animate your mosaic at home."

His words send me back to that moment in my hallway when the crickets' dead legs kicked and the glass beads glowed. Is he saying my curse-magic caused that, too?

"You understand the logic behind the illogical, Alyssa. It's in your nature to find tranquility amid the madness. And that's what we're doing here. We're giving our food a fighting chance." He winks at me. "Now, if you'll pardon us, my comrade and I have some bartering to do." He and the pig leave the table. Morpheus bends down to keep their heads together as they stroll to the far wall.

"Twinkle!" the white ferret shouts. He scrambles onto the table with spoon in hand, only to get toppled by the roasted duck. I catch my furry companion before he falls headfirst off the edge. His spoon jangles to the floor beside his helmet. With his cap gone, his bald scalp is revealed—the skin so thin, his brain shows through. He doesn't even have a skull.

He snuggles in my lap. "Datum. Datum very much, angel light!" Beady pink eyes study me, soft with morbid adoration. I'm so captivated by the strangeness of the creature, I don't realize a mob is coming our way, flailing their mallets in a chaotic rush for the prize.

Jeb jerks my chair from the table to save me from getting pounded while the ferret holds on to my tunic for dear life. Then Jeb sidesteps to the corner diagonally across from me, maintaining our distance. His expression strains with the effort not to make eye contact.

"Ye know the rulessss!" a serpentine wolf hisses in midpummel, just missing the duck as it hurtles across a dinner plate. "Firsssst to ring hissss bell getssss to carve!"

A bloodcurdling howl breaks the chaos as someone rips off one of the duck's legs. It drags itself free while several of the pursuers gnaw on the ripped drumstick.

The duck climbs atop a hovering wine bottle and takes to the air, all the while giggling deliriously. He taunts the others to catch him by tearing off and dropping pieces of his flesh.

He *wants* to be eaten.

A sick twinge spasms in my belly, tempting me to join in, teasing me with the thrill of the chase. My legs twitch in their desire to jump up. I suppress the impulse.

Any creatures capable of flight follow with mallets in hand, floating over everyone else. The grounded ones scuttle to the tabletop or rush along the floor, tumbling over dishes and chairs in hopes someone will knock the main course down to their level.

I cover my mouth to keep from screaming or laughing hysterically. It could go either way at this point. I'm beginning to enjoy the madness.

That's not good. Not at all.

My new ferret friend pats my fingers, his tiny pink pads soft against my skin.

"Hale be angel light," his flutelike voice soothes. "Hale and agreeable. Sort and sing. Be royal smiles for me." He grins, his sharp teeth glimmering beneath the chandelier's glow. His canines are as long as a rattlesnake's fangs.

My instinct stirs, and I do what Morpheus suggested—I follow it. I tickle the creature's left ear like I would a puppy's. He purrs in response.

I shut out everything—the pursuit of dinner, the crazy hoots and laughter from the animated guests, the affectionate, furry creature in my lap—as I watch Morpheus pass the fan and gloves to the pig.

In exchange, the pig slips Morpheus a small white bag tied with a black ribbon. Then the pig snatches up his mallet and waddles off to join the festivities, which have moved to the kitchen. The clang of pots and pans in the other room echoes loudly in the sudden hush of the abandoned dining hall.

I startle as the ferret grasps both sides of my face. "Dust-sweet, angel light." He licks my chin with his cold, forked tongue, then drops to the floor, snagging his spoon and helmet. "Twinkle. Gust and begone!" With that, he returns his helmet to his head and runs into the kitchen.

Once he disappears, only Jeb, Morpheus, and I remain in the room. Free of prying eyes, I look at Jeb from my seat and he stares back from against the wall, neither of us moving.

A strange pressure starts to penetrate my chin where the ferret's snaky tongue left a wet mark. It worms into my skin and winds into my mouth, both warm and cold at once. I swallow the taste of it—bitter yet sweet, like a confection made of tears.

The sensation doesn't stop there. It flows into my throat, then my chest, pinching with a deep, profound sadness. At first, I hurt for myself and Jeb, for how there's still so much between us to work out. Then I hurt for Alison and Dad and their lost years together. I hurt for Queen Red and her broken heart, and for Ivory, who's always suffered in solitude, now locked alone in the prison hatbox. The sadness escalates, as if all the grief of the world converges in one spot, just above my heart. I ache to cry . . . ache so much, it takes my breath away.

Jeb rushes to me, crouching at my feet. "Al, it's all right. It's over." He feels my forehead. "You're so cold. Say something, please."

I can't respond for fear I'll start to weep uncontrollably.

"She's turning blue!" Jeb shouts at Morpheus. "That ferret freak did something to her!"

"Tut. Don't get yourself worked into a snit, pseudo elf." Morpheus tosses his hat onto a chair and joins us. He bends over me. Jeb reluctantly inches aside to give him space.

Morpheus lifts my chin and tilts my face from side to side, like a physician conducting a checkup. "You are fortunate he liked you, little plum. The Mustela netherlings are notorious for their tempers, and they have the venom of a thousand asps in one snap of their canines. Their heads are soft and vulnerable. Had you touched him anywhere but his ears, he would've taken it as a threat. You would be writhing on the floor right now, choking on your last, excruciating breath."

I try to speak but can't. The sadness grows steadily stronger. Each beat of my heart sucks against my rib cage like a leech. I want to slide to the floor, curl into a ball, and cry forever. But I'm frozen in place.

"You sat her next to that deadly thing on purpose, didn't you?" Jeb asks, though it's more of a shout. "To punish her for kissing me!

You sick son of a—" He attacks Morpheus, spinning him into his wings and slamming his back onto the tabletop. Plates and utensils shake at the impact. Forearm pressed across our host's larynx, Jeb holds him down. "Fix. Her. *Now.*"

"There's nothing to fix. He gave her a gift." Morpheus grunts as Jeb's arm grinds into his throat. He tries to break free, but Jeb has him wrapped so tightly in his wings, he can't move. "If you'll let me up"—he grits out the words—"I shall show you."

Snarling, Jeb pulls away and kneels beside me again, taking my limp hand. He curls each of my fingers through his. "C'mon, skater girl. Stay with me, okay? Whatever's going on inside your head, don't let it win."

The worry pinching his features piles onto my already weighted chest and suffocates me. He needs me to answer him. But if I open my mouth to respond, I'll wail like a banshee until I'm an empty husk.

"Give me some room." Morpheus crouches down and Jeb eases back while keeping our fingers laced. Morpheus holds a cloth napkin close to my face. "Let it out, luv. I know it feels like a dam will burst, but I assure you, one tear, and you'll be right as raindrops."

It isn't possible. One tear will never be enough. I double over. A keening cry erupts from my throat, so deep it strains my vocal cords and hollows my abdomen. The cry ends in a sob. And then one single tear streams down my left cheek.

Just like that, I'm myself again. I squeeze Jeb's hand.

Morpheus ties the napkin around what looks like a clear glass marble, though it's soft and pliant like a bath oil bead. "This is yours."

"That's my tear?" I ask.

"It's a wish. Your new little friend has the gift of invocation. They only give out one in their lifetime, and he chose you. I shall keep it safe for now. You're not quite ready to wield this much power." Tucking the napkin into his jacket, our host starts to stand, but Jeb grabs his elbow and stalls him on one knee.

"No way. You give it to her now. Give it to her, and she can use it to wish us both home."

Morpheus pulls free. "And leave the curse unbroken? Besides, I'm afraid it's not quite that simple. For this can only be used for her and her alone. She must be the subject of the wish, for she's the one who cried it. No one else can ride its power. So it cannot carry you home, as well. If you're both to get back, the portals are your only chance."

Jeb and I exchange frowns.

"I'll wish for more wishes," I offer.

Morpheus laughs. "Oh, of course you would. Just like Alice did. She asked for an endless supply of wishes. Then her tears wouldn't stop falling. That's how the ocean was born in the first place. We almost never got that fountain stopped. If you try to outsmart magic, there's always a price to be paid." Morpheus pushes to his feet.

I catch his wrist. "You had me sitting next to him for a reason. You wanted me to get this wish. Why?"

Silent, he loosens the cravat tied around his neck in a relaxed gesture while holding my gaze. The left side of his mouth tweaks into a half smile.

"Hey . . ." Jeb raises our joined hands and presses his thumb against my sternum to get my attention. My heart beats against the pressure, remembering his caresses in the mirrored hall. "You were turning blue, Al. That same ferret-snake could've just as easily killed you. This creep took a chance with your life purely for his entertainment. He didn't have any noble motives."

"The Mustela netherlings are exceptional judges of character," Morpheus intones. "I knew Alyssa would rise to the occasion. I've complete faith that she can fend for herself. You, on the other hand, can't seem to grasp that concept."

Jeb helps me up from the chair and pulls me in for a hug. It feels good to be in his arms, even if I'm unsure of his motives.

Our host settles his hat into place. "Bless me that I didn't eat; elsewise, I'd be qualmish at such a nauseating display."

Jeb kisses my forehead to spite Morpheus. I pull back, because I'd rather he kiss me for myself.

"The pig." I offer up a change of conversation; I'm in no mood to play referee to any more of their wrestling matches.

"Yes," Morpheus answers without breaking his scowling match with Jeb. "The pig is in fact a hobgoblin, born to the duchess."

Bits and pieces of Lewis Carroll's story drop into place. Someone was making soup for the duchess with lots of spices. That's why the fan and gloves smelled like pepper. And she had a baby that became a pig. "So, what did he give you in exchange for the gloves and fan?"

Morpheus holds up the small white bag. "The key for waking Herman Hattington at the tea party—free of charge." He hands it to me, and Jeb starts to work at the ribbon.

Morpheus's thumb flattens on the bow. "You don't want to do that. It is the most potent and priceless black pepper this side of the nether-realm. And you've only enough for one dose."

Jeb's forehead wrinkles. "Black pepper. What kind of subpar magic is that?"

Before Morpheus can answer, a horde of sprites floods the dining hall, fluttering in from the main door.

"Master, we have company," Gossamer cries. "Bad company!"

"Go," Morpheus says to Jeb, bending down to grab a mallet.

Jeb tucks the bag of pepper into his pocket, then takes my hand. We've only taken two steps toward the secret exit when a deck of cards—each one complete with six sticklike legs and arms—marches through the main door. The card guards keep pouring in until the walls are lined with them.

On closer examination, these guards have bugs' faces with trembling antennae, and their paper-thin torsos are actually flattened shells, jagged at the edges and painted red and black to resemble suits of cards. With their oddly jointed limbs and piercing mouthparts crisscrossed at their mandibles, they look more like insects than cardboard.

All these years I've been killing bugs, and now karma's here to make me pay, in spades.

The bugs separate into suits: five hearts and five clubs on one side, five spades and five diamonds on the other, with Rabid White in their center. The sprites, tiny and helpless, look down on the situation from where they're gathered around the chandelier.

A red waistcoat and matching gloves hang off Rabid's short, skeletal frame. One hand holds a trumpet and the other a rolled-up scroll. He tilts his antlered head to blow three loud blasts from the instrument. Then, with a flick of his wrist and a rattle of bones, he throws open the parchment.

"Alyssa Gardner of the human court is hereby beckoned to the presence of Queen Grenadine of the Red Court." His glittery pink eyes turn up, locking on me. A shock of terror races through me.

Both Jeb and Morpheus shove me behind them. So much for fending for myself . . .

"She's going nowhere with you, *Rabid*." Morpheus raises his mallet.

"Otherwise, Queen Grenadine says." Froth slathers around Rabid's mouth, and his eyes glow like lit coals, red with fire. "Otherwise, her army commands."

On his signal, the cards against the wall shuffle together and leap toward us, as if dealt by an invisible hand.

The sprites drop from above, trying to run interference. Morpheus spreads his wings wide to block me and Jeb from the attack. Spears hit his wings, stretching them but not breaking through. My palms flatten against Morpheus's back, absorbing the shock as his muscles strain with every swing of his mallet. His grunts drown out the clatter of guards hitting the floor.

"Get her out of here!" he shouts over his shoulder as he backs us toward the secret exit to the mirrored room, still using his wings as a barrier.

Jeb grips my elbow and drags me over the threshold.

"No!" I wrestle against him. "We can't just leave him to fight alone. There are too many!"

Gritting his teeth, Jeb scoops me up over his shoulder. "He's handling them. And you're all that matters." His arm locks around my thighs, my head and torso hanging upside down across his back. The winding black marble stairway bounces by beneath us, and blood races to my head.

I squeeze my eyes closed, listening to the battle in the dining hall grow farther and farther away.

The memory of how Morpheus and I played in our childhood, of the way he healed my bruises today, the sound of his beautiful lullaby—all of it boils over in a confusing brew of emotion. I think of the wish tucked within his jacket . . . the wish he wanted me to have for some reason. If I had it now, I'd wish to be in the dining hall, helping Morpheus fight.

I'm just about to make an escape attempt when I hear the sound of pots and pans clanging.

"Twinkle! Twinkle them all!"

Next there's a rush of screeches and roars—the same bestial voices I heard at the feast. The beasts have returned from their chase, and Morpheus is no longer alone in his fight.

Jeb and I slip through the secret passageway leading up another flight of stairs. Soon, we're far enough away that the only sound is his boots pounding the mirrored floor.

"You can put me down now," I grump.

"I don't know. It's a lot easier to save your ass when I have it riding on my shoulder."

"You don't need to save me."

Jeb barks a sarcastic laugh. "I don't have much choice when you keep running headfirst into risky situations for this crusade of yours. Now you've gone and dropped us smack into the middle of a magical war."

I pound him. Right between the shoulder blades.

"Hey . . ." He eases my feet to the floor so we're facing each other and rubs his back. In spite of his frown, he looks impressed.

My knuckles are throbbing. The guy could put a boulder to shame. "I already feel bad enough for bringing you into this. Okay? If I had it to do over, you wouldn't be here at all." I shake out my fingers. Gossamer hasn't come yet to open the mirror portal, and an urgency to get to the tea party jitters through me.

Jeb lifts my aching knuckles and presses his lips across them. "I'd still want to be here with you, even if we had do-overs. But if we're going to make it out of this, you need to stop taking moth man at his word like he's some kind of saint."

"His name is *Morpheus*." My throat clenches as I'm reminded of what's happening some three flights down. "Do you think he's losing in there? You think they'll hurt him?"

"Why are you so worried about him?"

"I grew up with him. I care."

"That makes no sense. It was in your dreams. Your friendship wasn't real."

"It feels real. Because he believes in me. He lets me take chances and learn from them. That's something a friend does." Clenching my jaw, I glare at Jeb.

His features darken, as if a shadow falls across his face. "So, because the freak boosts your ego, you're willing to overlook all his lies? He hasn't told the truth about anything since we've arrived."

"Then he fits in well with you, seeing as you're both liars." I hate the accusation in my voice but can't seem to contain it. I break our handhold, noticing the bag on the table—the one containing the jabberlock box. "Why's this still here?"

Frowning, Jeb steps up next to me as I unwrap the box. "Probably the safest place. You shouldn't mess with it."

"I want another look at the inscription." I'd like another look at the queen, too. What is it about her that holds Morpheus so enthralled?

Jeb covers the lid with his palm. "You know, you can't just call someone a liar and let it drop. Maybe I wasn't honest about London. But you lied, too."

The moth spirits skim by in my peripheral vision, as if riding my racing pulse. "Not about my feelings. You waited until we came down here to own up to your so-called crush on me. Back in the real world, where it counts, you chose Taelor."

He forces me to face him, pushing the hatbox to the back of the table. "Where's this coming from? Has that cockroach been swimming inside your brain again?"

"No. But Gossamer was in yours when you were knocked out. And she saw you dreaming of another girl. When you kissed me . . . it was just to convince me to give this up and go home so you could get back to Tae."

"What?" His fingers feel hot and tight even through my sleeves. "The dream I had was of Jen and Mom. I'm worried about them."

"Right," I say, wanting to be convinced but not quite there.

He jerks away and strides to the other end of the hall, silent and stoic.

My arms chill with the absence of his touch. The pain is crushing, but I'm glad I said something. I would've had that doubt forever, thinking I was stealing kisses meant for another girl. I drag the pewter hatbox toward me again, concentrating on the lid's inscription to keep the hot tears behind my eyes from flooding out. If I focus and unfocus through the blur, the letters move, forming legible text. I trail it with my fingertip and whisper the words:

"Behold the box of jabberlock's, the fairest rests inside. But free the dame and ease her pain to slip into her tide. An ocean red from bonds of love, and paint the roses' hearts thereof, applied with wisps of finest strand and guided by an artist's hand. One trade of souls will shut the door, and blood shall seal it, evermore."

"It is the key to freeing the queen if you're not the one who imprisoned her." Gossamer's chiming voice pulls me out of my meditation. "Individualized to the box's inhabitant." She lights on my shoulder so I can see her up close—a woman's perfect form, dusted green and naked but for the strategic placement of glistening scales. Her hands rest on her hips. "An ocean red from bonds of love." Her dragonfly eyes glitter. "The roses must be painted with the blood of someone willing to trade places with her for the noblest of reasons. Love initiates the transfer."

The famous Lewis Carroll scene passes through my mind—the card guards painting the roses red in the garden to keep from being beheaded. How ironic, that in *this* Wonderland, someone could *lose* their head forever by painting the roses upon this box.

"So Morpheus wasn't completely honest," I say. "There's another way to free her and open the portal. It's not just up to the person who put her there." Jeb is standing behind my reflection, his expression smug. I can almost hear the "I told you so" emanating through his eyes.

"It isn't such an easy decision," Gossamer scolds, then lifts off my shoulder, wings buzzing. "Once the trade is made, no one can ever free the replacement soul. The blood makes the seal permanent, eternally. *One trade of souls will shut the door, and blood shall seal it, evermore.*"

"So, what you're saying"—Jeb steps up—"is that it has to be an unselfish love. Which Morpheus is incapable of giving. He lacks that kind of courage."

Gossamer flaps her wings in midair, arms crossed over her chest. "My master has a great capacity for courage. He saved my life once." She glances at the hall's entrance and back again. "No one knows what he or she is capable of until things are at their darkest. That is why the key to opening the box is the essence of the heart. Therein lies the world's most potent power." Her cryptic words hang in the air.

She ducks beneath the table and drags out my dad's army knife, leaving it by Jeb's foot. He tucks the weapon into his pocket. I want to ask what the sprite means about a heart's essence, about the dark. I want to ask how Morpheus and the solitary netherlings are faring downstairs. But my tongue is tied up in the jabberlock poem and Jeb's reaction to my questions.

Gossamer has us face one of the mirrors, and she touches the glass with a fingertip. The moth spirits vanish from the in-between plane, flying into other mirrors along the walls.

Palm splayed over the reflective surface, the sprite initiates that same splintering effect I saw in the cheval glass in my bedroom. A long table filled with pastries and teacups appears in the mirror, sitting under a tree in front of a country cottage that's shaped like a rabbit's head—complete with chimneys for ears and a fur-thatched roof. It looks as if the sun has overpowered the moon this time, because daylight shimmers on the surroundings. With a key almost the size of her forearm, Gossamer unlocks the portal, smoothing the glass.

Pounding footsteps echo from the adjoining hall. The fight has made its way here.

"Just go!" Gossamer prompts.

Jeb won't even look at me as he lifts the backpack onto his shoulder, his complexion almost as green as Gossamer's. I leap through the mirror, more desperate to escape my hurt and confusion than anything Rabid White and the Red army could unleash.

Hattington

My boots end up on a plate loaded with pastries. Once the dizziness subsides, I lift a foot and shake off some sugared crust.

Before I can explore the table I'm standing upon, something crashes into me from behind. I trip face-first into a pie filled with succulent purple berries.

"Al . . . I'm sorry." Jeb lifts me by my elbows, pulling my shoulder blades into his chest. "You okay?"

I refuse to answer on the grounds that he didn't specify physically or emotionally. With his help, I regain my footing between a plate of buttered bread and a bowl of candied violets. Some of the pie filling coats my mouth.

I lick it from my lips, then flap my fingertips, trying to get the sticky stuff off.

From our end of the table, the landscape we saw refracted in the mirror is in full view. The bunny-shaped cottage sits on a hill—a green and lush oasis smack in the midst of a desert. Sand dunes in the distance look like a chessboard—squares of black and white like the ones I'm always tripping over in my nightmare. I yearn for a canvas and raw materials so I can capture the warped vista forever.

A temperate breeze sways my braids, birds twitter in a mulberry tree overhead, and sunlight warms my shoulders. It reminds me so much of Pleasance that a wave of homesickness crashes over me. I wish I could talk to Dad; even more, I wish I could hug him.

It's Saturday. At least I think it is. If I were home, Dad would be grilling steaks. I'd fix a fruit salad, because it's my job to see that he eats well-balanced meals.

What if I can't pull this off and get back home? Alison will blame herself forever and plunge into the deep end for real. Shock treatments will make her worse. Then Dad will be sitting alone in the kitchen eating cold cereal with nothing but his grief to keep him company. And then there's Jeb's mom and Jenara. His job at Underland helps pay the monthly bills. They rely on him. What will they do without him?

If I screw this up, I screw it up for everybody.

Jeb—still behind me—offers a napkin. I wipe my face and mumble, "Why didn't you land at the other end of the table?"

"It was occupied." Jeb turns me around.

I nearly choke at the sight of the tea party guests—Herman Hattington, March Hairless, and Door Mouse—all seated at the far corner and frozen solid beneath thick, glittering sheets of bluish gray ice.

"Mothra has a twisted definition of *asleep*," Jeb says.

Morpheus has a twisted definition of everything. Shaking my head, I start toward them. As I step over the teapot's spout, steam licks my calf, dampening my leggings. Hattington and his crew are suspended like glaciers, but the food looks fresh and the tea's still hot.

"Where's that pepper?" I hold out my hand. It's awkward playing at teamwork. My family's been in upheaval mode since I can remember, but at least over the last few years, I've had Jeb's friendship to count on. Now it's hanging by some weird emotional thread; I don't know whether to believe him or Morpheus. It was easier to be mad up in the real world, when I knew for sure that he'd chosen Taelor.

Jeb digs the bag from his pocket. I loosen the ribbon while breathing through my mouth. I won't chance inhaling any of it. Just the faded scent of the pepper on the fans and gloves was enough to make me almost sneeze.

Sneeze . . .

That must be what Morpheus intended with this little bag of spice.

"You're not going to waste it on trying to make the hat guy sneeze, are you?" Jeb asks. "He's an ice sculpture. There's not even an opening where his nostrils should be. And there's only enough pepper for one dose. We have to be sure."

It's uncanny how well he reads me at times, yet is so oblivious at others.

Tying the bag shut, I hand it back. He's right. We'll never be able to wake Hattington with pepper. He doesn't even *have* a nose.

I edge closer. He's holding up a cup of steaming tea, as if he was in the middle of punctuating a point with it.

"Jeb, something's not right with his face. It's just a blank space of nothing." The glittery, bluish gray void reflects my likeness, more unsettling than a stranger's frozen snarl would be.

"Maybe the ice is so thick, it covers his features," Jeb says.

"I don't know. But check out that hat." It could be a medieval torture device—part top hat/part cage—made of metal pins with a hinged flap at the crown that's open like a lid. On second glance, the metal's actually growing out of his head like bones. The cage pokes through holes in his flesh, just like the chess piece in Morpheus's room.

"A conformateur," Jeb says, his voice tense. "He's got a conformateur sprouting out of his head."

Most people wouldn't know about a nineteenth-century tool used for customizing hats to fit specific head shapes, but Jenara has one in her room. Persephone ran across it at an estate sale once and, knowing Jen's love for anything fashion related, bid low on it and just happened to win because no one there knew the value of the artifact.

The ribbed metal frame molds around a customer's head where a hat brim would sit, and the pins conform to the ridges and bumps of the skull. An oval of cardboard is inserted into the hinged lid and pressed into place at the crown, causing the pins to punch holes in the shape of the head. It forms a pattern the hatmaker can use to custom-fit a hat to that individual.

Why this one is physically attached to Herman's skull is beyond me, and I don't even want to imagine how he uses it in his craft.

I force my attention from his reflective face and turn to the "hare," who is twelve kinds of hideous. Mostly because he seems to be turned inside out—no fur, only gaunt flesh. It's like looking at a skinned rabbit. But at least he has a face. His expression is demented, with a wild glint in his white eyes. A teacup balances atop a pastry on his plate. His paw is tucked into the cup from his wrist down, as if he's dunking something.

Of the three guests, the mouse is the only one that looks normal. If a mouse wearing a doorman's jacket could be considered normal.

"I don't know how to solve this," I say. "They're all frozen, so how do we make them all sneeze with one dash of pepper?"

Jeb shakes his head. "Let's look at the book." He wades through place settings and steps from the table to an empty chair. Pushing aside a rickety, three-tiered tea wagon, he drops to the grass. "Come here," he says, urging me to take his hand as he sits at the table and settles the backpack next to him.

I let him help me down but pull free the instant my feet hit the ground. Blotting the remaining berry juice off my face with a cloth napkin, I check my clothes to make sure they're clean. "I'm hungry." An understatement. I'm famished. And I can't remember the last time I ate something.

"Well, we shouldn't eat this stuff." Jeb gestures to the tea party spread. "Who knows what it might do to us?" He finds an energy bar in the backpack and hands me half. He motions to an empty chair next his. Instead, I take another one two places down. He stares hard at me while we eat; the only sounds are the rattling wrapper, the birds, and the breeze.

Avoiding his gaze, I count the peach and gray stripes in my leggings. My legs are starting to remind me of peppermint sticks. Tasty, curvy peppermint sticks.

My mouth waters.

What's wrong with me? I need to be helping Jeb figure things out, but all I can think of is food.

After I wolf down the last of my bar, the hunger still hasn't abated. I remember how good that purple stuff tasted and wish I'd never fallen into that pie to begin with.

On the other hand, it must've been hilarious to watch. I picture myself tumbling into the pastry and snicker out loud.

"What's so funny?" Jeb asks. He has the *Wonderland* novel open on his lap and drops the last of his snack into his mouth.

"Nothing." Another bout of giggles tickles me. This wave is so strong, I bite my inner cheeks to keep from giving in.

Oblivious, Jeb flips a few pages. "It says in chapter seven that the Dormouse kept falling asleep at the party, and the Hatter poured hot tea on its nose to wake it. The passage is underlined, so maybe that's a hint. What do you think?"

"I think the mouse must've had a nose for tea." I slap a hand over my lips, embarrassed by the senseless reply.

"Okay. Enough pretending everything's cool." Jeb drops the book into the backpack along with the wrapper. He comes over and catches my chin, lifting my gaze to his. "You really think I faked wanting to kiss you?"

An odd sense of playfulness blossoms inside me, completely inappropriate for the seriousness of our situation. "Ah-ah-ah, elfin knight." I peel out of his grasp and jump to my feet—flirty, giddy, and totally not myself. "You're not to touch my precious booty, remember? Get thee behindeth me, Jebbeth." I swivel my back to him.

He grasps my elbow. "Would you look at me, please?"

I yank free and skip around the tea wagon to the other side of the table so the place settings form a barricade between us. To my left sits the Door Mouse. He's the size of a gerbil, but his thin tail is furry like a squirrel's and covered in white frost. Pillows are piled high on his chair, boosting him so he can reach the table. His head rests next to a cup half-full of hot tea. He must've frozen while napping.

I lean close to his ears—silvery with ice and oblong. "I don't blame you for sleeping your life away," I whisper to him. Jeb's gawking at me like I'm from Mars. "Wish I'd slept the last few hours of mine."

Jeb's expression falls, and I know I've hurt him. That wasn't my intention. I feel anything but spiteful. Aside from being hungry, I'm whimsical, light-headed, and uninhibited. It's very liberating.

"Al, c'mon. I don't want things to be like this . . . not with us." Jeb starts around the table and I'm about to bolt, thinking a good chase could be fun, when I hear a sniffle. It's so soft, at first I think it's the leaves rustling overhead. Then I see the mouse's nose wriggle. It's shiny, wet, and pink, like a teensy ball of strawberry icing. I'm about to pluck it off and eat it when Jeb steps up behind me.

The mouse sniffs again.

"What do you think, Jeb? Use the pepper to wake him up. He can be our sidekick. We'll call him Skittles, like the candy." The things coming out of my mouth are nonsense, but I can't seem to stop them. Any more than I can stop the colossal stomach growl that follows.

Watching me with an uneasy frown, Jeb takes the seat next to me and drags out the bag. "Its nose must be defrosted from the tea."

I can't concentrate on anything but my body. My skin feels itchy, like I need to *do* something. I climb on top of my chair, then onto the table, kicking some dishes aside.

"Al, what the—?"

Music plays in my head . . . not Morpheus's lullaby. Something with a sensual, addictive beat. I twist my hips back and forth. The rubies on my belt sparkle, and the rings jingle—belly-dancer style. I didn't know I could move like this. Must be from all those years of hula-hooping with Jen.

Jeb's eyes look like they might pop . . . so do the veins in his neck. He makes a sound—somewhere between a cough and a moan—mesmerized by my rocking hips. He stands. "Would you get down? You're going to hurt yourself."

"No. Come up here with me." I raise my arms over my head and roll my pelvis seductively. "It's a wake-up dance for Skittles. You know, like the Native Americans used to do to bring down rain."

Jeb gawks. "I seriously doubt any Native Americans moved like that."

Feeling the groove through every pulse of my body, I envision the chains on Jeb's belt dancing to the music, imagine coils of energy running through the links, inducing movement. I beckon them toward me with a fingertip.

"Hey . . . hey, wait!" Jeb's chains lurch, forcing him up onto the chair. He tries to grab the links with his hands, but they break free, tugging until he's standing in front of me on the table.

I catch his hips, coaxing his body to sway with mine. Pressed against him, I nuzzle his neck, dropping kisses over his soft skin as I rake my fingers through his hair. His ponytail comes undone. "You taste good enough to eat," I whisper.

The chains wind around his thigh, squeezing. Tensing all over, he grabs them. "H-h-how are you doing that?"

I laugh, running my palms across his biceps and chest. "Morpheus showed me I could animate objects. Isn't it spectacular?"

I'm concentrating too hard on how good his muscles feel, and it breaks my connection with the metal links. The minute he's free, Jeb climbs to the ground and lifts me down. I drop into my seat, giggling as he clasps both my hands crossways over my chest.

"You're freaking me out, Al. Come on."

"Come on where?" I break a hand loose and run a fingertip down his shirt, tracing the line of sheer black fabric over his yummy navel and stopping to clutch his waistband.

A muscle in his jaw jumps.

I purr. "Poor control-freak Jeb. Your world's way off-kilter when little Alyssa's not tripping over her chastity belt. Is that it, bad boy?" I tap the button at the top of his fly.

"Uhhh . . ."

"Why don't you wake up Skittles, and then we'll go home and have a real party?" I'm smiling so hard, it hurts my face—a provocative, teasing smile. For some reason, I can't stop.

"You need to quit looking at me like that," Jeb says, a husky rattle in his voice.

"Or else what?" My insides tickle with an unfamiliar power, knowing that he's flustered. Knowing that I caused it.

Swallowing hard, he fishes out the bag of pepper again. "'Home.' Right. Maybe if we wake the mouse, the others will wake up, too."

"Yeah! Let the tea party begin!" *Then I can finally eat something.* I play a drumroll on the table's edge with my forefingers.

Jeb shoots another bewildered glance my way. It's delicious being able to unbalance him. Like when his blood turned green over Morpheus earlier. I've never known any girl to be in control of Jebediah Holt. Sure would rock to be the first.

A tiny voice inside me tries to break through, tries to remind me this isn't *me* . . . that I wouldn't say these things, not to Jeb—that I wouldn't take pleasure in his pain. Something's wrong and I should tell him so he can help, or at least defend himself. But the hunger inside crushes my conscience. It's more than just an ache for food. I'm starving for power, too. Power to bring the guy I want to his knees. To make him pay for not wanting me back.

With one eye on me and one on the bag of pepper, Jeb packs the mouse's nostrils. The tiny creature inhales sharply. A sneeze gathers, then erupts on a hiccup. His icy shell shatters with the force of it. Clumps of frost slide from his brown fur and red jacket as he sits up to rub his nose.

The instant he sees us, he scrambles behind his teacup. Braving a peek, he blinks black dewdrop eyes our way. They look like chocolate chips. That fierce hunger rolls through me again.

Drooling, I scramble on top of the table.

"Eep!" The mouse's voice is a high-pitched squeak as he scuttles out from his hiding place.

"Al, stop. We need his help." Jeb tries to grab my ankles, but I'm too fast.

Shoving platters and plates aside, I crawl after the mouse as he skitters toward his friends, fuzzy tail jouncing behind him. He skids to a stop when he sees their condition. Whiskers drooping, he twists to look at me.

"Miss Alice, you must wake them!" he squeaks. Hesitant, his tiny feet patter backward. "You're not Miss Alice." He pats the edges of his eyes while staring at mine. "You're much more—"

"Hungry." Now I understand the octobenus's preoccupation with his stomach—intimately. I smack my lips and veer to the left to escape Jeb's attempt to snag my waist. My palm lands in a pastry, and I fling off the squished crust. I've got my sights set on live bait.

The mouse backs up, squeaking nervously. Tiny clawed hands reach for his whiskers, drawing them down under his chin. He's close to tripping into the broken crust that I landed in earlier, and I'm rooting for that to happen. I could really go for a slice of mouse pie right about now.

Jeb steps onto a chair and climbs from one to the next to follow me. "Listen, little guy." He talks softly to the mouse. "I'll keep her from eating you if you'll help us wake the others. Do you remember how Alice put you to sleep?"

The mouse wraps his tail around himself, hugging it. "She dropped the watch into the teacup." He studies me warily from the middle of the table, stepping closer to the purple pie.

Sitting up on my knees, I gouge my fingernails into my kneecaps to distract myself from my stomach. Eyes shut, I concentrate on the book. The story's details are hazy, but I remember an argument over the inner workings of the Hatter's pocket watch. Something about the hare buttering—mmm . . . butter. Butterscotch candy, buttercream icing, butter cookies.

I growl and pound my fist on the table, rattling silverware and plates and sending a jolt of pain up my arm, which gets my brain back into gear. *Gear!* That's it—the hare buttered the gears with a bread knife and mucked up the insides with crumbs. In the *Wonderland* book's version, that's why the March Hare dropped the watch into his tea—to rinse it off. But maybe he wasn't the one who dunked the watch at all. He must've been trying to get it out. By submerging it,

Alice suspended the mechanism and froze the guests in time. That's what I have to fix. The gears. I just need to dry them off and start them up again.

I open my eyes, and Jeb's way ahead of me, book in hand. He's already next to March Hairless's place setting. Jeb tilts the teacup, careful not to break off the rabbit's frozen paw. I crawl over as tea sloshes across the pastries on the plate. The pocket watch glides out, dragging its chain behind it. Jeb flips the lid open. "It stopped on six o'clock."

"Teatime!" the Door Mouse chirps excitedly, clapping. His enthusiasm knocks him backward into the broken pie.

My focus lasts only long enough for me to take the watch from Jeb, blot the gears dry, move the hands to one minute after six, and rewind the clock. I lose all train of thought after that, because the mouse clambers onto the edge of the pie pan, eating berries and dripping with purple syrup.

Luscious purple syrup.

Saliva trickles from the edges of my lips. The insatiable hunger I've been fighting explodes. My surroundings disappear. In my mind, the Door Mouse is that roasted duck from the banquet, which makes him fair game.

I chuck the watch, barely even hearing the clank of metal. Jumping to my feet, I give chase. My prey dives behind pastries and tunnels through breads, managing to elude me each time I almost have him. I skate past dishes, slip over platters, and skid through cakes. I don't even realize Jeb's on the table until he catches me and slams me down, his solid weight flush across my back. "Al, stop! Have you lost your mind?"

Like an animal, I growl and claw at the tablecloth until it snags on my fingernails.

"Al." Jeb's breath is hot on my neck. "Come back to me. Be my skater girl again."

My skater girl. The tender entreaty almost brings me back.

Only almost.

Maybe it's the adrenaline, or maybe it's whatever demon possessed me when I fell into that pie and tasted that purple junk . . . but something gives me enough strength to thrust Jeb aside like he's a twig. He rolls off the table with a grunt and I snag the screaming, sticky, mousey delicacy. Purple syrup oozes through my fingertips and down my gloves. I'm just about to bite his head off when I'm tackled from behind, and he escapes.

"Let me up!" I snarl, my momentary burst of superhuman strength all but gone.

Someone flips me onto my back and pins me in place. My vision blurs, and I can barely make out the two forms bent over me.

"She's sampled berry juice from the Tumtum Tree," the silhouette wearing the hat-cage says in a voice that bounces between tenor and alto. "She must eat the berries whole, else she'll go mad." The speaker then bursts into giggles so loud and absurd, he sounds like a hyena on a pogo stick.

"Oh, now . . . being mad's not all bad," the shadow with two long ears intones, adding his giggles to the mix. "We could let her eat *us.* Hold her mouth open, and I'll climb in. I've always wanted to see the inside of a stomach."

A paw stuffs itself into my mouth and gags me, nearly cutting off my breath. I chomp down. The intruder jerks free and I spit out the taste of scorched flesh.

"She bites!"

Laughter and howls explode all around.

"Get away from her!" Jeb's outburst shuts them up. He strokes my hair to soothe me. It has the opposite effect. Being close to him makes the hunger pierce my gut—like a thornbush taking root deep inside.

There's nothing funny about the way I feel now. "Jeb, please! I'm so hungry! Feed me or I'll die!"

"Okay, okay—" His voice cracks, and I realize that I've brought him to his knees, after all.

My intestines blaze as if fire ants are gnawing through them. I close my eyes but can still smell the food—everywhere.

After a pause that seems to take forever, something cushiony and cool nudges my lips. I open my mouth, greedy, and take every plump berry that can fit inside. They burst on my tongue, juicy and succulent. Gulping, I beg for more.

Five mouthfuls later, I can concentrate with no more pain.

I sit up, blinking at the tea party guests who have settled at the other end of the table. The rabbit's preoccupied with the pocket watch, dabbing it with a napkin and doling out apologies to Father Time. His white eyes sparkle like marbles as he smiles, his lipless mouth revealing three crooked yellow teeth. The Door Mouse is taking a bath in a teacup, his teensy stained uniform laid out on the saucer. And Hattington—he really is faceless. He keeps flashing from the mouse's likeness to the hare's, as if someone's switching channels between them.

Jeb leans over the table. "You all right?" He looks worried.

Guilt slashes through me for the way I wanted to punish him. "I was . . ."

"Uninhibited and impulsive. In a big way."

I look at the broken plates and crushed food around me. "I have another side to me, Jeb. And I'm not sure it has to do with the curse. I think maybe it's always been there."

He joins our hands. "It's okay that you have a little bad inside. So do I. We're a great match like that." He helps me off the table, folding his arms around my waist. As he kisses my forehead, his labret presses between my eyebrows, cool and comforting.

I pull back. "So, you weren't faking that you want to be with me and not Taelor. This . . . us . . . is real?"

His thumb and forefinger pinch my earlobe gently. He's so quiet and thoughtful, I'm afraid he's not going to answer.

Taking a breath, he looks down. "I dated Tae . . . to try not to think about you. Hoping that it might get you out of my system. Just like with the pencil and sketchbook, it didn't work. Then I wasn't sure if you felt the same way. And if you did, I was afraid of . . ." Jeb studies the cigarette burns on his forearms through the sheer black stripes of his sleeves.

"Go on . . . ," I press.

"Of unloading my baggage on someone as sweet as you."

I can't keep the smile off my lips. "Oh, wow."

"What?"

"I guess we're both oblivious. That's the same reason I kept running from my feelings for you."

"Because I'm sweet?" That dimpled, boyish grin flashes over his face.

Running my fingers through his messy hair, I giggle. "I didn't want to pull you into my family's madness."

A clatter of dishes shakes the other side of the table where the mouse and hare wrestle over a spoon, both trying to see their reflections in the silver.

Jeb cups my jaw, recouping my attention. "Listen, I never meant to hurt Tae. She gets enough crap from her dad. But when she came to pick me up for prom, we had it out. I told her it was over . . . that we should break up. I was just going to keep it quiet for the dance because she asked me to. She'd already bought her dress, and I'd rented a tux, you know? But she knows the truth. That you're it for me, Al. Only you."

They're the most beautiful words I've heard in my life. My stomach feels wonky, like when I was a kid and the merry-go-round at the playground finally stopped spinning and I just lay there facing the swirling sky—dizzy and blissful and exhilarated—until the world came back into perfect clarity. "Oh, Jeb."

He raises my hand and kisses my knuckles. The labret on his lip glistens in the light, reminding me of Morpheus's jeweled eyes. I hate that I let him put doubts into my head about the most devoted guy I've ever known. I can't let Morpheus get to me like that again— ever.

"You're it for me, too." I link my fingers with Jeb's. "I'm sorry for the things I said to you in the Hall of Mirrors. And that I lied to you about Taelor's purse . . . and stealing—"

"Shh." He leans down to kiss me, so tender-sweet, it chases away everything but his touch. "Let's forget it all. Except one thing," he whispers against my lips. "When we go home, can you keep the chain trick? That table dance was very hot." He growls.

I laugh, shivering at the sultry vibration in his chest. He laughs, too, then pulls my hips close and kisses my ears, my temples, my lips—immersing me in a thousand different sensations, each so delicious, I almost forget what I have left to do.

I break our embrace. Jeb's half-lidded expression looks back at me, questioning. "Be right back," I say. I peel off my soiled gloves, cast them aside, and scramble onto the table, stopping beside Hattington. "The vorpal sword. Alice brought it to you, before you were frozen. We need it."

The flat screen of his face blinks, flashing between a reflection of mine and Alice's. The effect is creepy, like a movie screen snapping between two different eras. Jeb steps closer, waiting.

"Sword?" Hattington glances at his two companions. "Either of you remember anything about a sword?" They all burst into chuckles—a sound that rattles me.

"Perhaps you swallowed it, Herman," the hare says between snorts. "Open your mouth, and let's have a look."

"Better take a flare gun," the mouse squeaks. "It's dark and wide as a canyon in there!"

More snorts and giggles.

Jeb grabs the hare by the ears and holds him above the table, ending the laugh-fest. He points to Herman and the mouse. "A little cooperation would go a long way toward you two keeping your hides."

Hattington's face flashes to Jeb's image. "You're barking up the wrong tree, woodchuck." He glances at the mulberry overhead. "Someone sent you on a wild duck chase. Wonder who?"

The leaves rustle, and Morpheus appears at the top of the canopy. "That would be me," he answers, a smirk on his face.

14

CAGES

I shade my eyes to look up at Morpheus, an angry knot forming in my chest. Jeb was right. All he can do is mislead us. "You lied."

His smile fades as Gossamer peeks out from under his hair. "I was misinformed," he says.

Jeb's entire body visibly tenses. "'Misinformed'? You sent Al out here, into danger, on *misinformation*?"

I clamber off the table, fingertips resting on his bunched-up back muscles to calm him.

Morpheus grins again from his perch atop the tree—regal and pompous with his wings spread high, a backdrop of sleek satin shading his pale complexion from the sun. "It was foolish, I know. Taking hearsay for fact. I was in my cocoon when little Alice escaped with the sword. I didn't see for myself what happened. I'd heard through the rumor mill that she came here with it. But now I've learned the truth. The sword has been hidden all this time in the Red castle itself . . . guarded by the bandersnatch."

"Right." Jeb's voice is choked with strained self-control. "And we're just supposed to take your word for that."

"My spy only learned of it today. Alyssa believes me, don't you?" Morpheus trains his gaze on me.

I don't answer. Truth is, I don't trust him.

"Take her silence as a no, bug for brains." Jeb stays focused on the canopy.

"Neither of you is even curious about the battle I waged to keep you safe? Pity the ingratitude." Morpheus straightens his gloves while Gossamer flutters around his jacket, checking for snags. His clothes are rumpled and ravaged, even sooty in places. He's lost his hat and his hair's a shock of wild waves. "Had to torch the dining hall to smoke them all out. But they'll soon be spreading over Wonderland in search of you. Queen Grenadine has a dinner party planned, and she's determined to unveil a new pet to entertain her guests."

Jeb's shoulder blades fidget beneath my palm. "Pet?"

"Grenadine has wanted a replacement for Alice for decades. A caged bird, as it were." Having dropped that bomb, Morpheus takes a graceful leap and glides to the tabletop, landing next to Hattington and crew. "Good to see you fellows again. How was the nap?"

The three netherlings greet Morpheus with hugs and handshakes.

I grab Jeb's hand, my pulse racing. "Do you remember the psych report? Alice told the therapist she'd been in a birdcage for seventy-five years in Wonderland. But she must've come back. She got married and had a family. Or else I wouldn't exist. Right?"

He pulls me close. "I don't know what's happening. But we need to get you out of here quick."

"Now that the curse is broken," I say, although I don't feel any different.

Morpheus seems oblivious to our urgency. He pats Hattington's conformateur. The blank-faced little man comes only to his thigh. "Splendid to have you back among the living, Herman. I'm in dire need of a new Cajolery Hat."

"Can do!" The lid flips closed on the hatmaker's contraption. His bone structure and skull contort and crack into place as the metal pins squeak and mold around his head until he and Morpheus look like a matched set of nesting dolls.

That's why he's the best hatmaker in the realm. He becomes his subject's head and face until he finishes a project, making for the perfect fit. What would that be like? To never have an identity of your own? No wonder they call him mad.

"Mayhap you'd like a derby style?" Hattington says as he feels his temporary cheekbones. "I have some fine red felt back home."

"Hmm . . ." Morpheus brushes soot off his lapel. "I was thinking one of buckram might be nice."

"Hey!" Jeb slams a fist on our end of the table. The group turns to us. "Al's in danger of becoming someone's human parakeet. She's finished what she came to do. Fulfilled the requirements to break the curse. Now we need to get back to our world. Like yesterday."

"Yesterday, you say?" the hatmaker warbles in his bouncing timbre. "Yesterday is doable."

Guffawing, the hare slaps a knee and adds, "Although two yester-days would be impossible."

The Door Mouse snickers, slipping back into his uniform. "No, no! You can retrogress as many yesterdays as you please. Simply walk backward the rest of your life."

They all bend at the waist, holding their ribs as they laugh hys-terically. Their lack of sobriety stuns me, and Jeb looks like he might snap at any minute.

With a flick of his wings, Morpheus lands on the grass beside us. Gossamer nestles in his hair. "There's more bad news, as per your leaving here."

Jeb narrows his gaze. "How can it get any worse?"

"When the Red army raided my home, they found the jabberlock box and stole it back again. It is no longer under my protection, and without the Ivory Queen, her portal will remain closed. That makes it ever more imperative we get the sword and defeat Grenadine and her king."

Jeb inches closer to Morpheus. "And how do you propose we defeat them when the sword is at their castle under the keep of some mutant watchdog?"

I grip his shoulder from behind, reminding him to use restraint. Morpheus is our only ally, however infuriating his tactics are.

"All is not lost," Morpheus says. "Chessie can subdue the bander-snatch since his other half resides within." He tickles his sprite's tiny swinging feet with his finger. "You will get Chessie's head for me. He'll have full control, and I can steal the sword and defeat Grenadine, then send you both home via whichever portal you like, Red or White."

"No!" Jeb lunges in a move so swift, it almost jerks my arm out of its socket. He catches Morpheus by his lacy shirt and lifts him onto tiptoe so his wings drag on the ground. Gossamer dangles from a strand of blue hair. "This is all a ploy to get Al to do another 'task.' Right? Another *test*. What I want to know is what she's being tested for. What happens when she passes them all?"

Smug, Morpheus taps Jeb's fingers, one by one, as if he were playing a flute. "Ah. Gossamer's been running her little pretty mouth again, aye? Jealous little nymph." The sprite scrambles off his shoulder and flitters into the tree overhead. "You know, you should never trust a woman with green skin. Just ask any man who's had a hangover from absinthe." Morpheus gazes at me. "All I've ever wanted is to free Alyssa and return her to her proper place."

"And where would that be?" Jeb moves his head in front of me so Morpheus has to look at him.

"Her home, of course." The jewels at the edges of Morpheus's tattoos turn clear and sparkle like liquid, mimicking the sincerity of real tears. "I'd like nothing more than to get Chessie's head myself. But, because of our misunderstanding over the moth spirits I harbor, the Twid Sisters and I aren't on the best of terms. They'll not let me set foot nor wing anywhere close to their gate."

"Wait." I step up. "What does this have to do with the cemetery?"

"That's where Chessie's head resides," Morpheus answers. "Because he's technically 'partly' dead, he was able to find solace there. So the solution is simple: Save the cat to subdue the bandersnatch, free the Ivory Queen with the sword, and then you get to go home."

"What a load of crap." Jeb shoves Morpheus away. His netherling wings swipe wide, maintaining his balance before he crashes into a chair. Gossamer drifts down from the leaves, hovering over him.

Jeb takes my hand. "Let someone else go after the cat. Al's in danger out here. We need to hide until we can get home. She's done everything you asked. The curse is broken, right?"

Morpheus looks at me, not Jeb. "What good is breaking the curse if you never go home? If Alison never sees her daughter again, she'll be worse off than she is now. Her insanity will no longer be an act."

I shudder. Morpheus is right. Alison would never forgive herself if I was lost for her sake.

Morpheus glances over his shoulder toward where the tea party crew argues over who gets to drink the mouse's bathwater from the hare's boot. The edge of his mouth curls. "The inner garden is hallowed to our kind. We're forbidden to walk upon those grounds. You're the only ones I can send."

I squeeze Jeb's hand, hating what I'm about to say. "We have no choice, then. We'll go."

Jeb presses my knuckles to his chest. "No. I'll go. You fly back with bug snot."

"Of course," Morpheus interrupts, his voice edged with something between sarcasm and suggestiveness. "I'll be happy to take Alyssa back with me. We can pick up where we left off in my bedroom, right, luv?"

I scowl at him.

Jeb pushes me aside and snaps out the Swiss Army knife, the blade pressed against Morpheus's sternum. "Better idea. Give Al her wish—now."

My stomach turns. "Jeb, I won't leave without you."

"It won't come to that." He slides the blade up to Morpheus's throat. "You can wish you never came at all. You'll still be the subject of the wish, and it'll get us both out of this. I never would've come if I hadn't seen you leap into that mirror."

He's right. That would work. The only problem is, I'll have done this for nothing: Alison will still get shock therapy and my family will be cursed again because I'll have never come to fix things.

"Give it to her," Jeb says, "or she'll have a king-size moth to use in her next masterpiece. Got me?"

Gossamer flies in Jeb's face in a frenzy of wings. Her distraction gives Morpheus a chance to catch Jeb's wrist and hold him back. "I don't have the wish," he seethes. "It fell out while I was trying to save your bloody little lives, and now it's in the hands of Rabid White."

Jeb twists his arm free. "Lies."

"Doesn't matter," Morpheus answers, watching Jeb warily. "Alyssa wouldn't use her wish so lightly. Elsewise, her family will forever suffer the curse she risked life and limb to break. "

The heat from Morpheus's knowing gaze is a thousand times worse than the spotlights on the miner's caps at Underland, and there's nowhere to hide my bared soul. "He's right."

Jeb glares at me. "You've gotta be kidding. Your mom wouldn't want you in danger!"

I look down at my boots. "Why are we talking about this? He said he doesn't have the wish, anyway."

Jeb's laugh has a bite of venom behind it. "That's amazing. You just keep playing into his hands." His face hardens. "You know what I'd do if I had a wish? I'd wish you would trust me like you used to. The way you trust him now."

The insinuation cuts deep. He can't really believe that. Can he?

Jeb turns to Morpheus, brandishing the knife's blade again. "Anything goes wrong—she gets even a scratch—and I'll gut you from head to toe." Forcing himself to pull back, he turns to retrieve our backpack.

"Get directions to the graveyard," he says to me before he moves to the edge of the hill, stopping at the border of the chessboard desert. He snaps the army knife closed and looks off into the distance with all the patience and composure of a wild, caged animal while Gossamer flutters around him.

"Your boyfriend has some real trust issues," Morpheus baits.

"Shut up. He had a rough childhood."

"He should be grateful he had one at all."

"Stop fishing for sympathy. You had a childhood. I was there, remember?"

The black marks around Morpheus's eyes crinkle in a snide grin. "No, Alyssa. It was poor little Alice I was referring to."

"What do you mean by that?"

"You will need a weapon." Morpheus sidesteps the question. Reaching a gloved hand into his jacket, he digs around in an inner pocket and draws out a small, thin cylinder of wood. He turns it, revealing holes in the body and a mouthpiece at one end.

"A flute? How's that supposed to protect us?" I ask.

Morpheus steps closer and tucks the cylinder into my blouse. He slides it against my bare skin until it fits snugly in my cleavage. Gossamer must be distracting Jeb, or he would've already thrown the jerk off the hill. Personally, I'm considering shoving the instrument up his nose.

His gaze holds me in check. Somewhere behind the fathomless black glitter is sincerity, maybe even concern. My heart pounds against the flute's cool, smooth wood.

"Let us hope you remember those music lessons your mumsy

had you take." Morpheus leans his hip against the table. His wings relax behind him. "A cello should suffice for knowing the musical scale. You've played one instrument, you've played them all, aye?"

For the first time, it hits me point-blank. "You're the reason she wanted me to play."

"Even though she hoped with all her heart you would never come here, she still prepared you, just the same. And thus far, you've proven yourself gloriously capable. How proud she would've been of your antics upon the table earlier."

A blush creeps hotly into my cheeks. Did he see my dance? Or maybe he's referring to my barbaric race to eat the Door Mouse. The possibilities are equally unsettling. "You were watching?"

"By the by . . ." He glances at Jeb's back and leans closer, murmuring low. "Tumtum juice alters a person's inhibitions, magnifies their hunger. But it's not hunger for food. It's experiences they crave. Had it been me instead of your toy soldier, I would've found a means to slake your ravenous hunger without resorting to berries."

His arrogance simmers my blood. "You don't have the equipment to satisfy anything. *Moth*. Remember?"

He laughs, dark and soft, under his breath. "I am a man in every way that counts. Just like you are a woman, even if some people believe you're nothing more than a scared little girl in constant need of saving."

I ignore the barb. "Of course. You're an expert on women." Ivory's lovesick ogling from behind the glass plane bobs to the surface of my thoughts. That strange, possessive pang follows, but I suppress it.

"Do I sense jealousy?"

"As if."

He smiles, dragging a wing over his shoulder to preen it. "I've been in this form for some time. I had to get some practice in. But only one lady is my equal in every way. Intellectually, physically, magically."

"It's all about her, isn't it?" My envy is almost palpable. "You'd endanger anyone to have her in your arms."

"Absolutely, I would."

"I hate you."

"Only because of the way I make you feel."

My fingernails eat into my palms. "Only because you bring out the worst in me."

"Oh no, luv. I bring out the *life* in you." His intense gaze pulls me in. The lullaby trills through my blood, carrying my pulse on its rhythm: *"Little blossom in peach and gray, grew up strong and found your way; two things more yet to be seen, until at last you'll . . ."*

The ending to his verse—that final puzzle piece—still drifts just out of my reach. I squeeze my temples to shake him from my head. My fingertip grazes my hairpin, and it pinches. "Just stop it!" I snap at him. "Where is the cemetery?"

Gossamer comes back to light on Morpheus's shoulder as he points down. "After the abyss . . . just there."

He indicates a drop in the chessboard sands at the edge of the dune, not too far from where Jeb's standing. It's hard to make out from here, but it appears to be a fissure in the earth.

"There's an abyss?" I ask, more doubtful by the second.

"It separates the desert from the valley—a bit too wide for a mortal to leap across. The cemetery is on the other side. It's cloaked in a thicket of vines and ivy that protects the spirits from sunlight."

My courage does an about-face at the thought of trudging through some dark thicket filled with ghosts—netherling or otherwise—but I rein in my fears. Jeb will be there; I won't be alone.

"Unless you can find a way across the chasm," Morpheus continues, "you will have to hike on foot. Take the upper ridge that winds around it."

The ridge's sands seem to stretch on forever. If we go around, it could take a day. Maybe two. We don't have that kind of time if we're going to stop Alison's treatments. I'm about to object when the Door Mouse shouts out: "Jubjub birds!"

Gossamer tunnels into Morpheus's hair as he flaps his wings hard, taking to the sky. The back draft rushes through me on a licorice-scented gust. The tea party crew scrambles into the hare's cottage and slams the door shut. Puffs of black-and-white dust rise in the distance.

The dust clouds clear to reveal an army of card guards riding birds. Huge ones, built like ostriches with peacock tails and the heads and wings of giant grasshoppers. Although the birds can't seem to fly, their long legs cover the distance between us with ease. It's like a swarm of mutant grasshoppers coming to devour us.

I'll never kill another bug as long as I live . . .

Heart striking my ribs like a gong, I yell up at Morpheus, "Help us!"

"Beware the shifting sands," he shouts back. "Use the flute if you need to gain ground. Assuming you make it to the valley, head straight for the cemetery gate. The army won't follow you within." He swoops away in the opposite direction of our attackers. Gone. Just like that.

Assuming we make it? I'm so outraged, my eyes burn. "You swore you wouldn't leave me again! Your wings are going to shrivel up, you coward!" I scream.

But you aren't hurt . . . yet.

It's his voice, though I'm not sure if it's from my memory or if he's still in my head. Either way, I'd forgotten about the stipulation to his life-magic vow. He's the master of technicalities.

A hammering shatters the air. I turn to see Jeb pounding the wooden tea wagon against the tree trunk. Before it even registers what he's doing, he's separated two of the shelves from the frame. He pushes his bangs out of his face and flips the boards over to study the bottoms. They're smooth and seamless with a slight upward curve on the ends.

He holds one out to me. "Let's go!"

I take the piece of wood, confused.

Jeb shoulders the backpack, sprints to the edge of the dune a few feet away, and places his shelf on the ground at the border where the sandy slope begins. With one shoe on the wood to tilt it downward, he turns to me. "Now, skater girl!"

I run to him, arms trembling as I settle my board into place. He expects us to ride down on the boards—like sand surfing. But doesn't he see the chasm between the desert and the valley?

The end of the slope slants upward, like a launch ramp. He can't possibly expect us to . . .

"Today you master an ollie," Jeb says, finishing my thought.

My pulse drums in my neck. "No way."

"No choice." He reaches out his hand. "If we start to fall, use your magic trick. Make the boards float across the chasm."

"What if I can't? I broke the curse, fixed all of Alice's mistakes. Maybe I'm me again."

"You still look like one of them. I'm betting you don't go back to normal until we get through that portal. At this point, what do we have to lose?" His hand waits for me.

I grasp it and glance behind us. Clouds of dust consume the slope as the army overtakes the hill. They'll be at the plateau any second now. I squint against the swirling grit.

Close up, the incline is about three times steeper than the skate bowl's highest drop in Underland, and I've never even scaled the top of that one. We're so high, my vision swims, and my knees go all buttery.

"Whoa." Jeb wraps an arm around my waist to balance me.

"Jeb . . ." I hold his wrist. "We'll get separated."

"Won't happen." He unclips one end of the metal chain hanging from his belt loops. He unwinds it, leaving the other end still locked on his pants. By latching the chain to a ring on my belt, he forms a lifeline. When stretched out, the links allow a three-foot span between us while still providing security.

"Ready?" he asks, looking over his shoulder at our impending captors.

"Yeah." But my pitching stomach screams, "No."

Every part of me begs to turn back . . . to run in the opposite direction. But the Jubjub birds screech from behind—as earsplitting as giant pterodactyls from some prehistoric soundtrack—and raise the hairs on my neck.

I slide my foot on top of the wood.

"Now!" Jeb shouts.

My stomach falls as we shove off together and plummet into the checkered depths.

LIFELINES

The first half of the drop swoops by in a blinding rush. We stay ahead of our attackers, the wood gliding smoothly over the sand. By tweaking the pressure with our feet and legs, we control our direction and speed. My muscles fall into a familiar rhythm, distracting me from how high we are.

The rush of wind lifts my braided hair to flap behind me. Beneath my erratic pulse, a sense of hope nudges—quiet, easy, and strong. Is this what Morpheus meant by finding tranquility amid the madness?

My tentative smile stretches out to Jeb, and he winks in encouragement. His hair thrashes in black waves around his head. Sunlight glows through the strands like a halo. He's like some rebel guardian angel.

"We'll launch at the same time," he says across to me. "When we hit the other side, we'll unsnap the chain so we can roll into the landing without getting tangled."

I nod. A yank at my belt reassures me I'm safe . . . that we're locked together.

Behind us, the gallops and screeches escalate. Nervousness tugs against my chest. I breathe in dust vapors and stifle a cough, watching the chasm come into view.

The valley on the other side has a clearing of plush grass before the thicket overtakes it. That should cushion our landing and slow our momentum enough that we can get to our feet and scramble to safety.

We can pull this off without any magic. We just have to make our acceleration count this last half . . . gather enough velocity to launch into an ollie that will carry us across the space.

Which means it has to be a straight shot from here on out.

I prep my feet, positioning my back heel to smack against the tail of the board and my front toes to pull up on the nose when it's time. A bump knocks the bottom of my board, and I bounce slightly, veering off course and losing precious speed. Jeb skirts toward me to coach me back on route. Then the same thing happens to him, his board bucking hard enough that he almost loses his balance.

He guides himself back into place. "Something's moving under the sand!" he shouts.

Another thump jolts through my feet. Morpheus's warning of shifting sands whispers in the back of my mind. As Jeb and I struggle to stay on our boards, the black-and-white squares we've been sliding on shift, collide, and converge—snapping the terrain into a jagged jigsaw puzzle, as if a thousand tiny earthquakes have buckled the landscape. Déjà vu hits me. It's just like my dream.

Our boards come to a complete halt where the squares intersect and fold. We slump in place, panting. The queen's army makes its way toward us, the giant birds picking paths around the uneven surface.

The sun beats down. We're totally exposed with nowhere to run. Above is the army . . . below a chasm too wide to leap across from a standstill. The first row of riders tops the ridge and stirs a whirlwind of sand, which plumes into a mushroom cloud, then puffs down to envelop us. I cover my nose and mouth. The birds are close enough that their powerful gallops thunder through the wood under my soles.

"Pick up the board and use it for a weapon when the dust clears!" Jeb's command barely leaves his mouth before I remember the flute. Morpheus said to use it if we needed to gain ground.

He knew this would happen . . .

He's behind the scenes and pulling strings like he's always been.

I take the instrument out and lift the mouthpiece to my lips, blowing as I tap my fingers across the holes in a pattern that plays out the melody of his lullaby. Though I've never attempted to use a flute—and wind instruments are a completely different animal than string ones—the notes come to me effortlessly.

Jeb gawks, as shocked as I am. If he only knew the half of it . . . how long this song has been dormant inside me.

The tune echoes over the chaos—loud and magical. As soon as the last note fades, a clatter explodes behind our pursuers. In a sweep of dingy gray, a thousand clams come rushing like a landslide over the ridge, carrying the queen's army on the surge.

The flute slips from my hand and gets whisked away. Jubjub birds who've lost their footing, and fallen guards attempting to scale the clams like mountain goats clambering for ledges, are also caught up in the rattling flood. The shells part like the Red Sea on either side of Jeb and me, leaving us untouched. They still remember what we did for them.

We're not going to be captured, but we've already lost our chance at acceleration. We'll never make it across the chasm now, and the climb back up—with the terrain so jagged—could take hours. I've lost track of time in all the excitement. We might've been here for hours already.

"Get on your board!" Jeb positions himself in front of me, shouting over the cacophony. "We're going to jump onto the clams; somehow they're clearing the chasm . . . we'll hitch a ride to the cemetery."

I watch the clams as they fly across the rift to safety by using the jacked-up Wonderland physics to their advantage. They catch the Red army in their momentum and forcibly tilt their shells to chuck the Jubjub birds and guards into the depths like trash from a car window. For a split second, I worry they might do the same to us. But I have to believe they won't. They came in answer to the flute and are here to help.

Jeb bends his thighs like he's doing squats. He's getting ready to jump on. "At the count of three," he says. He levers his board several inches above the clams and props his left foot atop it while balancing his right on solid ground.

"One . . ." His voice spurs me into action. I hold my slab of wood aloft in one hand and mimic his stance, balanced on one foot and ready to drop my board when he does. "Two . . ." My free hand curls around the chain hanging from Jeb's belt loop. "Three!"

Simultaneously, as if we've practiced the move a hundred times before, we slap our boards onto the advancing shells with our one foot already in place and shove off with the other to blend into the flow. This ride isn't nearly as smooth as the sand surfing. My board bumps from one clam to another, hurdling over a card guard here and there. Each impact jiggles the chain and juggles my bones. My skeleton will be as cragged as the landscape before long.

Our speed picks up as the chasm draws nearer. My heartbeat is in my throat, drumming against my larynx.

"Grab the board, and don't look down!" Jeb yells over his shoulder.

I grip the wood with my free hand and draw up my knees as we launch. I'm holding so tightly to the chain links that my fingers feel like they're made of metal, too.

Eyes closed, I gulp the fishy air surrounding us, trying to ease my fear.

"Wooooo-hoooo!" Jeb's cheer forces my eyes open.

For one instant, I believe in the impossible. We're soaring— crouched on our boards—just a few feet away from the valley's edge, and it looks like we're going to clear. I'm not even using any magic. It must have something to do with the curve of the shells and the curve on our boards, because the same bizarre gravitational lapse that's allowing the clams to soar is working in our favor, too. The wood is actually floating on its own. Wind rushes through me and I lift my chin to the sky, drifting into the blueness that surrounds us. I'm buoyant, and it's amazing.

"Woo-hoo!" I mimic Jeb's triumphant cry. He casts a glance over his shoulder, grinning.

I smile back, no longer scared, until Jeb breaks our gaze to look ahead and my attention drops down.

The chasm isn't endless. That would be so much better than seeing the corpses below us. We're about twenty stories up, a front-row seat to the gore and carnage. The remnants of our pursuers hang in bits and pieces along the spikes of rock that jut out where the sides of the canyon narrow toward the bottom.

Wooziness bleeds into my periphery. My balance careens out of control and I topple off my levitating board.

I inhale a soundless scream. Jeb hasn't noticed yet. A whimper lodges in my throat as I fumble to unhook him from my belt, determined not to kill us both. The chain's latch won't budge, and he's jerked down. He passes me with a shout.

I attempt to yell back, but my lungs suck all the sound inside me. Jeb's weight tugs at my waist, and the sides of the canyon pass in a rush of jagged stone. He drops the backpack to try to delay our descent.

It feels like we're falling in slow motion. I see our deaths in excruciating detail. Jeb will be the first to hit, his limbs and torso ripped apart as he bounces from one craggy outcropping to another. Then my head will hit a stone and burst like an overripe melon.

Outrage and regret almost incapacitate me, until something clicks inside . . . an indescribable knowing.

I. Can. Fly.

The memory of my grandmother Alicia's leap through a hospital window blinks on in my mind. Maybe she didn't jump from high enough. Her wings didn't have time to burst through her skin.

As if triggered by the thought, there's an itch at my shoulder blades. Then a sensation like razors slicing my skin. The screams earlier clogged in my throat break loose as something erupts from behind each shoulder, like umbrellas popping open.

Jeb tugs on the chain and shouts, "Al! You've got wings! *Use them!*"

I recall Morpheus's words from the feast. *"Stop thinking with your head, Alyssa."*

So instead, I think with my gut. By clenching my shoulders and arching my spine, I control the thrust of my new appendages. Two seconds before Jeb reaches the first jutting rock that would've torn him to shreds, we stall in midair.

Wow.

Jeb whoops his gratitude from below. "You're beautiful, baby!" He's so relieved, he laughs. I do, too, until I start to lose altitude. I hold the chain with both hands and flap harder to counteract Jeb's drag. My waist feels like it might break in half.

"Lower me." His voice sobers and carries on the wind. "I'm too heavy for you." Dust coats his pants and the cross on his thigh has lost enough jewels that it looks more like an inverted L. The fabric of his shirt gapes at his elbows, where there are bloody cuts and welts from pushing himself off the canyon's walls to miss jutting rocks.

The chasm narrows, and it's obvious my wings won't fit. We'd have to separate before his feet even touch bottom. It's no higher a drop than from the trees we used to climb as kids, but I can't leave him. I won't.

"I can fly us up," I stall, trying to envision that the chains are alive . . . that they wind around him and lift him on their own. Either I'm too nervous for the magic to work or he's too heavy, because I can't make headway.

"Uh-uh," Jeb says. He sways to the left and props his feet on a boulder to help support his weight. "I dropped the backpack and the money. We have to get it. My girlfriend's not spending summer break in juvie."

His girlfriend. Just hearing that makes me push harder. I try to grasp the boards floating above with my mind. If I could snag one, I could guide it down for Jeb to use as a ride back up.

They drift across to the valley, as if purposely ignoring me. My new wings strain with the effort to catch them, and my spine tilts and stretches. I yelp.

"Stop hurting yourself!" Jeb loses his balance and swings below me, side to side, like a pendulum. "Either you lower me, or I take off this chain and free fall. Your choice." His fingers hover at his waist.

"But I can't come with you!"

"So you're going to drop me here, and then find something. Rope, vines . . . an extension for the chain that can pull me out. Okay?"

"All right," I say, wishing it really was all right.

He nods, and I ease him down along the canyon wall, offering an anchor line from the sky, just like the times we went rappelling.

Lowering him is the hardest thing I've ever done. Not only because of the icy dread winding inside my chest, but because my wings have to alternate between the rigidness of a hang glider and the relaxed swoops of a bird to pilot us through the maze of rocks.

"How're you holding up?" I attempt to sound lighthearted.

"Other than a colossal wedgie?" he squeaks out in a deliberately high-pitched voice. "My boxers have stretched five sizes."

I snort halfheartedly. "Karmic payback for those Boy Scouts you hammered in seventh grade."

He laughs, though it echoes hollowly in the chasm.

My wings stutter as I clench the chain with both hands to counteract his drag.

"We're almost there." His words have a serious edge to them now. "Am I getting too heavy?"

"I'm good," I manage. Sweat dribbles from my hairline as I feed him through to the narrow opening at the bottom. He's collected a few more scrapes along the way but doesn't complain.

We've made it as far as we can go together. Even though there's only a three-foot span between us, it might as well be a football field. We can't touch. I can't hover any lower without scraping my wings against the cliff walls, and he's balanced between two rocks holding him centered above his drop. From here, the fall looks less intimidating. But it's not the drop I'm worried about. What if I can't find a way to pull him out?

"Al . . ." We meet gazes, and I see something new in his eyes. Astonishment mixed with reverence. He shakes his head. "Your wings are amazing. Do they hurt?"

"No." Fluttering in place, I reach back and touch a shoulder blade through the blouse's slit. "I'm not even bleeding. They just feel heavy. Like I'm wearing a huge backpack."

"But you look like you're in pain."

I grip the taut chains, our one solid connection, wishing it could be his fingers interlocking with mine. My eyes sting. "Jeb, what if I mess up your rescue?"

"Not gonna happen." He loops his fingers through the links on his end. "You remember when my father died . . . that night?"

I nod.

"We came over to your house. Your dad made us hot chocolate. He went to bed after a while. Jen and Mom fell asleep on the couch. But you and I sat up in the kitchen and talked until five in the morning."

I'm not sure where he's going with this. It's not making me feel any better about leaving him. To be reminded of how much he was hurting makes my insides feel as heavy as bricks.

"You lifted me out of the darkest night of my life," he says. "Even after, you were the one who kept me going. You went skateboarding with me every day, texted me all the time."

"Came over to watch you work on your bike and paint."

Our gazes touch in a way we can't, and rough and sturdy Jebediah Holt looks vulnerable. "You're the best friend I've ever had. Even if things get screwed up, you'll still find a way to help me."

His faith makes me sob. "I don't want to do this without you."

He glances at my wings, and his mouth tightens into a stern line. It's obvious he's fighting the urge to pull me down to him. "One thing Morpheus didn't lie about . . . you can take care of yourself. I should've already realized that, since you've been taking care of me for years. So, be tough, Alyssa Victoria Gardner."

My chest swells with hope. He actually makes me believe I can do it. "Okay."

"And Al," he says, his jaw tight. "No matter what happens, we'll find each other again. You're my lifeline. You always will be."

The sentiment spurs the strangest reaction in my heart—breaks it and heals it all in the same breath. Before I can respond, he releases the chain. I've been flapping so hard to hold us both steady that, with the lessened weight, I catapult up from the chasm as if on a bungee cord.

The propulsion forces me against the wind. My braids whip around my face, bringing back the image of Alison fighting her hair in the asylum's courtyard. But I won't be the victim she was. I'll embrace the power she kept running from. It's the only thing that can keep me alive and get me back to Jeb.

I slap my hair aside and angle my wings to steer a turn toward the valley. My fear of heights returns, and I dip too low, too fast. The grassy ground races up to meet me, and I scream.

I squeeze my eyes shut. A jolting slam rocks my bones upon impact, and I roll into a ball to ride out the momentum. My wings and the chain twirl and tangle around me—so tight I can hardly move my limbs by the time I trundle to a stop.

Wiggling to make sure nothing's broken, I splay my palms against my wings, straining to free my face. The very things that saved my and Jeb's lives are now suffocating me like a straitjacket. Each breath pulls the milky membrane tighter against my nostrils and lips.

Air still filters through, but, smothered in a cocoon, I can't see anything around me. A rank smell seeps in, as if I've fallen into a raw-sewage treatment plant. Hot puffs of breath circle my body. Something is surrounding me . . . sniffing me. Panic shrinks my lungs.

I play dead as ropes wrap my ankles and drag me. A scream struggles to break out. I smother it, and it burns in my chest.

I'm moving downhill, which means I'm being pulled away from the chasm, toward the cemetery thicket at the lower end of the valley.

Three things are wrong with this scenario: I'm trapped with no chance to fight or see what's dragging me; I'm getting hauled farther away from Jeb; and, last but not least, I'm about to be alone, deep inside Wonderland's garden of souls, with nothing but dead things for company.

HUSH

Escape is futile. No matter how hard I concentrate on the chains and rope that bind me, I can't animate them. I'm too distracted by the claustrophobia.

I try to tell myself I'm wrapped in a snuggly blanket, but my brain's not buying it. When we finally come to a stop, my wings ache and my back and tailbone throb from the uneven terrain we bulldozed on the way here.

I breathe quietly as a strange argument takes place over me.

"Stupidesses! Stupid, stupid! She usn't smellum deadish!"

"But she lookum deadses. She lookum it!"

Bad news is, they've figured out I'm alive. Worse news, I can't be sure about *them*. Their decomposing stench burns my throat. They don't sound very big. Maybe they're pygmy zombies.

I creep myself out with that thought and have to suppress a whimper.

The ropes loosen around my ankles. They'll have me out of my winged cocoon soon. Then I'll have to face whatever they are. Nervous anticipation makes my pulse jump.

"Usses are only to brung the deadses. Twids usn't approve of 'stakes being missed," one of the creatures says shrilly.

"Missing 'stakes aren't the worsest of our oblems-prob."

"Eps and yesses. Mistakens usn't our aults, f's or any other. Sister One asks usses to brung her here."

"Asks or notses, Sister Two will hang usses by our necks! No iving-lees are to be brunged. No breathers or talkeresses. None, none, none!"

Their language is a mix between pig latin and utter nonsense. The best I can tell, they work for the Twid Sisters as the gatherers of dead things. They're worried Sister Two won't be pleased that something living has been brought onto the hallowed grounds. Sounds like she might hang them for that mistake. If they think on it long enough, they might decide to *make* me dead to save themselves.

I clench my teeth to stave off a stab of fear. Maybe Sister One won't let them hurt me, since she assigned them my capture. Which raises a new question: Why did she want me here?

A distant thrum of thunder rolls through my bones. I force myself to breathe, inhaling the scent of moist earth over the stench of my captors. The cemetery must be watertight, because rain's hitting what sounds like leaves overhead, but I'm not getting wet.

What if Jeb is in the middle of the storm? What if he gets caught in a mudslide?

I've got to get back to him. I can use the rope around my ankles as an extension to the chain.

My captors are still arguing about what to do with me, and the reality hits that no one's going to come to my rescue here. It's up to me to save myself.

Insecurity sinks its teeth in, vicious and biting.

But wait. I'm no stranger to this world—I'm acquainted with its secrets. Maybe that was only in my dreams, but I still learned things that have saved me more than once on this journey. I'm not the helpless and vulnerable little girl I was when I used to play here.

I'm not even the same girl I was when I arrived in the rabbit hole with Jeb. I'm stronger.

For one, I have wings now; and, as I've seen with Morpheus, they can be used for more than just flying. They can be weapons and shields.

Hoping for the benefit of surprise, I thrash my legs where the ropes are loose. The creatures ricochet off my bucking shins, no heavier than guinea pigs.

They scream as I shift to my side and the chain jingles to the ground. I unlatch it from my belt and my wings snap open. Gasping air into my lungs, I kick out my legs and roll to my feet, keeping a brave front in case the creatures are like dogs and can smell fear. I even manage a decent roar while I balance my weight against the new appendages.

The creatures scurry around my feet, hissing. They're wearing tiny miner's caps, and the lights bob all around like reflections from a disco ball, disorienting me.

I immediately recognize them from the Wonderland website.

They're like the paintings of pixies trapped in cages, crying silver tears—gruesome yet fascinating.

Their long tails and primate faces remind me of spider monkeys, except for their hairless hides. Silver slime oozes from their bald skin, the origin of the noxious scent I've been gagging on. Their bulbous eyes are silver, too, with no pupils or irises, so they glimmer like wet coins—almost glaring, even in the dim light.

Oily droplets trail their footsteps. A glance at my feet reveals the same silvery slick residue around my boots. They must have used their tails to drag me here, not ropes, which means I'll need to find another way to make a cable for Jeb.

A few of the pixies pause at my feet and look from the chain to me, debating whether it's worth the effort to bind me again. I pick up the links, then swoop my wings low to bowl the creatures over, stomping my feet for good measure. The pixies squirm into some hedges where the others have already hidden.

Whimpers shake the leaves, along with flashes of light from their caps. The creatures sound more scared than I feel.

I'm in a covered garden, dark and musty. Over to my left, I spot a smattering of glittery items—from bracelets and necklaces to unset jewels—and a pile of bones along with several reels the size of bicycle tires filled with gold, shimmery thread. I'm reminded of the creepy staircase Jeb and I climbed down to get into the heart of Wonderland; it could've been built from these materials. Maybe the jewelry is the pixies' payment for their creations.

I pick up a reel of gold and tug on the thread. Though it looks elegant and fragile, it's deceptively strong, like telephone cord. Strong enough to hold Jeb's weight.

As I loop the chain through the hole in the middle of the reel to fashion a sling, a few of the pixies scurry out to drag the remaining reels, bones, and jewelry into their hiding places, hissing at me.

I size them up, searching my memory for anything Morpheus taught me about them, trying to assess if they're a threat. I remember a sketch he drew. How his long, elegant fingers pointed to their likenesses. He said they're docile and shy and love anything that glitters. Like snakes, they shed their skin when they grow, but, unlike snakes', their skin decomposes in greasy patches before falling off, giving them a unique rapport with the dead. In fact, they feel more at home with corpses than living things.

I'm nothing but a novelty to them. They have no reason to hurt me. The staccato beat of my heart slows.

I turn on my heel, looking for an exit. The wings tangle under my boots, causing me to step all over them. Twinges of pain shoot through my spine and shoulders, proof the appendages are attached to my skeleton.

A few wayward giggles shake the bushes and I glare at my invisible audience while freeing myself. My wings can't stretch all the way up, due to the low-hanging thorny vines and briars of the roof.

I pull a wing over my right shoulder to make sure I didn't hurt it. Contact with the veinlike cross sections sends pulses through my back. It's like touching sunlight and webs. Warm, ethereal, but not sticky . . . fine-spun.

I'm struck by how something so delicate can give me such a sense of power. My wings are not black like Morpheus's. They're closer to white frosted glass with spots of glittery jewels that blink every color of the rainbow like the jewels under his eyes. The pattern reminds me of butterflies.

Butterfly. Ironic, that all these years Dad has called me that. Now I really am one. A trapped butterfly.

I look around again. The air down here is motionless and clammy. Judging from the sharp-cornered hedges, I'm smack in the middle of a garden labyrinth worthy of any gothic suspense novel. There are three openings branching off from here. One of them is my escape route.

Rain slams harder on the leaves overhead. I have to hurry.

Slinging the chain and reel over my shoulder and underneath my wing, I jingle a warning to the pixies for good measure—*I won't go down without a fight*—then choose the opening on my right, where a soft glow radiates. I weave my way through the maze, stopping to work the chain free from underbrush each time it gets snagged.

Soon the path branches off again, this time to five options—all equally bright. I take the opening in the middle and keep moving.

Ten steps in, and I plunge through an archway, ending up where I first started. The pixies have crawled out of hiding. Their miner's caps bounce light all around as they snicker. I glare at them and they scrabble back to the hedges, leaving oily tracks behind.

Maybe it's time to bargain for some answers.

Taking off my belt, I wave it in front of the hedges so the dim light catches the rubies. "I'll give this to whoever shows me the way out of the maze."

Murmurs erupt, but no one volunteers. I plop to my knees and part the leaves at the base of the closest hedge. A set of reflective eyes peers back from the depths. The light on the creature's cap is turned off.

"Hi." I amp up the charm, trying to be diplomatic like I was with the ferret creature at Morpheus's banquet. It's not easy when the subject smells like rotting meat. I thread the belt through the leaves, letting the pixie see the jewels up close. "Pretty, right?"

It yanks the belt out of my hand and dons the accessory like a scarf. Petting the sparkly rubies, it purrs.

"Do you know why Sister One wants me here?" I ask.

The pixie blinks its long lashes demurely. Its eyelids are vertical, closing side to side like stage curtains before snapping open again. Just plain freaky.

"Usses usn't know," it murmurs.

"Okay." I can buy that. "But Sister Two *doesn't* want me here, right?"

The creature shudders in answer.

"Then help me get out, and the big bad sister will never know. You won't get strung up that way. Make sense?"

The pixie nods. "Uses the ee-kay, sparkly talkeress," it whispers before withdrawing deeper into the leaves.

"The key?" I ask aloud. He can't mean the one Jeb left in the rabbit hole door. But what other key is there?

In my dream, Morpheus called my birthmark a key when he showed me how to open the diamond tree.

I shove my wings out of the way to sit down, peel off both my boots, and wiggle my toes, rubbing the swollen arches of my feet. I've been wearing platforms for way too long. Two days straight now. Is that right?

I can't remember.

Frowning, I roll up the leggings on my left leg until I see the birthmark. I'm reminded of how my skin reacted to Jeb's touch when he caressed my ankle in the living room. And then how it felt in that moment Morpheus pressed his flesh to mine to heal me.

Jeb is stable, strong, and genuine—my knight in shining armor. Morpheus is selfish, unreliable, and transcendent—chaos incarnate. Impossible to compare.

Yet here I am, all of those things. Both light and dark at the same time. If I were to give in to one side of me, would that mean I'd have to give up the other? My heart aches at the possibility. Somehow I feel like I need both to be complete.

I study the birthmark and shut down any other thoughts. It's possible that this is a map of the maze I'm in. The pigmentation follows a continuous right curve and winds into itself. Assuming I'm in the very middle of the maze, I'll need to take left turns to get out again.

Unless I'm looking at the thing upside down.

Disorientation makes my head spin. The feeling of being trapped constricts my chest again. I stand, holding my boots by their laces in one hand and the chain and reel in the other. If I just keep going left, I'll end up somewhere eventually. I hope . . .

"You guys coming?" I ask the pixies. As strange as they are, their company comforts me. Leaves rattle from behind when I start through the left opening. I step wide to avoid prickly patches in the ground cover. My companions follow in my footsteps, little lights bobbing, and I imagine how comical our caravan must look. If Jeb were here, he'd come up with some funny nickname for the pixies.

My smile at the thought is bittersweet. *Just be okay, Jeb. I'm coming.*

It's too quiet with only the rain pattering above us, and I consider talking to my pixie companions, maybe even the hedges. Silence isn't all I once thought it would be. Throughout most of my adolescent life, I tried to shut out the bugs and plants, longing to fit in. But I'm starting to think I might need those other voices in order to fit into my own skin. In order to be myself.

I feel the same way about my wings . . .

I flew.

I. Flew.

I wasn't afraid. I was in control, strong, free. *Alive.*

As if in response to my thoughts, my left wing droops down and butts me in the head. I push it behind me, then spin on my heel to walk backward, studying my companions. "Why is it the longer I'm here, the more I feel like I belong?" I ask them.

They slow their steps but don't answer. The one wearing the belt as a scarf smiles a gruesome smile, and thirty-some other pairs of metallic eyes glitter back curiously beneath their caps.

Morpheus's remark about Alice's lost childhood niggles like a dripping faucet in my head. Two things don't add up: Alice's claim that she'd been held captive in a cage for all those years, and the missing birthmark when she was an old woman. Morpheus is hiding something. If only I had time to stop and reason it out.

A distant thrum of thunder spins me around again. I've lost count of how many leftward turns my entourage and I have taken, but this path seems longer than any other. I stop at an archway—the tallest and brightest I've seen. It has to be the way out.

The pixies' mining lights disappear into the hedges. It doesn't matter if they come or not. Nothing's stopping me from leaving this place.

My determination falters the minute I step through the archway. The boots, chain, and reel slip out of my hands, clunking to the path beneath me.

A tunnel of massive webs curves ahead, heavy with dots of amber light.

Once, in Pleasance, after a summer storm, I found a spiderweb in a tree with rows upon rows of dewdrops on every radial. The sun sliced through a cloud and lit the droplets as if they were on fire. It was amazing, water . . . on fire.

That's what this looks like—magnified by the thousands. But these are not dewdrops clinging to the giant cobweb. These are roses: crystalline and cabbage-size. Their scent is different from the roses' back home. It's spicy with a hint of scorched fermentation, like autumn leaves.

I step deeper within. The lights pulse like a heartbeat, hypnotic. Another roll of thunder quakes overhead. Fog drifts along the ground—a carpet of mist spooky enough for a horror movie.

I inch closer, captivated by the electric fluctuations in the center of each glassy rose. Awareness surges through me, that same knowing that hit when I sprouted wings. The light inside these flowers is the residue of life. This is the garden where Sister One plants and tends spirits. And I'm standing smack in the midst of Wonderland's dearly departed.

The ground is hallowed here. No wonder the pixies didn't follow me. Unnerved, I back up.

"Do not fear. Come closer, fair child. I have what you seek." The whisper stops me in my tracks.

"Chessie?" I mutter. There's no way the quest could be this easy.

"You'll not find that treacherous creature in this web. But I can serve you better than he."

The voice is coming from one of the roses. A red swirl gilds its transparent petals, reminding me of stained glass. I bend low and part the bloom's center, expecting a hard, slick surface. Instead, my fingertips meet a soft velveteen fuzz, an incandescent fur that coats the petals like a fiber-optic novelty.

As if responding to my touch, the light brightens, then takes on the shape of a face, eerily lifelike, just like the cameos of white smoke Morpheus blew from his hookah.

"He found you at last," the face whispers, *"bearer of my pin."* A scowl stretches her features. *"I assumed your hair would be red . . . well, no matter. We can amend the color. You will do beautifully."*

I touch the ruby hairpin, words frozen on my tongue. The woman's tattooed eyes look like mine, and I recognize her vaguely but can't place her. Before I can draw back from the petals, the light separates from the bloom then shoots into my fingers on a shock wave. A fizzy sensation jitters through my veins and illuminates them beneath the skin on the back of my hands so they appear green—like chlorophyll. My veins sprout leaves at every turn, making them look more like vines than channels of blood.

Then, just as quickly as they brightened, my veins blend once more into my flesh, as though nothing happened.

I could have imagined it. One thing I didn't imagine, though, was the sense of intrusion. For a minute, someone else shared my body.

With a snap, the rose cracks and withers beneath my hand.

The minute the rose dies, the thousands of surrounding blooms shake on their webbed trellises, all whispering at once.

The cacophony surges through my eardrums. I clutch my ears.

Their murmurs rise to a harrowing screech, as if someone has taken a cello's bow and scratched it across a chalkboard—back and forth, again and again—feeding the vibrations through subwoofers turned full blast in my brain. I fall to my knees, screaming.

"You've gained a square." A woman's singsong voice cuts through the chaos. As she scurries by, a rustle of skirts touches my sleeve.

Her long, pale fingers tug on the web that surrounds the shattered rose, playing the anchor lines with the mastery of a harpist. The other blossoms—still trembling and murmuring—grow quieter until their whispers are tolerable again.

I look up into her face, eyes sky-bright blue and lips the lavender of November dusk. Her skin is so translucent, she's like a drawing on a piece of tracing paper—shimmery and gauzy, with hair the color of pencil shavings. A red and white striped dress, fitted at the bodice like a candy striper's uniform but with a long, flowing hoop skirt, gives the illusion she's from the Regency era.

I stand, shaky, and back away. She follows. The lacy hem of her skirt kicks up and sweeps fog from around her feet. If she had ankles and shins, they'd be showing. Instead, eight jointed limbs, black and shiny like a spider's, glide underneath. It's as if someone took her torso and snapped it into place atop the thorax of a black widow.

I swallow a groan. The hoop skirt must hide a globule abdomen along with the spinnerets used to make this tunnel of web. I suppress the urge to run for my life. Wouldn't do any good. The roof's too low for me to use my wings, and there's no way I can outrun that many legs.

"Sister One?" I croak, surprised I can get anything out of my compressed voice box.

"How do you do?" She offers an open palm for a shake. I can't bring myself to reciprocate, for fear she'll spin me up and tuck me away for a late-night snack.

Her hand drops. "You gained a square but lost the queen." She grows taller in one smooth motion, as if raised up on a mechanical platform. "That was not in my bargain with Morpheus." Her hands settle on her waist.

"Morpheus?" Suspicion defeats horror. He's the reason she had me dragged here? Was it to ensure I'd find Chessie's head? But he said she was holding a grudge, so why is she helping him?

"Have you stolen the queen? Or is she on the loose?" Sister One's blue eyes glimmer, her feathery black lashes narrowing.

"Um." I shoot a sideways glance at the rose I ruined, now splintered like the mirror in my room. And then it hits me why the smoky white silhouette looked familiar. "That was Queen Red!" *The netherling who cursed my family.* "I didn't know she was dead . . ."

"Yes, was." Sister One leans down to wave a finger at my nose. "And this was not part of the bargain."

The roses on the web start to shake again, more volatile this time. The movement rocks my equilibrium, as if I'm spinning inside some carnival ride. Sister One holds out her palms to me.

"You woke them! You must help me lull them back to sleep!" She starts to sing a familiar tune . . . not Morpheus's lullaby but something else from my childhood.

"Ring around the rosy . . ."

Her eight feet tap to the rhythm, waiting for a dance partner. Trying not to think about the spinnerets beneath her skirt, I take her hands. Her skin is smooth and smells of sunlight and dust.

Soon we're whirling in a circle like children. One scene in Lewis Carroll's version of Wonderland comes to mind . . . when Tweedledee and Tweedledum danced with Alice to the tune of "Here We Go 'round the Mulberry Bush."

But Sister One is partial to the *rosy* song—for obvious reasons. Though it's a different version than I heard growing up:

Ring-a-ring-a-roses / The body decomposes.
Hush! Hush! Hush! Hush! / You'll all tumble down.
Down, down, into the deep / Give the Twids our souls to keep.
Silent slumber on a web / Ne'er to raise a restless head.
If we wake the First will come / And sing us back to sleep as one.
Hush! Hush! Hush! Hush! / We're all slumbered down.

We turn in dizzy circles beneath the bouncing web. I lift my chin and laugh, actually starting to enjoy the clamor around me. It's so freeing, my wings whirling like clouds, soft and silky when they bat my head and shoulders. We spin and spin and spin until finally the roses stop their uproar and join our chant. Sister One releases me to face her spirit charges. I lean my elbows on my knees and catch my breath.

The flowers' voices converge to finish the final verse. Sister One leads them, her arms raised and snapping in time like a band conductor:

If we fail to find our rest / Sister Two will raid our nest.
She'll make us live as broken toys / Discarded by the girls and boys;
And there will no more slumber be / For we'll be locked in misery.
Hush! Hush! Hush! Hush! / We'll all tumble down.

At the end, stillness falls over the garden. The only sound is the swish of grass slapping Sister One's sticklike legs as she moves about the web to tuck the flowers into the clingy gauze.

Euphoria fades as I'm taken back to a time when Alison would tuck my blankets around me and kiss my head good night . . . moments before I'd drift off to sleep to meet Morpheus. The memory swirls to a blur, like food coloring dropped into water.

I can't remember how long I've been here . . . minutes, days, weeks?

I have to find Jeb.

Sprinting for the archway, my bare feet crush the grass with each step.

"Wait!" Sister One screams from the tunnel's far end. "You must get the smile I stole for you!"

Ducking my head, I leap over the chain and rope I dropped earlier and keep going. Fear has taken up residence inside my heart, and I don't know how to send it packing.

Skirts rustle behind me as the spider gives chase.

I skid onto a pathway and pick up speed. My lungs ache from panting. The drag of my wings slows me down. I reach behind and draw them around me like a shawl.

Coming to the only archway left, I plunge through. One look around, and I fall to my knees.

Just like in the Alice nightmare . . . I'm as good as dead.

STOLEN SMILES & BROKEN TOYS

I kneel, too horrified to move.

I've stumbled into Sister Two's lair of despondent souls. That's the only explanation for the moans and wails rattling my spine. A chill hangs on the air and clings to me like a second skin—dry and stale, softened with a hint of snow.

Clenching my hands, I force myself to stand. The cries and laments silence. Every hair on the back of my neck grows rigid. Drifts of white powder, grainy with bits of ice, coat my naked feet and pack between my toes. It's cool but not biting like the snow at home.

The passage widens to a vast hollow filled with dead weeping willow trees—branches drooping sinuous and thin, all the way to the ground, each one bare and slick with ice. The thicket's roof reaches high and filters what little light there is. It gives the scene a brownish tinge. At first glance, it could be the front of a sepia Christmas card, complete with ornaments hanging from the serpentine branches.

Only these aren't ornaments. An endless array of teddy bears and stuffed animals, plastic clowns and porcelain dolls, hang on the branches from webby rope. In the human realm, we'd call them love-worn and threadbare—playthings that were hugged and kissed by a child until the stuffing fell out or the button eyes popped off. Toys that were loved to death.

I reach up and tap the leg of a ragged stuffed lamb who's missing an ear. The toy sways on a noose of spider silk. The movement is so silent and tranquil, it's disturbing to my core.

Tranquil. That bothers me . . . the fact that the instant I stood up, everything hushed. Bone-deep quiet. After all those years of yearning for silence, why is it that I seem to feel more at home amid mayhem and noise now?

Finding a sleepy doll that's eerily similar to one I loved as a little girl—complete with time-yellowed vinyl skin and moth-eaten lashes over eyes that open and close—I touch its foot. The leg swings, hanging by a thread to the stuffed body.

The doll's eyes snap open, sucking my courage away. Something in its empty gaze begs for escape . . . something that's trapped, unhappy, and restless, aching to get out. The toy is harboring a soul. They all are.

I wait, mouth drained of all moisture—for the doll to scream or to weep out all the pain I see in its eyes. But the movement slows, and her eyes close once more.

A rustle stirs behind me. Prickles of awareness clamber up my spine, spreading through my shoulders and all the way to my wing tips.

Maybe Sister One followed my footprints in the snow.

Please be the nice one . . . please, please, please be the nice one.

Reluctantly, I turn on my heel. A shadowy face bends down to mine.

"Why ye be standing on this hallowed ground?" The voice—like branches *tap-tap-tapping* a frosted windowpane in the dark of night—rushes over me. Her breath smells of freshly dug graves and loneliness, sending shivers of terror from my toes to my fingertips.

"I can explain," I whisper.

"Dandy that would be." She draws back. Her clothes, body, and legs are duplicates of her sister's. But on her face, scars and fresh lacerations dribble blood. On her left hand, a pair of gardening shears takes the place of fingers. She must have caused the cuts herself.

Compared to her, Sister One is the sugarplum fairy.

My odds of getting out with my head intact just plummeted to almost nil. "I—I took a wrong turn."

"I'd say ye did." Her other hand eases out from behind her hoop skirt, covered by a black rubber glove. She carries a trio of ragged toys on a web like fish on a line. Her scissored deformity edges close to my neck—*snip, snip*. Puffs of air graze my skin as the blades open and close. "Ye don't belong here." *Snip, snip, snip.*

"I don't want to belong here." The stuffed atrocities in her hand cause fresh dread to bubble up in my chest. I step backward and nearly slip on the snow. Spreading my wings low, I catch my balance.

"Well, ye won't. So long as ye're still breathing."

"Right," I answer, gasping to assure myself I am.

"It's when ye stop breathing that ye're mine." Her scissors rake my sleeve's shoulder seam. "Once I cut out yer lungs, ye'll belong then."

Self-preservation kicks in, and I back up two more steps, breaking through a curtain of branches to get closer to the trunk of the tree. Heavy with decrepit toys, the limbs bow over me almost to the ground, like a morbid parasol dimming the light.

Sister Two's silhouette moves on the other side, scuttling around the circumference. Taking strained breaths, I turn with her, keeping her in my sight through openings between branches.

The instant she parts the curtain to come inside, I fold my wings around me, watching through a translucent shell.

She laughs—a grinding, hollow sound. "The pretty butterfly is now the cocoon. Isn't that backward from the natural way of things?"

As if anything is natural *here.* I ease against the tree trunk to protect my back.

The point of her blades nudge the juncture where my wings hide my windpipe. Even through the gossamer layers I can feel the cold metal compressing my air passage.

"Ah, yer wings are yet young. Thin as paper. I can chop them into little pieces and dance in yer confetti. Face me, or suffer that fate."

She steps back. Considering how much it hurt just to step on my wings earlier, I let them fall to my sides and stand against the tree trunk.

Smiling, she snips at the air in front of my face, blowing sharp wisps around me. "Now. Ye've stolen something from me. Give it back, or I'll bleed ye like a pig until ye squeal."

"I haven't stolen anything!"

The scissor-like tips drag down to my abdomen, trailing a chilling line through my clothes. Wings folded around either side of the trunk, my spine grinds into the icy bark and my stomach rolls over.

Her face leans closer—a bloody and horrific sight. "Tell me what ye did with Chessie's smile." *Snip,* and a strand of red lace falls from my tunic onto my bare feet.

My heart nearly stops. "I—I don't know what you're talking about."

"Liar." *Snip, snip,* and a rain of tattered fabric gathers around me as my baby-doll tunic peels open at my waist, leaving only my blouse covering me. "Yer lungs have to be in here somewhere," she says, digging around the fabric.

Growling, I jut out a knee, knocking her hoop skirt lopsided and unbalancing her. Her eight legs regroup before I can escape, and she rams forward until our noses touch.

The cold, sharp point of her blade crimps the bare skin above my throat. "I know why ye're here. Ye seek the next square. The one that will win ye the crown."

Square? Crown? My mind bounces back and forth, caught between confusion and the will to live. I swallow, and the tip of the shears bites deeper into my skin. "No," I whisper, slipping my fingers around her bladed hand to alleviate the pressure. I push against her. "I won't make this easy for you."

"Good. I like a challenge." Her bumpy tongue rakes over her lips as she snakes the blades toward my sternum, pushing harder against my resistance. "Less'n ye wish to watch me hull out yer heart like a nut's meat, ye will tell me where ye hid the smile . . . now."

I close my eyes, willing my erratic pulse to calm, to become steady and confident. There's only one way out of this. Only one thing I can rely upon.

Pandemonium.

I envision the branches around us filling with rabid sap—a snarling, feral energy sweeping through each branch. The movement jostles the toys awake, and they let out a mournful howl. Every branch on every tree across the lair joins in and twists, restless spirits awakened and angry.

"Devil's child!" Sister Two screeches and lifts her scissored hand to stab me. Trapped between her and the tree, I scream and raise my arms to protect myself from the blow.

The doll I roused earlier swoops between us and grabs the shears, wrestling Sister Two.

Seeing my chance, I break through the swaying branches. Snarling toys claw at me as I make my way out, tugging my hair and wings. I burst through and sprint for the entrance, colliding with Sister One.

She shoves me behind her as her twin crashes out of the tree, a bloodthirsty scowl on her marred face. "Move out of my way! The little thief is mine."

"Wait!" Sister One says, out of breath. "*I* took the smile!"

I wither in relief, panting and slumped against the back of her hoop skirt.

"What do ye mean, ye took it?" Sister Two asks. "Ye're not to touch my wards!" She waves the stuffed toys in her good hand, effectively stilling the trees all around us as the spirits cower in fear.

"Morpheus gave an oath," the good twin explains. "If I should help the girl get into the garden and cross off the last two squares, he'll relinquish the moth spirits into my keep."

"Ye never use any sense, nohow!" the murderous sister screeches. "I told ye to stay out of it. It be none of our concern."

"Contrary that! We *must* have the spirits. One spirit in exchange for a thousand. 'Tis fair price to keep the dead contained here, so they'll not possess the living. 'Tis our sworn purpose, after all!" Sister One pushes me through the archway back into the labyrinth.

"Where ye be taking her?" Sister Two asks, her blue eyes aglow with suspicion and fury.

"To the looking glass." Sister One cups my elbow and leads me down the path. I nearly slip once in the snow, but she steadies me. "She yet has a game to win. And you have a queen to catch."

Sister Two follows, her eight legs sifting through the powder as her long skirt leaves drag marks behind her. "What mean ye by that?"

"Queen Red has escaped her slumber. She's on the loose and restless. Best to hurry before she finds a way to the castle." Having said that, Sister One guides me back into the maze, leaving her twin screaming in outrage. The spirits join the tantrum, wailing once more.

I shut it all out. Queen Red was dead and imprisoned, but now she's on the loose. That means I released the witch who put a curse on my family nearly a century ago. What will she do to us now that she's free? "Will you be able to find her?" I ask, swallowing against the knot in my larynx.

"She's of no consequence to you." Sister One slides her grasp to my wrist, whipping around turns through the maze with such speed, I can barely keep up. "The queen's always been trouble. I'm glad to be done with her. My sister is responsible now. She'll capture the restless soul and contain her—permanently."

The wails and laments from Sister Two's lair fade with the distance. "Why are there so many unhappy souls in Wonderland?" I ask.

"Some had unfinished business or lost loves. But the unhappiest died imprisoned by the curse of their name being spoken."

"But I've said Morpheus's name many times."

She laughs, and it sounds like the warble of a songbird. "Morpheus is not his true name. He is glory and deprecation—sunlight and shadows—the scuttle of a scorpion and the melody of a nightingale. The breath of the sea and the cannonade of a storm. Can you relay birdsong, or the sound of wind, or the scurry of a creature across the sand? For the proper names of netherlings are made up of the life forces defining them. Can you speak these things with your tongue?"

A blur of green hedges rushes by. I pump my legs to keep up. My feet, which had been washed clean by the snow, gather more grass stains by the minute. "Can anyone?" I ask.

"Only a netherling at the end of his or her life can speak the language necessary. It must be spoken upon a dying breath."

"Language . . ." The description on the back of Alice's lab report. "Deathspeak," I whisper, unbalanced and confused.

"Aye, it is a volatile thing," Sister One answers. "The victim utters Deathspeak along with a challenge that the one who wronged her must meet. Any netherling who dies under the Deathspeak curse, unable to meet the challenge, is left as a broken spirit, eternally unhappy and seeking escape. Until Sister Two puts a stop to it."

I cringe, thinking of how close I came to being stuck inside one of her toys. "How can an empty plaything hold a spirit? That doesn't make sense."

"Contrariwise. It makes the rightest sense of all. Only toys from the human realm be chosen, and only the most beloved of the lot. Those accustomed to being filled with hopes and dreams and all the affections their children pour into them. For that is the essence of a soul. Hopes and dreams and love. When the most cherished toys are abandoned in junkyards and trash heaps, they become deprived of those things that once filled and warmed them. They become lonely and greedy and crave the essence of the life they once had. So we send our pixie slaves through the portals to carry the toys down for us, and my sister fills them with what they want most—souls. Like thirsty sponges, they hold on to them with every portion of their strength and will."

Straitjackets for spirits. So disturbed by the image, I don't utter another word until we come upon a small house surrounded by hedges and ivy on all sides. It appears to be made of leaves.

"Come in, warm your toes, and eat," Sister One insists. "Then I'll give you what you came for and send you on your way."

"I'm in a rush." I have a headache from all the confusion. Food might help but not the kind they serve in Wonderland.

"You will have tea first, at the very least."

How can I argue? She has a looking glass hidden somewhere, and a key around her neck. Until she's ready to send me through the portal, I'm her hostage.

Inside, there's only one room—furnished like a kitchen except everything is upholstered in cushiony fabric, even the appliances. A puffy white sink, table, and chairs, and a fluffy stove of the same hue, all arranged on a plush white floor that's springy and warm beneath my wet feet, like a marshmallow. There's a tall pantry with stuffed velvet doors, also white. Along all four pillowed walls are circular windows with milky curtains. Odd to have windows when there's nothing to look out at but leaves.

The sterility of the room reminds me so much of a padded cell, I want to run away again. But I can't miss the chance to use Sister One's portal and find Jeb.

The most vivid splash of color in the room is a bowl of bright red apples on the table alongside a silver and red chessboard.

"Are you waiting for tea, too?" Sister One asks, directing her query to a large egg-shaped creature sitting in a chair. I jump when he moves. He blends into the background so well, I would've missed him if not for his yolk-yellow eyes, red nose, and wide mouth. A band of fabric wraps around his widest end, under his mouth, and just above spindly arms and legs that are hinged and green like a praying mantis's appendages. Two triangular flaps of blue gingham serve as a makeshift collar. An orange scrap of linen takes up the space where a necktie might've been.

"It is hardly clever to ask if one is waiting for tea," he says, "when he's sitting at a table set with teacups and sporting a napkin tucked within his collar." His mouth takes on a sour slant as he polishes a spoon with his napkin's corner.

Humpty Dumpty? This whole thing keeps getting weirder and weirder.

Draping my wings over the back of a chair, I drop into the seat opposite the egg-man, mesmerized by the hairline fractures across his pearly shell.

He averts his eyes. "Some people have no business attending a dignified tea. Gawking as if I belong in a zoo, when they're the ones who have all the manners and fashion sense of a monkey."

"Sorry." I smooth my ragged clothes and reach for an apple the size of a plum. I'm starving but still nervous about the food. "What will this do? Make me invisible? Or maybe make me sprout a stem and some leaves?"

"Ungrateful little twit." The egg-man scowls at me. "Looking a gift spider in the fangs. See if you're invited to tea again."

Sister One smiles. "I do not play games with my food . . . unless it's wrapped within my web," she says.

I cringe at what I hope is her attempt at a joke, then bite into the crisp fruit and chew while glancing down at my grass-stained feet. It's only a matter of seconds before my gaze creeps upward again. I can't resist. "So, you're Humpty, right?"

"Humphrey." He sneers. "Youth these days. Can't even manage a proper introduction."

I take another nibble of fruit, encouraged that it tastes like the apples in my world. "Your shell. Did you fall from the—"

"Wall?" Humphrey snaps the ending to my question. "No, actually. That was the first time. I tripped over Chessie's rolling head the second. Kind Queen Grenadine glued me together again, when all the king's horses and men failed. And if there be any other questions on the subject, I would bid you ask them with a mouth less filled with apple."

I swallow my bite. "The king tried to help you? I thought he was a greedy dictator."

"Greedy?" Sister One clucks her tongue, cinching an apron around her waist, then pulling a pan of fragrant cookies out from the stove. "Utterly ridiculous. He's very sympathetic. He brought this one to me so I could keep him in cushions to prevent further cracking, in case the glue doesn't stick. We can't have Humphrey's spirit leaking out to wreak havoc in Wonderland's commons."

Wonderland and *common* . . . two words that should never be in the same sentence.

"So, Humphrey's here because he's partly dead," I say after finishing the rest of the apple. "Partly dead like Chessie."

"Yes." Sister One scrapes the cookies onto a plate. "In fact, Grenadine herself brought Chessie's head here. Many years ago, when her stepsister, Red, was on her bloody rampage. But she's no doubt forgotten by now that he's here."

Wait. Morpheus made it sound as if Chessie came to this place on his own . . . found solace here. He never mentioned that Grenadine tried to help keep the cat alive. I dab my mouth with my napkin. "Partly dead . . . ," I mumble, mind whirling in confusion.

"What business is it of yours how much dead I am?" In a fit of temper, Humphrey slams his spoon to the cushioned floor. The utensil bounces back like a boomerang and thumps his side. Following a crackling sound, the fissures in his shell branch out to form new ones. Slimy, clear liquid drizzles from the fissures. His cheeks turn a deep pink and he glowers at me. The slime starts to sizzle and harden to cooked egg whites.

"You're hard-boiling your innards again," Sister One scolds.

"Now you've gone and done it!" Humphrey aims the accusation at me. "What glory is there to be had in bettering an egg, hmm? Will you make of me a soufflé or perhaps have me coddled?"

"Coddled?" I ask, confused. "You mean like a parent coddles a child?"

He wriggles in the chair until his short legs almost dangle over the edge, causing the new cracks to stretch farther yet. "Coddled in water, you speck. Cooked just below boiling until my brains are scrambled. What sort of empty-headed rot are you? Do you not have a proper vocabulary? And why are you even here? Don't see any cracks in your shell."

Sister One clucks her tongue again and reaches into her apron pocket, proffering a tube of glue. "You should be gracious to her.

She's the *One*." She gestures her chin toward me as she helps him apply the adhesive. "She woke the dead."

He stares, wide mouth gaping almost to the floor.

I can't stop the blush rising through my face. "Morpheus said that the king is bad. That he wants the crowns to both kingdoms for his wife, Grenadine, and will do anything to get them."

"Ha!" Humphrey says. "As seen through the eyes of a murderer."

"A murderer?"

"There's no proof of that," Sister One says, patting down Humphrey's shell to adhere it to the glue. "Morpheus carried Red's corpse to me many years after her banishment. But he shared nothing about the circumstances surrounding her demise, or where he found her. I'm not surprised he's lashing out at Grenadine and her king. He's always held a grudge about what happened to Alice after Grenadine hid her. The queen's intentions were good, to keep the child safe until they could capture Red. But after Red was banished to the wilds, Grenadine lost the ribbon into which she'd whispered Alice's whereabouts and so forgot where she'd put her. Alice became a cautionary tale told to netherling children as they were tucked into bed. The real child was forgotten. By all but Morpheus. Seventy-five years in a cocoon, and he still remembered her upon waking."

"Wait." I grip the table, fingernails puckering the cushiony top. "None of this makes sense. Alice went back into her world. *My* world. She had to . . ."

"Oh, no. She was here. Upon his metamorphosis, Morpheus left no sandbar unturned in his search for her. He found her hidden away in the caves of the highest cliffs of Wonderland. She'd been captured and kept in a cage by a reclusive old bird, Mr. Dodo. But

Morpheus's precious friend was no longer a child. She was a sad, confused, old woman by that time."

Panic chokes back any response. If Alice really did spend her life in a birdcage here, how am I alive? How are any of the Liddell descendants alive?

Scuttling to the stove, Sister One produces water out of thin air from a spoutless sink and fills a kettle. "Would one of you be so kind as to move the red queen to the next square on the game board?"

Humphrey minds the request, pink cheeks ballooned in concentration. "One more left to go," he whispers, thumping the last remaining silver square with his clawlike hand.

The game board has sixty-four squares, half of them red and half silver, with pawns, bishops, and rooks in positions that make no sense for real chess. Their arrangement reminds me of the board in Morpheus's room.

Out of the thirty-two silver squares, a diagonal line of seven glow like burnished metal—the one on which Humphrey centered the red queen, along with six others that lead up to it. On each glowing square, a script appears in floating, curvy letters—again, just like on Morpheus's chessboard.

This time, nothing stops me from reading them:

Burst Through Stone with a Feather; Cross a Forest in One Step; Hold an Ocean in Her Palm; Alter the Future with Her Fingertip; Defeat an Invisible Enemy; Trample an Army Beneath Her Feet; Wake the Dead.

There's one silver square left in the back row, waiting to be illuminated. I suspect that until that happens, the final words will remain hidden. "Do you know what the last one is?"

"Harness the Power of a Smile," Humphrey answers, surprisingly cooperative.

"I don't understand," I say, feeling weaker by the minute.

"Don't you see?" Sister One carries over a tray with the kettle and pours three cups of tea. A soothing, lemony fragrance rises on the steam. "'Tis a record of all you've completed. The tests you've passed."

"'Tests'?" I look at them again, unable to find a tie to anything I've done, aside from waking the dead.

Then I remember what Morpheus said in his room moments before I animated the chess pieces: *"It's all in the interpretation."* Illumination comes to me, flowing slowly into my mind:

I'm sitting beside Morpheus on the giant mushroom where I found him after Jeb and I drained the ocean, but I'm a tiny child of four. My seven-year-old guide positions a picture book in front of me. He's teaching me to decipher riddles.

"This," he says, pointing to a picture of a woman with puffed-out cheeks. "Something you can hold but cannot keep." He reads the words under the picture.

I shouldn't be able to understand them. I'm a toddler. But it doesn't matter. Because each time I visit him in dreams, I feel older somehow. Wiser. Gifted.

"You know the answer," Morpheus says, his young voice scolding. "You're the best of both worlds."

He takes a deep breath and holds it in his lungs. Lifting my palm to his mouth, he lets it out slowly, closing my fingers around the warm air. When I open my hand again, nothing's there.

"Breath!" I smile and clap.

Morpheus smiles and nods, pride shining in his inky eyes. "Yes. We can hold it but always have to set it free."

Back in the present, understanding blinds me, like a flash of sunlight across pupils accustomed only to darkness, dilating my perceptions to perfect clarity: *I'm the best of both worlds . . .*

Netherling logic awakened, I see my accomplishments imprinted on the board next to their summaries, like a checklist:

1. *Burst Through Stone with a Feather*—Used a quill to shove the sundial statue aside and open up the rabbit hole.
2. *Cross a Forest in One Step*—Rode on Jeb's shoulders as he stepped over the flower-garden "forest."
3. *Hold an Ocean in Her Palm*—Balanced the sponge in my hand after it had absorbed Alice's tears.
4. *Alter the Future with Her Fingertip*—Jump-started the tea party crew's futures by drying and resetting the pocket watch's hands.
5. *Defeat an Invisible Enemy*—Faced my darker side and suppressed it with the help of Tumtum Tree berries.
6. *Trample an Army Beneath Her Feet*—Rode across the card guards on a wave of clams.
7. *Wake the Dead*—No explanation necessary . . .

My dark side is thrilled at what I've accomplished, and pride swells my chest.

Then my other side takes the lead. "No," I say aloud to myself. "Not *my* accomplishments. Morpheus's." Dread winds itself around my heart, deflating me.

Jeb was right all along. The things I've been doing weren't to fix my great-great-great-grandmother's messes. They were elaborate tests. Why didn't I listen to him?

"What am I being tested for?" I take my teacup and hold it in trembling palms, willing the heat to seep inside me and stave off the chill in my heart.

Humphrey meets Sister One's gaze as she hands him a cookie dusted with cinnamon and sugar.

"That list represents the criteria for a queen," she answers. "The requirements were written after Grenadine took the throne. King Red heard rumors that his former wife had escaped Wonderland's wilds and remarried. Fearing the possibility of female offspring, he insisted that if anyone was to ever step forward as Red's lineage and try to take the crown from Grenadine, she would first have to pass eight impossible tests to prove her worth. The Red Court agreed to make the tests a royal decree. You are the first to ever pass them . . . well, almost all of them. Of course, you are the first of Queen Red's offspring to come forward and try."

I'm about to object, to say that it's impossible because I'm not of royal lineage. I'm about to stand on my chair and stomp like a two-year-old, to refuse to believe that any of this is real . . .

Until Morpheus's lullabies trickle through my mind, complete at last: *"Little blossom in white and red, resting now your tiny head, grow and thrive, be strong and keen, for you will one day* be their queen . . . *Little blossom in peach and gray, grew up strong and found your way; two things more yet to be seen, until at last you'll* be their queen."

Shivers run like icy drizzle through my wings. "No, no, no. I'm not—I didn't actually pass anything," I say to my hostess. "I stumbled into accomplishing each one . . . by accident, really."

She and Humphrey have no comment. They're too busy counting squares and sipping their brew.

They know, just like me, that nothing I did was by accident. Morpheus orchestrated all of it—set up familiar Wonderland scenarios by using Lewis Carroll's book and soliciting the help of other netherling natives, then stood back and watched as I completed each "test."

At the tea party he said he wanted to return me to my proper place, my home. Which realm does he consider home for me? Gritty discomfort fills my throat, as if I've swallowed the entire desert. I gulp down half my tea.

Jeb . . .

I need him to put his arms around me and promise it will be okay; I need him to make me feel human again.

"I want to use the looking glass to find my boyfriend." I stand so fast, one of my wings hits the table and tips the kettle of tea.

Humphrey pats the spill with his napkin before the steaming puddle can reach his lap. "I was right! You do mean to coddle me!"

Sister One leads me to the tall pantry and opens the left door, revealing a looking glass. "Your mortal escort is already where you're going. My pixies were in the chasm gathering Grenadine's dead army when they saw your mortal leave in chains with Morpheus and the elfin knights. Thanks to your help defeating the card guards, the White army successfully raided and took control of the Red castle tonight in search of their Ivory Queen."

The beat in my chest almost comes to a halt. "Morpheus has Jeb imprisoned at the Red castle?"

She pats my hand without answering. "You'll need this." From one of the pantry shelves, she pulls down a tattered teddy bear. She doesn't have to explain. I already know it holds the part of Chessie that will somehow be my final test—his smile—although I've no idea how I'm supposed to harness it.

"Remind Morpheus that my end of the bargain is met," Sister One says as she waves her hand across the looking glass. It crackles like ice, revealing a chamber in a castle with lush red carpets and curtains of gold. There's a canopied bed and a fireplace; a tall Victorian parlor chair, with its back to me, faces the hearth. A silver fedora trimmed in red moths hangs from one arm of the chair. Smoke rises into the air and a gloved hand stretches into view, a hookah's hose perched elegantly between two fingers.

Morpheus.

If I refuse to bring the teddy bear, does that mean I level his plan to dust? And Jeb—how will we get home? I bite my lip and tuck the toy beneath my left arm, snug against my rib cage.

Sister One draws out a tiny key and turns it so the surface opens to the portal. Her eight feet tap impatiently.

Everyone in this place has an agenda. In exchange for her precious spirits, she's delivering me straight to the one who's manipulated and used me this entire journey. *My entire life.*

Tears blind my vision as I step through the glass.

If only I hadn't stepped through the first portal; if only I hadn't found the rabbit hole.

If only I'd never been born.

CHECKMATE

I land in the Red castle, a few feet behind the chair I saw in the portal. My heels sink silently into the spongy carpet and Morpheus doesn't even stir, still puffing in front of the fire. The scent of his licorice tobacco lights a flame inside me . . . a burning need to trump him in this warped game.

I squeeze the teddy bear under my arm.

"It wasn't little Alice who came back to the mortal realm, was it?" I ask, facing the chair's back.

"No." Morpheus's answer comes from behind me and I spin, almost falling. His wings sweep over him like an eclipse as he bends to steady me.

I shove him away.

Arching an eyebrow, he smooths his silver and black pin-striped suit. Between the suit and the punkish hair, he looks like an emo gangster.

"You were waiting for me to come through the portal?" I accuse.

"Then who's—" No need to finish. Rabid White tumbles over the chair's arm into view, pink eyes aglow. Of course. He's in league with Morpheus, which means he's only been pretending to be my enemy. They've both been playing me all along.

The cadaverous creature lays the hookah hose aside and bows to me. "At your service be I, fair queen." His high-pitched voice drips sincerity.

I exhale to steady my wobbly insides. "I'm not the queen. And I don't want your service." I turn back to Morpheus.

"I believe you're being dismissed, Sir Rabid." Morpheus keeps his fathomless gaze on me. "No doubt she'll call upon you soon enough, just as Grenadine once did. When she's officially queen, she shall covet your talents as an experienced and devoted advisor."

"Highness. Loyally and always, ever yours." Rabid bows so low on his way out that his antlers set him off balance and he almost topples. He catches himself, then hops across the threshold, a rattling bag of bones in a waistcoat.

The door latches shut and I'm alone with Morpheus in a room of shadows and flashing firelight.

"Your spy," I say.

"Yes," Morpheus answers. "It never set well with him what Grenadine and the Red Court did to Red. He wants to see Red's heir upon the throne almost as much as I do, to amend the injustice done to his true queen."

The play of the firelight across Morpheus's wild hair and oth-erworldly beautiful face spins me back into my memories. He was training me to be a queen. The Red Queen. And now I stand here, vulnerable, imprisoned by feelings he inspired in my youth-ful dreams: happiness and comfort, affection and admiration. But nostalgia is deceptive, and I shove it aside. Because everything has been a lie.

"What have you done to Jeb?" I ask, suppressing the urge to lunge at him and attack.

Morpheus's lips twitch a half smile. "He is here in the palace, safe. I'll allow you to see him soon. He wanted me to give you this." Fishing his gloved fingers into his jacket pocket, he draws a small crystallized bead between us so it reflects the firelight.

My wish. I thrust my hand out for it. I won't hesitate this time. I'll wish I never came at all, just like Jeb suggested . . . then we'll both finally be safe again.

Morpheus jerks back, holding it high. "It will stay in my keeping until the time is right." He tosses the bead into the air, then catches it with a deft twist of the wrist before tucking it back into his breast pocket.

Fury surges through me. I bide my time. I have to play this smart or I'll lose everything.

"Have a seat, Alyssa, princess mine." Morpheus gestures to the bed.

"If I sit anywhere, it won't be on the bed." I hug the teddy bear— my one bargaining chip.

"Surely you don't think I mean to seduce you? Wouldn't I have already taken advantage of your innocence at my manor, whilst I was watching you sleep?"

The reminder of that intimate moment, when his birthmark

touched mine, sparks uncomfortable heat in my abdomen. "This entire quest has been a seduction, Morpheus. It's time to come clean."

He lifts the end of his red necktie and scrutinizes it, then scrubs at an invisible smudge. "There's nothing clean about betrayal, luv. And that's where the story begins, as you well know. Queen Red's court mutinied against her, her own husband joined the traitors in order to marry her stepsister, and it upended the balance of the realm. But you will restore the equilibrium." He tucks the necktie back into place.

"Because I'm her heir," I murmur, nearly choking on the words.

The proud smile on his face is luminous. "Figured it out, did you?"

I suppress the ache in my throat. "It was never about me fixing things. My family wasn't cursed by Alice's messes. We're not cursed at all. We're half-breeds."

He splays out his wings and arms. "Isn't it glorious?"

"You brought me here . . . set the scenes to fit the Alice story. Everything's been a game. Everyone's been playing a part. That's why most of them were different from the characters in the book. Everyone helped you . . . they were your accomplices."

"Yes. Characters playing the parts written for them in a book from the human realm. Some, anyway. Others played along unwittingly."

"The octobenus."

Morpheus nods. "Despicable. Murdered his best friend to appease a wave of gluttony. He deserved what he got. And the card guards? They are always expendable. Now, quench my curiosity, little plum." He gestures to the chair behind me. "Make yourself comfortable, and enlighten me on how you came to be a netherling princess."

I refuse to sit. A bitter taste burns my tongue. "A masquerade."

He frowns. "Pardon?"

I twist one of the teddy bear's ears. Filthy toes rooted into the carpet for support, I unleash the theory that came to me when I saw Sister One's chessboard. "The website. It said some netherlings take on the appearance of existing mortals. After Queen Red was exiled, she snuck through the Red castle's portal into the human realm."

"Pray tell, how did she manage that?" His voice is teasing, meant to goad me.

"She shares my magic . . . she found a way to distract the card guards. She coaxed the ribbon off Grenadine's hand by animating it—the ribbon that held a reminder of Alice's whereabouts. Then Red stepped into the mortal realm as the child. She grew up as Alice, fell in love with a mortal man as Alice, married and had children as Alice. Half-magical, half-human children, and heirs to her lost throne. The netherling characteristics only pass to the females, because Wonderland is ruled by queens." I'm hugging the bear now, so tightly I can feel Chessie's essence clawing for escape . . . begging to be free. Or maybe it's my own.

"Tell me more. You hold a captive audience." Morpheus's voice has changed, the teasing edge replaced by something ravenous and exposed.

I can't bring myself to watch his enthralled features, so I look at the fire's flames instead. "Red came back to Wonderland, a few months before the real Alice died. Somehow they traded places again. That's why the older Alice in the picture had no birthmark, when the younger one did. That's why she remembered nothing of her mortal life. It was stolen from her. She had no childhood, just like you said." My chest constricts with sadness almost as potent as when I cried out my wish. "Poor Alice."

"Yes. Poor, dear little Alice."

I search his expression. His reverence seems sincere.

A pained, poignant tenderness warms his eyes. "I tried to return her home, in her old age. I thought I was doing right by her, letting her die among her own. I stole into the Liddell house late one night, hoping to convince Red it was the right thing to do . . . hoping that with her family asleep in other rooms, we could make the switch undetected. Red was compliant, said she was tired of being old and feeble." A soft smile lifts one side of his mouth. "I tucked Alice into the bed where she would awaken among those who should've been her family all along. They were strangers to her, so I tried to prepare her, but her mind was too far gone to grasp it all. I held her hand until she nodded off, then left with Red for Wonderland. Upon our arrival at the rabbit hole's opening, the wretch changed her mind and turned on me, refusing to leave her family behind. She intended to murder Alice, then drag all the Liddells to Wonderland. To use her lineage to win back the throne she'd lost."

Morpheus regards the flames, the corners of his mouth tugging down. "I wouldn't let her go. We fought on the ground beside the sundial, then on wing in the trees. Red had me pinned to the uppermost branches of one, meaning to snap my neck. I cast her off, and she landed hard, impaled by the iron fence just below us. The metal went straight through her heart and poisoned her blood. I carried her down into the rabbit hole. I attempted an apology. But she would not forgive me. And she made sure I could never forgive myself as she took her last breath."

"*Deathspeak,*" I whisper.

His gaze snaps to me, shock apparent on his face. Flickering light exposes the remorse in his eyes

I turn to the hearth again. "That's why you dragged me here. It was never about saving your friend Chessie. It wasn't even about Ivory being trapped. You're the one who's cursed. You need me to save your spirit from an eternity as a worm-eaten toy in Sister Two's lair."

"You judge too harshly. I do want to save my friends. It just happens that I can save myself in the process. I've been enslaved for too many years, racing against a ticking clock. Now, at last, I can make the hands stop. I can dethrone Grenadine and set the rightful heir in her place."

"Even if the heir is unwilling."

A heavy silence hangs between us.

Gently, Morpheus captures my chin, shifting my gaze to him. "What of the book I used as my storyboard, that one by the mortal bard Carroll. What are your thoughts on that?"

He's relentless, leading me deeper into a place of both darkness and light. "Carroll came up with the story. But Wonderland, the place, the characters and names . . . I think that Red, as little Alice, inspired him with the half-truths she used to explain her short absence. Her family all assumed she'd wandered off to have a dream beneath a tree." I frown. "Red became a child in every way, just like you once did. Her mind was innocent again. It's a good thing her little-girl's imagination took over. If she'd been completely honest about the dark, twisted creatures here, she would've been locked up in an asylum on her first day as a human." My attempt at sarcasm is wasted because I'm one of those dark, twisted creatures. I always have been. Only now I look the part.

"Splendidly told," Morpheus says. "And every bit of it, exactly as it was." He taps my nose. "Do you wonder how the details come to you with such ease?"

My answers were more than lucky guesses. It's as if the words were scripted on my tongue. Mentally, I thumb through each dream spent with Morpheus to see if he ever told me, but he didn't.

Morpheus draws me closer to the fireplace, studying my hairpin in the light. He brushes his thumb across it. "Anything of particular interest happen in the cemetery, other than your retrieval of Chessie's smile?"

I touch my hairpin, recalling my encounter with the rose. "Queen Red's spirit . . . it flashed through my veins before escaping into the garden. She must've imprinted some of her memories on me! That was part of the Deathspeak, wasn't it? You had to set her free, and you used me to do it."

With a sound somewhere between a sob and a laugh, Morpheus pulls me into his arms and strokes my hair. His scent enfolds me, his chest solid and warm. As a child, his touch used to make me feel secure when he'd hold me under my arms during flying lessons. But not now. I stiffen for an instant before realizing I'm face-to-face with his lapel. Nothing but a layer of silver and black pinstripes stands between me and my wish. Instead of pushing away, I snuggle closer—drawing my hands up between us.

A tremor travels the length of his body in response, fingers weaving through the braids at my nape. "Lovely Alyssa. What a grand pupil you were," he mumbles, his mouth on the top of my head. "Yet you taught me more than I taught you. You are far more worthy to wear the crown than any other. Courage, compassion, and wisdom. The triad of majesties. You have something I could see even through the eyes of a child. You have the heart of a queen." His voice cracks on the end of his statement, as if he's saddened by it.

Gloved fingers—silken and confident—glide from my shoulders to my wrists. I curse him silently for moving my hands as he raises them to study the scars. He kisses them, his lips a fluid brush along sensitive flesh, then places my palms on his cheeks.

Mouth inches from mine, he whispers, "Forgive me for bringing you into this. There was no other way." His skin is softer than clouds must feel, and the tears gathering around my fingertips are hot and tangible. But are they sincere?

Our breaths swirl between us, and his black eyes swallow me whole. My heart knocks against the bottom of his rib cage. I know what's coming next. I fear it. But it's the surest way to distract him and get the wish. And if it has to happen, I'm going to be the instigator.

Rising up on my toes, I press my mouth to his. He moans, frees my wrists, and sweeps me into his arms—sealing the teddy bear between us. My ankles swing at his shins, and my hand creeps toward his lapel. *I'm in control.*

But it's a lie, because now I've tasted him. His lips are salty-sweet with yesterday's laughter . . . digging in the black sands beneath Wonderland's sunshine, playing leapfrog atop mushroom caps, and resting in the shade of black satin wings.

I try to shake off the spell, but he angles his face and deepens the kiss. *"Embrace me . . . embrace your destiny."* He breaks the barrier of my lips, touching his tongue to mine, a sensation too wickedly delicious to deny. As our tongues entwine, his lullaby purrs through my blood and bones, carrying me to the stars.

Behind closed eyes, I'm floating against a velvet sky, lungs filled with night air. On some level, I know I'm still in the middle of a fire-warmed chamber, yet my wings pantomime flight on a cool breeze. I'm dancing with Morpheus in the heavens, no longer imprisoned by gravity.

Fluttering our wings in unison, we twist and whirl a weightless waltz among stars that coil and uncoil in feathery sparks high above Wonderland's warped and wonderful landscapes. Each time we spin, then return to each other's arms, I laugh, because at last I'm me.

I'm a me I've longed to be in my innermost fantasies—spontaneous, impetuous, and seductive.

Morpheus promises a lifetime of dancing, a world where everyone obeys my commands. He shows me every piece and parcel of Wonderland that is mine. Down below, past the stars and night sky, I can see myself seated on a throne at the head of a table, hosting a feast with mallet in hand, prepared to strike the main course dead. Maniacal laughter echoes in the marble halls, sweet to my ears.

The scene makes me drunk with power. I kiss him again. He holds me tighter.

Beneath my feet, the stars burst into a thousand glittering colors: silent fireworks, just like the ones Jeb and I saw in the boat on our first night here.

Jeb . . .

The image of his dimpled smile slams into me like a gasp of ice-cold air. Memories of my mortal life intensify the frost: the pride and satisfaction of finishing a mosaic, the maple-sweet flavor of Dad's Saturday morning pancakes, Alison's tinkling laughter that feels like home, Jenara joking with me at Butterfly Threads, and Jeb . . . his loyalty, and his kisses, so magical yet so real.

The spinning in my head slows, like a top falling to its side. I'm back at the castle, pressed against Morpheus in a passionate embrace.

I have to finish what I started, or risk becoming what he is.

I coax my palm into his lapel in search of my wish, returning his feverish kisses. "Checkmate, you son of a bug," I say against his mouth two seconds before my fingers find an empty pocket.

"Sleight of hand, blossom," he says right back. "'Tis in fact in my pants pocket, if you'd like to search there."

I shove him off and drop to the floor, wiping my mouth. "It's mine!"

"And you'll receive it when the time is right." His lips, all I can look at, tilt into that smug smile that I've come to detest. He motions toward the chair. "Sit. You've just been soundly kissed. No doubt you're short of breath."

"Don't flatter yourself." I huff in an effort to hide a gulp of air and hold the teddy bear against my chest. "That kiss meant nothing. It had underlying motivation."

"Oh, to be sure. That kiss was nothing if not motivational."

Maybe it's wishful thinking on my part, but his pale complexion looks flushed as he turns the chair around so its back is to the fire. Considering that my stomach is a pendulum in full swing, I hope he's at least a little rattled.

Cheeks hot, I sit on the warm cushions, my wings ornamenting the arms like lacy, jewel-studded doilies. I can't pin down my emotions. I shouldn't have kissed him. How could I do that to Jeb? But I did it for us, so he'll understand, right? As long as I never mention how it affected me, how I almost drowned in Morpheus's seduction, in my own darkest desires . . .

"Have I commented on your loveliness tonight?" Morpheus asks, compelling me to look at him. His eyes follow the lines of my gauzy appendages. "There's something about a lady in wings. You wear them well. You're exquisite, in fact. Just like a netherling princess should be."

The drag of his gaze alerts all my nerves, forcing me to relive his lips on mine. A touch of his hand would've affected me less. I reach for his hat balanced on the chair's arm and flick the red moths so they dance. "Cut the crap, Morpheus. My clothes are shot, and I look like a marshmallow exploded on my back."

He chuckles, masculine and deep in his chest. "You've always been irresistible when you're cranky." He sits on the floor in front of me, pinstripe-clad legs crossed like a Boy Scout's. Too bad Jeb's not here to pound him to a pulp.

I punch the hat's brim, exasperated.

Morpheus flinches as if I hit him. "Careful. That's my Insurrection Hat. I've ne'er had occasion to wear it until today. The red represents battles and bloodshed, in case you were wondering."

"Doesn't interest me in the least," I answer, flinging it to the floor.

With a hiss through white teeth, he gathers his prize. "Bah. You're a descendant of Queen Red. You crave chaos. You're happiest when the world is in an uproar. You thrive on madness. Even your magic is at its best when it's the catalyst to confusion. You still can't admit this?"

I shake my head, not wanting it to be true.

He places his hat on his knee and shrugs, as if too busy to drag the truth out of me. "You will wash up and change. I've picked a stunning ensemble for you. A queen must dress properly for her coronation."

"I'm not going to be queen," I grumble.

"Perhaps not forever, but you will be temporarily. It is the condition of Red's Deathspeak. You must be crowned with the ruby tiara. Oh, and did I mention it's the only way to free your mortal knight?"

My chest constricts, the guilt overwhelming. *Jeb.*

"Take me to him. Now." I start to stand, but my wings refuse to cooperate. My tired muscles prove no match for their weight, which is suddenly overwhelming. I plop down in resignation and groan.

Morpheus clasps his hands in his lap. "You need a warm bath and some rest. As I said earlier, your pseudo elf is safe. How long he stays that way, however, depends entirely upon your performance tonight."

"You can't touch him!" The only things keeping me from tearing off those flashing jewels on his eye patches are my deadweight wings. "You made a vow you wouldn't hurt him. A *vow.* If you break it, you'll lose your wings, your dream manipulation . . . everything that makes you who you are."

"True. Wouldn't wish to lose my powers at such a precarious juncture." Firelight blinks across his clothes in swathes of orange and purple, intensifying the gangster circus-freak image. "But there was a stipulation, was there not? That I wouldn't hurt him as long as he stayed loyal to your worthy cause. Well, he proved himself an obstacle. He and I discussed your destiny a bit ago, and he has no desire to see you become queen. In fact, he became rather unmanageable at the suggestion." Morpheus lifts the hair at his forehead, displaying a goose-egg-size bruise. "Imagine that . . . most men would leap at the chance to be in bed with royalty."

"Shut up." A sob catches in my windpipe.

Be tough, Alyssa Victoria Gardner. I can almost hear Jeb's voice, can almost see the sincere faith in his green eyes. I'm not going to let him down again.

Patting the bear's mustard-scented fur, I take a steadying breath. "You said I could just be queen temporarily. Explain."

Morpheus relaxes, elbows on knees. "I want the vorpal sword to free my friends. But we need to crown you as queen to fulfill my Deathspeak. As luck would have it, King Red has the frumious bandersnatch guarding both sword and crown because his absent-minded queen kept misplacing her bloody tiara. So for us to get them, you must subdue the creature."

The jade chess piece with the wide, snapping mouth and spiked tail scrapes along my memory. It struck terror into my heart as a child, and that was just a plaything. *Frumious.* Anything that inspires its own adjective is a force to be feared. "Wait. No. Since you have control of this castle and the cooperation of the card guards, why can't you just force the king at swordpoint to get the items for us?"

"Grenadine is the only one who has the command the ban-dersnatch was trained to obey. It's a word passed down from queen to queen. But in the confusion of our takeover, Grenadine lost the ribbon that held that secret."

I bite my inner cheek, determined there has to be some way for us to skip this step. "Okay, but if Chessie's smile can tame the beast, then we can just cut him out of the toy here and release Chessie into the bandersnatch's lair. We can all wait out of danger until the bandersnatch is subdued."

"Ideally, yes." Morpheus drags the teddy bear out of my lap. Straining, he yanks the stitches apart. Before I can blink, the threads mend themselves, closing the gap. "You see?" he explains. "Because Sister Two's toys harbor the residue of a child's innocent love, the world's most binding magic, the only tool that can permanently sever these stitches is—"

"The vorpal sword itself," I mumble, rubbing the knot in my stomach. I take the teddy bear back and trace the pits where it once had eyes. "What happens if . . . *after* I tame the beast?"

"The White army has agreed to leave this castle upon the condition that the Red Court crowns a new queen and frees Ivory. Both courts will accept you as the rightful heir once you've fulfilled the final test and harnessed the power of the smile." An arrogant smirk crosses his lips. "I suspect King Red originally penned that with a knack for diplomacy in mind. But this interpretation hits all the high points. No one can argue that."

Apprehension snakes through me at the thought of standing before both courts. "So, I'll get crowned. Then Jeb and I can leave?"

"Once you're queen, you can force King Red and Grenadine to free Ivory. Wonderland will be in balance once more. Both portals will be open to you. And then"—Morpheus runs a finger along the bridge of his hat—"you may use your wish to cleanse your blood of netherling traits, which in turn will save your mum, and your children thereafter. The Red Court will appoint a new queen once you and your toy soldier return to the human realm."

Something about that last step doesn't sit right. First off, who else would they crown as queen? Second, how exactly would half of me—the netherling half—just disappear? Would I be wiped clean by some magical eraser?

Before I can air my reservations, Morpheus hits me with the only words that could cause me to forget everything else: "Would you like to see your mortal knight now?"

I'm at the edge of my seat, about to get up, but Morpheus kneels in front of me, ever the obstacle in my path.

"No need to stand, plum. You can see him from where you sit."

Next to my right leg, he shoves his hand between the chair's cushion and frame. The nerve endings in my thigh sizzle. Eyes locked to mine, Morpheus drags out a small handheld mirror, its frame embossed with shimmery silver. He flips the glass side to me.

In some dank, dark place, Jeb bangs his head against prison bars. Blood trickles down into his face, and he totters backward, dazed.

My heart breaks in half—a pain so acute, it could launch a thousand wishes and fill a sea of tears. "Jeb, stop . . ."

"For reference"—Morpheus studies my reaction—"that is a birdcage. Our pseudo elf is the size of a sparrow. Upon word from me, the guards will feed him to Queen Grenadine's notoriously hungry cat, Dinah."

"No!" I skim my fingers over the cold glass and the image vanishes. I'm faced with only my reflection. The girl whose selfish desires brought Jeb into this journey to begin with. All because I wanted him to myself. But I never wanted *this*.

The sob I've been holding back rips loose. I was delusional to think I could sway this game to my favor. The checkmate's already been played. Morpheus has won.

"What will it be, Alyssa?"

The fire crackles behind me, a cat-o'-nine-tails whipping harsh tongues of light across his ruthless expression. I wipe my tears and level my gaze on his. There's no need for another word between us, because he already knows.

I'll do anything he asks of me now.

CHESSIE

Morpheus escorts me down a long, dim corridor on the first floor. Candles in brass sconces light the glittery red walls. The lace and bustled skirts of my coronation dress sweep the black marble beneath my feet. This is exactly why I didn't want to go to prom. I hate being on display, especially in something I would never choose to wear on my own.

From my hands to my feet, I'm dripping crimson velvet, ivory lace, and ruby jewels. The elbow-length sleeves and floor-length skirt pouf out like the princesses' ball gowns in the picture books I used to read as a kid, and the gloves are made of stretchy velveteen.

My hair's dressed up, too; long curls pile atop my head, studded with jeweled barrettes that flank my great-great-great-grandmother's hairpin. Morpheus instructed my sprite attendants that Queen Red's ornament should remain the focal point.

I'm the epitome of royalty. I even smell royal—perfumed with sandalwood, roses, and a hint of amber. But I'd rather be Sister One, awash in the scent of dusty sunlight and hiding spinnerets beneath my skirt, so I could wrap Morpheus in a web and leave him to hang.

As if intuiting my thoughts, he squeezes my velvety palm to his satin one, locking our fingers tighter. His jaw is set in the same severe expression he wore earlier—just after the sprites put me on display for his approval—when I told him how much I despised even looking at him.

He seemed hurt by that. I wouldn't think he'd care. I'm only his pawn, after all.

Our wings accidentally brush, and I reposition the bear tucked beneath my arm to subdue my anger.

Five card guards from the Red Court lead the way, and five elfin knights from the White court follow closely, their military boots imprinting echoes on my eardrums. I can't keep from staring at the red jewels that sparkle in pinprick designs on their temples and chins, the same color as Jeb's labret. Other than the pointed ears, they do bear an uncanny resemblance to him, size and coloring-wise. Almost human but for their lack of emotion.

They've all come to offer protection and to report back to their respective parties after bearing witness to my final test. Just like Morpheus said, the Red Court has agreed to let me be crowned, but they can't just hand the honor over. I have to prove myself worthy.

Harness the Power of a Smile: Subdue the bandersnatch with Chessie's head.

When my legs turn to jelly at the thought, all it takes is the memory of Jeb bleeding in his birdcage, trying to get to me, and my strength returns. I will do this—for him and Alison and Dad. I will put an end to this crazy nightmare and win our passage home.

My entourage and I take a right turn, arriving at an arched wooden door painted red and fitted with brass fixtures in the shapes of card suits: diamonds, spades, hearts, and clubs.

Before opening the door, Morpheus turns. He takes both my hands in his. His fedora's brim casts a crescent of shade across the upper half of his face. "We must keep the chamber dark. The bandersnatch's weak vision is to our advantage. He will be slow on the uptake but swift on instinct. In turn, we shall be stealthy and expedient. We'll have only a matter of minutes before the beast registers us with his other senses. He attacks with his tongues . . . like a frog would capture its prey. You will need to stay behind me, and that's easier done if you're grounded, so resist the urge to take flight."

Maybe it should flatter me that he's so protective. But my safety is an afterthought. He just doesn't want his hand trumped.

"Once we get the vorpal sword, you can free Chessie's head. After that, ready the cello's bow. Chessie will guide you on what to do. Are you clear on our strategy, Alyssa?"

I don't answer, refusing to look him in the eye. I've welcomed my darker side over the last few hours, embraced it, because it's taught me how to manipulate Morpheus. Indifference affects him more than anger. Too bad I didn't figure that out earlier.

Hindsight is for losers.

"Please look at me . . ." His voice is pleading.

And again, he falls into my trap—too little too late.

"I want this to be over just as much as you do," he says with a sweet sincerity that could melt all of Greenland. Lifting my chin so I have to meet his gaze, he takes the cello's bow offered him by an elfin knight and holds it out to me. "A trade for the toy?"

I flash both the knight and him an acidic glare, then take the bow and hand off the bear. The first time I ever held a bow, Alison was kneeling behind me, supporting a cello that was three times my size. She held my wrist to guide the bow across the strings. The instrument wailed beautifully, the most resonant and heartbreaking sound I'd ever heard. That was only a few days before the incident that sent Alison away to the asylum. Thanks to Morpheus.

"Our plan will work," Morpheus promises as he traces his knuckles down my temple, disregarding our escorts. He must sense the sadness in me, because he's very gentle. "Chessie's body wants to be reunited. You're simply enabling that to happen. Think of yourself as the bridge."

I don't answer. I give the bow my full attention. It's wider and has a larger arch than mine at home. I turn the screw to increase the tension, then tap it once on the floor and meet Morpheus's expectant gaze. "Ready."

My hands are sweating inside my gloves, and I'm barely able to ward off the tremors in every muscle. I grab Morpheus's wrist before he turns the key in the latch. "My wish?"

He pats his pants pocket, the residue of a hungry smile hovering over his lips. He's remembering our kiss, but my mind flees in the opposite direction, desperate not to fall into the memory alongside him.

"You'll give it to me?" I ask.

"I vow on my life-magic. When the time is right."

I move behind him. In response to Morpheus's hand signal, the soldiers spread out in a V-formation on my left and right sides.

The door creaks open, slicing the darkness with light. A humid stench slaps us, as if someone baked an oyster and sauerkraut casserole inside a sweaty sauna. The definition of *frumious* is vividly clear. Hand over my nose, I stifle a gag.

As the opening widens, our shadows blot out the light in front of us. Still, I can see that the roof stretches almost as high as the one at Underland, and the room is twice the size of the massive skating bowl. A smattering of windows lines the top quarter of the domed ceiling to coax in a filmy silver haze, just enough light to differentiate between outlines and shadows but not to see anything clearly.

I have a vague sense of the layout from Morpheus's description. A thick chain binds the bandersnatch to the back wall. It's long enough to allow him access to his pen and the radius of the stage that holds the crown and sword, but that's the extent of his range. This allows the bandersnatch's keepers to toss in food from the doorway while staying out of reach of his tongues. My eyes adjust so I can make out the shape of the stage. There's a podium centered in the middle and a hole carved within it. A light is tucked inside the stem, allowing a beam of soft yellow to radiate up from the center into the glass case on top, a gentle beacon in the darkness. Inside, a red crown and a shimmery silver blade are nestled on a plush pillow. From where we stand, the weapon looks as small as the fillet knife Dad uses when he prepares fresh-caught fish; the blade and handle can't be more than eight inches long. It's more like a knife than a sword.

A heavy chain drags on the floor somewhere in the pool of darkness behind the stage. Snuffles fill the air, then escalate to a low, spine-guttering growl.

Dark dread knots in my throat. Morpheus steps farther into the room, urging me behind him. My mind screams for me to turn back and run. Instead, I force myself to follow. The guards and knights sidle along the walls, backs pressed to the stone, spears and swords drawn, for all the good that will do. A bandersnatch's hide is indestructible. If the creature attacks, their only hope will be to wound his tongues and buy themselves time to escape.

Morpheus and I creep within inches of the stage. Gripping the bow, I wait for my cue . . . heart pounding. The bandersnatch must hear my pulse, because he lashes out a tongue to investigate. The slimy, snakelike appendage slithers by, leaving a glistening streak of mucus in its wake.

Morpheus's wings fold around me, and together we sidestep the tongue as it backtracks. Knuckles pressed against Morpheus's back, I feel his muscles straining.

"Easy, Chess, old boy . . . easy," he whispers. He's wrestling more than fear. He's wrestling the cat's eager spirit. Chessie must sense his other half and is struggling to get to it.

We reach the stage, and Morpheus hoists me up in my awkward gown at the same instant the bandersnatch lumbers out of the darkness and into a splash of moonlight. One of the card guards along the wall gasps, and the creature staggers in his direction, as clumsy and erratic as a boxcar derailed from its train—except three times bigger.

Tense, Morpheus edges us toward the glass box on the podium. The beast jerks its head in our direction, chain jangling. We freeze, hand in hand.

Milky white eyes pass over me, unable to focus. Nothing could've prepared me for what I'm seeing: a rhino's gray hide, pitted and bulging, head triangular and feline with fangs, like a reptilian saber-toothed tiger. The creature's giant lizard legs bow outward, and its spiked tail whips from side to side as he cocks his head. One of the elfin knights makes a clucking sound for a diversion. Snarling, the bandersnatch turns in that direction, drool lagging like shoestrings from his muzzle.

Morpheus eases his grip on my hand when we come to the glass case, and he hands me the teddy bear. He slips a key into a brass lock on the front, wriggling it to trigger the mechanism. On some kind of instinctual reflex, my wings flutter. I wince and meet Morpheus's concerned gaze, but it's too late.

The movement snaps the bandersnatch's attention back to me and he roars—his putrid breath rushing over us with all the heat, thunder, and wetness of a wicked summer storm. No longer under the protection of Morpheus's wings, I scream in response, almost turning my lungs inside out.

Morpheus shoves me behind him as three tongues lunge toward us. At the ends of each appendage, a snakelike face opens toothless jaws and hisses. They're like giant eels, though not nearly as peaceful and charming as my pets at home. Every drop of saliva evaporates from my mouth as one tongue comes within inches of Morpheus's face. He ducks, but the tongues snap back, winding around his ankles and waist. They topple him to his knees and drag him to the edge of the stage.

"Morpheus!"

I want to believe I'm only worried for my wish. But seeing him captured awakens that child who once loved him. Racked with terror, she pushes her way out of the recesses of my heart, casts off the cello's bow, then launches me forward to reach for him.

I land on my stomach in a pool of fetid slime, hoop skirt bubbling above me. "Take my hands!" I stretch my arms and lace his fingers with mine, but he pries them away.

"No, Alyssa! The test! Get the vorpal sword . . . free the smile—"

The tongues lug him offstage and toward the slobbering mouth. His wings wither against his back, caught up in the appendage wrapped around his waist. His hat flutters to the ground.

I struggle to stand with the contraption beneath my skirts, rocking back and forth until momentum gives me ground. As soon as I'm on my feet, I spin around and lift the glass lid. The vorpal sword's handle feels warm even through my gloves. Everywhere I touch, I leave prints glowing blue on the silver metal.

A shout draws my attention back to the fight. Graceful and lethal, the elfin knights catapult onto the bandersnatch's back, hacking away at its hide with their swords in vain. The card guards spring into action. They perform elaborate feats of acrobatic skill to build a card tower above the beast's head. Then they topple and prick at his tongues with their spears on the way down.

Their combined efforts help Morpheus escape the tongue at his waist. He dives to the floor, flapping his wings for leverage against the other two appendages still on his ankles. The bandersnatch thrashes. The card guards flutter like leaves caught in wind and slap against the walls. The beast bucks again, toppling three of the elves. They hit the floor, knocked out cold, swords spinning next to them with grating sounds.

Urgency surges through me. Fingers clamped on the vorpal sword's handle, I gut the teddy bear's stomach seam. Stuffing bulges and parts as something struggles to push its way out.

Morpheus wails. The knights and card guards litter the floor, all of them either unconscious, wounded, or dead. Eelish and slimy, the tongues writhe against Morpheus, holding him upside down. The bandersnatch's lower jaw unhinges and widens to a chasm, preparing to swallow his prey whole.

Chessie still hasn't emerged from his prison of stuffing. Tucking the bear into my bodice, I grab the cello bow and vorpal sword, then flap my wings and take to the air. I don't even care how high I am. Hovering over the snarling mass of monster, I shout down at Morpheus, "Catch!" I balance the sword just over his raised hand and drop it.

With lightning reflexes, he snags the handle and slashes the blade in three sweeps, slicing the head off one tongue. The creature bellows and releases Morpheus, who joins me in midair. Below, our attacker slinks back to its pen, howling.

Hair a mess and clothes slimed and rumpled, Morpheus tucks the vorpal sword into his lapel and nods his gratitude. Together, we descend. My feet have barely touched ground when the teddy bear in my bodice jerks against me, dragging me toward the beast's pen.

"Chessie's trying to get to his other half!" Morpheus shouts.

It's as if someone has caught me on a fishing line and is reeling me in. Morpheus tries to grab me, but it's too late. I'm shuffled into the pen to face the bandersnatch. My knees start to give as he circles me, looming and snarling, his incapacitated tongue dragging on the floor and dripping green blood.

"Free the smile, Alyssa!" Morpheus swoops into the pen to distract the beast.

Shaking all over, I slide the toy from my bodice and drop it. An orange glow drifts up from the torn seam. The bandersnatch softens its growls, mesmerized by the light.

Cello bow clenched in my hand, I wait and wonder . . .

The orange glow grows from the size and shape of a penny to that of a football. Emerald green eyes with slitted pupils appear, and a bulbous nose follows in the center. Lastly, a smile bursts into view—glaring white like Nurse Poppins's at the asylum—with whiskers stretched above either side.

Another orange light answers from inside the bandersnatch's stomach. It illuminates the creature's undigested victims. The silhouettes of winged beings, big and small, flutter inside like a morbid baby mobile, casting shadows on the wall of his gut.

The beast holds his head low in silence, somehow aware of the change going on inside him. Chessie's orange head flips around to face me and morphs into an hourglass shape, whiskers stretching vertically over his teeth to form bow strings.

A cello . . .

"Be the bridge," Morpheus instructs me. "Subdue the beast."

I reach up for the floating orange instrument and coax it down. Leaning against a wall, I drag the bow over the whiskers, choosing a simple song we used to play in band to warm up. But it's not my notes that come out of the smile. Chessie's voice sings a melody, melancholy and contagious, and soon I find myself humming as I continue to accompany him—though I've never heard the tune.

The bandersnatch's eyes grow heavy. His legs bend, no longer able to hold his weight. With a loud, sloughing sound, he rolls onto his side, snoring. The light inside his stomach ascends through his esophagus, leaving the fluttering silhouettes to their prison.

Morpheus lands on the ground and drapes an arm around me. Still asleep, the bandersnatch hiccups, releasing the glowing orange bubble. My "cello" breaks free to unite with its other half, and when the bubble bursts, Chessie is in one piece, hovering in midair. He shifts into a tiny creature with orange and gray stripes—more a mix between a raccoon and a hummingbird than a cat. The smile on his face widens as he winks at me, nods to Morpheus, then vanishes with one swish of a striped furry tail.

My legs are weak, and my body is numb all over. Morpheus escorts me out of the sleeping bandersnatch's pen, shutting and bolting the gate to hold the chained creature within. "After such a battle with magic, he should sleep until morning, I would think."

The surviving guards and knights applaud.

Morpheus turns to them, one arm supporting my waist. "See to your wounded. Leave the dead for now. I shall ready Alyssa and the crown. Gather the courts and witnesses in the throne room. We will have the coronation shortly."

The able-bodied drag away the injured and close the door, leaving us in the domed room with their dead. I can't look at the bodies, sickened that they had to die for me.

Sensing my frayed emotions, Morpheus opens his arms. Without hesitation, I turn into his embrace and hug him in the moonlight. The vorpal sword's handle presses against my ribs under his jacket, and I battle the temptation to slide it out and cut his throat. But I can't. Not after what he did.

"You jumped in front of me," I whisper. "You could've died."

"You saved me back. So we're even." He says the last word in his most humble voice, just like when I used to beat him at games when we were little.

I clench his jacket and pull him hard against me, nose buried in his chest. I don't know how to put into words what I'm feeling. Fury for what he's done to Jeb and me all twisted and gnarled around the affection my child-self harbors for him. Except I'm no longer convinced it's just the child in me who's attached.

"I hate you," I say, the sentiment muffled against his heart, hoping to make it true.

"And I love you," he answers without hesitation, voice resolved and raw as he holds me tighter so I can't break away and react. "A crossroads, my beautiful princess, that was unavoidable—given our situations."

That cuts me, and I don't even know why. I'm adrift in confusion and disbelief over everything: our kiss, his confession, my standoff with the bandersnatch; most of all, that Jeb and I are about to go home.

Stretching to hold me at arm's length, Morpheus stares at my face, silent.

"So, now you crown me," I venture, needing to break the intense magnetism between us. "And I'm done."

He glances down at his shoes. "Yes. Then you're done." Without another word, he lights several torches along the wall, brightening the room. Then he retrieves his hat and settles it into place on his head.

His clothes are in a shambles, just like mine. I cast a glance at the sleeping bandersnatch locked inside the pen. Why did Morpheus have me wear my coronation dress to something that would leave it crumpled and ruined? A niggling of suspicion is reborn as he returns with the ruby crown in hand.

"If you like," he says, "I could crown you here and now—privately. No more performances. This can all be over in a matter of minutes."

His words shoot down my suspicions. He doesn't sound very convincing, but I like the part about doing this without all of Wonderland watching. "Yes."

His free palm opens to display my wish. "When you're ready, squeeze it to burst in your hand while thinking of your heart's dearest desire. But be sure to choose your words carefully. Say that you wish to be free of Queen Red's influence forever. That is the only way to free your family."

I nod.

For some reason, he won't meet my gaze. "All I ask is that you wait for me to crown you before you make that wish." His lashes cloak his eyes, and the jewels on his face blink three different shades of blue—as if he's indecisive about something.

I slip off my gloves and take the bead, still warm from being in his pocket.

He surprises me by offering something else—the jade carving of the caterpillar from his room. "So you'll never forget me, or your better side."

I take it, swallowing against the doubt in my throat.

He lifts the ruby crown over my head.

I clamp my fingers around the gelled wish, waiting for my cue, rehearsing to make the words perfect in my mind.

"I crown you Queen Alyssa, rightful ruler of the Red Court."

He's no sooner placed the circlet on my head than the door flies open. Card guards and elfin knights fill the room, expressions stern and solemn. Two elves point their swords at Morpheus and force him to his knees. Gossamer hovers over one of the knight's heads and Morpheus glares up at her.

"You spilled the magic beans, eh, traitorous pet?" he asks with venom.

An apology glimmers in her coppery eyes. "The guilt would've eaten you alive," her bell-like voice chimes. "To take an innocent girl from all she knows and place her in a foreign world, away from her friends and family. So blinded by fear, you could not see you were repeating what happened to Alice. You are my most beloved master . . . I will not watch you wither away in regret. Better you face your fate with nobility."

Morpheus hisses at her. "Nobility? Was it not noble that I saved your life? Now you're condemning me to death! I should've left you to be eaten by that fanged toad all those years ago." The elves tighten their stance over him, and Gossamer hangs her head in shame.

The knights and guards around me part to make an opening for someone coming through the door.

"What's going on—?" My last word clips short as a woman in ivory lace—flesh and gown glistening like ice crystals—steps forward. Her feathery white wings arch high and graceful, like a swan's, complementing the lovely turn of her long neck beneath waist-length silvery hair. Her face is familiar for its beauty and loneliness, and she carries the pewter hatbox that once imprisoned her.

The Ivory Queen.

How did she get out? Did Queen Grenadine and King Red release her?

One glance at the roses on the box, and that hypothesis falls to shreds. The roses used to be white. Now they're the color of . . .

Blood.

Ivory steps up, inches away from where Morpheus kneels.

"You seduced me," she accuses him, her voice cracking. In spite of the angry frost shooting from her bluish white eyes, tears roll down her cheeks.

"Recovered your memories, I see," Morpheus remarks, smug even in the face of the swords pointed at him.

"Along with my crown." She touches the glistening diamond tiara on her head. "You used such pretty words." She sobs. "All the nights we shared. You made me think you cared for me . . . used my affection to trick me into the box." Her delicate fingers brush the wetness from her face. "Then you framed King Red and turned my court against him, all so you could close my portal and hold the young princess here until she completed your plan! Have you told her yet? The truth of it all? What you intended to take from her?"

I look down at Morpheus. The guilt on his face sickens me. "He told me I could leave after I was queen." I throw the caterpillar carving at his feet. "What else is there?"

Morpheus stares at the chess piece next to his knee. "Nothing. To atone for all of the wrongs done to her, I was to see Red's blood heir crowned as ruler of the Red Court."

A queen in ruby-colored robes, with ribbons on her toes and fingers that match her flaming hair, pushes forward, her king and guards flanking her. It's Queen Grenadine. "There is more . . . the sprite told us . . ." She holds a beribboned hand to her ear, listening to the whispers. "Yes . . . there was one other stipulation to his curse, you see. One that will lock you forever to this place."

"He never intended for you to leave," Ivory tells me.

I curl my fingers around the gelled tear. If that's true, then why the charade with the wish?

"In your mad rush for freedom," Ivory says, her attention once again on Morpheus, "you have cost a noble mortal man his life and betrayed both courts. Amends will be made for your heresy."

The words *mortal man* ice my heart. I turn to the jabberlock box and the blood-painted roses. My chest cinches tight with a horrible intuition. "Where's Jeb?"

Ivory opens the box's lid, sympathy softening her expression.

My stomach writhes even before I see the matted dark hair in the black water, even before it spins to reveal a face so familiar it scrapes my soul bare.

SACRIFICES

"Jeb . . . no, no, no." Rivers of hot tears burn my face.

He looks confused as he watches me from inside the jabberlock box; then a flash of knowing brightens his eyes. "Al." His lips mime my name on a surge of bubbles. The muted word breaks me in half. I was supposed to be his lifeline . . . how could I have let this happen?

"Oh, you idiot!" Morpheus shouts up at Jeb. "Just had to be the hero, didn't you?"

"You are to blame for his state." King Red steps up to speak. "Your actions caused this earthly young man to make a choice . . . an irreversible one."

"You're one to speak of blame," Morpheus shoots right back, arrogant as ever. A knight whacks him on the head with a gloved palm.

Guilt gouges so deeply inside me, I almost double over from the pain. I kissed another guy, and Jeb bled his body dry for me. "This can't be happening," I say to Ivory, swatting tears away.

Her expression grows tender. "I'm so sorry. My court would never have listened to King Red's claims of being framed. The only one they would believe was their very own queen. Morpheus planned to set me free but only after he succeeded in trapping you here. Gossamer told your mortal boy, and he chose to take my place so I could stop Morpheus from completing his plan. He could not bear for you to be locked in our world forever."

"But now *he* is," I mumble. Jeb watches me through the liquid. Pain pierces my heart—as if the organ is being pecked by ravenous birds.

An ocean red from bonds of love, and paint the roses' hearts thereof . . . It was Jeb's love for me that opened the box. The same love that's so bright in his eyes, it reaches through all the barriers between us—breaking through the dark water and glass to remind me of his faith: *"You're the best friend I've ever had. Even if things get screwed up, you'll still find a way to help me."*

He's right. It won't end like this. I won't let it.

The clear bead sparkles in my palm. My wish can't be used directly for him, but it can still save him.

I glare through my tears at Morpheus. "You once told me if I helped you, I'd be helping myself. Setting things right in Wonderland would free me and my family, forever."

He nudges the caterpillar carving with a finger. It spins on the marble floor. "Have you never heard the saying, 'The truth shall set you free'? I gave you that. A glimpse of the real you."

He doesn't care that I can't hear Jeb's voice. That I can't touch his skin. He doesn't care that Jeb's terrified of losing control of his life but he gave up all control just to save me.

What's worse, soon enough, Jeb won't remember me. He won't even remember himself.

Morpheus doesn't care about any of that. All he cares about is carrying out Queen Red's Deathspeak challenge.

I bend down, level with his ear. "If I could, I'd make you take his place."

Morpheus's jaw clenches. "The magic is final. Your mortal knight saw to that. *One trade of souls will shut the door, and blood shall seal it, evermore.*"

Every muscle in my body tenses, holding me back from attacking him. Instead, I touch the red flocked roses. "I could join him. The wish can be used to put me inside."

"I'll not allow it!" Morpheus tries to stand, but the knights place their sword tips at his sternum.

"It will be a wasted wish." Gossamer lights on my shoulder. "Only one soul will fit in the box at a time. Besides, the portal will never open again—in or out."

Jeb mimes the words, "Go home."

Regret claws at me, juxtaposed with overwhelming anger. He had no right to make this sacrifice. No right to give up his life for me. No right to leave me here alone.

I stroke the glass above his face, memorizing every line. If I wish that we never came, neither of us will have been here for this to happen.

Morpheus struggles against his captors, still on his knees, reminding me why I came here to begin with. If I put everything back as it was, he'll be free again, too. Free to torment my family until someone stops him once and for all.

There's only one solution, and it's as clear as the blue sky when Jeb and I flew across the chasm on floating boards.

I kiss the cold, hard glass separating us, remembering his lips like they were in the Hall of Mirrors. Soft, warm, giving, and alive. Those first kisses will be our last.

"What you gave up for me," I tell him. "Everything you've done while we've been here is amazing. If I make it back home, I'll spend my life thanking you."

Jeb's mouth drops open. He shakes his head, forcing bubbles to churn all around him. His hair swirls like black moss floating on water.

"No, Alyssa!" Morpheus's screams are strangely synchronized with Jeb's silent ones. But it's too late. I've squeezed the tear, and the liquid drizzles down my wrist, warm with the scent of brine and longing.

In my mind, I send up my heart's deepest desire: that I had never answered the door on prom night when Jeb first came knocking, that I had stepped into that mirror alone.

Behind my closed eyes, a giant pocket watch spins, its hands turning counterclockwise. Everything happens in reverse: my wings sinking back into my skin; our ride on the clams shuffling us upward onto the crumpled chessboard, which levels to a smooth, sandy slant; surfing up instead of down and jumping backward onto March Hairless's table, face-to-face with icy statues; the kisses in the mirrored hall, all of them taken back—slipped away into a pocket of time never to be remembered by anyone but me; I see the ocean refilling, us leaping into the rowboat, then the octobenus sliding back into the water while we fall asleep once more, only to awaken on the white sandy beaches; me riding atop Jeb's shoulder as he walks backward, shrinking down to my size as we battle the flowers, then backtrack to the tiny door. Into the rabbit hole, then up, up, up to face the sunshine. Until at last, Jeb's gone, and I'm falling down the rabbit hole—me and no one else.

My lungs wheeze as if I've been dragged underwater. I open my eyes.

All the memories remain, and everything's the same: Morpheus pinned in place by knights' swords; the queens, side by side; the guards looking on in anticipation; and Gossamer on my shoulder.

Worst of all . . . the jabberlock box. The roses are still red. Ivory holds the pewter cube in her hands. I'm about to scream, because the wish didn't work, and I failed.

The tears in Queen Grenadine's eyes stop me.

I step closer to the box. On the other side of the opened lid, King Red stares back through black water. Without Jeb here to make the sacrifice, the king used his love for Grenadine to trade places with Ivory, saving both kingdoms. Maybe in some small way, that redeems him for breaking my great-great-great-grandmother's heart all those years ago.

I wonder if anyone remembers Jeb. The confusion in their eyes tells me they don't. But I'd bet my life Morpheus does. He's always been able to get into my mind.

"Foolhardy choice," he says, confirming my suspicion. "By being the martyr, you'll never see your family again. How do you think fragile little Mumsy will feel about that?"

"Oh, I'll see them," I answer. "It was never the netherling traits that were my family's curse. *You* were the curse. Today, I'm breaking you. I'm queen now. The portals are open for me. So I'm going back home, and my family will finally be free."

He glances down at his shoes, his jewels blinking black and blue, like bruises. "Such pretty delusions, little luv. Almost pretty enough for a fairy tale." A hoarseness scrapes his voice, tingeing it with remorse.

Tired of his mind games, I start to lift off Grenadine's crown.

My fingers lock up at the base of the rubies, unable to move. Underneath Queen Red's hairpin, my scalp flames. White-hot tendrils reach down from my skull into my spine, nailing my entire body into place.

The sensation migrates to my arms, setting my veins on fire. They glow green again, like in the spirit garden, sprouting into ivy. The same sensation runs up my legs beneath the wide skirt. This time, the vines don't recede into my skin. They grow larger, expand with my breath—a living, breathing plant growing out of me.

I scream as the vines strike like leafy snakes, snapping Gossamer from my shoulder and lashing out at everyone around me.

"What is happening?" Grenadine wails, the ribbons on her fingers all whispering at once.

"Your husband's sacrifice was for naught!" Ivory screams. "Red's spirit was in the hairpin . . . she's united with the girl . . . they are one being!"

The knights and guards, fearing for their queens, turn their weapons on me.

Morpheus uses the distraction to whip his wings closed around his chest, knocking the remaining knights off him. With a turn of his heels, he maneuvers behind Ivory and catches her around the waist, vorpal sword at her throat. "Step away from Queen Alyssa, or I slice Ivory in twain and awaken the bandersnatch for a feeding."

Everyone freezes. Even Gossamer hovers in midair. I want to make a run for the door, but I can't move. Queen Red is fighting for control of my body, and it takes every last drop of concentration and strength to keep her contained.

"All of you"—Morpheus gestures toward the door—"get out. This is between the three of us now. Or the four of us, if you count the queen you stabbed in the back a lifetime ago."

Gossamer's the first to leave, her green shoulders drooping. Grenadine takes the jabberlock box from Ivory and walks backward toward the entrance along with her guards, nearly tripping over some of the dead soldiers on their way out. The elfin knights stand at the ready, waiting for a command from Ivory.

"Do not test me." Morpheus spreads his wings high and presses the blade to her jugular until a puckered indentation appears.

"Go," she rasps.

A wave of frustration ripples through the knights as they back away, swords lowered. But the emotion can only be felt, not seen; their faces remain impassive. The door slams shut behind them.

Dragging Ivory with him, Morpheus locks and bars the door, then turns to me, narrowing his eyes at the crown on my head. "My part is done, wretched witch. I am now free of you."

"Well enough . . ." Red's answer rings through my head and forces its way from my mouth on a gust of air. *"But I have expanded my expectations. Being imprisoned for so long, I deserve retribution. Bring your captive closer. I want her crown-magic as well. Do it, and I'll offer you a position at my side as king, ruling over all of Wonderland."*

Ivory struggles, but Morpheus holds the blade steady at her throat. Locking my gaze with his, he grimaces miserably. "Why didn't you listen?" he asks, voice pinched. "The wish I gave you . . . if you had used it as I instructed . . . it would've saved you from this end. My challenge was for you to sit on the throne with Red possessing your body. I tried to offer you a way out."

If the queen wasn't holding me up, I'd faint dead away. My fate is to be a vessel—only one-half myself—tethered to Wonderland for all eternity? I want to tell him again that I hate him, to really mean it this time. I want to spit at him and scream that he's a coward in the worst way, to sacrifice me for his own worthless soul.

I avert my eyes instead, using that ploy that worked so well earlier so I can bring him to his knees. Because he's the only one with the power to free me now.

"Please, you must understand." His voice takes on that pleading quality, and my heart—the one part of my body that I'll never let Red have—picks up a beat, hopeful. "I'm not a coward." He tries to convince me, as if I'd already called him the name. "It wasn't the fear of death that drove me . . . it was captivity. Like you, I cannot be a spirit contained. I must be free. You understand, don't you?"

I suppress any response, wincing from the effort of fighting Red.

"Would you hurry and get over here, you fool? I need the added power of Ivory's crown to fight the girl. She's very powerful, this one." There's a hint of pride in the statement, which only feeds my resolve to beat her. Forget family ties. I'm not hers to be proud of.

Morpheus steps forward a few feet with his hostage. Red throws out a vine like a striking snake. It topples the crown from Ivory's head; she screams and faints.

Slowing her fall, Morpheus lays her out of the way, his toe on the diamond-encrusted crown. Red's vine rope tries to reach again but can't get any closer without me stepping forward. I refuse to budge.

Red manipulates the connection between her ivy strands and my veins like puppet strings. I bite against the tearing pain, jaw almost cracked from grinding my teeth so hard. Still, I don't relent.

"It was to be so perfect!" Morpheus all but cries the words, concentrating solely on me. "Your mortal suitor has already forgotten this journey. But you and I, we share memories of a childhood that I will never forget. You are the lady of my heart. My match in every way. I would've stayed at your side once we banished Queen Red, never left you to rule alone. We could've danced every night in the stars above your kingdom. For you, I would've given up my solitary life . . . been your loyal footman and cherished you eternally."

Red forces my face in his direction, but I keep my gaze on the floor.

"I should make you my footstool with that admission of heresy. But I'm giving you one last chance. Bring the crown if you wish to have any part of her. I'm sharing one-half of her mind. I can offer you her body, force her to surrender to your desires. Use her as you will. Wed her, bed her. Be her mate. Just let me have Ivory's crown."

The sole of his shoe scrapes the jeweled circlet along the floor toward her. Rethinking, he moves it back even farther out of her reach.

An ember of hope stirs inside me, until I look up. He's deep in thought, actually considering her proposition.

She can't do that, can she? Force my body to her will? As if in answer, my hair escapes several of its pins and thrashes around me, the strands no longer platinum blond but flame red. They reach toward Morpheus, taunting him like beckoning arms.

"Do you want her for your own?"

"So very much—" His voice breaks.

"Then do my bidding. She'll be yours physically, and there the heart and soul will follow in time. You can romance your way into her good graces. You shall have forever to win her."

The expression on Morpheus's face is torn between longing and a struggle for honor. The gems bejeweling his eyes flash from pink to purple. "Forever to win her." He's almost in a trance. He crouches to lift the crown but stops.

"Oh, for Fennine's sake! If you're too weak to hand it over, simply leave. The girl's only remaining strong because you're giving her hope. Begone, and I'll overpower her. I shall get the crown for myself."

Morpheus stands, takes one last lingering look at me, then starts for the door.

A cry erupts from my throat as I reclaim my voice. "That's it? You got what you want, and now you're going to turn your back on me like you did Alice? You'll leave me to my cage of ivy? Why not? It can't be any worse than living in a straitjacket, and you've forced enough girls into those."

He pauses, midstep.

"Don't listen to her! She will be yours to hold and cherish within the hour. You can kiss her tears away, make all her pain a distant memory."

As if in slow motion, he resumes walking, broad shoulders tense and wings low.

"You made a vow!" I screech, wrestling for control of my mind. "Not to leave me heartbroken and hurt again! You'll lose everything!"

Morpheus stalls at the threshold, his back turned and head hanging down. "I would give up all my powers to have you in my arms. Your love is the only magic I need."

Red forces me forward a step . . . then two.

"I'll be a corpse in your bed!" I try to get through to him, one last time. "You're killing everything that makes me who I am. The girl you taught, your playmate . . . the one you claim to love will be gone, with a puppet in her place."

The leafy veins in my legs jerk on another unwanted step as if in demonstration.

Just as Morpheus reaches his hand to unbar the door, Red snaps out her vines and reaches the crown.

"Good-bye, Alyssa," my one last hope says, his wings drooping in resignation. "I'm afraid neither of us is strong enough to defeat her."

"We'll see about that, Morpheus," I hiss back, then turn my attention to the vines possessing me.

I'm done letting everyone else dictate what happens to my life. I'd rather be dead than an eternal pawn.

Exerting the last of my will, I force my hands to grip the vines that are dragging the crown toward me. Slamming to my knees, I tug against the ivy, holding it taut where it joins my skin. Queen Red's scream rattles my brain. She drops the crown to concentrate on me. Her ivy winds around my palms and fingers until they're covered with leafy mittens. She forces my arms together and binds them and follows with my legs and torso, incapacitating me just like the flowers did on the beginning of my journey, except the pain can't compare. Any struggle against her shackles makes each bone in my body feel like it's going to crack.

The only way to stop hurting is to go limp . . . give up. She's won. I'm finished . . . I close my eyes and whimper.

I think of Jeb, Jenara, my mom and dad—all having to pick up their lives without me. It pierces my heart with a pain more acute than anything I've ever felt. And I'm glad for it. The intensity of the emotion proves I'm still alive . . . that I'm an individual. That I'm me.

Red has my body, but she doesn't control my heart or mind yet. That's where my magic lies.

Three of the elfin knight corpses lie only feet away. One's arm is severed, one's neck is buckled, and the other has a twisted leg, all from their encounter with the bandersnatch. They might be broken, but I can still use them.

Concentrating on their bodies, I picture them alive: Their brains become computers, hardwired to my thoughts; their hearts made of putty, pumping in time with my own; their legs and arms are pliant like pipe cleaners, moving on my command.

Shaky and awkward, they stand. Limping and swaying, they drag themselves toward me. Their fingers clamp around the vines and heave against Queen Red.

My ivy cocoon unwinds, spinning me on the ground. The vines grow taut at my ankles, wrists, and hands, where they're joined with my body. The knights continue to heave with all their weight and the vines rip my skin on the way out, like electric cords being jerked from a plasterboard wall. A knife-sharp pain guts me—a rotary blade hacking through my organs.

I gurgle a scream and strangle on the taste of blood, losing control of my macabre marionettes. They droop, almost releasing their hold on the vines. Driven by the desire to be free, I command the knights to yank harder.

Crimson streams spurt from my wounds and puddle on the floor. I grit my teeth, using my body's anguish to drive me, to give my creations the strength to fight until they've ripped Red out, until she's connected only to my fingertips by a tangle of weeds.

I collapse, and my trio of knights crumple into a pile, inanimate and dead again.

I'm so weak, I barely realize Morpheus is at my side. Vorpal sword in hand, he severs the leafy stems from my fingers, then slashes the vines away. Another piercing screech jars my skull as Morpheus works off the crown and hairpin to disconnect me completely from my puppeteer.

Without a body to inhabit, Red's spirit writhes in the ivy on the ground, dying like a mass of eels out of water.

Morpheus tucks the vorpal sword away in his jacket. I slump in a fetal position, drained of blood and energy. My wrists and ankles gape open, a thousand times worse than the wounds that slashed across my palms as a child. I wonder if I'm dying . . .

A black haze dims my surroundings.

"Brave, stubborn girl," Morpheus whispers into my ear as he tenderly cradles me in his arms, lifting my body. "You were the only one who could free yourself of her possession and win the crown. I knew you would be victorious. All you needed was a push to anger. And who better to drive you to the edge of fury than me?"

"Liar," I mumble, swimming in nausea and coughing up blood. My arms and legs feel weighted, and sticky streams ooze out of the gouges in my skin. "You left me."

"I'm still here, aren't I?" Morpheus guides me down beside Ivory and exposes her birthmark, touching it to mine. Heat flashes along my body. "I've always believed in your power. For the queen I saw in you even as a child . . . for the woman you could never see in yourself. My faith is as unchanging as my age."

"I don't believe you," I murmur, half-conscious. My veins refill, healing my skin. The agonizing lacerations both inside and outside my body ease to numbness.

He strokes my head. "Of course you don't. I've given you no reason to."

I snap open my eyes as a roar breaks from the bandersnatch's pen. The gate hangs off its hinges, the padlock crushed and useless as the monster rises over Morpheus's shoulder with Queen Red's ivy illuminating its veins. She found another body to inhabit . . .

"Morpheus!"

He leaps toward the monster to defend me. Two tongues and a lasso of vines cinch around his neck, jerking him high into the air. He loses his hat.

Still weak, I struggle to stand. "Fight back!"

But it's over even before I say it.

Morpheus clutches his throat. "Better to take my medicine, luv," he chokes out. "If you try to outsmart magic"—a strained cough breaks his words—"there's always a price to pay."

The creature swallows him whole. His wings slide down last—a flash of glistening black grace.

The creature is about to charge me but instead falls to the ground and rolls around, wrestling itself. Morpheus is still defending me from the inside.

When the bandersnatch rises to its feet again, it runs into the closest wall. Slamming its massive body against the rock until it crumbles and breaks open, the monster bursts out of its chain and leaps through the hole, escaping into the wilds of Wonderland.

I sit and stare at the giant gap in the castle wall—my hooped gown encircling my waist like a velvet globe—for what seems an eternity. As I breathe in the night air, I know it really can't have been more than a few seconds.

The pixies arrive to gather the dead. They first appear in the distance, mining lights bobbing in the darkness before they clamber in over the rocky ruins and set to work.

I scoot forward to pick up the tiny caterpillar carving from the floor and tuck it into the top of my dress. I stop to look at Morpheus's fedora, and a pang of regret stings my heart.

Crawling to Ivory, I tap her face to wake her so she won't be mistaken for dead.

The pixie brigade passes us, sniffing as they go. "No smellum deadses. Move longish and wide."

While they gather the corpses, Ivory and I help each other stand. I tell her everything that happened when she was unconscious.

I'm numb . . . my emotions rubbed so raw, I've become desensitized. "It makes no sense," I whisper, holding my chest where the carving, cold and lifeless, presses against my heart. "Morpheus defeated Red's Deathspeak, then gave himself up to the bandersnatch, the very fate he'd been running from—"

"To save you." Ivory finishes my thought. "It appears he did have the capacity for unselfish love, after all. Just not for me."

I rub at the tears and blood dried on my face, overwhelmed by the destruction surrounding us. "I came here to set things right. Instead, I made a mess of everything."

Ivory straightens my gown and wings. Her eyes are kind as she catches a strand of my loosened hair, studying the fiery red color. "Sometimes a flame must level a forest to ash before new growth can begin. I believe Wonderland needed a scouring."

I look down at my tattered and bloody clothes. "What happens now?"

She places the ruby crown on my head and repositions her own. "You are the rightful heir of the Red Court. You passed all the tests and received the crown. Grenadine is required by her court's own decree to step down. Whatever you bid your subjects do next, they will abide by it as law."

"Whatever?" I ask.

As she nods in response, the door bursts open with the help of a battering ram. Both courts pour in from the outer hall. Even the clams and zombie flowers have found their way through the hole in the wall.

Soon, I'm surrounded by a celebration of creatures both winged and wily, left to decide my own fate for what feels like the first time in my life.

"What will it be, Queen Alyssa?" Ivory asks.

I bend over to pick up Morpheus's hat and place it on my head over my crown, tilting it at an angle. "Let us feast."

LOOSE ENDS

In the realm of humans, a proper high tea would've better served negotiations between two kingdoms trying to reestablish peace, but watching my albino ferret friend pound the roasted goose into submission, and seeing all my guests plunder the giggling main course for its succulent, aromatic meat, I know I made the right choice.

The maniacal laughter, smacking lips, and uncivilized conversations provide a comforting backdrop while I square away things with my new royal friends. I sit at the head of the table with Ivory on my right and Grenadine on my left and catch a floating bottle of wine sent my way by the woolly-headed netherlings at the other end. Pouring a glass for myself, I toast them, then take a long drink.

The flavor of berries and plums rolls down my throat, thick and sweet like honey.

Dad wouldn't approve, even though this is nothing like the wine at home. All I know is, I need something to warm the chill in my chest that hits each time I see Morpheus's fedora on the arm of my chair—the red moths fluttering with the movement around me.

Morpheus's sprites share my grief. They bob and weave around the table like hiveless bees, unsettled. Gossamer hangs limp from the chandelier above, crying inconsolably.

Rabid White entertains Grenadine with a joke while passing a plate of moonbeam cookies. The ribbons on her fingers that reminded her of her king's whereabouts and the skeletal netherling's betrayal mysteriously flew off when we first sat down to eat. I tuck the red bows beneath my leg to be destroyed later.

Rabid has sworn a vow of loyalty to me and whomever I choose to rule in my stead while I'm gone. Grenadine will need an experienced royal advisor, and I have no reason to doubt his devotion after everything he did to see me crowned.

"You are resolved in your decision?" the Ivory Queen asks me.

"It's better this way," I answer, touching the necklace around my neck. This key is mine to keep. A ruby embellishes the top, in honor of my kingdom.

"You should know . . ." Ivory lifts a crystallized candy, sucking on one end. "Since you're a half-blood, the realm in which you live shapes your form. Your wings and eye stains appeared here but will vanish within hours there. Your powers are eternal but will become dormant if neglected. The more you avoid reminders of your stay in the nether-realm, the more human you'll become."

Nodding, I take another sip of wine to ease the ache in my stomach. I smooth out the dress Grenadine gave me after I cleaned up—a red strappy one-piece with black hearts, spades, diamonds, and clubs appliquéd just above the knee-length hem. The black petticoats rustle under my hands. She offered boots, but my arches are killing me, so I'm barefoot.

Attending an important political dinner only half-dressed. I couldn't do that in the human world.

I never thought I would feel so torn about going home. Then again, I never thought *this* place would feel like home. "I want to experience everything that Alice missed out on," I finally answer Ivory.

"I understand. Your heart belongs in the mortal realm for now, with the knight you told me of. He sounds very brave and noble." A dreamy look passes over her face.

A pang of sympathy hits me. She's always been so isolated—Morpheus must've seemed like a dream come true. Even if she can't find the right guy, there are other ways to curb her emptiness, friendships she can forge. Maybe she just needs a nudge in the right direction.

I glance over at Grenadine, whose mouth glows with moonbeams as she laughs, oblivious to us. "While I'm gone, would you and Grenadine meet once a week or so? Eat together, play croquet, whatever you like. You know, to keep foreign relations balanced. You could take turns hosting . . ."

Ivory's beautiful, icy features warm at the thought. "Of course."

"And you might take the sprites back to your castle. They'll be lost without Morpheus."

The queen smiles sadly. "Yes. They will. I would be glad to take them in."

We both pause as the conversation around us turns to stories of

Morpheus's antics throughout his life. The dinner guests snort and smile upon each telling—a transparent ploy to cover their sorrow.

I look down at my plate.

Ivory pats my hand. "He spoke of you often. His childhood with you was sacred to him. So few of us here ever experience that kind of innocence."

My wings grow heavy on my back as I think of our short time together. The memories I worked so hard to remember will now haunt me forever.

Anticipating the inevitable good-bye to these wondrously eccentric beings—to a very wondrous part of myself—leaves me even more bereft. I gnaw on a drumstick. The mutilated goose snickers and rolls around on his platter, as if he can feel my nibbles all the way across the table.

"We should discuss your journey home." Ivory places her candy aside. "Time is tricky as you step back through the portal between realms. Unless you envision a specific hour, the clock goes in reverse."

So that's what the flowers meant by time moving backward in Wonderland. "How far back?"

"It will drop you into the exact same moment you stepped through to begin with. This could work to your advantage. If you aim for your bedroom, you can give the illusion you never left."

Blotting my lips with a napkin, I meet her gaze. "No. I have another place in mind. There's something I have to do before my wings disappear, before I can start my life again."

❖ · I · ❖

The way the portals work, I'm supposed to envision where I want to land, but it has to be a room with a mirror big enough for me to fit through. Magic is stricter in the human realm. Since the only three places I'm really familiar with at the asylum are the registration desk, the lounge, and the bathroom, I squeeze the tiny key on the chain at my neck and choose the obvious one.

Crouching, I crawl through the portal and end up with my knees in a pristine sink, hands banked on the edges for balance. I almost crash into Nurse Jenkins, who was bending over to dig through her makeup bag. An eyebrow pencil clatters to the floor. She totters backward and falls on her butt next to the toilet, gawking at me. A small sound, somewhere between a whimper and a gasp, squeezes from her throat.

Maybe I could explain the eye patches and wings by saying it's a costume, but creeping through a mirror? Best thing to do is leave and let her convince herself she's overworked. It's unlikely she recognizes me, anyway.

I tuck my key into my bodice and breathe deeply, disinfectant stinging my nose. My petticoats crinkle as I hop down from the sink. Freshly mopped cold tiles meet my bare feet.

On my way to the door, I hear Nurse Jenkins squeak. I pause. She's still sprawled out, in such a state of shock, she's practically drooling. A full syringe has fallen from her pocket along with her keys. I almost pity her, until I see Alison's name on the syringe's label.

I kneel beside her and clamp her keys between my fingers. "I need to borrow these."

The nurse stares at me, gaping.

A sense of retribution takes over, and I give in to my wicked side. "You know, you seem a little high-strung today." I roll the syringe her way with my toes as I stand. "Maybe you should take something . . . sleep it off."

I tip Morpheus's fedora, turn to the door, and shake out my wings for good measure. Checking to make sure the hall's empty, I step out, biting back a smile.

The sterile corridors that used to intimidate me hold no terror now. I duck in corners and stick to the shadows, close to being caught once or twice, but since only the night crew is here, I'm soon on the third floor where the padded cells wait—alone. I don't have to guess which one she's in. Call it netherling intuition, but I know. Unlocking her door, I creep inside and shut it behind me.

Curled up in a corner, she turns her shaved head and squints my direction. "Allie?" Her voice sounds tiny and muffled.

I take the hat off and drop it. The dim lighting makes her look fragile and weak. My heart caves in. Maybe she's still too sedated to do this. She proves me wrong when she pushes herself up to lean against the cushioned wall, wrestling with her straitjacket.

"W-w-wings?" Understanding creeps over her features. "You found the rabbit hole."

"It's over, Mom," I whisper, moving cautiously toward her across the padded floor. I've no sooner ripped open the Velcro belts holding her arms in place than she pulls me into a hug. We kneel, clutching each other tightly.

"But you're one of them," she sobs against my neck. "The curse . . ."

"No more curse," I whisper, rubbing my cheek along the fuzz of her head. "There never was one. I have so much to tell you."

※·I·※

I wake up to a growling stomach. White noise buzzes all around and sunlight seeps under the curtains. Still groggy, I glance at the calendar over my bed. Saturday, June 1st. The morning after prom.

Perfect timing. When I used the mirror in the asylum's bathroom to come home, I made it back in time to change and crawl into bed for a few hours. Although I don't really remember anything once I stepped out of my cheval glass.

Maybe because I didn't step through. Maybe I never went to Wonderland to begin with. *Maybe I dreamed everything* . . .

Panicked, I throw off my covers and swing my feet over the bed's edge. Something drops to the floor: the jade caterpillar. It lands next to Morpheus's hat.

I feel around my neck and find the necklace with the tiny key.

Relief untangles the knots in my stomach.

Picking up the caterpillar carving, I make a beeline to my mirror—unbroken and as smooth as crystal—to face my reflection.

There it is: proof positive that I rode a wave of clams and captured an ocean in a sponge. The glistening skin and streaks of flaming red in my platinum hair are still there. The tattoos around my eyes are gone, as are my wings—although by wrenching my arm around, I can feel ridges at my shoulder blades. Buds ready to sprout if I need them.

I turn around and stare at my eels in their aquarium. The memory of the bandersnatch's tongues shakes my core. Then I glance at my cello and recount another memory . . . Chessie's song, warped and weird. Even looking toward my desk and the dried spider mosaic takes me back to the amazing spiral constellations I saw while in the rowboat.

Memories, real and irreplaceable, all of them. The happy ones, the bitter ones, the terrified and the poignant. Two guys willing to sacrifice their lives for me.

Morpheus, who's imprisoned forever in the belly of a bandersnatch. And Jeb, who probably spent last night at a hotel with Taelor after prom. It's possible they didn't break up in this reality. Since I never answered the door when Jeb first came by, he wasn't in my house when Taelor came to get him.

I race out of my bedroom, forgetting to throw a robe over my camisole and flannel boxers, half hopping and half sprinting into the hallway. I need to go next door, to see for myself that he made it out of the jabberlock box. To see where things stand with us.

"Whoa there, Butterfly." Dad catches me as my fluffy ankle socks lose traction and I skid across the wooden floor.

It's so good to see his face again, I laugh to keep from crying. "Trying to skate without a board." I motion to the slick floor.

He slaps me with the Elvis smirk. "Just be careful, or you'll hurt your other ankle, too."

I throw myself against his chest in a hug.

One of his arms wraps around me, and he holds the other one between us. "Hey . . . you all right?"

I nod, unable to speak over the torrent of emotions. I let my hug say everything for me. *I missed you. I love you. And I'm so sorry for fighting with you.*

The arm Dad holds between us wiggles. He has the cordless phone against his sternum. I pull back.

My first thought is Taelor. She figured out I stole from her. Maybe Persephone found the purse in the trash. I can't believe I didn't think to use the mirrors at the store and put the money back before coming home.

I was wrong to steal it in the first place. So I guess, just like Morpheus said before the bandersnatch swallowed him whole, I'll have to take my medicine. I'll have to tell her that I'm the thief and hope she won't press charges.

I squeeze the caterpillar carving between my fingers to give me courage. "Who are you talking to?"

Dad winks, then lifts the phone to his ear. "Hey, sweetie. Would you like to say good morning to our daughter?" He holds out the phone.

I'm relieved it's not Taelor but twist my face into a confused expression. I have a part to play.

"Patients in Alison's ward never get to use the phone," I say, making my voice tremble for effect.

Dad shrugs and grins.

The phone's cold against my ear when I finally take it. "Alison?"

"It's working, Allie." Her voice sounds strong and clear.

"Yeah?" I ask, still feigning shock.

"Dad will tell you the details. Come visit me later today, okay?"

"Have they given you anything this morning?"

"No," she answers. "I did what we agreed on. I'm letting them see that I'm sane. For some reason, they think it was the sedatives causing my delusions. How's that for irony?"

I smile. "It's so good to hear your voice."

"Yours, too. I want to see you again, to hug you . . . to tell you how proud I am. I love you—" Her voice cracks.

I tear up, and this time I'm not pretending. "I love you, too . . . Mom."

I stand there, rooted to the floor. Dad gently pries the phone loose and says his good-byes before leading me to the couch in the living room.

"The asylum called this morning, before the crack of dawn." His eyes mist, smile lines framing them. "I went and visited right after, while you were still asleep. She's lucid . . . *really* lucid. She's not talking to anything but people. And she ate an omelet off a dinner plate. A dinner plate, Allie! All of this without meds. The doctors are conferring . . . they think maybe all along she was having a reaction to the meds that somehow exacerbated her symptoms. Weird part is what led them to that conclusion. You know Nurse Jenkins?"

I nod, wary. Last I saw her, she was conked out on the bathroom floor with a hundred-volt smile on her face and an empty syringe in her hand. It looked like she took my advice.

"Well, a janitor found her in the restroom really late last night. She had given herself the same sedative they've been giving your mom. When she came to, she was talking about fairies walking through mirrors and stealing her keys. Thing is, the keys were right there next to her. The doctor thinks there's something wrong with the brand of sedative they've been using . . . they're sending it out for further testing." He sighs and chuckles at the same time. "To think, all this time it could've been bad medicine making her worse. I'm so glad we found out soon enough to stop the treatments we'd planned for Monday."

"Me, too." I catch his hand and hold his knuckles against my cheek.

"Say." He tugs at one of the red streaks in my hair. "This a new hairpiece?"

"Sure," I answer mechanically, not even realizing it's a fib until I've already said it.

"I like it. Well, there are doughnuts on the table. I'm going to spend the day at the asylum. Will you come by after work?"

"Nothing in this world could stop me," I promise.

It hits me that Dad hasn't asked about his recliner. I look toward the chair, expecting to see the appliqués torn and frayed. Instead, they're just as they always were. Which makes no sense at all, because that's another thing I forgot to fix . . .

Dad heads out the front door, turning once. "Oh, you might want to check your traps today. I found a monster moth in one of them. Must've come in looking to get out of the storm last night. It'll make a great addition to your mosaics. Never seen one so big."

Monster moth . . . a brick chucked at my gut would hurt less than those words.

I lay the jade caterpillar on the coffee table and have to force myself to wait until Dad's truck pulls out of the driveway.

In the garage, I open three buckets before I find him, lying atop a pile of assorted bugs. The stench of Kitty Litter and banana peel stings my nose. I lift him out—glowing blue body and black satin wings unmoving and lifeless.

He escaped somehow . . . he escaped the bandersnatch's belly and made it back here, only to be suffocated by me.

Cradling him, I walk numbly into the living room, wavering with a sick sense of guilt and loss. I place him on the coffee table next to his carved counterpart and nudge his wings with a shaky finger.

"What were you thinking?" I murmur. "Why did you fly into the pipe? You had to know better." It hurts to see him, once so pompous and full of life, now as hollow as the caterpillar carving. I pet his cold blue body. "I believe you now, okay? I believe that you cared. And I won't forget what you did for me . . . in the end."

I won't let you forget. Morpheus's voice slides into my head. I jump back as the moth body begins to vibrate.

The wings fold over and grow, opening to reveal Morpheus looming atop the table, in all his freakish glory. He's wearing a modern suit in sapphire silk that matches his jeweled teardrops. And, of course, a spectacularly eccentric hat.

I stand, struggling to mask my happiness. A smile breaks out against my will.

"I knew you'd miss me." He lights on the floor and moves in close, pinning me to the wall with his body.

"How did you escape?"

"It would seem"—he blots my tears with his sleeve—"that the bandersnatch's hide is indestructible from the outside in. Not the inside out."

Realization dawns. "Oh, my gosh . . . you had the vorpal sword in your jacket."

"I did indeed." He polishes his fingernails on his lapel. "Of course, all the other victims escaped with me. Now they're following me around like lollygagging pups. They've proven useful enough. Fixing things. I had one of them return the stolen money and place the purse under the store's counter while you were sleeping."

"You . . . what?"

He gestures to the recliner behind him. "Then I put several in charge of stitching up daisies on the chair."

A wave of disbelief and gratitude washes over me. "Thank you."

"Ah, I deserve better than a thank-you." His dark eyes simmer with seduction.

I cross my arms at my chest. "Huh. You owe me at least that. You preyed on my mind when I was a child. Forced my mom to leave her family and be boarded up in an asylum so she could protect me. Then you lured me into Wonderland so I could fix everything for you but be left with nothing in return."

Raising one hand, he tilts his hat to that sexy slant. "You want me. Admit it."

Even if he's partly right, I'll never tell him. "Why would I *want* you?"

He lifts three fingers to countdown. "Mysterious. Rebellious. Troubled. All those qualities women find irresistible."

"Such an optimist."

"My cup is never empty."

"Too bad your brain is." The words bite, but my smile softens with affection.

His answering smirk is edged with respect. "So . . ." He traces the necklace's chain where it glides over my collarbone, igniting little fires on my bare skin. "You left Grenadine minding the store?"

"With Rabid as her advisor. I told everyone I had unfinished business here."

"Such as?"

"Family and friends. Senior year and graduation. My art."

Morpheus raises an eyebrow. "And your knight?"

I glance down at my socks. "Right now, he belongs to someone else."

Morpheus grazes a fingertip down my temple. "Much as it warms me to the depths to hear that, I don't believe it. The blood already won."

"What are you talking about?"

"The boy bled for you—a whole body's worth of blood. There's no love greater than that. He belongs to you alone."

His words are surprisingly beautiful and kind, and somewhere in my heart, I know he's right. But how long will I have to wait for Jeb to have the courage to admit it to himself?

Morpheus touches the scars on my palm. "But let us not forget that you bled for me. So to whom do *you* belong, Alyssa?"

The reminder evokes a tangle of emotions. He's a pro at unbalancing me. "I've chosen the mortal realm."

"You're evading the question."

"I learned from the master."

He chuckles; then his inky gaze looks me up and down. "Fine, then. Play with your toy soldier. But you are a woman now, with the fire of the nether-realm coursing through your veins. You're a savage at heart, and you've tasted the ambrosia of power. One day you'll want to fly again. And rest assured, I'll be waiting in the wings. *Pun intended.*" His wings swoop over us, enfolding me in a black cocoon and pulling me toward him.

I'm not sure if it's the woman he's awakened or the blossoming Wonderland wildness in my soul, but I surrender to the embrace. His warm mouth grazes my nose, leaving a hint of licorice behind. I prepare to push him off before he can taste my lips—I'm not about to betray Jeb again, even if we're not together—but instead, Morpheus kisses my forehead, warm, chaste, and gentle. Then he lets me go.

An uncomfortable silence settles between us. Fishing some gloves from a pocket, he slips them on. I sense good-bye in the action. It twists my insides into a bittersweet tangle.

"Before I leave," Morpheus says, as if reading my mind, "you need to know. When I killed the bandersnatch, there was no sign of Red."

My pulse stalls as realization dawns. "You don't think she's still out there looking for me . . ."

"It's possible she crawled off and withered away somewhere, having no body to inhabit. But, if she did find someone, the portals are very heavily guarded now. I would ne'er have made it here if not for

Gossamer's guilty conscience. She and the spritelings distracted the elfin knights for me. I've alerted the Twid Sisters, and I'll keep an eye out myself. I've fought the witch once for you. I'll do it again if I must."

I have no doubt he would. I place a palm at his chest. His heartbeat knocks rapidly against my skin. "I never would have guessed."

"What's that?" he asks on a hoarse whisper.

"That you're one of those netherlings who has a rare penchant for kindness and courage."

"Tut." He presses his glove over my hand. "Only when there's fringe benefits."

Smiling, I rise to my toes, grip his lapels, and kiss each one of his jewels until they change to a captivating dark purple—the color of passion fruit. I ease back to the balls of my feet. "So beautiful," I whisper, tapping one of the sparkling gems.

Morpheus catches my palm and kisses the scars there. "I couldn't agree more."

We stare at each other, an invisible cord drawn tighter between us—a bond strengthened.

The doorbell rings, startling me. I flash a look at the clock in the kitchen on my way to the door. Motioning for Morpheus to be quiet, I steal a glance through the peephole.

"Jeb!" My heart races as I tuck the necklace's key into my cleavage and scramble to unlock the latch. "Could you"—I gesture to Morpheus's wings—"you know?"

He moves behind me, breath warm on my nape. "I'll be watching over you. We bent the rules. Outsmarted magic."

"And now there's a price to be paid?" I whisper against the sick nudge in my stomach.

"Perhaps. Then again, it could be that we're already paying the price." There's a hint of sadness in those words. He steps back and bows, wings forming a beautiful arch. "Ever your footman, fairest queen." He takes one last look at me, then transforms into the moth and flutters at the threshold, waiting.

The minute I open the door, he swoops out, trying to take Jeb's head off.

Jeb ducks. "Hey!" He stares at the moth hovering behind him. "Isn't that the bug from your car's air freshener?"

Amazing. He really doesn't remember . . . anything.

"Do you want me to catch it for you?" Jeb asks when I don't respond.

"Nah. I'm hoping it'll hit a windshield."

Liar, Morpheus whispers in my mind, then drifts away on a warm breeze. I bite back a smile.

"An insect like that would've been a great focal point for a mosaic," Jeb says, his voice demanding my full attention. That velvety, deep timbre is like music to me now, knowing I could've lost it forever. I have to fight back the urge to leap into his arms.

The breeze wraps his scent around me. He's wearing a ragged T-shirt and oil-stained carpenter shorts long enough to brush his shins. His hair is pushed back with a torn bandana, and his face is scruffy. He's here to work on Gizmo. Taking care of me, like always. My elfin knight.

I study his tanned arms, drinking in those scars. The night on the rowboat, how it felt to sleep locked in his strong embrace. All these memories are mine alone now. Something I have to keep from him, and I'm not comfortable with secrets between us anymore.

Kiss him, kiss him. You know you want to kiss him . . . A grasshopper lands on my shoulder. I tune into the white noise coming from the yard, picking out whispers where I can. They're all saying the same thing.

Kiss him . . . But I can't, because I want to do this right. I want to be sure he's broken up with Taelor first. That he's mine in every way.

"Al?" Jeb picks the grasshopper off me and sets it free.

The movement shakes me from my stupor. "Oh, sorry."

"Yeah, you were really deep in thought there. You okay?"

I shrug. "I was thinking about my mosaics. I'm done killing things. It's time for a change in mediums. Rocks and broken glass maybe. Beads and wires, ribbon." Why not? I have a full reserve of Wonderland landscapes reawakened in my memory, waiting to be immortalized.

"Sounds great," Jeb says. "I'm ready for a change, too." He draws something from behind his back: a bouquet of white roses wrapped in pink tissue paper. He must've had them tucked in his waistband. A sweet smile frames his crooked incisor as he hands them to me.

"Thank you." I sniff the delicate scent. "Where'd you find a florist open this early?"

He shoves his hands into his pockets. "Uh. I actually kind of borrowed them from Mr. Adams's bushes over there." His elbow gestures to the duplex across the street, where a rosebush suffers several obvious bald spots.

I snort. "You're so bad."

"Eh, I'll mow his lawn for free or something. Hey . . ." He lifts a thumb to my wrist, rubbing it. My entire body lights up with sensation. "I tried to come by to see you before prom last night. No one answered."

"Oh . . . is this about Hitch?"

"It was last night. Since I couldn't reach you, I made Hitch swear to let me know if you showed up. When you didn't, Jen told me what happened with your mom at Soul's. That's what the roses are for."

"White ones," I whisper, eyes filling with tears.

His eyebrows pinch in concern. "Please, don't cry. If you don't like white roses, I'll paint them red for you."

"No, never do that." My blood sprints too fast through my veins; I feel dizzy.

"I meant like in the Alice story." He winces. "Sorry. That was stupid. I know you hate that book."

I grasp his arm. We both stare at the point of contact when his muscle twitches. "Actually, I'm starting to see the charm in it. And the roses are perfect."

"Good." He shuffles his tennis shoes on the porch. "So, am I forgiven about the London thing, for keeping the part about Tae from you?"

Great. I'd forgotten that we haven't hashed this out yet.

When I don't answer, he continues. "Because there's something I need to tell you, something that's changed." He repositions the bandana's knot at his nape, looking nervous.

Before he can say another word, Taelor's Mustang convertible rips into my driveway and screeches to a halt, as if materializing at his mention of her.

Jeb curses and presses his forehead against the doorframe.

Slamming her car door, she stomps up to the porch. She slides her Fendi sunglasses to the top of her head. Rumor has it those shades are worth over two hundred bucks. More than my entire wardrobe of secondhand outfits.

"Figures you'd be here." She looks Jeb up and down after noticing the roses in my hand. "What, did you spend the night with your little virgin after our fight?"

My jaw drops. Prom obviously didn't turn out well.

"I just now got here, so don't go spreading any rumors, Tae." He rubs the iron labret on his chin. I hadn't noticed until now that he's not wearing the garnet one. My pulse kicks a beat faster, knocking against the key at my sternum.

Taelor taps her pedicured, sandaled foot. "So, you haven't told her yet?" Her eyes flick to mine. "He broke up with me last night. At prom. Then he left me there alone. Classy, right?"

The pained edge in her voice triggers a weird mix of pity and empathy.

Jeb grinds a knuckle into a place where the mortar's crumbling between some bricks on the porch. "You had your chauffeur."

"Oh, and I'm supposed to dance with him? The guy's like ninety years old." She clenches her designer lime green handbag against her matching wrap dress. "You weren't home after the dance, because we drove by. If you weren't here, where were you?"

"I went over to Mr. Mason's."

"Our art teacher?" Taelor and I both ask simultaneously. We give each other scathing glances while waiting for his response.

"You told me I was fired from Underland," Jeb answers, studying where his knuckles graze the bricks. "Mr. Mason once mentioned he could get me a job at that art gallery on Kenyon Street. He's good friends with the proprietor."

"Wait, why do you need a job here?" I ask, confused. "I thought you were leaving for London this summer."

"He can't, now that he turned down my dad's offer to rent him a flat. He has to save up money before he can have a place to live."

Taelor sneers in my direction. "Because of you, he's giving up his career."

Jebediah I-must-have-structure Holt is altering his life plan for me? "You can't do that," I say, forcing him to look at me.

Apprehension tightens his features, but so does resolution. "I'm just veering off course a little. I'm not giving anything up. Once I get the job at the gallery"—he steals a glimpse at Taelor—"which is as good as in the bag, I'll be able to sell some of my paintings there. I can make connections in the art world, help Mom with Jen's senior-year expenses, and still save money while I attend community college." Then his focus tightens on me. "You know, until after you graduate. Then we'll go to London together."

Go to London, *together* . . .

I crinkle the tissue paper between my fingers, unable to pin down the wonderful emotions rushing through me.

"Well, how sweet." Taelor's voice shakes. "Maybe you can sell that crap I found in your car the other day and buy her an engagement ring from the thrift store." Digging into her purse, Taelor tosses three rolls of paper inside the door at my feet—skinny cylinders bound with rubber bands. "Keep your rabbit eyes on him, Alyssa. He's an SOB, just like his sicko dad. He can't be trusted."

She starts to leave.

Jeb's shoulders droop, a blush tinting the tips of his ears. My blood catches fire. No way am I going to let her talk to him like that. No way is she going to make him second-guess who he is.

Chucking the roses to the floor, I step out onto the porch and catch her by the elbow.

She jerks free and twirls around.

With me on the step and her on the ground, we're at eye level.

She starts to open her mouth. I shush her. "My turn to talk. And you're going to listen. Then I never want to hear another word from you about Jeb or anything else again."

Her jaw clenches, but she waits.

"I'd trust Jeb with my *life*. He's everything his dad never was. And you know it, or you wouldn't be so busted up over losing him. He treated you with respect . . . and he never wanted to hurt you. Why else do you think he put up with your attitude for so long?"

Her gaze intensifies behind a sheen of tears.

Jeb stands there in stunned awe.

"And you know what?" I continue, unable to stop what I've unleashed. "Neither one of us has a perfect family. We could've been friends or at least tried to get along. But you killed it. Things suck for you sometimes—I get it. But you can't use that as an excuse to treat people any way you want." My cheeks burn hot at the purging of emotions I've suppressed for too many years. "Tearing down the rest of the world won't make you happy. Look inside yourself. Because finding who you were meant to be? What you were put into this world to do? That's what fills the emptiness. It's the only thing that can."

It's dead quiet all around other than a few chirping birds. Even the white noise has gone silent, as if the bugs and flowers stopped to listen to me for once.

Looking down at her feet, Taelor sniffs and runs the back of her hand across her cheeks. She turns her gaze up to mine, and in that moment, I see it. A connection. I got through to her. Thoughtful and quiet for once, she stumbles to her car and peels out of my driveway without so much as a wave.

"Holy wow," Jeb mumbles.

I spin on my heel and we're face-to-face. Alone . . . finally.

Staring at me with that same reverent expression as when he first saw my wings, he moves his lips to say something. A screen door opens across the street and interrupts him. Mr. Adams picks up his hose to water his yard. The old man scowls when he notices the empty spots on his rosebush.

"Jeb, you're about to get busted."

He gives me a sexy, sideways smile.

Grabbing his wrist, I tug him through the doorway before Mr. Adams looks in our direction. I close the door and press my back against the wood to hide my wing scars.

"Wait a minute." Jeb catches one of my strands of red hair, twisting it between his thumb and forefinger. "This isn't a hairpiece. You actually dyed it. What's gotten into you?"

"I guess I finally found my fiery side."

"I like it." He tilts his head, as if evaluating a painting. "So, this glittery stuff that looks like you've been swimming in pixie dust . . ." His knuckles graze my cheek. "Is it on every inch of your skin?" His intent appraisal of my pajamas heats me from my neck to my feet.

"Uhhh . . ." His touch is enough to make me stammer, but the pixie comment sends me over the edge. I almost groan when he pulls back.

"Thanks for saying that stuff out there, to Tae."

"I meant every word." *Because I love you.* I can't bring myself to say it out loud yet, but it's true. It's not something that hit me from out of nowhere; it was a gradual awakening. Kind of like a metamorphosis . . .

"Well, looks like you can do okay on your own. After seeing the way you just took care of me." He leans a shoulder against the wall, closing the space between us once more. "So weird. I had a dream about the same thing last night—you taking care of me."

The confession snaps me to attention. "Were we in Wonderland?"

He smirks. "Uh, no. We were in a house in the country, and you were sitting at a table playing chess while I painted pictures with a feather and some colored honey. A swarm of bees pounded on the window, yelling at me for stealing from their hive. I mean really yelling, like with people's voices. Then you sprouted wings and flew outside to chase them all away. Strange, right?"

I stifle a cough. "Yeah, strange."

"Yet somehow, it fits." He picks up one of the cylinders Taelor threw at me earlier, removes the rubber band, then hands it over.

I unroll it and gasp to see myself in pencil lines and shading—an amazing rendition of a gothic fairy complete with gossamer wings and eye tattoos—exactly as I looked in Wonderland. Since technically he was never there, it can't be a memory. So there's only one explanation: This guy sees into the soul of me and always has.

I meet his gaze, speechless.

"There's a hundred more like that. You're my muse, Al. My inspiration. I was hoping . . . maybe . . . you might want to be—"

Before he can finish, I clench his T-shirt and drag him down for a kiss. His eyes widen at first, then close, arms wrapping around my hips to lift me to his height. He presses me into the wall with his body.

I smile against his lips, intoxicated.

How many girls get to have their first kiss twice? But this time, I'm not in shock. This time, I don't forget to curl my arms around his neck and pull him closer. This time, I'm the one to nudge *his* lips open and find his tongue.

The sketch falls to the floor next to the scattered roses. Jeb moans, wraps my legs around his waist, and holds me tight. He breaks contact just long enough to whisper, "Where'd you learn to kiss like that?"

"You taught me." I recover my senses and realize what I said. "In my dreams."

"Oh, yeah?" He nudges the indentation on my chin with his nose. "Been dreaming of me, too, huh?"

"Ever since the day we met." Finally, the truth.

He flashes his dimples. "Guess it's time for us to make some dreams come true, skater girl."

Little does he know we already have; we went to Wonderland and back, after all. I smile, then give him a kiss he'll never forget, to replace all the ones he'll never remember.

ACKNOWLEDGMENTS

Thank you first and foremost to my family. My husband, children, brother and brothers-in-law, sisters-in-law, nieces, nephews, and cousins. Both sets of my parents, the ones who brought me into this world and the ones I inherited through marriage. My aunts and uncles on all sides of the family, and my grandparents, who are no longer with us. And, lest we forget, the red Solo cup crew in Kansas. You believed in me through the ups and downs and never once questioned that I would find my way. Your faith carried me through the toughest times.

Gratefulness and hugs to my super-agent, Jenny Bent, and her unwavering dedication to this story, my abilities, and my ideas.

Thank you to the prestigious Abrams/Amulet family (including but not limited to): Maggie Lehrman, my brilliant editor, who saw into the heart of this book and gave it not only a pulse but also direction; Maria Middleton, book designer extraordinaire, who, with the help of the mystical artistry of Nathalia Suellen, captured the story's essence in one gorgeously twisted and fairytale-esque picture; Laura Mihalick, my in-house publicist and stomper of grassfires; copyeditors; marketing advisors; printing press specialists, who oversaw the pages and special effects for the jacket; and many, many more. There is not enough space to thank everyone for their contributions in seeing the final product come to fruition, or for making the realization of my dream a lovely reality.

A debt of gratitude to my crit group, the Divas: Linda Castillo, Jennifer Archer, Marcy McKay, and April Redmon. I might be a lowly Kumquat, but because of your Wednesday night wisdom, I'm a published one.

A high five to my online critters and beta readers: My POM (aka Jessica Nelson), for always seeing the good in my bad boys; Rookie (aka Bethany Crandell), for talking me down, holding me back, and helping me find my inner Melvin; Katie Lovett, for reading even my earliest stories and still believing I had something akin to talent; Marlene Ruggles, for finding those typos I just couldn't see; Chris Lapel, my number-one fan; and finally, Kim Dickerson, for giving a whole new meaning to Godiva sweetness. Yes, words can be chocolate, indeed.

If it takes a village to raise a child, it takes a posse to write a book. Undying gratitude to my #goatposse for your support, advice, and witty repartee throughout this journey to the shelves. Also, a hollah to the WrAHM girls and to the folks at Crockett Middle School, with special mention to Cara Clopton, Christen Reighter, and the Vault Crew (you know who you are!).

Cyber hugs to my online support group: twitter friends, Query-Tracker.net pals, and the many bloggers who lit my footsteps on my sometimes dark and lonely seven-year-road road to publishing.

A very special thanks to Lewis Carroll and Tim Burton. Without their artistic geniuses, vivid characters, and warped dreamscapes, I would never have been inspired to write *Splintered*.

Last but not least, gratitude to the One who gives me my stories, the ability to write them, and continues to bless my life each day.

ABOUT THE AUTHOR

A. G. Howard wrote *Splintered* while working at a school library. She always wondered what would've happened if Alice had grown up and the subtle creepiness of *Alice's Adventures in Wonderland* had taken center stage in her story, and she hopes her darker and funkier tribute to Carroll will inspire readers to seek out the stories that won her heart as a child. She lives in Amarillo, Texas.

Alyssa's adventure continues in

UNHINGED,

the sequel to *Splintered*. Read the first chapter now.

BLOOD & GLASS

My art teacher says that a real artist bleeds for her craft, but he never told us that blood can *become* your medium, can take on a life of its own and shape your art in vile and gruesome ways.

I shove my hair over my shoulder, puncture my forefinger with the sterilized safety pin I had tucked in my pocket, then position the final glass gem on my mosaic and wait.

As I press the translucent bead into the wet white plaster, I shudder at the seeping sensation. It's like a leech at the tip of my finger where I touch the glass, sucking and siphoning my blood to the underside of the gem, forming a pool of deep, velvet red. But it doesn't stop there.

The blood dances . . . moves from gem to gem, coloring the back of each with a line of crimson—forming a picture. Breath locks in my lungs and I wait for the lines to connect . . . wondering what the end result will be this time. Hoping it won't be *her* again.

The last bell of the day rings, and I scramble to cover my mosaic with a drop cloth, terrified someone might see the transformation taking place.

It's yet another reminder that the Wonderland fairy tale is real, that my being a descendant of Alice Liddell means I'm different from everyone else. No matter how much distance I try to put between us, I'm connected forever to a strange and eerie sect of magical creatures called netherlings.

My classmates gather their backpacks and books and leave the art room, giving each other fist bumps and high fives while talking about their plans for Memorial Day weekend. I suck my finger, although there's no blood leaking from it anymore. Hips leaning against the table, I look outside. It's cloudy, and mist specks the windows.

My 1975 Gremlin, Gizmo, had a flat tire this morning. Since my mom doesn't drive, Dad dropped me on his way to work. I told him I'd find a ride home.

My cell phone vibrates in my backpack on the floor. I push aside the fishnet gloves folded on top, lift out the phone, and open a text from my boyfriend: *Sk8er grl . . . waiting in east parking lot. Can't wait 2c you. Tell Mason hi 4 me.*

My throat catches. Jeb and I have been together for almost a year and were best friends for six years before that, but for the past month we've only been in contact through texts and spotty phone calls. I'm eager to see him again face-to-face, but I'm also oddly nervous. I worry things will be different now that he's living a life I'm not a part of yet.

Glancing up at Mr. Mason, who's talking to some student in the hall about art supplies, I text my answer: *K. Can't wait 2c you 2. Give me 5 . . . finishing something.*

I drop the phone into my bag and lift the cloth to peek at my project. My heart falls into my feet. Not even the familiar scents of paint, chalk dust, and plaster can comfort me when I see the scene taking shape: a Red Queen on a murderous rampage in a bleak and crumbling Wonderland.

Just like in my most recent dreams . . .

I smooth the cloth back into place, unwilling to acknowledge what the imagery might mean. It's easier to hide from it.

"Alyssa." Mr. Mason comes to stand by the table. His tie-dyed Converse shoes stand out like melted rainbows against the white linoleum floor. "I've been meaning to ask . . . are you planning to accept the scholarship to Middleton College?"

I nod in spite of my bout of nerves. *If Dad lets me move to London with Jeb.*

"Good." Mr. Mason's wide smile showcases the gap between his front teeth. "Someone with your talent should take advantage of every opportunity. Now, let's see this latest piece."

Before I can stop him, he tugs off the drop cloth and squints, the pockets beneath his eyes magnified by his pink-tinged glasses. I sigh, relieved that the transformation is complete. "Rapturous color and movement, as always." He leans across it, rubbing his goatee. "Disturbing, like the others."

His final observation sends my stomach tumbling.

A year ago, when I used bug corpses and dried flowers in my

mosaics, my pieces retained an air of optimism and beauty, despite the morbidity of the materials. Now, with my change in medium, everything I create is gloomy and violent. I can't seem to capture lightness or hope anymore. In fact, I've stopped trying to fight it. I just let the blood have its way.

I wish I could stop making the mosaics altogether. But it's a compulsion I can't deny . . . and something tells me there's a reason for that. A reason that keeps me from destroying all six of them—from busting their plaster backgrounds into a thousand pieces.

"Do I need to buy more red marbled gems?" Mr. Mason asks. "I've no idea where I got them to begin with. I checked online the other day and can't seem to find the supplier."

He doesn't realize the mosaic tiles were clear when I started, that I've been using only clear gems for the past few weeks, and that the scenes he thinks I'm meticulously crafting by matching colored lines in the glass are actually forming themselves.

"It's okay," I answer him. "They're from my own personal supply." *Literally.*

Mr. Mason studies me for a second. "All right. But I'm running out of room in my cabinet. Maybe you could take this one home."

I shudder at the thought. Having any of them in my house would only invite more nightmares. Not to mention how it would affect Mom. She's already spent enough of her life imprisoned by her Wonderland phobias.

I'll have to figure out something before the end of school. Mr. Mason won't be willing to keep them all summer, especially since I'm a senior. But today I have other things on my mind.

"Can you fit just one more?" I ask. "Jeb's picking me up on his bike. I'll get them next week."

Mr. Mason nods and carries it over to his desk.

I crouch to arrange the stuff in my backpack, rubbing sweaty palms over my striped leggings. The hem brushing my knees feels foreign. My skirt is longer than what I'm used to without the petticoats underneath to fluff it out. In the months since Mom's been home from the asylum, we've had a lot of arguments about my clothes and makeup. She says my skirts are too short and she wishes I would wear jeans and "dress like regular girls." She thinks I look too wild. I've told her that's why I wear tights and leggings, for modesty. But she never listens. It's like she's trying to make up for the eleven years she was away by being overly invested in everything about me.

She won this morning, but only because I woke up late and was in a rush. It's not easy to get up for school when you've been fighting sleep all night, avoiding dreams.

I lift my backpack to my shoulders and tip my chin good-bye to Mr. Mason. My Mary Jane platforms clomp along the deserted tiles of the hall. Stray work sheets and notebook papers are scattered like stepping-stones in a pond. Several lockers hang open, as if the students couldn't waste the extra half second it would've taken to shut them before leaving for the weekend.

A hundred different colognes, perfumes, and body odors still linger, interspersed with the faded yeasty scent of rolls from the cafeteria's lunch menu. *Smells like teen spirit.* I shake my head, grinning.

Speaking of spirit, Pleasance High's student council has been working around the clock to tape up prom reminders around every corner of the school. This year, the dance is the Friday before our Saturday graduation ceremony—one week from today.

ALL PRINCES AND PRINCESSES ARE CORDIALLY INVITED TO

THE PLEASANCE HIGH FAIRY-TALE MASQUERADE PROM, MAY
25TH. NO FROGS ALLOWED.

I smirk at the last line. My best pal, Jenara, wrote it with bold
green marker at the end of each announcement. It took her entire
sixth period on Tuesday to do it and cost her three days of detention. But it was totally worth it to see the look on Taelor Tremont's
face. Taelor is my boyfriend's ex, the school's star tennis player, and
the student council's social chairperson. She's also the one who rat-
ted out my Liddell family secret in fifth grade. Our relationship is
strained, to say the least.

I run my palm across one of the banners that escaped half its tape
and drapes like a long white tongue from the wall. It reminds me of
my experience with the bandersnatch's snaky tongues last summer. I
cringe and rub the vivid streak of red in my blond hair between my
forefinger and thumb. It's one of my permanent souvenirs, just like
the nodules behind my shoulder blades where wings lie dormant
inside me. No matter how I try to distance myself from the Wonderland memories, they're always present, refusing to leave.

Just like a certain *someone* refuses to leave.

My throat constricts at the thought of black wings, bottomless
tattooed eyes, and a cockney accent. He already has my nights. I
won't let him take my days, too.

Shoving the doors open, I step into the parking lot and get hit
by a rush of chill, damp air. A fine mist coats my face. A few cars
remain and students cluster in small groups to talk—some hunched
inside hoodies and others seemingly oblivious to the unseasonably
cool weather. We've had a lot of rain this month. The meteorologists
calculated the accumulation somewhere between four and six inches,
breaking a century's worth of spring records in Pleasance, Texas.

My ears automatically tune in to the bugs and plants in the soggy football field a few yards away. Their whispers often blend together in crackles and hums like radio static. But if I try, I can make out distinct messages meant just for me:

Hello, Alyssa.

Nice day for a stroll in the rain . . .

The breeze is just right for flying.

There was a time I hated hearing their fuzzy, buzzy greetings so much I would trap them and smother them. Now the white noise is comforting. The bugs and flowers have become my sidekicks . . . charming reminders of a secret part of me.

A part of me even my boyfriend is unaware of.

I see him across the parking lot. He leans against his souped-up vintage Honda CT70, chatting with Corbin, the starting quarterback and Jenara's new main squeeze. Jeb's sister and Corbin make an odd match. Jenara has pink hair and the fashion sense of a princess gone punk rocker—the antithesis of a typical Texas jock's girlfriend. But Corbin's mother is an interior designer who's known for her eccentric style, so he's accustomed to offbeat artistic personalities. At the beginning of the year the two of them were lab partners in biology. They clicked, and now they're inseparable.

Jeb glances in my direction. He straightens as he sees me, his body language as loud as a shout. Even at this distance, the heat of his mossy-green eyes warms my skin under my lacy shirt and plaid corset.

He gestures good-bye to Corbin, who shoves a strand of reddish blond hair from his eyes and waves in my direction before joining a group of football players and cheerleaders.

Jeb shrugs out of his jacket on his way over, revealing muscular arms. His black combat boots clomp across the shimmery asphalt, and his olive skin glistens in the mist. He's wearing a navy T-shirt with his worn jeans. A picture of My Chemical Romance is airbrushed in white with a red slash streaked diagonally across their faces. It reminds me of my blood art, and I shiver.

"Are you cold?" he asks, wrapping his jacket around me, the leather still warm from his body. For that fleeting second, I can almost taste his cologne: a mix between chocolate and musk.

"I'm just happy you're home," I answer, palms flat against his chest, enjoying his strength and solidity.

"Me, too." He looks down at me, caressing me with his gaze but holding back. He cut his hair while he was gone. Wind ruffles the dark, collar-length strands. It's still long enough at the crown and top to be wavy and is a mess from being under his helmet. It's unkempt and wild, just the way I like it.

I want to leap into his arms for a hug or, even better, kiss his soft lips. The ache to make up for lost time winds tight around me until I'm a top ready to spin, but my shyness is even stronger. I glance over his shoulder to where four junior girls gathered around a silver PT Cruiser watch our every move. I recognize them from art class.

Jeb follows my line of sight and lifts my hand to kiss each knuckle, the scrape of his labret igniting a tingle that races all the way to the tips of my toes. "Let's get out of here."

"You read my mind."

He smirks. The butterflies in my belly clash at the appearance of his dimples.

We walk hand in hand to his bike as the parking lot starts to clear. "So . . . looks like your mom won this morning." He gestures to my skirt, and I roll my eyes.

Grinning, he helps me with my helmet, smooths my hair across my lower back, and separates the red strand from the blond ones. Wrapping it around his finger, he asks, "Were you working on a mosaic when I texted?"

I nod and buckle the helmet's strap under my chin, not wanting the conversation to go this direction. Not sure how to tell him what's been happening during my art sessions while he's been gone.

He cups my elbow as I climb into place on the back of the seat, leaving a space for him in front. "When do I get to see this new series of yours, huh?"

"When it's done," I mumble. What I really mean is, when I'm ready to let him watch me make one.

He has no memory of our trip to Wonderland, but he's noticed the changes in me, including the key I wear around my neck and never take off, and the nodules along my shoulder blades that I attribute to a Liddell family oddity.

An understatement.

For a year, I've been trying to figure out the best way to tell him the truth without him thinking I'm crazy. If anything can convince him we took a wild ride into Lewis Carroll's imagination, then stepped backward in time to return as if we'd never left, it's my blood-and-magic artwork. I just have to be brave enough to show him.

"When it's done," he says, repeating my cryptic answer. "Okay, then." He gives his head a shake before tugging his helmet on. "Artists. So high maintenance."

"Pot . . . kettle. While we're on the subject, have you heard from your newest number one fan?"

Jeb's gothic fairy art has been getting a lot of attention since he's been going to art expos. He's sold several pieces, the highest going for three thousand bucks. Recently he was contacted by a collector in Tuscany who saw his artwork online.

Jeb digs in his pocket and hands me a phone number. "These are her digits. I'm supposed to schedule a meeting so she can choose one of my pieces."

Ivy Raven. I read the name silently. "Sounds fake, right?" I ask, straightening my backpack straps under his jacket. I almost wish she was made up. But I know better. According to some Web searching I've done, Ivy is a totally legit beautiful twenty-six-year-old heiress. A sophisticated, rich goddess . . . like all the women Jeb's around lately. I hand the paper back, trying to stanch the insecurity that threatens to burn a hole in my heart.

"Doesn't matter how fake she sounds," Jeb says, "as long as the money is real. There's a sweet flat in London I've been looking at. If I can sell her a piece, I'll add it to what I've already saved and have enough to cover it."

We still have to convince Dad to let me go. I refuse to voice my concern aloud. Jeb's already feeling guilty about the tension between him and Dad. Sure, it was a mistake for Jeb to take me to get a tattoo behind my parents' backs. But he didn't do it to make them mad. He did it against his better judgment because I pressured him. Because I was trying to be rebellious and worldly, like the people he hangs out with now.

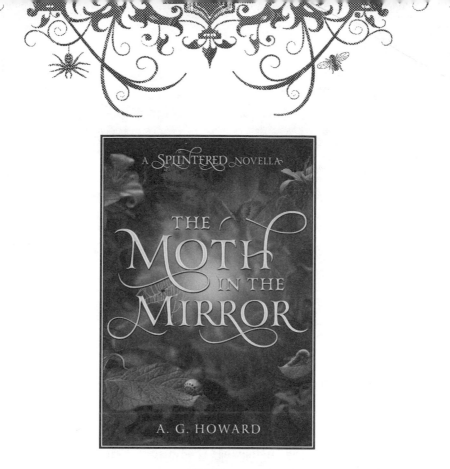

A SPLINTERED NOVELLA

THE
MOTH
IN THE
MIRROR

A. G. HOWARD

For more from A. G. Howard, read *The Moth in the Mirror*, a novella set in the world of *Splintered* and told from the points of view of both Jeb and Morpheus. Morpheus wants to know more about his rival for Alyssa's affections, so he digs into Jeb's memories of his time in Wonderland. But he may be surprised by what he finds . . .

This book was designed by Maria T. Middleton. The text is set in 10.5-point Adobe Caslon, a revival of the mid-eighteenth-century classic created by the legendary engraver and type designer William Caslon. Designed in 1990 by Carol Twombly, Adobe Caslon is based on William Caslon's original type specimen drawings. The display font is Yana Swash Caps I, designed by Laura Worthington for Umbrella Type.

This book was printed and bound by R.R. Donnelley in Crawfordsville, Indiana. Its production was overseen by Alison Gervais.

Jeb got a tattoo at the same time, on his inner right wrist—his painting hand. It's the Latin words *Vivat Musa*, which roughly translates to "Long live the muse." Mine is a miniature set of wings on my inner left ankle, camouflaging my netherling birthmark. I had the artist ink in the words *Alis Volat Propriis*, Latin for "She flies with her own wings." It's a reminder I control my darker side and not the other way around.

Jeb tucks the heiress's number into his jeans pocket, seeming a thousand miles away.

"I bet she's hoping you're Team Cougar," I say, half joking in an effort to bring him back to the present.

Making eye contact, Jeb works his arms into the sleeves of a flannel shirt he had flung across his Honda's handlebars. "She's only in her twenties. Not exactly cougar material."

"Oh, thanks. There's a comfort."

His familiar teasing smile offers reassurance. "If it'll make you feel better, you can go with me when I meet her."

"Deal," I say.

He climbs onto his motorcycle in front of me, and I no longer care if anyone sees us. I snuggle as close as possible, wrapping my arms and knees tightly around him, face nuzzled into the nape of his neck just beneath his helmet's edge. His soft hair tickles my nose.

I've missed that tickle.

He slides on his shades and tilts his head so I can hear him as he starts the motor. "Let's find somewhere to be alone for a while, before I take you home to get ready for our date."

My blood thrums in anticipation. "What'd you have in mind?"

"A roll down memory lane," he answers. And before I can even ask what that means, we're on our way.